SK

Daniel Easterman was born in Ireland in 1949. He is the author of eleven critically-acclaimed novels.

THE JAGUAR MASK

DANIEL EASTERMAN

HarperCollins*Publishers*

HarperCollins*Publishers*
77–85 Fulham Palace Road,
Hammersmith, London W6 8JB

www.**fire**and**water**.com

This paperback edition 2001
1 3 5 7 9 8 6 4 2

First published in Great Britain by
HarperCollins*Publishers* 2000

Copyright © Daniel Easterman 2000

Daniel Easterman asserts the moral right to
be identified as the author of this work

ISBN 0 00 651293 3

Typeset in Meridien by
Palimpsest Book Production Limited,
Polmont, Stirlingshire

Printed and bound in Great Britain by
Omnia Books Limited, Glasgow

To Beth, in the year of our silver wedding.
'It was always you.'

ACKNOWLEDGEMENTS

Thanks, first of all, to Eddie Bell, who wanted a jungle. Thanks, as always, to my long-suffering and inspirational editor, Patricia Parkin; to my untiring and caring agent, Giles Gordon; and to Beth, one hell of a wife.

1

Lacandón Forest
Chiapas State
Southern Mexico
12 November
Noon

The pyramid seemed to rock in the sunlight. Leo squinted his eyes and watched it regain balance. It was like a giant cardboard cutout, as fragile as glass, protected from the world by the dense rainforest that hemmed it in on every side. High up on its east flank, a sapodilla tree grew at an angle. On its flat top, a long rectangular temple seemed to teeter.

His pace quickened as he neared it, as it had quickened three times every day since his arrival. He still couldn't get over the thrill of having an untouched ruin of this quality under his own direction. He'd led the dig since day one, and for most of that time he'd been inside the pyramid itself, working with his hands. He'd been the one to find the tunnel that led from top to bottom of the structure, his hands had cleared away more rubble than anyone's.

The great stone edifice was high at two hundred and twenty feet, almost as high as the tallest pyramid at Tikal. The steps on each of its four sides were vertiginously steep and potentially dangerous. Centuries ago, the whole thing would have been painted bright red, but the rains and sunlight of all the years since then had washed it clean of pigment, leaving the original stone to crumble and crack at its own slow pace.

Leo looked up at the steeply-rising flank of the pyramid and pondered – as he did two or three times a day – on whether to take the stairs or the lift. There were one hundred and fifty-six steps in all, shallow steps that rose without interruption to the flat platform on which the temple was built. Some of the team couldn't cope with them, either because they were too steep and dangerous, or because they were just too damned punishing. A handful of the younger set made it their religious duty to take the stairs on every occasion.

The lift was a wonder. Built entirely from wood and ropes, it rose to the top, propped against the pyramid by elaborate scaffolding. A light cage was powered by an electric generator at the bottom. On reaching the top, there was a short walkway to get you to the platform. Anybody who couldn't handle the lift or the stairs stayed at ground level, clearing paths to the other buildings, still hidden behind thick curtains of trees.

Leo sighed and stepped into the lift. He was doing it more often now. At thirty-five, he was a geriatric to most of the expedition, but he liked to think he was still capable of making the climb, and resented every occasion he decided against it. He pressed the button that started the generator. The entire structure began to vibrate, then to quiver as the cage began its mad ascent.

Leo had lost count of how many times he'd watched a scene like this unfold before his eyes: green trees, flowers of every colour, birds with painted feathers, moss-covered ruins hidden deep among the foliage. Apart from teenage visits to the best-known tourist sites – Chichén Itzá, Tikal,

Palenque, Copán, and the rest – he'd taken part in an expedition every season since he was twenty. Yet however many times he came here, to one forest or another, to a half-reconstructed site or a freshly-discovered site like this one, he never lost the sense of wonder and excitement that had urged him to study Mayan archaeology in the first place.

The cage came to a shuddering halt and he stepped nimbly on to the walkway. Above him, the narrow structure called Temple 3 blocked off the sun. The pyramid below it was structured like a Russian doll. It had been built on top of an earlier pyramid, which had itself been constructed on top of a much older temple. Not long after starting to excavate the main pyramid, they'd found a secret entrance giving access to a network of passages and staircases. Treacherous, unlit steps led steeply down through the superstructure. They hadn't quite reached the bottom yet, but they expected to find a burial chamber of some sort when they did.

Leo stepped through the open entrance to the temple. Once inside, the thick stone walls blotted out the sounds of the forest. He was in another world here, a man-made world of shadows and mysteries, where nothing natural or bright belonged. They had run strings of electric lights from here right through to the temple at the foot of the stairs. A separate oil-fired generator powered the lights, chugging away contentedly in a corner of the temple.

In the artificial light, the brightly-coloured frescoes that covered the walls stood out almost jarringly against their stuccoed background. They were as familiar to him as the walls in any computer game he'd ever got stuck in. The cosy domesticity suggested by the proportions was belied by the painted images. This was a house, but not any

3

house: its builders had called it *u y-atoch k'uh*, the house of the gods.

All about him, now in shadow, now in light danced representations of men – never women – who had once lived and died in this city without a name. A king named Balam Ahau Chaan sat on his jaguar throne, dispensing justice. On another panel, men in huge *quetzal*-feathered headdresses fought a raging battle against their enemies from a nearby city. Some of the warriors wore costumes of jaguar skin, and their lances were wrapped in the same material. A third scene showed prisoners being condemned to death, and the acts of sacrifice that followed, each condemned man led in turn to have his chest torn open and his heart ripped out.

Catching sight of a lifted hand clutching a still-beating organ, Leo gave a little shudder and walked on. As he reached the top of the staircase that would take him down into the heart of the pyramid, he paused. A red light had gone on, showing that someone was coming up. The stairway was too narrow to allow two people to pass. After a week or so of arguments about who had right of way, up-goers or down-comers, they'd given in and asked Barney Kavanagh, the party's boffin, to rig up this advance-warning system.

Moments later, Diane Krauss's head appeared in the stairhead.

'Doctor Mallory. Great. I was just coming to fetch you.'

'Is anything wrong?'

He noticed she was wearing yet another fetching outfit, a cerise designer T-shirt over jeans so tight he was amazed her legs hadn't succumbed to oxygen starvation long ago. It would all be filthy by evening, but tomorrow morning she'd be wearing something completely different.

4

'Wrong? No, sir. We just broke through. There's a wall right ahead of us. Professor Jessop thinks it could be the chamber.'

'No sign of a door?'

'Not yet, but we're looking.'

'I'll come down. Are you staying up here, or . . . ?'

'Hell, no. I don't want to miss this. It's like Tutankhamen. Kinda.'

He pressed the button that would alert anyone at the bottom that they were on their way down. Diane led the way into the stairwell. She was a senior sophomore from Chicago, one of the two universities participating in the dig. The other was Cambridge, to which Leo was attached as a Senior Fellow at the newly-established Centre for Mesoamerican Studies. He caught sight of Diane's beautifully-rounded posterior preceding him down the narrow stairs, and decided he'd been cooped up in the forest for too long.

'Sir, are you eyeing my butt?'

'I'm sorry?'

'You heard me. Butt is plain English.'

'Not where I come from, Diane. And I'm not eyeing it. I'm admiring it. From where I'm looking, I don't have much choice. It's right ahead of me.'

'There's more to me than my butt.'

'There is, indeed, Diane, and I'm very well aware of it.'

'Why don't you close your eyes?'

'If I close my eyes, I'll fall. If I fall, I'll hit you and send you crashing to a well-deserved death at the foot of this staircase. You have a choice: death or admiration.'

They continued their mock bickering to the foot of the stairs. It was only as they came near the end that Leo realized why Diane had kept the banter going so long

5

– she was frightened to be alone in that sombre, claustrophobic passage, squeezed in underneath thousands of tons of rock.

He couldn't blame her: the pyramid scared the hell out of him as well. Breathless, he tried to imagine what it must have been like down there centuries ago, when the staircase had first been created, without electricity, in the presence of dark gods.

Maddox was there, wearing his battered panama for God knows what reason. The Filbert twins stood a few yards away, dressed in identical clothes, swaying imperceptibly to left and right, as if moving to music only they could hear. The Ramírez girl was just by the stairway, hand in hand with her newly-acquired American boyfriend, Leroy Lamont. She turned as he came to the foot of the stairs and smiled at him. That smile, he thought, as others had thought before him, wondering how he might burn it from his memory when they packed up here and he went home to a cold and frosty England.

Bill Jessop came shuffling out from behind the corner of the little temple next to which they were all standing. Leo sometimes wondered how Bill, with his outsize belly, ever managed to work his way down the stairs, much less get up them again. Bill was his deputy, fifteen years his senior, a full professor at Chicago, who had never built any sort of reputation in the field. That didn't stop him thinking he was the Messiah of Mexican archaeology. As a result, he resented Leo, and all the more so since it had begun to look as though this could be the start of the most important excavation in Central America since Lhuillier opened the burial chamber at Palenque.

'How are things down here, Bill?'

'Fucking awful. We should have gone in from outside, like I said.'

6

'We came in from above. If it goes wrong, let me take the blame. Now, what's the problem?'

'OK, you work it out. We just found a false wall. In the temple.'

'Like we expected.'

'Not me. I never expect anything on a dig.'

Leo took care not to point out that Bill had only ever participated in five or six digs in a career spanning thirty years. He wouldn't have been here now if it hadn't been that Leo required a counterpart from the Chicago side.

He looked up to see Diane smiling teasingly at him from further down. A narrow corridor separated the inner wall of the pyramid from the little temple it enclosed. The light was poor this far down, as though the generator was unable to push the waves hard enough along the wires. A musty smell pervaded everything. It was hard to work down here for long stretches. He smiled back weakly, telling himself that he mustn't let her get to him.

He stepped into the temple and walked across the rough floor. It scared him sometimes to think of other feet walking here centuries ago, performing God knows what ceremonies in the dark. All about him, the dimly-lit figures of gods and priests, warriors and ceremonial dancers stood frozen in time or out of it, their colours as fresh as they had been when the temple had been sealed up.

The false wall had already been breached, leaving a sizeable gap in the west side of the temple. A video camera had already been set up next to it, attached to a flexible endoscope that would permit visual access to most parts of whatever room or chamber lay beyond. Leo glanced at the extent of wall that had been torn down already and bit his lip, swearing silently. He'd have a word with Jessop later on, maybe more than a word.

'Anything visible through there?'

One of the twins appeared beside him. He genuinely couldn't tell one from the other. They claimed their extreme thinness made them an asset down here, but Leo was more impressed by their knowledge of Mayan archaeology. Leo understood that they came from Duluth, Minnesota, a city whose most celebrated sons were Bob Dylan and Ernie Nevers. On account of the baseball caps they sometimes sported, they were nicknamed the Minnesota Twins. They wore black at all times, and kept their hair short and flat against their skulls. Rumour had it that Bill was screwing one or both of them. Leo wished him luck.

'We can't see the back of this wall,' she said. Her voice was softer than the severe cut of clothes and hair suggested. Maybe she was Dorothy. 'But I've not been able to make out any frescoes or carvings ahead or to the side. Apart from . . .' She hesitated. 'Why don't you take a look at it yourself?'

He bent down opposite the little CCTV monitor, while Dorothy – if it was Dorothy – manipulated the camera. Behind them, the others had entered the temple and were standing silently, watching. Dorothy pressed a button, and a bright light came on behind the wall.

Leo watched as the endoscope panned over walls and floor. It revealed a short landing leading on to at least two steps down. His reading of the inscriptions had been right: there *was* a burial chamber underneath the temple.

He looked at Dorothy. Her sister Dorothea had come to stand beside her; or perhaps the other way round.

'Dorothy, you said . . .'

By way of answer, she swung the endoscope up. Over the steps hung a low corbelled vault. Just above its lowest point a skilled mason – probably a scribe belonging to the city's royal family – had carved a single glyph. Leo

8

strained to make it out, but the endoscope would not stretch far enough. For all that, the outlines of the square, elaborately carved figure awakened echoes at the back of his mind.

'Do we break it down?' Bob Maddox, the expedition's photographer, was standing behind Leo. He'd finished work on the temple interior, and now he was hot for something fresh to shoot. What he was looking forward to were human remains, preferably those of sacrificial victims, their hearts torn out or their heads severed. *National Geographic* would pay a lot for something picturesque and gruesome.

Leo stepped back from the opening. He turned and saw them watching him, waiting with bated breath for the go-ahead. A royal burial, if there was one, might be mere feet away.

He didn't like being pressed, but he knew when it was time to bow to the inevitable. It was unlikely that there were any frescoes behind the wall. The landing ahead was clear of artefacts. If they were going to find anything, it was down the steps, not up here.

'Fine, let's go ahead,' he said. 'But we'll take it easy. Don't just go tearing the wall down. I want every stone labelled and located on a grid. You all know the routine.'

He watched them form themselves into a coherent group, well-organized and extremely skilful. Letting Bill Jessop take charge at such a crucial stage had been a mistake: he wouldn't let it happen again.

They worked for four hours, dismantling the wall slowly and sending the individual sections back up to be stored in case later researchers decided they wanted to look at them. Leo sent Bill up top to supervise that end of the work. Down in the temple, he found himself working side by side with Diane, whose fingers had discovered a way of coming in contact with his more than was strictly necessary.

When enough of the wall had been removed, Leo picked up a large torch that had been charging nearby.

'What do you think?' he asked. 'Should we break for something to eat, or shall we just see what's down here?'

'We're wasting our time,' said a voice from the back, the Ramírez girl. Funny, he could never remember her first name. 'I mean, all that's down there is a hole in the ground and a piece of paper saying "I got here first, Hernán Cortés".'

'Is that Mexican humour?' he asked.

'Hernán Cortés was an ancestor of mine,' she said. 'He got my great-great-something grandmother pregnant. She was a pretty Spanish girl, she had no choice. It's said that when my great-great-something grandfather married her and wanted to sleep with her, he looked down and there on her belly was a tattoo, saying –'

'Don't worry, we get the idea. Since you're the descendant of such an illustrious man, why don't you keep up the family tradition?'

'I'm sorry?'

'Come over here. It's your turn to go first.'

Nervous, she came over. He handed her the torch. She smiled and he nearly buckled at the knees. Maybe her grungy boyfriend would fall off the pyramid. Or wander into the forest and never be seen again. She had the most seductive smile in the world, but he hadn't known that when he hired her – it was her Ph.D. thesis on the Sun and Moon pyramids at Teotihuacan that had convinced him, that and her first book, published a year earlier, *Interpretación Matemático-Astronómica de la Piedra del Sol.*

He had not let on to anyone else, but he thought she was the brightest mind in the entire expedition.

Dorothy – or perhaps it was Dorothea – approached him and asked if she should switch on the video camera. He nodded absentmindedly, distracted by the girl and the shadow-covered steps beyond her at the same time.

'Yes, why not? I want this recorded.'

She switched on the light, illuminating the recess and the top of the steps. The Ramírez girl took a couple of hesitant steps forward, then halted as she came to the staircase. She stood frozen, looking upwards.

'What is the glyph?' she asked. 'Do you recognize it, Doctor Mallory?'

He stepped forward dutifully. Up close he could smell a faint perfume from her skin; she'd been working hard all day, sweating like the rest of them, but somehow she remained fresh.

'I don't think I can work it out, Doctor. That looks like part of the glyph for *chum*. Something to do with a king sitting on his throne, is that right?'

He looked up at the glyph over the stairs, and for a moment his heart stopped beating. More than once before he'd seen a drawing like it, and had hoped never to see it again. Caught unawares, he almost blurted out the glyph's true identity, but at the last moment caught himself.

'It's one of the glyphs for the god Chac,' he said, hoping no one would look too closely and spot the lie. In the poor light, he could just get away with it.

There were seven steps down. At their foot was a door of hammered gold. The Ramírez girl – Leo suddenly remembered her name was Antonia – made her way down carefully until she stood on the bottom step. A blurred and hazy image of her body appeared in the

11

irregular surface of the door, as though she had somehow entered it from the other side, or from a dream. She reached out a hand and touched the gold, running her fingers gently over it.

'It's covered in hieroglyphs,' she said, and her fingers brushed them, like those of a blind woman reading a book in Braille.

He stepped down beside her, so close their hips touched, and he could smell her perfume again. When he looked he saw that his own image had been trapped in the gold next to hers.

'How do we open it?' she whispered.

He looked for a clue, but there was no handle, and he could find no hinges at the sides.

'I don't know,' he said. 'It may have been lowered from somewhere above here. There could be wood behind this, or a stone slab six inches thick. Dorothy, could you film this quickly, then let Bob down to photograph the inscriptions. I suggest the rest of us take a break while he does that.'

Nobody wanted to return to the surface. Usually, an hour or two was enough to drive anyone back up in search of fresh air and sunshine. That had changed the moment they set eyes on the golden door.

Coffee was brewed, and fudge brownies made by Diane the day before were devoured. Leo sat back from the others, thinking. He could call the dig off temporarily, until the problem of the door had been solved. That would be unpopular, but sensible. Or he could sit in front of the door until he got it to open.

He sent Leroy, the boyfriend, up top, with instructions to send a couple of the Lacandón Indians back down with crowbars and jacks. As the boy turned back towards the stairs Leo called to him.

'Don't say anything about the find. They don't need to know till later.'

Leroy nodded and vanished into the shadows. Leo doubted that he'd be able to keep quiet about the discovery. The entire team had been expecting something like this for some weeks now. By the time the downstairs shift got to work on the door, the whole expedition would have crammed itself alongside them just for the frisson of being there when it was opened.

He looked down to where Bob was working with his digital camera, the flash bouncing brilliantly off the door's sun-bright surface. From time to time he would pause in order to polish a section, then start again, working his way systematically round the door until it shone like a mirror.

Leroy returned carrying one of the jacks, the first heavy work Leo had seen him perform since their arrival. The kid wasn't cut out for field archaeology, and Leo didn't think he'd be back for another season. Unless he was really keen on Antonia Ramírez. A few minutes later, an Indian appeared, deposited a second jack, and went back up the stairs.

Bob was almost finished. Later, they'd have to take a proper mould, something that would reveal the inscription down to the finest detail. He'd want a sharp copy of the inscription to include in his report, together with the translation he would make from it.

At the thought of the report and the publications that would inevitably follow it, it began to dawn on Leo just how significant this moment would prove for his career. Everyone pretended that archaeology was not about finding lost treasure or cities or the jewel-filled tombs of kings and emperors, that it was no more than hard work to add pieces to a vast jigsaw assembled by a host of others.

That, anyway, was what they told undergraduates and graduate students embarking on an academic career. But Leo had learned some time ago that it simply wasn't true. Size did matter. Big finds were important. They stimulated public interest and they encouraged donors to contribute to future expeditions. And he was about to make a major discovery. In a matter of minutes. Behind that door.

They had to use chisels to cut the bottom step back far enough from the door to allow the jacks access. One jack went at either end. After that, it was a matter of pumping the door up inch by inch. Everyone held their breath as the little contraptions began to take the strain, and the door started its slow lift from the bed in which it had been set over one thousand years earlier.

He waited until the bottom of the door was three feet above the ground. Braces were added until he was satisfied that the door would not come crashing down again while he was inside – or under it. When he stood up at last, he realized there was no point in putting it off any longer. The atmosphere around him was electric, and he found that he was trembling, as though with lust.

'Pass me that torch,' he called out. Antonia Ramírez passed it to him and smiled. Her fingers grazed his as she relinquished it to him. He smiled back, then bent down and took his first step through the door.

2

St-Raphaël
Département du Var
Southern France
10 November
9.10 a.m.

Declan Carberry looked down over the beach in a fit of fake nostalgia. He'd never been in the place before, had no memories of it or any beach quite like it. But if he half-closed his eyes . . .

When he'd been younger, beaches like this one had figured prominently in his fantasies of the good life. His dark, Dublin-bred soul had painted the beaches of his youthful imagination with the lightly-clad forms of every beautiful woman between Donegal and the Wicklow Mountains.

The water beyond the beach was blue enough to pass as ink, the sort of ink that had filled the wells on the rough desks of his old school, a Christian Brothers establishment on the Stillorgan Road. Stillorgan: God, they'd made the most of the name, and with good reason too. 'May God forgive them,' he thought, thinking of the Brothers – Brother Nagle, Brother Horgan, Brother O'Keefe and the scarlet-faced and stormy Brother Ferriter. 'But weren't they a terrible bunch of tossers in the end? And cruel too, they were sadists nearly the lot of them.'

The Brothers would have hated this place, run from it in fear and loathing, their cold Irish eyes shut tight for fear they might see too much naked flesh. Or the wrong sort of naked flesh.

Not that Declan himself found the bare-breasted, sun-worshipping, long-legged young ladies of St-Raphaël easy to cope with. Ignoring them was like trying to keep cool in the close vicinity of a steel furnace. He was fifty, with a paunch that grew bigger by the hour, balding hair, and the nervous, furtive look of a dirty old man written all over his face.

There'd be no good protesting that he was the Deputy Director of Interpol's Liaison and Criminal Intelligence Division, a man of proven virtue and kindly thoughts. The reality was a plump man in a panama hat and dark glasses, feeling intensely out of place. The trouble was, he thought, that if you so much as looked at the beach, you became a species of paedophile. A lot of the naked breasts down there had barely celebrated their first birthdays.

It was still refreshingly early in the morning, and not many of the bronzed beauties or their biceps-ridden friends were about. They partied late, rose late, and waited till well after lunch before descending to the warm sand. These early hours were for the old and the lonely. Declan reckoned he fitted both categories well.

As he watched, a white-haired man walked a baby leopard along the water's edge, like a figure out of a Soldati novel, elegant and depraved at once. Declan closed his eyes. He could feel one of his headaches coming on. The Mincer, by the feel of it. This was his second day in the place, and he still hadn't set foot on the famous beach. The golden sand seemed to stare back at him, mocking and challenging. He'd brought shorts, but every time he tried them on . . .

He'd been forced to take a fortnight's holiday, and, at a loss, he had headed south in the vain hope of reliving the summers of his pallid youth. His first thought had been to take a plane back to Dublin and the first bus out to Ballina. Two weeks on Lough Conn with the fish moving hard beneath the cold water would have set him right. But Ireland had nothing and no one in it now to draw him easily back.

Concepta, his wife, had died a year earlier in an ecstasy of cancer that had ripped through her body like a tide. He'd never loved her, never hated her, and his indifference had ruined his life and hers. His daughter Máiread had died a few years before her, the victim of a terrorist attack in Dublin. He'd been in charge of Ireland's anti-terrorist squad then, and been able to do nothing about it.

His appointment to Interpol had come within weeks of Concepta's passing, courtesy of her brother Pádraig Pearse Mangan, a former prime minister and currently the Irish member on the European Commission. Declan had not been easily persuaded to his new role. All his married life, he'd fought against the political influence of his brother-in-law, and it didn't seem right to capitulate the moment Concepta was in her grave. But he'd been persuaded all the same, in part by a visit from some senior Interpol officials, and in part by his own desperation to get away from Ireland.

Most of his work had been little more than an extension of his Irish anti-terrorist activities, tracing gunmen and bombers in and out of the webs they had spun across Europe and into the world at large. In the past few weeks, however, he'd been tied up more than he liked by a case that might or might not have been linked to terrorism.

Arnaud Nougayrède, the French Foreign Minister, had

disappeared without warning three weeks earlier. Reports of sightings had been received from several countries, but so far nothing concrete had emerged. Three weeks into the investigation, Declan was tired. He had been due a holiday for three months, and in the end his boss had insisted. M. Nougayrède had been handed to Declan's assistant, Frédéric Leparmentier.

The beach had been a mistake all the same, he thought. At his age, he should have been pottering about the fortifications of nearby Carcassonne, or admiring the paintings in Menton's Cocteau museum, or playing roulette in the Salle Europe at Monte Carlo. He had the money to do it, and the common sense not to. Concepta, indifferent to his indifference, had left him her private fortune on her death. She'd have left him the money anyway, even if he'd divorced her under the new legislation.

A speedboat went past, leaving a trail of frothing water in its wake. Maybe the rowboat on Lough Conn would have been the business after all.

'Monsieur Carbeurry?'

The voice did not sound familiar, but he did not turn round to check. If it was somebody who knew him, it could only mean one thing.

'Je m'excuse, Monsieur Carbeurry, mais . . .'

He swore under his breath.

'Yes? What is it?'

'I'm sorry, sir, very sorry; but I have orders to take you back to Paris immediately.'

He sighed deeply and turned. The young plain-clothes man standing a respectful five feet away was a stranger. A local, presumably.

'To *take* me back?'

'I was told I should accompany you, to help you with your luggage.'

'I'm perfectly capable of doing all that myself. I'm not a geriatric yet, you know.'

The young man's face fell, and Declan realized he must have been looking forward to a break in Paris.

'Who asked you to come for me?'

The policeman reddened visibly. He'd been roped into something that made him feel uncomfortable.

'My station commander,' he said. 'But he had his instructions from Paris. From the Préfet de Police himself. He told me I should let you know that. It's very urgent. You have to leave at once.'

Declan was furious. Whatever it was, it would turn out to be a waste of time. He found the French fussy and inclined to exaggerate little things. Suddenly, he remembered that Ireland was playing Paris St Germain at the Parc des Princes. The match was tomorrow night, and no doubt somebody had worked himself into a lather, lumping English and Irish fans together in a single, roaring monster come to devour French civilization.

'When's the next train?' he sighed.

The young man licked his lips.

'There's a private plane waiting for you at Nice airport. A helicopter will take you there.'

Declan thought about the last helicopter ride he'd taken, in a storm over Bantry Bay. He'd vowed then he'd never set foot in one of those things again.

'What's wrong with the road?' he asked.

'There are jams from here to Menton. Please, we have to hurry.'

'I've got to pick my things up at the hotel. And pay my bill.'

'That's all been taken care of. Your bags are on the helicopter.'

'My drugs? The pornographic videos? The whip?'

19

The young policeman's face froze. Declan continued looking at him. It took a while to dawn, but it did.

'Oh, yes, I see, sir. Yes, all discreetly packed up and on board.'

'Good. We'll make a decent Irishman of you yet.' Declan winced. The Mincer was getting into its stride. 'Do you ever get headaches?'

The young man shook his head.

'Not even after sex?'

Another shake of the head and a reddening of the cheeks. Declan started to walk with him away from the beach.

'Got any idea what this is all about?' he asked.

'I was only told to put you on the helicopter. Except . . .'

He hesitated. The air was full of the scents of fruit and flowers. They walked a little further. Declan squared his shoulders: he was no longer a tourist, no longer an innocent passing by shimmering beaches.

'They said I was to warn you.'

'Warn me?'

'To prepare yourself.'

'I don't understand.'

'You're to go straight to the Louvre. Someone will be waiting to take you there from the airport.'

'I don't understand. Has something happened there?'

'In the Louvre? I don't know. I don't think so. He said you were to empty your mind.'

They turned a corner. A helicopter stood, rotors turning, on an empty square of grass.

They took off into a blue sky. He looked down on the little town, then past it to the sea.

'Shit,' he said, to no one in particular.

3

He halted an inch or two inside the door, and straightened slowly, not knowing how high the ceiling might be. It occurred to him that he could have sent someone in ahead of him to set up a battery of lights. They would have filled the chamber with more illumination than it had ever seen, at the same time stripping it of all magic, robbing it of darkness and silence at a single stroke.

He stood upright in the dark, with his eyes tight shut, listening. He could smell faint scents, as though long-dead flowers continued to exhale their odours. Or perhaps funeral incense still burned softly in the endless dark.

He switched on the light. The beam wavered, and at first he could make no sense of anything. He held the torch steady, and bit by bit things started to come into focus. But even when the last fragment had been illuminated, it still took time for it all to come clear in his brain. He had expected a few offerings perhaps, two or three sacrificial victims, a sarcophagus. Not this. The torch swooped and hovered in astonishment, cutting an image from the darkness here, a glimpse of something half-hidden there.

What he remembered most afterwards was the gold. They must have brought every last quill of it that they possessed, and left it here. Two golden discs rested against one wall, each the size of a locomotive wheel. They had been engraved with astronomical symbols, very like the great calendar stone of Tenochtitlán. With a thrill of pleasure, he realized that the discs would make Antonia Ramírez's reputation: he'd ensure she was given the job of transcribing and translating them. Not because she had a pretty smile or a perfect figure, but because he knew she could do the work better than anyone else.

Above the discs stood a four-foot-high model of a *quetzal* bird, its long tail feathers fashioned alternately from gold and silver. In a wide golden bowl lay scattered hundreds of emeralds, and beside them a *chacmool* figure, its belly overflowing with enormous pearls.

Against one wall stood cloth-wrapped silhouettes cut from chert, and next to them bowls overflowing with shark vertebrae, jade beads, and oyster shells.

The room was not large, only about twelve feet by twelve, as far as he could make out. The ceiling rose to around ten feet. Lances tipped with transparent *itztli* grazed its surface, while others lay heaped in bundles on the floor. Near them lay perhaps half a dozen yellowed and grizzled skeletons. He shuddered, knowing they would have been brought here at the end to have their hearts ripped out, as final sacrifices to the lord of the city.

At the centre of all these offerings stood a huge stone sarcophagus, every square inch of which was covered in pictures, with a lengthy inscription running along its edges. Leo crossed to it and laid a shaking hand on the top, next to a carving that showed the dead man in the jaws of the earth monster. He'd be wearing a death-mask of jade, Leo thought, and his wrists and ankles, his shins and arms would be encircled by ornaments of jade. He started to circle the inscription, looking for the dead man's name.

'Leo! Is everything all right in there?'

It was like snapping awake out of a dream.

'I . . . Yes, I'm fine. Everything's . . . Wait a moment, I'll come out.'

He squeezed his way past the tomb offerings again, re-emerging on the other side of the doorway. Faces peered at him, anxious and perturbed. He'd entirely lost track of how long he'd been inside.

Bob came forward. 'You've been in there a long time, kiddo. So, what do we tell the folks back home? All that money for nothing?'

Leo shook his head, but he couldn't bring himself to describe what he'd seen.

'It's better than we expected,' he said.

'"Better" like in "Wow!", or "better" as in "it could have been worse"?' asked Leroy. He was standing near the door, holding Antonia's hand.

'You'd better see for yourselves.'

He ordered battery-operated lights set up inside, and said three people could go in at a time.

'Antonia, why don't you go in first?' he suggested. 'There's something in there you're going to like.'

She took his torch and went inside. The twins followed her, carrying the portable lights. Minutes later, the interior of the tomb lit up as though someone had sliced the pyramid away. Inside, someone swore beneath their breath. The Filberts started to hum a little tune that they alone could recognize.

Diane edged up to him.

'Doctor Mallory, are you all right? You look kinda pale.'

He looked round. 'What? Oh, I'm fine, I'm OK. Just a bit . . .'

'You look shocked. What did you find in there? Martians?'

'Maybe. You should get in line, Diane. I'm going up top for a breath of air. Once everyone's had a chance to see inside, I want the chamber sealed again.'

'Sealed? But . . .'

'Come on, Diane. Give me a break. I need time to think about this, decide what we do next. Ask Bob to see the slab's put back in place. However much he may want to, tell him he's not to start filming or taking photographs.'

'Where will you be?'

'You'll find me in the canteen. I want everybody there in half an hour.'

They argued for hours that evening. It was a Friday, and there'd been a plan to send everybody back up to San Cristóbal de las Casas for a long weekend. They'd been in the forest for eight weeks now, working without a break, and Leo didn't think he'd be able to get more out of them if they didn't have some R&R. Till that afternoon, they'd all been of the same opinion. Now, it seemed that things had changed.

'I'm delighted you're all so eager to work at last.' Leo found himself confronting a sea of hostile faces. 'When you get back on Tuesday, you may not be so keen. Let's face it, we've got more work ahead of us than any of us guessed. If you don't get some relaxation now, you won't get a chance later.'

'I think that's our decision to make,' said Steve Sabloff, the team's British-born computer expert. The comment sounded rich to Leo, coming, as it did, from someone who wouldn't choose tea over coffee without first running the question through a computer program. Steve was an old friend, and someone Leo felt he could depend on; but at times he could be awkward, as now.

'As a matter of fact, Steve, it isn't. The final decision in all matters affecting this expedition rests with me. That's why I'm called expedition leader, if you haven't entirely forgotten.'

He surveyed them again. He could understand their frustration, but he knew he had to hold it in check. A find like this was too important to be left to the whims of a group of postgrads or anybody else who might want to stick their heads in.

'OK now, just listen to me. If we let anybody on the outside know what we've found before the time's right, this patch of forest is going to be overrun by TV crews from Mexico City to Tokyo. If anybody here thinks giving interviews to the press is a more useful way to spend their time than actually working on the dig, then I'd rather they didn't come back after the weekend.'

'Christ, Leo, you're getting the wrong end of the stick. We're more than happy to avoid the attentions of Japanese television. All we want is to be left here to get on with our work.'

'It's not that simple. We need our monthly supplies flown in. And it looks like we're going to need things we didn't plan on. The expedition was booked in at the Casa Mexicana months ago. They expected you last month, and if you don't show up as planned, somebody will start asking questions.'

Leroy got to his feet. He looked angry. Leo thought he could be a troublemaker. He was a clever kid from a broken home in the ghetto who'd worked his way through college. He'd finish his Ph.D. next year and start looking for a teaching post with prospects. It was one hell of an achievement. But Leo disliked him. He thought Leroy was pursuing Antonia because her family had money, lots of it.

'Doctor Mallory, I don't understand what you're saying

here. You talk about "you". "If you don't show up as planned". I thought you had a room booked at the Casa Mexicana along with the rest of us. Or am I wrong?'

'No, you're not wrong. I do have a room. But somebody's got to stay behind here to look after things. We could argue about who that should be, but it wouldn't get us anywhere. Until I hear to the contrary, I'm in charge here, so I'm taking responsibility for the site during your absence.'

'You're not planning to help yourself to a handful of emeralds, are you, Doc? I mean, it looks like a great opportunity.'

'I'll pretend I didn't hear that, Leroy.'

'You can pretend all you want, but the boy has a point.' Bill Jessop looked like he might turn purple. He'd been eaten up ever since hearing of the discovery of the burial chamber.

'I'll disregard that as well. Just remember that I'm not going anywhere.'

'What about the Indians?'

Antonia was referring to the casual labour the expedition recruited from a nearby tribe of Nahá Lacandón Indians.

'They won't be here either. They already spend most weekends back in their encampment anyway. This won't be any different.'

The arguments went back and forth for hours, but they gave way in the end, except for Leroy, Bill, and one or two others, who sulked and formed a small and insignificant faction. It was past midnight by the time anyone got to bed. The last thing Leo heard that night was the thin cry of a jaguar prowling beyond the trees.

The helicopter landed almost bang on schedule early Saturday morning. José, the pilot, had worked for Pemex on one of the Chiapas oil fields, ferrying personnel and equipment from place to place. He didn't treat archaeologists any different to oilmen, and he didn't handle the helicopter any differently to the horses he'd ridden down in the Guatemalan highlands, at the festival of Todos Santos.

The chopper was a half-tamed Chinook, a brute of a thing painted unevenly in olive green, that José had bought thirteenth-hand from a dealer in Quintana Roo. According to José, it had fought on every side in every conflict in Central America over the past twenty years. If you looked closely, you could make out Guatemalan, Honduran, and El Salvadorean decals under the drab paint. Leo had his suspicions that its front-line life wasn't exactly over, especially when it came to smuggling illicit substances.

It came down out of a blue sky, its fast-spinning blades throwing the forest into confusion. Birds fled from the shaking trees in a flurry of colours, their cries crushed by the craft's powerful engine. A tribe of spider monkeys threw themselves screaming from branch to branch in their desperation to escape. The Chinook sank down slowly to the plaza that had been cleared in front of the pyramid, as though that had always been its place. With the usual exceptions, the group cheered and whistled as it set down. This was their bridge to civilization.

It took half an hour to unload the supplies, mainly cans of gasoline for the generators. José would pick up the empty cans when he returned after the weekend.

While the team was busy unloading and stacking crates of water and packs of beer, Leo took the opportunity to speak to Bill Jessop. They walked down to the forest's edge. Behind the trees, it was silent, as though life had ceased.

'Bill, I'm going to come straight to the point. I don't want you on the return flight. I think you should go back to Chicago. Make some excuse, say you're ill; I really don't care.'

'What the fuck are you talking about?'

'I'm talking about you cocking up. I don't just mean last night's careless language, though God knows there's been plenty of it since we got here. What I mean is the way you broke through that wall yesterday. You damaged a fresco in the top temple last month, you got the measurements on the bottom temple completely arse-backwards, you've let some of the kids working under you make finds without making proper records. Shall I go on?'

'We all make mistakes, Mallory.'

'You make more than most. The truth is, whatever you may think, you're not a field archaeologist. I want you off this team and off this site. You can make it hard for yourself, or you can make it easy by pleading illness or whatever takes your fancy.'

Jessop had reddened visibly. He seemed both hurt and angry, and Leo could not tell if he was about to shout abuse at him or burst into tears.

'You can't do this to me, Mallory.'

'I'm offering you an easy way out.'

'You're offering me forced retirement. This project was important to me. I haven't published anything significant in five years or more, and my faculty board's getting edgy. A good report from this dig would have put everything right.'

'I'm sorry. But you have tenure, don't you?'

'Have I fuck! They're removing tenure in my department next year. My post comes up for review. That's why I need this. Especially since it looks like we've got something big. This discovery could put my career right back on track. You and I can co-author the main report. If you like, you can put your name first, I don't give a fuck.'

Leo felt uneasy. He hadn't reached his decision lightly. His mind had been made up by the previous afternoon's find. He simply had to keep Bill Jessop and his clumsy fingers away from the treasures in the burial chamber.

'Bill, I'm sorry to hear about your tenure problem. That can't be a lot of fun at your age. But your name isn't going on that report. To be honest, I've been covering for you ever since you got here. Every one of your progress reports has been re-written by me and Antonia Ramírez. Now, I could send Chicago your original, uncorrected versions. But I'm willing to provide them with the polished text, as long as there's no fuss about my dismissing you. Take a few days to think about it. Now, I think it's time you got on board.'

Bill's mouth opened and closed a few times, then Leo could see he'd already started to weigh up the pros and cons. Up on the deck of the helicopter, José was growing impatient. He'd have a job waiting for him back in San Cristóbal or Villahermosa; that was the way he cut things, very close to whatever edge there was. Bill turned and headed for the ramp. As he reached it, he turned back again and looked at Leo, like a condemned man turning to eye his judge.

'Fuck you, Mallory. Fuck you to hell. I may be back here sooner than you think. See if I'm not. I sure as hell ain't going to let you build some frigging British Empire at my expense. You understand me, son? You're on American soil, boy, near as makes no difference. This ain't fucking Wembley-on-Thames.'

Leo walked away slowly. He'd stopped listening, but he was shaking inside.

At the last moment, Diane came running across to him.

'Doctor Mallory, are you sure you don't want to come? Nobody's going to touch any of this stuff. You could leave it here a year, nobody would touch it.'

'Thanks, Diane, but I wouldn't feel easy in my mind.'

She was wearing hot pants. He dreaded to think what they were doing to her circulation. As for what they were doing to his libido . . .

'In that case, I'll just have to do my best to make you feel easy.'

'How's that?'

'Well, San Cristóbal doesn't really have a lot to offer a girl like me. I'd just as happily stay here.'

'Diane, I don't think that's such a good idea. Your mother wouldn't like it.'

'It's a great idea. My mother's dead, and my old man's a long ways away. If you like, I can spend the nights with you. Keep you from getting too cold and lonely.'

'Diane, I'm old enough to be your –'

'No, you're not. My father's forty-five and not half as attractive as you. Anyway, I like older men, just as long as they aren't bald and fat. You do find me attractive, don't you?'

His head had started spinning. Off in the trees, a Black Howler monkey had started to screech defiance of the helicopter. Its cry had been picked up by the rest of its group. Leo could tell the roaring, barking cry of the males from the wailing and groaning noises put out by the females. And now a host of other animals were joining in. Macaws were screeching, and blue manakins darted in and out of the foliage. Leo started to stutter an answer, then closed his mouth. When he was in control again, he grabbed her and started pushing her towards the helicopter.

'Diane, you've been cooped up in this jungle too long. It's gone to your head. Your clothes are much too tight. Believe me, you don't need all this. Hell, I don't need this.'

'Don't be such a hypocrite. You can't take your eyes off me. My body fascinates you. My backside drives you mad.'

'Those hot pants are cutting off the blood supply to your head. Diane, I swear, I think you're very attractive and very sexy; it's just that I . . . don't fancy you.'

'Well, Doc, I fancy you like mad. I don't want love, I want a week or two of hot-blooded passion. What's the harm if we snuggle up to one another?'

If she hadn't said 'snuggle', he might have weakened. Pushing harder than ever, he managed to get her to the helicopter steps.

'Remember, I'm off the menu after this, Doctor Mallory. What do you say?'

'Bye, Diane. Have fun. And, speaking of menus, why don't you bring me back an *enchilada* or two?'

She turned, raised a finger, and almost spat at him.

'Fuck you, Doctor. Or maybe not.'

He handed her up to José, who was shaking his head in wonder at Leo's fortitude. The door slid shut, and moments later, the rotor was turning again, pushing the animals further back into the forest. They usually took about a day to recover.

When he looked again, the helicopter was a tiny thing against the sky. Then it passed beyond the first trees and was hidden by the forest. The chopping of its rotors faded at last, leaving Leo with no one for company but a band of monkeys. He was already regretting his haste in sending Diane off with a flea in her ear.

4

Paris
11.30 a.m.

'How many were there?'

'How many what?'

'Bodies.'

'Eight.'

He'd been met at the airport by Gustave Seurel, Chief of the Paris Homicide Squad. Seurel had wasted no time in giving a rundown of what to expect when they got to their destination. Declan felt his stomach wrench, as though there was a little man inside, desperately trying to get out. And the headache proceeded with slow violence. One moment, paradise, the next, back on the job with a sick gut and a head full of razor blades.

'Who found them?'

'The porter, a Moroccan called Dris Benani, forty-six. No work permit. Doesn't want to talk. I'll see to it he does.'

'He's afraid he'll be deported.'

Seurel thought about it. 'I'd say he's just afraid. After what he saw . . .'

The Citroën wriggled through the traffic like a weasel in heat. Declan wondered why there hadn't been a helicopter at this end. As if reading his thoughts, Seurel turned to him. He was in his mid-thirties, Declan guessed, an assured product of a conservative CEG and police academy. He was handling this well. Too well, if his account of the killings was dependable.

'I'd have had a chopper pick you up, only . . . it's not so easy to land back at the Louvre.'

'Why there? Hmmm?'

Seurel shook his head. His suit was so well pressed, Declan feared the creases might cut him.

'No idea. It's maybe just random. Killers don't always have a reason for the choices they make.'

'You're sure of that?'

They edged out from the Boulevard de la Madeleine, did a turn of the square of the same name, and pushed their way down into the rue Royale. Their motorcycle escort cut a narrow swathe through a thick bouillabaisse of cars in front. A woman in furs stepped elegantly out of Ladurée carrying a tiny dog and crossed right in front of them without turning a hair or slackening her step. Declan thought of stopping for a *cramique* and a cup of tea.

'Sometimes the scene of the crime is just coincidental,' Seurel volunteered.

'And usually not.' Declan looked out on the grey winter streets, so far removed from those he'd stood on earlier that morning. 'Have you spoken to Boulanger yet?'

Boulanger was the new Minister for the Interior; he had a reputation for small-mindedness, and his views on crime and criminals were regularly deleted from government statements on law enforcement. He had rashly vowed to bring back the guillotine and even volunteered to operate it with his own hand.

'Boulanger was the one who insisted on bringing you in at this stage. If it had been left to me . . .'

'You don't have to explain. I'd have resented you too, if our roles were reversed. But why on earth did Boulanger –'

'You don't need me to tell you that. Interpol means this isn't a French crime. If that's the case, it must be the work of foreigners, probably dark-coloured ones. Boulanger is a racist. *Ça s'explique . . .*'

They turned on to the Quai des Tuileries. Declan squinted through the tinted window at the Seine, rolling past on the right. He wished it was the Liffey: French rivers were too turgid for his liking. The French annoyed him, with their pathological dread of foreigners. He remembered something his father had told him, years ago. The old man had been an unreformed Sinn Feiner with little time for the English. 'It's like this, Declan,' he'd said, 'the British conquered an empire and told everyone in it that the greatest thing in the world was to be ruled by Englishmen. The French, on the other hand, had an empire of their own, and they told everyone in it that there was nothing greater to aspire to than to be a Frenchman.' He turned to Seurel.

'We don't know it was the work of foreigners, though, do we? That's pure surmise, surely.'

'Boulanger doesn't surmise. And the *a priori* evidence –'

'Fuck the *a priori* evidence. I want to see this for myself. I hope to God nothing's been tampered with.'

'No more than necessary. The crime scene was sealed off pretty quickly. Benani called the *flics* from the Bourse Commissariat. It's more or less round the corner.'

The entrances to the Louvre had been cordoned off. A gaggle of uncomprehending tourists stood before each one, preferring to be locked out of the Louvre than to go elsewhere. A light drizzle had started, bringing the

35

Japanese out in a sudden rash of brightly-coloured rain-coats. An enterprising seller of pocket umbrellas wound his way among them, extending and compressing his wares.

Police cars waited like oversized beetles in the Cour Napoléon. Policemen hung about with an anxious air, not knowing if their presence was needed any longer, or whether this was to be the start of a very long day.

'I'd like to see it from this level first,' said Declan.

'You can't see much.'

'Nevertheless. And I want photographs. Be sure that's done.'

They walked up to the glass pyramid that dominated the courtyard. He'd never been able to make his mind up whether he liked it or not. No doubt what he was about to see would give him a permanent aversion to the place. He had places at home like that, none worse than the ice-cream parlour where his daughter Máiread had been murdered.

The rain had already smeared the glass with a film of drops that grew coarser by the minute. Declan bent across and rubbed his sleeve over one pane, exposing the scene underneath. It took some time to distinguish one thing or one person from another – a chair from a tripod, a policeman from a photographer, a photographer from an Interior Ministry dogsbody, and any of the foregoing from a victim.

Then, as the glass cleared, things came into focus one by one. The first things Declan could make out clearly were the victims. They were easy to pick out now. They lay on their backs, they were naked, and a trail of blood led away from each one.

'Monsieur Carberry, won't you come inside? It's getting uncomfortably wet. After all, you're wasting your time up here. My men scoured this area hours ago. They found nothing.'

Declan continued to stare down. The space underneath was the reception area and public entrance to the Louvre.

'You surprise me,' he said. 'The courtyard here is open to the public. I've been here myself and seen people hanging about the pyramid, chatting and smoking. Now, isn't it wonderful your men never set eyes on so much as a Gitane or a sweetie wrapper. God Almighty, they'd be better employed by the Department of Sanitation. They'd have this city as clean as the Pope's arse by Sunday.'

Seurel looked at him thinly.

'Monsieur Carberry, my men found plenty of cigarette stubs and sweet wrappers. But there was nothing that had the slightest connection to this crime.'

Declan continued to stare down. 'He arranged them to be seen from up here,' he said. 'They make a rough pattern that won't be obvious at ground level. How many bodies did you say there were?'

'Eight.'

'So. They're all visible from here. More precisely, they're all under the pyramid. No coincidence, Gustave. This site was carefully chosen.'

Seurel let his gaze follow Declan's. He was tight-lipped and ashen-faced, and he could feel control of this case passing out of his hands. When the dust had settled, he'd have questions to answer, especially if Interpol took charge. He looked up as another black car arrived, spraying everything with rainwater. A middle-aged man stepped out and headed for the entrance.

'That's Monsieur Arlaten, the City Pathologist. His assistants have been here since soon after the discovery. I expect he's coming to get the bodies back to his laboratory.'

'In that case, let's get down there double-quick. I don't want him putting a hand on anyone till I've had a chance to look at them properly.'

'Monsieur Arlaten, our paths haven't crossed in some time.'

The pathologist, hearing his name, turned and scanned the faces behind him. He recognized Seurel, of course, but they'd last met two days ago. The man beside him looked familiar.

'Ah, Monsieur Carberry. *Dia's Muire dhuit.*'

Arlaten spent a month of every year in a fishing boat on a lake in County Kildare. He spoke enough Irish to spit and swear with, drank a lot of Guinness, and was lucky if he caught two fish in a season. He didn't mind about the fish: they weren't the reason he sat in a wet boat on a lake while the rain sluiced down from a sky that had been in the Atlantic only an hour earlier. The reason he sought such refuge was all around him now.

That wasn't all. In a long career, he had known himself grow unsettled perhaps a dozen times. Some murders remained caught in the eye and frozen in the mind because they deviated in some explicit and shocking way from the ordinary run of such things. Most murders were mundane, tawdry affairs, small acts of sudden violence done with a brick or a metal bar or a rusty kitchen knife, the pathetic products of stale, pathetic lives. Most murders inspired disgust in him, or pity, or common hatred. But the others, the ones that made even his long-inured skin crawl, ones like that, they looked you straight in the eye and challenged you to comprehend. Or to forget. That was the case here, eight times repeated.

'I needn't ask what it is that brings you here, Mr Carberry. Have you been looking round the bodies?'

Declan shook his head. 'I haven't set eyes on them yet. Do you mind if I hold you up for a bit while I do so?'

Arlaten, angry at the delay, yet too polite to say so, told Declan he could do as he pleased.

'Perhaps, Monsieur, you'd be kind enough to give me a guided tour. This is the Louvre, after all.'

Declan hated to sound flippant; but it was part of his defence mechanism. He avoided murder scenes wherever possible. Especially ones like this.

The eight bodies had been laid in pairs, one pair aligned to each flank of the pyramid, their legs straight out, their arms tucked in by their sides, like soldiers at attention. In the middle, directly underneath the apex of the pyramid, stood a heavy stone shaped like a dome. There were traces of blood on it, and lightly-incised carvings all round its perimeter. The fingerprint boys were working on it as Declan approached, brushing and photographing every detail.

'Mr Carberry, why don't you come over here?' Arlaten was stooping over one of the two bodies laid within the north triangle of the pyramid. It was naked except for a loincloth tied tightly about the hips. Declan guessed that the victim had been a man in his thirties, fit, but by no means an athlete. More than that escaped him at the moment. There was nothing to guess from the face, since the man's head – like those of all the others – had been skilfully detached from the torso and hung a few yards away on a free-standing frame.

The victim had suffered a second appalling injury: his chest had been cut open, and the heart removed from it. The hearts of all eight victims had been placed in a row before the stone.

'Do you see anything of interest about the chest wounds, Mr Carberry?' Arlaten asked.

'That's your job. As far as I can see, they were cut open, their hearts were cut out and left over there.'

'Well, look more closely. Perhaps it will help if I explain that there are only four ways of opening the chest cavity in order to excise a heart. Whoever did this – and it was not one person, by the way, he had assistants – seems to have been experimenting a little. Here, let me show you.'

The pathologist knelt down, taking great care to keep the fabric of his expensive suit from any traces of blood. Reluctantly, Declan knelt facing him.

'This poor devil,' Arlaten said, 'is the only one with a vertical incision. Do you see? It runs from the suprasternal notch' – he put his finger on a spot just below where the Adam's apple had been – 'all the way down to the bottom end of the sternum.'

Declan felt sick. His headache was pretending to be something else. A mortar bomb, possibly. The gaping wound looked like a baited trap that the slightest touch would spring.

'If I were performing an operation, I would describe this as a midline axial sternotomy. In a modern hospital, the first incision would be followed by a direct cut through the breastbone with an electric saw. The killer didn't have such modern equipment. My guess is that he used a hammer and a sharp stone to break the bone apart. Once he was in, getting the heart out would have been easy.

'But it's not an ideal way to excise the heart, especially when you're performing a ritual – which I take it was the case here. A much neater way' – he stood – 'is just over here.'

'Have you been here earlier?' Declan asked, straightening.

'But of course. I only came back now to supervise the

transfer of the bodies to the mortuary. They've been here too long already, but I was told we had to wait.'

They went round to the east flank. The rain had stopped, and a pale city light pressed itself against the wet panes like a bloodless face straining to see what lay behind them.

The bodies on the east side were those of a man and a woman. Both had deep cuts running for several inches under the left nipple. Arlaten bent down beside the male victim.

'This is a left anterior intercostal incision. We use it nowadays to give open heart massage. It's not an easy way to get to the heart, though on the whole I'd prefer it myself. Our killer knows about cardiac operations, I think. He's seen them or taken part in them.'

'How do you know?'

'I hope I'll have more evidence for you by tomorrow. But take a look here. The problem with this approach is getting at the heart through the ribs. Let me show you.'

Before Declan could move to stop him, the pathologist took a thin rubber glove from his pocket and slipped it over his right hand.

'You see,' he said, barely pausing as he inserted his hand into the wound and moved it towards the space where the heart had been, 'my hand goes into the cavity very well.' He wiggled his hand about, making the flesh above it roll and distort. Declan hated the way some pathologists handled the human body.

'There's no need. I can see perfectly –'

'No, you don't see. This is not enough. I have to get through the rib cage somehow, and quickly. I don't have all day. A complete beginner might not know just how well protected the heart is. But he knew. As far as I can tell, he managed to get through quite easily, and that means he must have used some sort of "rib-spreader", probably one obtained from a surgical supply company.'

'How do you know he got his hand through easily? Couldn't he have pulled it through the ribs?'

'If he had done so, the heart would almost certainly have torn apart. None of the hearts on display seems badly damaged.'

'Could we be looking for a heart surgeon?'

Arlaten shook his head. 'I'd almost certainly say "no". The incisions are amateurish. They're not the work of a surgeon, not even a junior one. But the killer could have been a nurse or even an orderly, someone regularly present at heart operations. On the other hand . . .'

'Yes?'

'Take a look round you. This wasn't set up to imitate an operating theatre at the Salpêtrière. It's a primitive ritual.'

'You said there were several ways to carry out this operation.'

Arlaten straightened and scratched his nose. Whatever stress he might have been under, neither his features nor his manner betrayed it for a moment. Whereas Declan, as he looked round the bloody chamber to which he had been brought, felt shabby, dishevelled, and sad.

'Four, to be precise. One involves cutting through from the abdomen upwards. It doesn't feature here, and to be honest it's not the best method. What our killer favoured is the last approach, a bilateral transverse thoractomy. Take a look.'

Five of the bodies had been dissected in this manner. Each one had been cut across horizontally, from one side to the other, leaving a large gaping wound.

'They'll have held them on their backs across the stone, one man holding each arm, and one each leg. In that position, the chest would be lifted and curved. The killer will have cut across with a saw or something like that. In the process, he'll have caused the lungs to collapse as the blade penetrated the pleural spaces, here and here. Now that has two advantages. It exposes the heart very well, and it causes the victim to lose consciousness.'

Declan turned to him in horror.

'I'm sorry, Doctor – are you saying they were conscious up to that point?'

Arlaten nodded drily.

'I'm fairly sure,' he said. 'Though they may have been anaesthetized or dulled in some way.'

'All of them?'

'I would imagine so. You must remember that he wants to keep them alive as long as possible. The purpose of the exercise is to remove a beating heart. That isn't easy, not unless you know what you're doing.'

'You're sure of this?'

'My dear man, of course I'm sure. They may not have been conscious, but they will have been alive. He was performing a ritual. His victims were not the real sacrifices. His aim was to extract the living heart. When I've had a proper chance to examine the bodies, I'll tell you whether he succeeded or not.'

'Jesus Christ Almighty! What sort of lunatic would do something like this?'

Arlaten shook his grey head softly.

'I think you will find, monsieur, that he is not a lunatic. Not he and not his assistants. Don't look in the asylums for this man. Look in the schools, look in the colleges.'

'Why there?'

'Because he has studied what he does. He has gained proficiency somewhere. I can't tell you how much, that is not my expertise. But I think it very likely that he has done this before. More than once.'

'But you said – a ritual of some kind. Are they Satanists? Voodoo worshippers?'

Arlaten shook his head again.

'I don't think you will find your answer among that crowd, though God knows there are plenty of bizarre cults in this country. Satanists are a surprisingly insipid bunch. They like to boast about how dreadful they are, about their willingness to perform human sacrifice; but in practice few of them have the guts for it. Most of them would faint at the sight of a cut finger. I'd say you should look further afield. Was it the ancient Aztecs who used to tear out their victims' hearts?'

'Yes, but I don't expect we'll find too many ancient Aztecs in the near vicinity of the Louvre.'

'Perhaps not. But old habits die hard. Bear it in mind. Consult an expert in religious studies, or one of these sociologists who specialize in cults. Now, let me get these corpses away from here before they begin to stink.'

5

He didn't feel the force of his isolation until the sun went down, quickly and effortlessly beneath a western horizon he could not see. Diane's burst of anger still troubled him, and awakened fears that she might cause some sort of trouble when she got back to base. She had spoiled brat written all over her. What made things worse, he was starting to regret his decision. Every time he closed his eyes, her small, prominent breasts and tightly-curved hips would tantalize him, and he thought he must have been mad to order her away. How to win friends, influence people, and get laid.

He reflected that he hadn't made love to a woman in two years, not since Dorana. Even now, he didn't like to think about it. Dorana had been a Romanian gymnast who'd made Cambridge her home soon after Ceausescu's fall. She'd been seventeen then, and twenty-three when he met her in 1995, at a reception for Romanian academics looking for money and books with which to rebuild their national university library. God knows why she'd been there, he thought; she hadn't the slightest interest in books or libraries or universities. Her only interest was sport.

None of that had mattered to him then. He'd thought it refreshing to be with someone so lovely and so unformed. And perhaps, if he was really honest, he'd imagined he could change her, transform her into a first-rate intellectual with the physique of an athlete and the body of a siren. Some of his friends had warned him, but he'd judged their remarks as the product of jealousy and spite and blind academic prejudice. But as time went by, he realized that however much those things may have played their part in making a scandal of their match, they had contained more than a nugget of common sense.

Dorana became impatient with everything that mattered to him. When he had to prepare lectures or finish papers for a deadline, she would pout and seethe and go off for hours on her own. She stopped attending her English classes, despite the fact that her command of the language was still atrocious. He refused to learn Romanian, knowing it would make her even lazier. In the end, they exhausted all the things they could talk about with the vocabulary of a twelve-year-old. Meals became silent affairs, dinner parties drab exercises in how not to talk to Dorana. She ceased attending college events, he stopped making the effort to see her perform at gymnastic competitions. The gap between them grew intolerable. And one morning in August he woke to find her gone.

He remembered very little of her now. Her swiftness, her agility on the high bars and in bed, the smoothness of her motions, the fluidity of her limbs, their strength as they gave her momentary flight, and her long hair uncoiling as she came to him, unadorned, at the end of day.

He looked up and saw her standing in the open doorway of the common room. She was dressed in a blue leotard, and her feet were bare; he could sense her muscles beneath the thin cloth, taut, like those of a cat about to leap. He closed his eyes and rubbed them with his fingers, and when he opened them again, she was gone and the door was closed.

He made himself a meal of *frijoles* and rice around seven, and washed it down with a can of Nochebuena beer straight from the fridge. With the sun down, the temperature dropped alarmingly. Up here was *terra fria*, the cold country, where the winter nights were vicious. He went back to his bedroom and lit the oil-fired heater that stood in its centre. The thought of a cold bed ahead of him made him regret Diane's absence all the more keenly.

After eating, he made a tour of the generators, topping them up where necessary, and making a note of their oil levels in the little book provided for the purpose. Their constant throbbing allowed him the pretence that the camp was inhabited by more than himself.

At least he could be sure the forest was alive. At regular intervals, the sounds of nightbirds and prowling animals drifted in his direction. Every so often, there would be a screech and a cry of agonizing pain as a predator sank its claws or teeth into the neck of a fresh victim. A tree frog croaked its way through some sort of eerie anthem that had neither beginning nor end. And a monkey, high in the trees, gibbered menaces to an unseen enemy.

He finished stacking and storing the day's shipment of food and equipment, then sat down to compile a list of things they might need for the weeks ahead. If he radioed through tomorrow, there might be time to load some of them on the Chinook. But most of what they would need to handle a find this size would have to come from further afield.

When he finished his tasks, he went back to his room. It was hot inside, maybe too hot. He turned off the heater and got into bed. It was almost eleven o'clock.

He yawned and switched off the light. Darkness rolled over him like dust. There was only one place darker than this, he thought, and that was deep in the heart of the pyramid.

He breathed deeply, urging himself to sleep, and sleep came quickly, trotting across the floor and jumping into bed beside him, urging itself upon him like a wanton.

His first, broken dreams were of Diane, teasing him, urging him on until he could scarcely bear it. He would see her somewhere in the city, naked and beckoning, and set off to join her. But each time he reached a destination, he would look for her in vain. In the end, he was left alone in an empty city at the heart of a great, empty forest from which all but the spiders had gone.

He plunged more deeply into sleep, and for a time no dreams came. He tossed and turned on his camp bed, but if he cried out, there were no words. And then a darker dream began.

He found himself standing naked at the top of the pyramid, just inside the temple. It was night, and there were no sounds. He listened hard, and it was then he heard what sounded like a child crying bitterly. The sound seemed to come from below, from the heart of the pyramid, where a man without a name lay buried beneath layers of antique jade.

He found the entrance to the stairway and began to make the long descent. There was no light, and several times he lost his footing and almost fell headlong. The crying grew louder. Who the hell had left a child down there? he wondered. He reached the bottom step. Lights had been lit all the way through to the burial chamber.

The crying had turned to a thin wail that made the hair on his neck prickle and curl. He felt goose pimples rush across the surface of his flesh. He made his way down to the burial room. Someone had lifted the slab and kept it in place with columns of heavy books. He squeezed through and stood up. A baby lay on the flat top of the sarcophagus. Towering above it was the figure of a man dressed in ancient Mayan robes, a huge back-frame supporting a massive arrangement of *quetzal* feathers. In his hand he held an obsidian knife, its polished point directed at the child's undefended chest.

With a surge of panic and a gasp of breath, Leo came awake. The room was still far too hot. For a moment, he thought he could still hear the baby wailing, but in the same instant the sound was swept away into the silence. He sat up in bed and switched on the light.

Slowly, the dreams ebbed away, leaving no more than faint traces of themselves on his mind. He tried to read, but felt the words tangle and knit peculiarly in his brain. Switching off the light, he made a second attempt at sleeping; but within fifteen minutes he had put the light on again and was sitting on the edge of the bed, staring at the mud wall.

He struggled to his feet. There was no point in fighting it. From long experience he knew that, no matter how hard he tried, sleep would not come again till morning, if at all.

He dressed and shuffled back to the common room, pausing on the way to take another beer from the fridge. It was freezing in here, so he switched the heater on and slumped beside it, sipping beer and tuning in to Radio Universidad out of Mexico City. They were playing dance tunes from the fifties and sixties, louche numbers that worked their way through every variety of the tango, the mambo, and the samba. If nothing else, it was soothing. Maybe it would even help him nod off to sleep, he hoped.

It didn't. He got up and went to a window, staring out on pitch darkness. Behind him, the music played for ever. On reflection, he thought he shouldn't have stayed on. There would be days of this isolation before the rest of the team returned. It was Saturday now, no, early Sunday, and their party weekend stretched to Tuesday morning. He had a long wait ahead of him.

What, after all, had he stayed here to protect? The others had been right – no one was out there waiting to pounce on the burial chamber and carry its treasures off into the forest.

But if he was here, he reasoned that he might as well put himself to some use. It wasn't hard to guess what that ought to be. Ever since he'd set eyes on it, he'd wanted to get the sarcophagus to himself, to start reading the inscriptions that snaked their way across it.

He went back to his room and found what he needed. On his way out, he paused to slip on a down-lined jacket. It was warm and comfortable, and for a moment he wondered what the original inhabitants of the city had worn on nights like this.

Outside, a quarter moon had slipped free of the treetops and was sailing self-consciously in an old sky pebbled with stars. A pale light drifted down and laid a faint luminescence on trees and stone. Right ahead of him, the pyramid loomed out of the darkness, strange and forbidding. The forest sounds continued, unsettling him. He wondered what it would have been like to live here in a different darkness, listening to the fear of prisoners waiting for sacrifice, watching the forest for the coming and going of the oldest gods. And for a moment he sensed the city come alive, felt himself surrounded by curious eyes. It made his sense of isolation all the keener.

He switched on the generator and cranked upwards in

the wooden lift. Now he was up here with only the ill-lit stairway ahead of him, he wasn't so sure he wanted to head down there alone. But no real archaeologist could have resisted for long the thought of that room with its treasures and the sarcophagus in its centre.

The walls closed in on him, heavy and austere; the stone exuded a thin miasmatic air that lay on his lungs like the breath on the surface of a stagnant pool. He clambered down more carefully than usual, knowing that, if he had an accident, he'd have to lie here in the half dark for days.

When he finally reached the lower temple, it seemed both desolate and remote, as if he was the first human being to set eyes on it in centuries. He had never been here without the company of others, without jokes or snatches of song to fend off the total strangeness, the unlikeness of it. Just because he could read the words on the walls, or interpret the paintings, did not mean that he was comfortable here. If anything, his detailed knowledge of what they had done down here made it harder for him to like it, or feel at home.

As he passed towards the burial chamber, his eye was caught again by the strange glyph over the doorway. It was not the glyph for the god Chac, as he'd known all along. This was a simpler sign than that, the sign for Xiknalkan, the Flying Serpent. It was the name the ancient Mayan astronomers had given to the constellation Serpens. For part of the year, Serpens hung directly above their heads, the very image of a snake twisting through the heavens. At its head one star burned more brightly than the rest, the Serpent Star, Kan Ek . . .

Leo had seen it several times before, in scattered inscriptions, and always with the same meaning – a curse, or a foreboding of some dreadful thing to come.

Normally, he'd have laughed at himself for bothering with it at all; but down here alone it seemed a terrible thing. He could never have learned to decipher their horrendously intricate inscriptions had he not, in some measure, become a Maya in part of himself.

As he walked through, his footsteps sent curious echoes ringing round the pillars. He walked softly in order to deaden them. The golden door was back in place again, but the jacks were still underneath it, ready to raise it for a second time.

He worked the jacks up slowly until the door was high enough to let him comfortably inside. A startled spider scuttled away from him, its long legs hammering against the floor. He shivered and tried to put it out of his mind as he started to rig up a set of electric lights.

When all was done, he stood at the heart of the dead room, putting gold and feathers, serpents and spiders out of his mind. His fingers touched the cold stone of the sarcophagus, and he started the long process of unravelling the complex hieroglyphic text.

Within minutes, the inscription had captured him. He ceased to be conscious of his surroundings, focusing his mind entirely on the elaborate strings of pictorial writing that an unknown scribe had chiselled so carefully into the stone.

Balam Ahau Chaan, he read in a half whisper, *Lord of Komchen, King of the Kekchi people, sixth ruler of the Yax Kuk Mo dynasty, may he live for ever . . .*

The inscription continued along the edge of the sarcophagus lid, recounting the exploits of the man they had buried. Leo read on into the night, pausing only to note down what he had deciphered, or to consult one of his Mayan lexicons.

He could not be sure what brought him out of his

reverie of *tuns* and *baktuns* and *katuns*, the building blocks of vast Mayan eras in which the life of the world was no more than an instant. One moment he was concentrating on the inscription, the next he was fully alert. He stood stock-still, listening, thinking he must have heard something.

The silence could not have been more complete. His own breathing was enough to fill the room. A page that had been left half-turned fell back on itself, and the sound seemed to crash through the tiny chamber with the force of a collapsing wall. He held his breath until the silence returned. In spite of his insulated jacket, he felt cold; his naked fingers chafed against the stone.

There – he thought he could hear something, faint, impossible to make out, but undeniably there. He went across to the entrance and bent down. Moments later, he heard the same sound, but amplified this time, so that he knew what it was: it was the lift docking at the top of the pyramid. Someone must have called it down and then ascended in it.

His mind raced, trying to guess who it could be. It couldn't be any of the team – if they'd returned he'd surely have heard the helicopter. That left only the Indians, but that was equally impossible. The natives would never enter the forest at night, and certainly never come near the pyramid under cover of darkness. Their very worst fears centred on this place, and he doubted that the lure of gold – assuming they knew about the burial chamber – would have been enough to make them risk the terrors it held.

He wanted to call out, but something kept him back. Quietly, he moved behind the sarcophagus and began to wait. His heart moved in him like a fish on a baited hook. At some point he made out footsteps descending the stairs. Later, he was sure the interloper was bare-footed. An Indian, then? But he came down without hesitation, like someone who knew the way.

The steps reached the temple and then came through to the area in front of the chamber.

'Who's there?' Leo called out. His mouth was dry, and he admitted to himself that he was afraid. There was no answer. 'Is that one of the team?' Again, no response. Not knowing why, he reached out and took one of the lances from a nearby stack. It felt good in his hand, it made him feel protected.

The lights went out. And someone started shuffling under the low entrance. When the first blow struck him, Leo did not even have time to cry out.

6

Every time he heard footsteps, he thought they had come for him at last. How his heart started beating when that happened, as though it knew; as if it was leaping at the thought of the blade.

Rafael said it was good to die like this, that all his sins would be wiped away the moment his heart was plucked from his chest. It would be all the more cleansing were Ralph to stay fully conscious right to the last moment. He'd heard apocryphal tales of men and women who spoke even while their hearts were in the hands of the *nacom*. Rafael said he had herbs that would help with that; they would ease the pain a little, while giving the brain strength with which to survive the transition by half a minute or more. Ralph hoped that would happen.

He was scared and he was alone. He'd seen too many sacrifices to think he might enjoy a pain-free death. Often enough, Rafael or one of his *nacoms* would prolong the pain over a period of days. They could spend days singing and praying while their captives suffered terrible agonies as they were prepared for the act of sacrifice. Some gods demanded more than others. Some were cruel, some were kind, most were indifferent. But in the end, they all demanded blood.

It never occurred to him to question the sentence that had been passed. It had seemed at the time such a small betrayal, but to Rafael it had been total, as bad as betraying him to the authorities, who were always on the watch. Rafael was a shaman, a *zahorín*, constantly in touch with his own higher consciousness and with the heavenly powers. Ralph would never have doubted Rafael's judgement, not in this or in anything else. A shaman was not like other men, he had passed through many births and many guises to become what he was. Total allegiance was due to such a man, and Ralph bitterly regretted that he had neglected that truth.

Still, he did at moments feel he'd been treated a little unfairly. Death was a high price to pay for trying to make contact with his wife and child. He'd been wrong to do so, of course, but surely it was understandable. After all, he hadn't seen them in over three years, and they didn't have a clue where he was. He thought of them often, though he knew it was wrong to do so: his beautiful wife Samantha, and their little girl, Ramona.

It had always puzzled him that they'd called her Ramona. At the time he'd known nothing of Rafael or Mexico or what the Spaniard found all those years ago. It had just been a pretty name, one that reminded them of the Mona Lisa or Desdemona or the bird-girl Rima in a book he'd read when he was twelve – he couldn't say quite what, or why they'd chosen the name in the first place. But later he'd been sure it was a token of his destiny, and perhaps of her destiny too.

You could never be sure with names – Rafael had taught him that. Rafael wasn't his real name anyway, that was something hidden, something that had only been revealed to Ralph after a full year in the shaman's service. His true name was an Indian one, Karinhoti; but sometimes he called himself Huitzilopochtli and Tlaloc Tlamacazqui, which are the names of gods. Ralph knew that no mortal would have dared take those names unless entitled to. Whether you thought of the gods as actual beings with inhuman bodies and supernatural powers, or as mysteries hidden within nature, or as the actualization of our highest selves, it was still sacrilege for a mere man to appear before others bearing such names.

He calmed himself with the thought that Rafael was beyond the reach of scepticism. The divinity that radiated from his face, that sat in his every movement, that pronounced itself in every word he spoke or wrote was something close to tangible. He'd sensed it the first time he'd been ushered into Rafael's presence, and known it for sure when he'd first seen Rafael slip his thin hand inside a dying man's chest to draw the heart out, intact and still beating.

Samantha and Ramona were in Birmingham. He expected they'd be living with Samantha's parents in Selly Oak by now, unless Samantha had found someone else and gone to live with him. The thought pained him, but he didn't really believe it. Samantha wasn't like that: he'd always been sure of her fidelity, just as he'd been sure of his own. She'd be with her parents, he didn't need to worry, and she'd still have her job in the public library.

He hadn't liked her working there at first. It meant her going out and seeing other men, speaking to them, maybe even flirting with them. The job brought in money, and he was grateful for that, but it left him alone most of the day, going for walks through the neighbourhood, or reading. He loved reading, even if he didn't fully understand much of what he read. His lack of a full education frustrated him. For one thing, it got in the way of his finding a proper job. It made him angry to think that his wife was more employable than he.

Sometimes he'd be reading a book, on Buddhism, as it might be, or the *I Ching* or the lost continent of Mu, and he'd come across words he didn't know, whole sentences he couldn't make head nor tail of. Words like 'cosmology' or 'theosophical' or 'paraphysical' tripped him up and left him feeling inadequate. When Samantha came home in the evenings, he'd snap at her, not meaning to, only it was all those long words, and not having a job like hers, and wondering about all the men she'd have met that day. Sometimes he'd interrogate her for hours, sometimes she burst into tears and offered to give up the job.

And then he had a better idea. He realized that home was the worst place for him, with all his reading. He needed the convenience of a good library, some-where with shelves stacked with dictionaries and encyclo-paedias. Her library, where he could keep an eye on her from time to time. Like the time he found her climbing ladders in full view of half Selly Oak. They could almost see her backside, something which was his prerogative, had he but known the word. She wore trousers after that, he made sure of it. And Ramona too. Catch them young and you can't go wrong became one of his many mottoes. At that time, they helped him on his pitiful journey through life. He got most of them from *Reader's Digest*, which he found in his doctor's waiting-room, his least favourite place.

The doctor was a woman, and they'd told him he had no choice in the matter, doctors only came in one shape, colour, or sex at a time. An Indian she was, a Dr Sidhani. He often wept at the thought. At first, he'd tried to bring her out, telling her about his interest in the Bhagavad Gita, and what did she think of Ayurvedic medicine, and did she believe in chakras; but she turned out to be a great disappointment, she said she had no religious beliefs whatsoever, and no spiritual aspirations, and would he please roll up his sleeve and behave himself. That's when he'd started to have misgivings about Eastern spirituality.

Which is why it was all the more exciting that things happened the way they did. Some would have called it serendipity; Ralph described it as luck. One day as he was working at his usual desk upstairs, reading a book about a Russian seer called Gurdjieff, Samantha came in and asked if he fancied having a go at the Internet. The library had just gone on-line, as she called it, and they were offering free facilities to the unemployed. Why didn't he have a go?

So he did, and that was how he first made contact with the world of Rafael, how he first set foot on the slow-moving walkway that had brought him to the edge of the knife, here in this room with bars on every window.

He thought back, without pause. Rafael had taught him how to strip his memories of the false emotions they carried. He'd gone to the library the following day, sat at one of the three terminals, and learned to surf the Web in a matter of minutes. Of course, it took a lot longer than that to learn how to be discriminating. For every hit that looked promising, there must have been a dozen or more that were just plain rubbish.

He used an ever-expanding range of key-words. 'Chakra', 'Sufi', 'Ouspensky', 'Atlantis', 'Tao Te Ching', 'Ley Lines'. He explored links when he could, writing down addresses and any other information he thought might be useful.

It must have been about a week after this that he keyed in the single word 'Shaman'. He tried it on Yahoo first, then on other search engines. Plenty of sites came up each time, but always the same one at the top. Naturally, it was the one he entered first.

The first thing, and for a while the only thing he saw was a man's face. The quality of the reproduction was not particularly high, and the image was only a few inches square. But the moment he looked into those eyes . . . He shivered to remember it.

The site's second page carried just a name: Rafael. The third had a box in which to fill one's details 'in order to receive literature'. He filled it in, and waited. He said nothing to Samantha, not then, not later.

The literature, which arrived two days later, was not much of an improvement on the Website. It said that the man Rafael was a shaman, a Maya Quiché Indian, descended from the ancient Mayan ruler Shield-Jaguar. That he was in the world in a location known only to his closest associates. And that he travelled to heaven every night, beyond the stars, into infinity. That was all. Not even an address or a telephone number.

He went back to the library, quarrying deeper for whatever it was he sought, not really knowing if it was a man or a movement or an idea. Every so often, he would return to the Website just to look at the photograph. After a while, someone whispered to him that he was hogging the computer, making it difficult for anyone else to have a go. He left the library and did not go back. His old anxieties began to surface again. He found himself in Dr Sidhani's surgery again, crying. The tablets didn't help. He stopped making love to Samantha; just to be sure.

One month later, everything changed. He'd almost forgotten about the Rafael Website when, out of the blue, an invitation arrived, asking him to attend a meeting in London. There was a chance he might get to meet Rafael in person. Not just a photograph, not just a name. He cadged the money for a bus ticket off Samantha. All the way there he stared out of the window like somebody who wasn't coming back.

He'd expected – he couldn't say why – a packed auditorium and some form of happy-clappy revival meeting, with this man Rafael taking the place of Christ or Billy Graham. Hands uplraised, faces lifted, eyes shining. It wasn't like that at all.

The meeting was held in a hotel in Knightsbridge, in a small, elegant room with chandeliers and gilded chairs. Only thirty or forty people attended, most of them, he would later learn, already adherents. Non-alcoholic drinks were served. A table at the back carried books and pamphlets by the Master. His portrait – the very one that had graced the Website – hung above a small podium at one end of the room.

Later, Ralph could not remember a word of what had been said. All he recalled was a man of medium height, dressed in a white robe, coming to the podium and looking right at him. No, not at him – inside him. At that moment, Ralph became a stranger to himself. The jaguar of truth, they say, takes a man's soul from his body and gives it to the shaman for safe-keeping. The shaman preserves it or destroys it at his will.

There were orchids in every part of the room: white Allegria, red Petit Port, purple Zygopetralum. He did not know their names. In all truth, he had never set eyes on an orchid before that day. Sometimes he looked at them, sometimes at the man.

Rafael spoke a language Ralph did not understand, but somehow that did not matter. He did not need to wait for the interpreter to interrupt with his clumsy English, he understood everything at once, even though he could not speak a word of what was spoken. It was

61

only long afterwards that he discovered Rafael spoke perfectly fluent English.

Later, Rafael saw his new acolytes separately, in a room nearby. It was not a long meeting. The shaman looked deep into his eyes. It was known as the jaguar gaze, the long stare of the hunter for its prey. Ralph was snared and netted, or perhaps it is better to say that he found himself caught firmly between Rafael's sharp teeth and raking claws.

When Rafael blessed him, he knew he was free of his past. Nothing mattered now but life in the truth. That night, he threw his tablets away, never to use them again. They reassured him about that: Rafael was a *curandero*, a healer, a shaman, whose very presence opened the soul to its natural, uninterrupted state. His hands bestowed healing and life, even eternal life. They did not tell him then that the same hands could as readily snatch life away. It would be Rafael who took his heart tonight, not one of his seven *nacoms*.

He said he had to return to Birmingham that first night, but they dissuaded him, saying he had finished with that life. He saw no reason to contradict them. He was taken to a flat somewhere south of the river, and the following day flown to Munich along with two other new converts. They'd had a passport waiting, made out in his name, all but for the photograph.

He'd wanted to write to Samantha and Ramona, but they'd said it was not allowed, since no one outside the People must ever know the whereabouts of the believers, lest that lead to Rafael himself. Rafael had enemies, they said, evil men who would stop at nothing to destroy his influence, above all his work of universal salvation. Ralph remembered the shiver he had experienced on learning that, knowing that he was to be persecuted, not for his own self or his personal shortcomings, but for his love of Rafael.

He'd spent the intervening years moving between centres across Europe and Central America. He had witnessed things none of his old acquaintances would have believed. If only Sidhani had seen half of it, she'd have changed her tune. The only things he'd missed had been his wife and daughter. 'What if they converted?' he asked. 'What if they too gave themselves to Rafael, as he had done?' 'In time,' was the constant reply.

There were quick footsteps in the corridor, and a man's voice raised in command. The door opened, and one of the *nacoms* entered, a man called Chac-Zutz. That was his Mayan name, but Ralph knew he had originally been French. He was dressed for the altar.

'It's time,' the *nacom* said.

Another *nacom* entered, and together they hustled him out of the room and through a long stretch of corridor until they came to the altar room. There was no need to bind his hands or feet: he had bound them in his own mind long ago.

Rafael was waiting. On the floor beside him lay the still-warm bodies of his first two victims. The heads had not yet been severed, but the hearts lay in the great chafing dish, where his heart would join them. *Make it quick*, he thought, knowing death was seldom speedy in coming.

They took him and led him to the altar. Without warning, one of the *nacoms*, a Mexican much loved within the community, came to him and tied him with cord at the wrists and ankles. He was still standing when Rafael called out something.

A second door was opened and closed again. He lifted his head to see who had entered. His head was spinning, and his eyes were full of tears, and at first he could make out nothing. Then the new arrivals came a little closer, and this time he saw it was a woman and a little girl, and that they were both naked like him.

He heard his name called, then strong hands lifted him and stretched him, back downwards, over the altar.

'I love you!' he shouted. 'I love you!'

An outsider might have thought he meant the wife and child who were to follow him to the sacrificial stone. But he shouted the words in Mayan, and he directed them at the man now standing over him, knife in hand, contemplating the first cut.

7

Institut Médico-Légal
Paris
15 November

The long corridor deadened his footsteps, as though eager to eradicate all traces of a live human being. Declan had never been here before, but it looked and smelled and sounded like all the other forensic labs he'd ever passed through in a long career. The monotony of these places was surprising, given the rich variety of ways in which it was possible to be dead.

From somewhere came the sound of a deep humming. It pervaded the place. Declan assumed it was the air-conditioning, constantly struggling in its attempt to balance two wholly contradictory needs: warmth for the living, cold for the dead.

The corridor ended at a T-junction, from which two further corridors, each white-painted, rubber-tiled, and fluorescent-lit, progressed to a dim distance. That to the left was signposted 'Laboratoire d'Analyses', that to the right 'Salons de Dissection'. He went on walking until he reached Salon No. 5.

Arlaten was waiting, dressed in a heavily-starched lab coat, engrossed in the *Le Monde* crossword. he looked up as Declan entered.

'*Monsieur Carberry, vous êtes en retard. Mais, dites-moi, s'il vous plaît: "Piquent, cousent mais ne font pas la manche"?*'

Declan lifted his shoulders.

'No idea. I leave crosswords to intellectuals like yourself. Especially if they're in French.'

In one corner, a long-haired orderly sat on a rickety metal chair, reading a comic entitled *L'Ombre d'un homme*. He lifted his head and spoke, as if to no one in particular.

'*Giletières*,' he said, and resumed reading.

Arlaten started to shake his head, then opened his eyes wide and nodded. He wrote the answer in the grid and showed it to Declan, who shrugged again.

'I believe they do a very fine job of these in the Chinese language,' he said. 'They call it Mandarin, like the oranges. There are around four thousand characters in daily use. I have an imperfect knowledge of five of them, none of the slightest use to me.' Arlaten put down the paper and replaced the pen in his pocket. 'What can I do for you, Monsieur Carberry?'

'You can tell me if you've discovered anything yet. People are yelling at me down the line from Lyon. I'm getting e-mails from men and women I've never heard of. And I've got shitty little journalists after me who think, if they chase me fast enough, I'll crash and tell them all they want to know. And I find you here, doing crosswords while your assistant reads the latest episode of the Obscure Cities series.'

'It's our break,' said Arlaten. 'We have one every five minutes. However, I am entirely at your disposal now. What is it you wish to know?'

'Anything you can tell me. The results of your autopsies, to begin with. Anything out of the ordinary.'

'Well, it is all out of the ordinary, don't you think? No one gets his head cut off every day. And certainly not on the same day he gets his heart ripped out. Besides, your expectations are far too high. I may be a Frenchman, but even we are only human beings ninety per cent of the time. Post-mortems are not done in a flash, even when some of the work has been done for you. It took me long enough to match heads to torsos. The hearts will take even longer. We have to do DNA cross-checks. And Pharmacology are working flat out on the blood and tissue samples we gave them. Some of the people in these drawers were filled to the brim with very strange cocktails of drugs.'

'What are you saying?'

'I don't know, it's still much too early to make a clear statement.'

'I don't want clear. I just want to know what you mean by "drugs".'

'Monsieur Carberry, did anything occur to you about these killings? Apart from the obvious, that is.'

'Lots of things occurred to me. The big one was how they got there in the first place.'

Arlaten nodded. 'It's the first thing I thought of. They didn't walk there, which means they must have been sedated or anaesthetized. We don't know how many killers there were. It could have been one person. But as I said to you, it's my firm impression he had assistants. In any case, he'd have kept his victims unconscious and transported them to the Louvre in a van of some sort. After that, I think he must have brought them in one at a time and executed them.'

Declan made a mental picture of the scene. He or they would have used some form of trolley on which to wheel the victims in.

'He wouldn't have killed them while they were unconscious. I think he wanted to take the heart, not just from a living human being, but from a living and conscious human being.'

'That fits some of what we've found. Morphine salts are present in all the bodies. Most of them seem to have been administered in water mixed with granules of morphine sulphate. Some were given injections of morphine and atropine. That suggests an illegal or limited access to the drug, since the atropine isn't necessary for the purpose he had in mind, but he probably had no choice. But that's not all. All the bodies have high levels of a drug called naloxone hydrochloride. Are you familiar with it?'

Declan shook his head. 'I used to be with the anti-terrorist branch, not the drug squad. Tell me about this naloxone.'

'It's a drug used in cases of opioid-induced respiratory depression. Let's say you take an overdose of morphine, and it causes you breathing problems, I'd have to give you naloxone or another drug like it. But if I gave you too high a dose, it would reverse the effect of the morphine. That's why it's given to comatose patients suspected of narcotic overdose.'

Declan watched as, high up, an unbending shaft of sunlight perfused a small window.

'You mean, he knocked them out, drove them to his execution ground, and woke them up?'

'One by one. Who knows in what order?'

'But he woke them so he could rip their hearts out while they watched?'

'Basically, yes. Except . . . Did I say "rip" earlier? If so, I apologize. The hearts were not ripped from the chests. Quite the contrary. They were severed very skilfully. This is why the assistants were necessary – to hold down each victim in turn while the executioner did his work. They may have remained conscious for several moments after the heart was removed, assuming he worked at speed. It will have been a very cruel death. Not even the Chinese emperors invented anything so bestial. Funnily enough, one of your victims –'

'Was Chinese. Yes, I knew that. To be precise, his name was Lu Dingyi, a Hong Kong citizen. He's last known to have lived there in nineteen ninety-four. The Chinese authorities weren't particularly cooperative. But they did say that Mr Lu had no passport, from either the British or themselves.'

'Nevertheless, here he is.'

Arlaten nodded at a drawer half-way down the wall. It was cold in the white-tiled room, and the odour of chemicals was strong enough to permeate even stainless steel.

The orderly put down his *bande dessinée*, got to his feet, and slouched to the drawer.

'His name is Christian Thouement,' whispered Arlaten, nodding discreetly in the direction of the orderly. 'A doctorate in literature from the Sorbonne. Did his thesis on a group of literary figures called the Petit Cénacle. Won a prize for it. Can't think what he's about, working in a place like this.'

The drawer ran smoothly open, and the orderly drew back a white sheet, revealing a naked man's body the colour of putty. The dead look so helpless, Declan thought, and so malleable. The head lay an inch or two apart from the torso. Tramlines of stitching marred the smooth, almost hairless skin.

'He's on file with the Hong Kong police,' said Declan. He was still waiting for a full transcript of the English-language dossier that had been compiled before the take-over.

'Anything interesting?'

'I told you, they weren't too cooperative. Their report

69

contained nothing that would explain what he was doing in Paris. No drugs connection, for example, no history of antiques smuggling. A list of petty crimes, mostly connected to the local porn industry. Lu Dingyi rather fancied his chances as a photographer. Little girls, mainly.'

'I see. A paedophile. He should be on some registers.'

'Oh, yes, we're getting print-outs of those. We may turn up some leads. But that's not what this is about.'

'You sound very sure.'

Declan produced a piece of paper from his pocket, a dirty envelope covered in his particularly illegible scribble. God, he remembered the Brothers trying their damnedest to beat the rudiments of good handwriting into him. He squinted at his notes.

'Put him away,' he said. 'I'd like to look at number three.'

'Three's an ugly bugger, Carberry. *Un vrai sale type*. Why don't we slide out the woman in number eight instead? Legs to die for.'

'Are you scared of women or something? Your dissection-room humour would do credit to a first-year medical student.'

Arlaten sniffed. 'All real men are afraid of women. It's only natural. Look at them. Don't you think they're frightening?'

He nodded to the orderly. The Chinaman was put away and a second drawer rolled out.

'An ugly bugger as you say,' Declan remarked. 'He hasn't changed since I last saw him, and I doubt he'll change for the better now. His name's Liam O'Neill. Forty-five years old at the time of death. You'll have noticed the tattoos.'

'Naturally. But I can't tell you what they mean.'

'They were done while he was interned in the H-Block. They all had them done. This is the work of a man called Billy Milligan. Billy was a Loyalist, but he was happy to decorate anyone. The tattoo on the left arm is in Irish. It reads "Long Live the IRA", which was asking a lot even when this was done.

'Mr O'Neill was Quartermaster-General for the Provisionals for about ten years. He worked out of Dublin, which is how I came to know him; but a lot of his time was spent in the United States touting for money from sympathizers. He was able to buy great quantities of arms as a result.

'The weapons sometimes came to Ireland direct from the States, but as often as not there'd be a boatload from Brazil or Lebanon or Libya. O'Neill had dumps built round the country, and he organized trips to the North so's he could supply his brothers-in-arms with whatever it was they needed. He was arrested by the RUC shortly after crossing the border one night about seven years ago. Arrested, tried, and slung in the H-Block for I couldn't tell you how many years.'

'A very interesting man. But he doesn't seem to belong here, does he?'

'None of them do. Which means there's something we're missing.'

'There is something else,' Arlaten said. 'I don't know if it will mean anything to you.'

Declan followed the pathologist's fine-boned hands as they bent and picked up O'Neill's head.

'It's heavy,' he smiled, rotating it on the palm of his right hand. He turned it again, and with his left hand lifted the right earlobe. 'Just there,' he said. 'Beneath the lobe. Can you see anything?'

Declan leaned forward, squinting. Thouement brought

a portable lamp and switched it on, angling it to provide a clear light right beneath the ear.

'I can see something,' Declan said. 'But it's small enough not to be there at all. Flann O'Brien would have given his eye-teeth for a look at it.' He looked up. 'What the hell is it? The first sign of a deadly disease? Something the fucker picked up in Lebanon?'

'It's a tattoo. All the victims have one in exactly the same place. I've already had photographs taken and enlarged.'

He replaced the head and drew a set of photographs from his lab-coat pocket.

'Over here,' he said, indicating one of the dissection tables that stood proudly in the centre of the room. He threw the photographs on to the stainless steel surface. Declan picked them up and laid them back down one by one. They made no sense to him at all. Each print showed a square-shaped drawing or diagram, some of which appeared to be caricature heads, others of nothing recognizable. As he tossed the last photograph on to the table, it almost seemed to jog his flagging memory. He felt that, if only he could dig deep enough down, he'd find something very like this buried in memory.

'May I keep these?' he asked.

'Be my guest.'

'Have you any idea what they are?'

Arlaten shook his head.

Declan slipped the photographs into his jacket pocket. They were a clue of some sort, he supposed, but a clue to what he couldn't begin to say.

Arlaten nodded briskly, and Thouement, the orderly, long-haired and grave, began to slide O'Neill back inside his narrow home. Declan noticed that he frowned as he did so, and that his hand shook, as though the job was heavy for him, and an ordeal.

'That's it, is it?' Declan asked, knowing it was not.

The Frenchman shook his head. He looked troubled, like someone who has stumbled across something obscene where they had expected to find only purity.

'Well, there's one thing that disturbs me greatly. I should have mentioned it before this.'

'I'll make it easy for you, shall I? You've not been able to match one head and one body. That's it, isn't it?'

Arlaten looked at him in astonishment.

'How on earth do you know that? I haven't released anything yet.'

'Well, it wasn't too difficult. We ran a fingerprint check which came up positive and gave us the name of someone we knew. Unfortunately, none of the photographs matched our man. Now, what I need to know from you is whether the other seven heads and bodies are genuine matches.'

Arlaten uttered something resembling a laugh. For a moment, a horrid fear passed over him like a shadow, that the death toll had just doubled to sixteen.

'I told you earlier,' he said, 'that the first thing I did was to match them up. I used blood and DNA samples, all the tricks of the trade. The circumference of the two ends of each neck was measured. I'm one hundred per cent certain that the only mismatch is the one you mentioned. Who did the body belong to, by the way?'

Declan looked at him coldly, as though the pathologist had just challenged him to volunteer for a dissection.

'I'm afraid that's classified,' he said.

Arlaten folded his arms across his chest.

'Christian,' he said, 'could you leave Monsieur Carberry and myself alone for a few minutes?'

The orderly picked up his comic and made himself scarce.

'How far can you trust him?' Declan asked.

Arlaten shrugged. 'More than most, less than some. I've never really had occasion to put him to the test. But I find him *sympathique*. He has no ambitions that I can discern, no motives for betrayal.'

'Very well, but he must be told that not even this matter of the mismatched head and body can be divulged. Do you understand?'

'I would not expect anything to be divulged anyway. Now, what is it you want to tell me?'

Declan hesitated. He'd been over it again and again in his head, and still it made no sense.

'What I'm about to tell you, Monsieur Arlaten, is classified information. I don't mean that in the ordinary sense. The only people who know this are myself, my boss, Greg Dyson, the head of the French national police, Alain Planchais, and the French President, Alain Dutheillet.'

'And the Prime Minister?'

'Will be told in due course. I am only telling you now in case it helps your own investigations.'

'Well, hurry, monsieur, in case you forget this important information.'

'I told you that we have fingerprint evidence establishing the identity of our mismatched corpse. The body in question belongs to Arnaud Nougayrède, the French Foreign Minister. As soon as I leave here, I'm on my way to break the news to his wife.'

8

The American–British Cowdray Medical Center
Av. Observatorio
Las Americas
Mexico City
23 November
8.15 p.m.

He must have woken ten or twenty times without really waking. It had been like that before, in the darkness, when his eyelids would flicker open only to reveal the blackness at the bottom of the pit, and a silence deeper than that again. He'd convinced himself of that, of the reality of whatever hell he was in, and imagined tall figures with black leather wings and sunken incandescent eyes swirling about him, their fingers only inches away from his skin. Each time he'd gone back into that deeper darkness inside his own head, and each time he'd been a finger's span closer to death.

And then he seemed to rise a little bit above the surface of the pit. His eyes were still tightly shut, but he thought he could hear something, voices from a very long way away. He tried to see, but there was blood behind his eyes, and a pain that felt like knotted cords in the centre of his skull. He tried to hold on to the pain, because it brought him moments of consciousness. It was like that for a very long time: darkness through which only dreams swam, and moments when there was pain and the sound of voices.

'*¿Señor Mallory? ¿Me escuchas? Despiertese.*'

He tried to nod, but it felt as though any connection between his neck and his head had been severed. Perhaps that was what was wrong: he'd been beheaded in his sleep. Better have a word with the hotel management about that. They'd need to clamp down on head-stealers, stop this sort of thing happening to somebody else. He tried to open his mouth, but it must have been with his head, on its way out of the building.

'*¿Señor Mallory? ¿Puede abrir sus ojos? ¿Puede escucharme? Es muy importante.*'

He tried to do all he was asked, to open his eyes, to wake up. But his body would not obey him.

'Doctor Mallory? I think you can hear me. Don't try to speak. You aren't ready for that yet. Just lift this finger for "yes" and this one for "no". Do you understand? Good, now, try again. Can you hear me?'

The questions continued for a day and a night. He had his own time, in which hours and minutes did not figure. Weeks could have passed, or years, he would not have known. There were different voices, belonging to two men and three women. They spoke in Spanish, slowly, always the same questions, 'Can you hear me?', 'Can you see me?', like some sort of cheap Latin-American rock opera. 'Open your eyes', they'd command, 'Wake up', 'Move your finger', 'Smile'.

Then the voices dissolved into another silence, and different voices took over. These spoke in English ('Hello, Leo', 'Hi, Doctor Mallory') and seemed familiar, though for some reason he could put no names to them. They all sounded worried and distressed. Some of the voices held long conversations with him.

'Doctor Mallory, hi, this is Diane, how are you? Diane Krauss? Remember? I guess I shouted at you when I was leaving back there, but, hell, you know that was just playing about. I just want you to know we all hope you're going to come out of this coma or whatever, and once you're back on your feet, I'd like for us to go out on a date. How would you like that? There are lots of cool nightspots here in the big city. And if you had any thoughts about getting, you know, intimate, I've got a great hotel room just off the main drag.'

She prattled on like that, not really knowing how to speak to a man who might not even have heard her, and who wasn't able to answer her anyway. He tried to put a face to her, but was left instead with images of a perfectly sculpted body, a naked woman's body that he ached to touch. It was his first step towards regaining a physical self.

Pictures of Dorana moving between high bars flickered through his brain like taut images in a zoetrope. She whirled naked through his unshifting sleep, while voices hovered above the surface, vainly trying to draw him up. They thought he was as good as dead, that he would remain this way for ever, and they doubted their power to revive him.

'Leonard? Leonard, darling, this is Mum. Dad's here as well, he's sitting just behind me. We just got here a few minutes ago. Well, when we got the news we couldn't just stay in Bradford, could we? Your Dad said we had to get over. Just in case. Gran sends her love. She says, why haven't you written to her in over a year? Old bugger, she thinks the world revolves round her. I've met some of your colleagues, they seem very nice, that girl Diane's very friendly. Even if you don't want to come back for your old Mum, you can't just leave a lovely girl like that waiting, now, can you? I'm sorry, but I'm near passing out myself, that plane journey is just murder, isn't it, Dad? We haven't sorted out a hotel yet, we thought we'd come here to see you first, see how you were, talk to the doctor. Not that there's many of those around, and I'm not sure about the nurses, some of them are black, though I suppose that's no different to what it's like at home, I suppose you'd tell me off for being a racist, but it's only your own good I'm thinking about. I see that Dorana hasn't flown out. I don't know what you were thinking about moving in with her in the first place . . .'

The long-familiar voice droned on, lulling him into a deeper sleep. The thought of waking filled him with dread. There'd be hours of lectures, and complaints about every member of the family, alive or dead, and 'Why haven't you written to Doreen?' or somebody else, a list as long as your arm; and his Dad butting in from time to time with 'Len, listen to what your mother tells you for once.' He pictured Doreen in a sad skirt and handknit sweater, alone in a rented room in Reno or Albuquerque or one of those diminished cities on the edge of everything. She was the big sister he'd never really known, already flown the nest when he was born, with an American hippy with hot eyes. She hadn't come home much after that, not even when Ol' Hang-loose had hung loose. Leo had been the biggest surprise in his parents' life. His mother was forty-six and, as she often told him, 'They'd put all that behind them.' Somewhere in an empty bar in Nebraska, Doreen was sitting listening to 'Sylvia's Mother' and watching her cocktail come adrift.

They tired at last, and one of the doctors returned, or perhaps a new one arrived and started a fresh spate of

Spanish. There was no respite now, as though all that mattered was to keep his wandering attention by one means or another. His parents had brought tapes, tapes of music he hadn't listened to in years and had hoped never to listen to again. Some sadist had clamped huge headphones on him and was now blasting his exhausted brain with endless tracks by Duran Duran, Spandau Ballet and the indefatigable U2 in the naive belief that this would recall him to himself. He crept further inside and shut any mental doors he could find behind him.

A long time passed. His parents came again, but gradually lost interest and turned up less frequently. They were thinking of moving on to Doreen, wherever she was. He grew conscious, not in his mind, but in his body, that someone else was sitting beside him, had been sitting beside him all along. Not long after that, he felt his hand in someone else's. Was it Diane? he wondered. Had she persisted, had she come every day to sit with him? Or was it Dorana, acting on an impulse that signified nothing?

For a long time, there was nothing. It was as if they had turned their backs on him, all but the presence by his bedside. There were no more exhortations to wake, no blasts of familiar music, no tears, no pleading, no questions. All he could hear was the susurration of the equipment by his bedside, a soft rhythm of air and buoyant fluids that lived his life for him. But as he listened, something slipped or kicked within him, and he could hear the blood in his arteries, beating a slow passage through his head, running in thin streams through the folds and troughs of his brain. And out of the silence a voice came that was none of those other voices.

'Leo. Viene la madrugada. ¿Puede escucharme? Soy yo, Leo. Oa, mi amor – no ves. Quedes conmigo. Quedes conmigo . . .'

Her hand tightened on his, echoing the desperation of

79

her words. She spoke as though he was dying, and he realized that that was exactly what was happening, that he was dying, and that the dying would go on unless something happened to stop it.

He tried to speak, but he couldn't open his mouth. He tried to move his hands, but they remained immobile. Then, desperate, knowing his life hung in the balance, he tried to open his eyes. They felt as though they were sealed together. But he could feel the little muscles twitch behind his eyelids. He made another effort.

'Stay with me, Leo,' she repeated, this time in English. And she stroked his forehead with her free hand. This time he knew. He made another effort, knowing that, if he died and did not see her, he would enter some sort of blackness and never again come out.

His eyes opened on a room lit by low green lights. For a moment or two, he was dazzled by the brightness of everything. His eyes fluttered, but he was awake. He was propped up in bed, his hands flat against a starched white sheet. Dim as it was, the light stung his eyes, and he had to fight to keep them open. To his surprise, his neck moved, and he was able to rotate his head by a few inches.

She was sitting on a low chair next to the bed, her head bent.

'Antonia,' he said. His throat was as dry as a brush, and his lips were parched. '*Quedes conmigo.*'

Her head lifted and she looked at him as though she had always been there.

9

A bright November sun the colour of lemon juice glazed the street outside the quiet café. Water from the morning's rain strayed through the street gullies, its passage dammed every so often by rolls of cloth and miniature sandbags. An odour of aniseed rose from the pavements, wafted into every doorway by the light breeze. A woman passed, carrying half a dozen freshly-baked *miches* under one arm and a bag of vegetables in the other hand.

Declan squinted through a poster-cluttered window, straining to distinguish passers-by from one another. A pretty girl with a white terrier in her arms stopped to cross the road. She had short hair and a dark blue scarf that billowed out from her neck like a streamer at a fair. Tired of waiting, she walked out into the steady stream of traffic, the terrier tightly clutched to her bosom, moving between cars and *motos* like a dancer swaying to music only she could hear.

'She works in the florist's in the street next to us,' said a voice behind him. 'My wife wonders why I bring her flowers so often.'

Declan turned to find Arlaten standing close to him. He stood, bracing himself for the ritual of cheek-kissing.

81

Arlaten let him off with a firm handshake, and they both sat down, facing each other.

'*Ça va?*' asked Arlaten.

Declan nodded. He was wondering who he knew to send flowers to. Perhaps he'd have to wait for a death or a wedding. Perhaps he could send them to himself.

The café had started to fill for lunch. A bustling waiter with a handlebar moustache and slicked-back hair took their orders and passed them to the kitchen.

'You're sure that's all you want?' Arlaten asked. He removed the foil from a packet of Winstons and offered them to Declan, who shook his head.

'A *croque-monsieur* for lunch?' asked Arlaten. 'I thought you Irish had better appetites than that.'

'No, I'm fine. It's all I ever have this time of day. Back home, I'd have a pint of Guinness. But you go ahead. I'm amazed you can eat at all, the job you do.'

'I'll order a good bottle of wine, at least. Guinness is all very well, but beer is something of a brutish drink. I see its ravages too often in the bodies I dissect. Wine, on the other hand, has positive qualities. You are drinking, I hope?'

'I'll have a glass.'

'Nonsense. We'll have a bottle at least. The *patron* keeps an excellent Morgon, and I wouldn't want to insult him by asking for anything else. And don't worry, it's all on me.'

Declan smiled. In spite of the man's affectations, he was growing to like Arlaten.

'Business must be booming,' he said.

Arlaten permitted himself a reciprocal smile.

'Business is always good, not least since you and your multiple killer came on the scene. We pathologists have nothing to fear but the day all men die natural deaths. We are not so different really, you and I.'

Arlaten looked the Irishman up and down. He could tell so much about a man with his naked eye. Hadn't he seen inside hundreds like him, sliced them to the bone, sewn them up again with thick thread? Carberry was a thinker, a man too troubled for the job he did. He'd have been better off running one of those pubs in which Arlaten liked to down his pints of Guinness when he came off his heron lake at the height of summer.

He'd heard all the rumours that were doing the rounds about Carberry. The policeman spent most of his time at Interpol's General Secretariat in Lyon, and when he did visit Paris, he kept himself pretty much to himself. He owned a small apartment in the Marais, to which, it was said, no one, male or female, had ever been invited. Nevertheless, rumours clustered about the man like paparazzi about a celebrity. There was talk of a long, loveless marriage that had ended only on her recent death. The wife had been the sister of Ireland's Prime Minister. She'd left Carberry very well provided for indeed. A lot of women of a certain age – single women, widowed women, women of limited means – made it their task to attract his attention, to seduce him, perhaps; but he fended them off like a horse shaking aside dull flies.

Rumours of a different variety popped their heads out from time to time, among which Arlaten was most taken by reports that there had been an affair with a Lebanese intelligence officer. What had become of her no one seemed to know.

'Anything more on our Monsieur Nougayrède? I see you've given nothing to the media.'

Declan nodded.

'Not for the moment. I can't see that it would do any good to tell the public that their Foreign Minister was one of the Louvre victims. Perhaps later, if we find out what really happened. At present, what was given out at the press conference yesterday still holds: Monsieur Nougayrède fell over a steep precipice while hiking alone in the Gorges du Verdon last month. His widow's happy to go along with it. She didn't ask to look in the coffin, and we didn't encourage her.'

'How'd he get to be in the Louvre all the same? Was he really hiking in the Gorges du Verdon?'

At that moment, the waiter arrived with their meals. Arlaten gave the wine order, which appeared moments later, as though by magic. The waiter uncorked the bottle effortlessly and filled their glasses. Arlaten gazed admiringly at his, tasted it, thanked the waiter, and tucked straight into his plate of charcuterie.

'No, he wasn't hiking anywhere, so far as we know,' said Declan, cutting a corner from an enormous *croque-monsieur*. 'Of course, it was his pastime, and he did like to go alone. But none of that helps us decide where he really got to after he vanished. There's a gap of about three weeks between his disappearance and your presumed date of death. That period is a total blank. We don't know if he was travelling or staying in one place, whether he was free or held captive somewhere. I've got operatives going over the month or so before that, but his official diary gives no obvious clues and his secretary either knows nothing or isn't talking.'

He forked the slab of ham, cheese and *pain de mie* into one corner of his mouth and started chewing. It brought back memories of cheese on toasted Bewley's bread when he'd been a boy.

'Not bad,' he mumbled. 'Now, there's one thing that does bear looking into. Nougayrède spent the entire week before his disappearance in Mexico. There was a meeting of foreign and economic ministers of the NAFTA member states in Mexico City. EU ministers were invited as observers.'

'NAFTA?' Arlaten speared a lovely slice of boar's head-cheese on to his fork and let it slide into his mouth. Declan wondered if any of the staff knew what this man did for a living.

'North American Free Trade Agreement. It just covers the US, Canada and Mexico, but it's still the biggest free-trade zone in the world. The summit lasted five days, and all the EU ministers flew straight home. Except for Nougayrède. He spent a further two days in Mexico – or at least that's what we think. Actually, we don't know where he was during that period. He could have headed north or south into several countries.'

Arlaten relished the headcheese for a few more moments, then swallowed it and turned his attention to a generous helping of *rillons de canard*.

'Surely there'd have been a record if he'd crossed a border. The French Minister for Foreign Affairs would hardly have gone unnoticed.'

Declan munched on through his *croque*. He swallowed and took a long sip from the wine glass. The wine was terrific, but it hardly went with cheese on toast.

'If he was travelling under his real name. The cross-border theory is only guesswork. But if it could be proved ... well, it might open up cans of worms you can't imagine. However, I have other reasons for thinking this could be the crucial connection.'

'Does this really concern me, Declan? International conspiracies are more in your line than mine, I believe.'

He poured more wine into Declan's glass. The scarlet liquid swirled, then steadied itself.

'Not necessarily. I'm looking for connections between this group of eight victims, then between each individual and the wider world, and finally between the entire group and the world. I've issued a series of black notices, official sheets carrying the details of corpses whose identity is unknown. If we get responses, we can start to build up the wider picture. You need to know what I know, because I may come up with information that triggers off ideas or lines of enquiry for you.'

The pathologist trimmed beads of fat from a *saucisson de Lyon*, sliced it, and slid a forkful into his mouth. He followed it with a mouthful of wine.

'Such as?'

'According to my notes, your body number one is a thick-bellied man in middle age. Somewhere around fifty. His hair is thinning from the forehead back, and he has no facial or body hair. Does that seem to fit?'

'Absolutely. Christian has christened him Baudelaire.'

'Yes, I noticed a resemblance in the photograph. Well, I now have a better identity for the poor man. His photograph and fingerprints were on a yellow and black notice I sent out early on. The strangest things and the oddest people find their way on to police computers. A few years ago there was a killing in Guatemala, in a little village called El Remate, just on the shores of Lake Petén Itzá.'

Arlaten put down his fork. 'Not a million miles from southern Mexico.'

'You French catch on quick. At the time this killing occurred, there was a Catholic mission from Belgium about a mile down the road, and when the police took fingerprints, they took those belonging to the priests as well. They weren't really suspects, but what the hell, it probably made somebody feel industrious. And it put a set of fingerprints and a photograph on the Guatemalan police computer, and hence into Interpol files.

'The man is Father Justus de Harduwijn. I've double-checked with his records in Belgium, and this is him all right. He'd been in Guatemala recently, but disappeared about two months ago in the course of a trek into the jungle. He and his expedition were making renewed contact with an Indian tribe in the hills. He went to sleep one night, and in the morning he was gone. *Disparado*.'

'Like Mr O'Neill.'

Declan shook his head furiously.

'Oh, no, not at all like that. This was much more abrupt. One moment our man was in his tent, the next thing they're all up shouting his name and scouring the jungle for a sign of him. His bishop has been paying a private detective to track him down, so far without so much as a sighting.'

'They think he's still in Guatemala?'

'Not any more, they don't. But they have done until now. The detective's flying in to Belgium tomorrow. Maybe he'll have something we can use.'

'Anything else?'

'We now think number six is a German called Jürgen Habermayer. Habermayer comes from Stuttgart, where he ran a small art gallery. He was thirty-nine years old, unmarried, and without children, but living with a voluptuous young woman called Helga.'

'A Rhine maiden, eh?'

'Not quite, but she's in training. According to the photograph we have on file.'

'And Herr Habermayer was recently in Central America?'

Declan shook his head. 'I don't think so. But he was a known neo-fascist, a leading light in the FAP.'

'The . . . ?'

'Freiheitliche Deutsche Arbeiter Partei. It's a small right-wing group with terrorist inclinations. They have affiliations with neo-Nazi groups in Belgium, like the Vlaamse Nieuwe Orde, but none, as far as I can tell, with groups outside of Europe. But I do know that Habermayer did get mixed up in a plot to import Semtex from Poland several years ago. He did three years in jail for that. I've got Frédéric Leparmentier looking into it. Now, perhaps you can tell me why you have that glazed look in your eye.'

'I'm thinking about dessert. They serve a fresh Fontaine-bleau, made from *fromage blanc*. Believe me, it's worth a try.'

'You were thinking about something else, and it wasn't the fish you caught this summer.'

Arlaten played with the last of the meat on his dish.

'I was thinking that there may be yet another connection between the victims you mentioned.'

'What might that be?'

Arlaten frowned. 'Have you ever heard of something called the pineal gland?'

'Vaguely. Why?'

'Eat up. When we're finished, I'll show you a couple.'

10

Mexico City
23 November

Once the first hurdle had been passed, and her face and voice and temperament imprinted on his mind, it was just a matter of time. He dreamed of her now, always the same dream. She came to him smiling, with her hair down, her long, black hair. Then one day he woke up fully, and she was still there, with her hair tied up, but smiling that extraordinary smile. His parents had vanished to Nebraska, leaving nothing, not even an address.

'I don't understand,' he said. '*¿Qué hubo?* What's going on? How did this happen?'

'You being in hospital, is that what you mean?'

'No. Your being here. Your waiting after everybody else has gone.'

'They haven't gone. They just don't come here, that's all.'

'And you?'

She reddened and looked away. Nothing had ever been said between them, nothing like that.

'Do you live here?' he asked. 'In Mexico City?'

'My family has a house here, yes. In a *colonia* called Lomas de Chapultepec. Have you heard of it?'

He shook his head. But he guessed it wasn't a poor *barrio*.

'It's a ghetto for rich people,' she said. 'You don't want to go there.'

'Is that where you live?'

She hesitated. She thought he might despise her for her family's wealth.

'My mother lives there most of the time now. She finds it dull at home.'

'This isn't your home?'

She shook her head.

'No. Our family home is out by Cindad Camargo. We're really country pumpkins.'

He laughed, correcting her, and as he did so, his hand struck the bedclothes, and his fingers grazed hers, and he caught her eyes.

'My family have lived there for a long time,' she rushed on. 'My great-great-great-grandfather fought with Iturbide. In return, he was given land. That was in the 1820s. Maybe I left out a great or two.'

'You have a house out there?' He felt stupid, not knowing about these places and events. Whatever blood ran in her veins, it was different to his. He'd been a fool even to wake for her.

'*Una hacienda, sí*. My father is a *hacendado*. He also owns a *ganadería*, a ranch for breeding fighting bulls. It's his passion, my mother's too.'

'What sort of man is he?' he asked.

'*Es muy grande, muy famoso*.' She smiled. '*Pero, non muy simpático*. Not a very nice man to know, I think. I don't want to talk about him. I want to talk about you.'

'I'd rather talk about you. Where do you live? On the ranch or with your mother?'

'It's more complicated than that. I was brought up on

the ranch, but when I went to university I stayed with my mother. Since I'm going to be doing some teaching at the National University, I took an apartment near there with a friend. It's down in San Ángel. It's nice there, you'd like it. My mother worries that it's too full of intellectuals.'

He tried to sit up more easily. It was then he noticed the various drips to which he was attached.

'Shouldn't you be calling one of the doctors?' he asked.

She shrugged. 'I don't think they care very much. If you died it would be so much better for them.'

'Doctors don't like their patients to die.'

'These ones do, I think. You're taking up an expensive bed. Soon your insurance will stop paying. Then what do they do? They can't keep you. You can't go back to England . . .'

'Can't go back . . . ?'

At that moment, the door opened to admit a nurse wheeling a trolley. She was an Indian, and Leo guessed she had not been in the city very long. Her nurse's uniform fitted her badly, and she still wore a plain *chachal* round her neck. Leo thought how hard she must have worked to get where she was. When she caught sight of him, eyes wide open, smiling lopsidedly at her, she let go of the trolley, put her hands on her hips, and smiled back at him. Then she turned and left the room.

'She likes you,' Antonia said. 'All the nurses like you.'

'Where's Leroy?'

'Leroy?'

'Your boyfriend. Isn't he the one you share the apartment with?'

She smiled. 'Leroy was never my boyfriend. He just wanted it to look that way.'

'We all thought you two were together. You always gave that impression.'

'He was a nice boy, I liked his company. But . . .' She looked pleadingly at him, as though desperate that he understand. '*Mi padre* . . . my father would never have allowed it, even if I had wanted it. He would . . . he would have killed him.'

'Your father is that old-fashioned?'

'Oh, my father is the last word. But don't say anything about him – you may need his help before very long.'

'Help? For what?'

'Did you know they call you the English Patient in here? They think you look like Ralph Fiennes.' She pronounced the name Rafe Fee-enes. 'One of the nurses they call Juliette now, because she looks after you.'

'She'll be sad that I'm leaving.'

'Yes – if they let you leave.'

Again the door opened. The same nurse came in, followed by a doctor, a tall man of about thirty, dressed in a white coat and gold spectacles. He seemed impassive, a patrician among thieves. Leo glanced at him. He knew the spectacles would be solid gold, the qualifications North American or European, and the hands cold to the touch.

'Mr Mallory. I was told you'd returned to us. It is very good news. Naturally, we shall want to administer some tests. Nothing very painful, I assure you. But we have to be sure that all your normal responses have returned. I'll give you a going-over now, and maybe we can start on the tests tomorrow, depending on how you seem to be.' He turned to Antonia. 'Perhaps Miss Ramírez would like to leave us. There's a waiting-room just down the corridor.'

He spoke to her quickly in Spanish, and Leo noticed how deferential he was, as though his life depended on not offending her. When the door closed behind her, his manner changed again.

'Where exactly am I?' Leo asked.

The doctor looked at him as though this was something he ought to have known all along.

'You're at the ABC,' he said, assuming this was explanation in itself.

'The what?' To Leo, the name sounded like a cinema.

'The American–British Cowdray Medical Center. The best hospital in Mexico City. You were very lucky that Miss Ramírez insisted on having you brought here.'

'How long have I been here?'

'How long? I don't know exactly. Nurse, when did Mr Mallory arrive?'

She picked up one of the charts at the bottom of the bed.

'Seven days,' she said. 'He arrived here on the seventeenth.'

The doctor nodded and held his hand out for the chart. He barely looked at the nurse.

'What's the date today?' asked Leo.

'The twenty-third.'

'But that's . . .' Leo shook his head in astonishment. Neither the doctor nor the nurse seemed inclined to comfort him. 'I've lost over a week. My work . . . The dig . . .'

'Please don't worry about that. Your dig has been suspended. You don't have to be there. Nurse, would you unfasten Mr Mallory's pyjama top?'

The doctor placed his stethoscope in his ears and bent to listen to Leo's chest. He moved systematically across him, then removed the ear-pieces from his ears and clicked the stethoscope shut.

'*Es muy guapa.* She's very beautiful,' he said. 'You're a very lucky man. At least, I think you are. You must

93

enjoy sleeping with her. But . . . I take it you've met her father?'

Leo shook his head. A headache lay, barely visible as yet, among the furniture at the back of his head.

'I only know he's a *hacendado*. And that he's very conservative.'

The doctor smiled and sat down on the side of the bed.

'Don Ortiz Rocha y Ramírez. Does the name mean anything to you?'

'I don't think so. No.'

'What about his hacienda? It's one of the best-known in Mexico. It's about forty miles from Ciudad Camargo, south of Chihuahua. The Hacienda de Nuestra Señora de Guadalupe. The name is not very original, I admit – but originality has never been a Mexican vice. We want to be *Conquistadores* or we want to go back to the woods and play Indians.'

'You sound disillusioned.'

'What would an *extranjero* like you know about my disillusionment? Better you lie back and let me examine you.'

Bit by bit he tapped and looked at every part of Leo, and from time to time, he would talk. His hands were cold, as Leo had expected, and they seemed incapable of warming.

'Her father is a proud man. A true *criollo*. The family has only Spanish blood, even now. You can see it in the girl, can't you?'

'She looks beautiful, that's all I can say.'

'Mm. Can you just . . . Thank you. Now, the other side. OK, that's fine.'

'You haven't told me your name, Doctor.'

'Haven't I? You mustn't be misled by my Spanish

bedside manner that I'm a European doctor who believes in fraternizing with his patients. You don't need to know my name. All you have to do is lie back in bed and let me make you better. Open your mouth now, please.'

The doctor leaned forward and shone a light down Leo's throat. As he did so, he went on talking.

'The father is also a very wealthy and influential man. For many years now he's been making large donations to the National Action Party. He was close to Alvarez, and the new man Peraza spends his vacations at Nuestra Señora. Has she ever told you about her aunt?'

Leo shook his head. He didn't want to hear all this, yet he was in no position to put up a fight. And part of him was curious.

'Consuela. She is younger than Don Ortiz, the daughter of his father's second wife, Consuela is perhaps fifty now, an old woman.'

'Fifty isn't . . .' Around him, lights flickered, green ghosts in a dim room. The nurse watched without emotion. The lights and the equipment were as alien to her as to Leo. In some ways, she was a ghost of herself here in the middle of this dead city.

'Listen. Consuela Ramírez is still a well-known name in some circles. She sang for several years at the Palace of Fine Arts here in the city, and there was much expectation that she would tour. She had the makings of a diva. If you had seen photographs of her, you would understand. Very like Callas. She was part of the musical set here, she knew everybody.

'Unfortunately, she allowed herself to become involved with a *mestizo*, a young man of her own age, a musician. Her father got to hear of this liaison. He ordered her back to Nuestra Señora. She refused. A few days later, she was abducted from the apartment where she was living with her lover. He tried to save her, but he was shot. The police enquiry later concluded that he had committed suicide.'

Leo shook his head. 'How terrible.'

'I'm not finished. Can you lift this leg at all? Good, excellent. And the other. Very good. They brought her back to Don Oritz's bull-farm, a place called El Turuño, and she has remained there ever since. No one ever visits her. Outside certain musical cirles, no one in Mexico City ever asks about her. She's a forgotten name. Here and there, you can pick up some old recordings. That's about it.'

'You're saying she's been locked up there for – what? – twenty years?'

The doctor shook his head. 'You misunderstand me,' he said. 'Not locked up. She has her own bungalow within the *finca*, she's free to go outside if she wishes to.'

'Then . . . ?'

'She remains indoors because there is nothing for her outside. Not at Nuestra Señora, not in Mexico City. When he brought her home, he ensured that she would never want to leave again. He paid a doctor to come to the ranch, a man he could trust. They performed an operation, on a table in the kitchen. *¿Entiende?* The doctor cut her vocal cords. *Créame. Es cierto. Todo es cierto.*'

The doctor's face shrank back away from Leo.

'You say it's all true,' Leo said. 'But how can you know? This can't be public knowledge.'

'Many people know about it. He intended it as a warning to others. We are to believe that the honour of the family is sacred above all things. Women threaten that honour. Their freedom imperils family and religion.'

'And Antonia?'

'Antonia is his concession to President Zedillo and his plans for political reform. Don Ortiz wishes to be thought open to suggestion. To be capable of compromise. That way he can disarm Zedillo and the PRI, while waiting for a chance to drive them from power. So he sends his daughter to university, and he allows her to pursue a career as an archaeologist. But believe me, he has her watched the whole time. Now, we've talked too much. You're still not out of the woods. I just say all this so you will know to be careful. A man in your position has no defences.'

'You still haven't told me how you know.'

The doctor stepped away from the bed.

'I think you should sleep now,' he said.

'I'm afraid to sleep. I've slept enough for a lifetime.'

The doctor paused with his hand on the door, looking back at Leo's supine form, at his pale face, at the white bandages on his head.

'If you must know,' he said, as though speaking to no one in particular, 'the doctor who carried out the operation on her aunt was my father. He's an old man now; he does not like to be reminded of the matter. I would not have told you this, but for a certain sympathy. You may not die of a broken head. Be sure you do not die of a broken heart. *Buenas tardes.*'

11

The light table flickered into brilliant life, as though set there on purpose as the platform for a modern séance. Arlaten, restored to his white lab coat and sporting the horn-rimmed spectacles that were his affectation in this arena of death, laid several large acetate sheets on the flat surface like a gambler setting forth his hand. Set against one avocado-green wall were tall cabinets storing files of X-rays, radionuclide cerebral scans, CT scans, magnetic resonance imaging scans, cerebral angiography readings, and old pneumo- and echoencephalography. Other walls held the files for other parts of the body.

As they took light, the acetates seemed like icons of a spirit world far removed from the blood and bone of the dissecting rooms below. Arlaten tapped the one nearest Declan.

'This is a section from a CT scan I had made this morning. The subject arrived around five o'clock this morning, an Algerian car mechanic aged about twenty-five who committed suicide by slashing his wrists. I don't know the reasons: those are for the coroner to decide. But I am satisfied that that is precisely how he died.'

'So why a scan of the poor bugger's brain?'

'I'm using him as a control for your benefit. I expected to find his brain looking perfectly normal, and it was. Now, you're looking downwards at a cross-section of the brain cut horizontally and penetrating quite deep. What you're looking at shows ventricles and choroid plexuses here and here. This spot' – he tapped his finger against a roughly circular white image that came close to occupying the centre of the brain – 'is the pineal gland. This is what I wish to draw your attention to.'

'I can't say it looks particularly interesting.'

'I'm afraid this is a CT scan, not the Mona Lisa. The interest comes later.'

'Jeez, you could have fooled me. They're only white spots on a man's brain, after all.'

'Clearly, you haven't spent much time looking at CT scans. All I want you to note is that this is how a normal pineal gland looks like from above.' He moved across to the next acetate. 'This is a sagittal section through the midline of the same man's brain. You can see a lot more this way. If you look closely, you can see the pineal gland just above the colliculus, just here. That's the corpus callosum just above it, and the cerebrum wrapped round it. Can you see?'

'Just about. But I don't think this is a very good likeness.'

'We do what we can. Strictly speaking, the pineal gland isn't part of the brain, though it develops from the roof of the interbrain. Now, please look at these two scans. They show horizontal and vertical sections through the brain of our Irish victim, Liam O'Neill. If you take the trouble to compare it with the normal scans I've just shown you, you'll see that O'Neill's pineal is over twice the size it should be.'

'And how big is that?'

'In an adult, it's around 0.64 centimetres. O'Neill's is 1.36. It should weigh about 0.1 gram. O'Neill's weighs more than double that. And before you ask, there is no known medical reason for it to be so. In fact, the normal trend is for the pineal to shrink as we grow older.'

'How on earth did you come to find a thing like this?' Declan asked, bending over the table and scrutinizing the pictures.

'Ordinarily, I'd have missed it,' the pathologist confessed. 'In a case where the cause of death is obvious and can be tested, there's generally little point in chasing down every last inch of every body system. As a matter of routine, I'd cover all the main organs, and only go further if something odd turned up.'

'Which it has done.'

Arlaten nodded. 'In this case, I had no doubt whatsoever that the cause of death was excision of the heart. I can dress that up in all sorts of medical jargon for the inquest, but that's what it amounts to. Decapitation followed the excision, probably quite quickly; in no instance did it play any part in the deaths. In all eight cases, my conclusions were cut and dried. But . . .'

He looked down at his neatly-manicured fingers, as though seeking to find on them some stain, some blemish that might lead him to the simple truth behind this complex obscenity.

'But you may remember my telling you that I'd found traces of substances that I called, for want of a better word, drugs. Not ordinary drugs. I found no cocaine or heroin or opium. I tested for prescription drugs, but that was a blank as well, apart from the ones I told you about before. So I started to look at plant derivatives.'

'You can't be serious. Parsley, sage, rosemary, and

thyme? You're suggesting they'd all been overdosing on herbal tea?'

'Monsieur Carberry, I know you Irish are a backward race, but even you must know better than that. Let's say you were a German, and you went to your GP suffering from depression. What would he give you?'

'Prozac, like anybody else.'

'He'd be ten times more likely to send you away with a prescription for a herbal extract of a plant called St John's Wort. It's more or less the standard treatment there. Not because the Germans are peculiar buggers – though, God knows, some of them are – but because clinical trials show the harmless little plant is every bit as effective as an SSRI or Tricyclic antidepressant. Herbs can be as powerful as synthetic drugs. Have you forgotten about belladonna? Or aspirin? What about digoxin and digitalis, what do you think they're made of?'

'I've no idea.'

'Foxglove leaves, of course,' Arlaten trumpeted impatiently. 'I wonder they let you loose.'

'All right, I take your point. We're not talking about nettle soup.'

'To be honest, I'm not sure what we *are* talking about. I've found about a dozen separate substances, but I'm not entirely sure how to put them together. I've found indole alkaloids including aspidospermine, quebrachamine, and quebrachine, which add up to a South American plant called white quebracho. Another set of indole alkaloids include gelsemine and sempervirine, and alongside those there are traces of methyl aesuletin and monomethyl ester of emodin, which fits the picture of a Central American plant called gelsemium. It's a powerful sedative, and an overdose will kill you.'

'Do I notice a certain geographical tendency here?'

'It's possible. I still have a lot of work to do on this. I think there may be several substances involved which we've never come across before.' He paused.

'What is it? There's something else, isn't there?'

'Well, I . . . Yes, there is. Several of the bodies have very minute marks on the skin, all in different places. The marks vary in size and colour, but taken together they seem to suggest that these individuals have been bitten by spiders at some time, probably not too long before their deaths.'

'You think this could have been the cause of death?'

Arlaten shook his head. 'It's unlikely. But I have found traces of material contained in a number of spider venoms. One body contains traces of ω-agatoxin-TK or ω-agatoxin-IVB. That's a 48-amino peptide which occurs in the venom of the American funnel-web spider. Its effects are mainly felt in the brain, where it blocks voltage-dependent P-type calcium channels in brain neurons. Along with that I've isolated a steroisomer called L-Ser46-ω-agatoxin-TK.

'Another body contained proteinous Robustoxin along with some small compounds such as γ-aminobutyric acid and spermine and a peptide toxin called Verustoxin, all of which suggest that the subject was bitten by another funnel-web spider, Atrax robustus, which is native to Australia.'

'Which body was this?'

'The German, Habermayer. I also found traces of alpha-latrotoxin in the Belgian, which is a product of the Black Widow. The blood also contained a variety of related components: ATPase, esterase, hyaluronidase, phosphodiesterase . . .'

'Enough, enough. I get the idea. Can you sum this up?'

'Well, apart from the Australian spider toxin, I'd say that all the arachnids involved come from the Americas. Some spider toxins share similar components, but they are, in fact, quite diverse.'

'You think our killer might have used these drugs or exposed them to spider bites to kill his victims *before* he cut their hearts out?'

'You haven't been listening to me. I explained that the cause of death in all cases was excision of the heart. And I told you that some standard drugs were used to knock the victims out for their journey to the Louvre.'

'Then, why these plants and the spider toxins?'

'I already think I've discovered strong traces of two Amazonian drugs called *ebene* and *yopo*, both of which have hallucinogenic properties. I believe I will find more. Some of the spider poisons can cause changes in brain chemistry. The most famous example is, of course, the bite of the tarantula, which sets some victims dancing in a manic state.

'And, to answer your question, it was after finding these substances that I decided to carry out some CT scans. I wanted to see what effect, if any, the drugs and venoms might have had on the brain or the brain stem. The only indication of any abnormality I came across was in the pineal glands of four of the victims.'

'So at least we know what caused that.'

Arlaten shook his head. 'No, I don't think we do, not as far as I can see. We have four expanded pineals, but eight bodies with varying amounts of herbs. We have three pineal glands with moderate growth, and another that is about seven times over its normal size. Except that the brain with the largest pineal increase happens to have the smallest quantity of unusual chemicals.'

'Which one had this large increase?'

'Let's go downstairs. I'd like you to see this for yourself.'

Christian Thouement was waiting for them in the dissection room. Music was playing from a portable CD unit in one corner. Jacques Brel's gravelly voice sang of the low country, conjuring up images of low, grey skies and mists, east winds and marshes, canals losing themselves against a flat horizon.

'You remember Christian?'

'Of course,' said Declan, reaching out his hand and shaking the assistant's. 'Nice music, though I'd sooner have Chris de Burgh myself.' He coughed. 'What did you think of *L'Ombre d'un homme*?'

'Startling. As good as the Urbicande stories. Have you read them?'

'I've got the whole series at home. I got the bug when I came to live here. We've nothing like it back home.'

'Monsieur Thouement,' Arlaten's voice boomed out. 'We'd like to take a look at Mr O'Neill's brain, if you have it to hand.'

Thouement walked slowly to a refrigerated cupboard at the far end of the room. He returned carrying a stainless steel salver, on which a human brain lay like a moulded jelly.

'Just set it down there for the moment.' Arlaten directed him to the dissecting table in the centre of the room.

'Right now,' said the pathologist. 'This bowl of noodles is the brain of the not-so-lamented Liam O'Neill. You will observe right away that it is a normal brain, with no overt signs of pathology. I've already split it along the midline, so . . .' He pulled the two halves of the brain, and they came apart without difficulty.

'Now, this little fellow is the pineal gland, the very

same one whose picture you saw upstairs just now. *Très mignonne, n'est-ce pas?'*

With a dainty pair of tweezers, he drew out a tiny object shaped like a pine cone and pinkish-grey in colour.

'It's a bit calcified,' he said, holding it up to the light. 'If you looked at it under a microscope, you'd see these little deposits more clearly. We call them brain sand. *Sable du cerveau.* In the old days, doctors thought they caused psychiatric illnesses. In fact, they're perfectly natural, not the result of drugs or bad habits or belonging to a terrorist organization. Even policemen get them. Their sole medical value is that they let you see the gland on an X-ray.'

'Well, I don't doubt this is interesting stuff,' broke in Declan. 'And I don't doubt you've got brain camels in there as well. But wouldn't it be more to the point if you told me what one of these things does? I take it I have one upstairs myself. Tell me, would I miss it greatly if it happened to escape?'

Arlaten looked pensive, then severe. With exquisite care and a steadiness of hand that might have been the envy of a stage magician, he popped the gland back into the hole from which he had taken it, and placed the two halves of the brain back together again.

'That's not an easy question to answer. Twenty-odd years ago, I'd have had to say, nothing at all. The ancients thought it was a sort of valve controlling the flow of memories. *Le troisième oeil.* The Third Eye of the Hindu mystics. Descartes believed it was the seat of the soul. For a long time, that wretched system we laughingly call medical science was of the firm opinion that the poor old pineal gland was of as much use to the body as a ten-inch cock to a new-born baby.

'Fortunately, we've moved on since then. We still don't

know that much about it, but we have a better idea of what it does. It's an endocrine gland that contains several peptides and a number of neurotransmitters, like serotonin. More importantly, it secretes a hormone called melatonin. Melatonin's a funny substance. It seems to control our relationship with time.

'Children have large pineals and plenty of melatonin, but at some point the gland shrinks and sexual development starts to take place. During the day, you have less melatonin in your system as long as there's daylight; once it grows dark, the pineal starts pumping out more, and you feel drowsy and fall asleep. Some people attribute more to it, that it cures jet lag, perks up your sexual vitality, protects against cancer, and so on; but there's no evidence for any of it.'

Declan wished there was a chair to sit in. He hated deskwork, but you had to admit it was kind on the legs.

'Does knowing any of this help my case at all?' he asked.

'How on earth should I know? I merely draw your attention to it. *Le flic, c'est vous*: it's up to you to make sense of it all, if that's possible. In any case, I haven't finished yet.'

He straightened. The music had changed from Jacques Brel to Lucienne Boyer, who asked to be spoken to of love. And why not? This was the perfect place for a love-song, after all, thought Declan. If not here, where?

Thouement returned the brain to its shelf in the cupboard and, on Arlaten's instructions, opened four of the drawers. One after the other, Arlaten swept the white sheets from the torsos, exposing them naked beneath the bright lights.

'Well,' he said, 'what do you make of these?'

'What are we talking about now? It was pineal glands a few minutes ago.'

'I think it is still pineal glands. You'll have guessed that this is O'Neill,' Arlaten said, indicating the nearest body.

'The top of his head missing, you mean?'

'Yes. And this is Habermayer. Next is Nougayrède. And finally, our Belgian priest, de Harduwijn. We'll leave him to last. Now, what can you see? Does anything strike you as out of the ordinary?'

Declan scrutinized the torsos and heads, but saw only what he had seen before, what he would have expected to see. What was he overlooking?

'Perhaps you think all corpses look like these.' Arlaten seemed irritated by Declan's obtuseness, as though what was obvious to him should be obvious to anyone. 'Or perhaps you're just not used to looking at naked men. Take a look at O'Neill, take a good look at his private parts, please don't be shy, he's past worrying.'

This time, Declan guessed what Arlaten was getting at.

'He's got no pubic hair,' he said.

'Precisely. Nor do the others. No bodily hair at all, just a fine down. Their faces are completely free of stubble. Now, it is a myth that the nails and beard and hair continue to grow after death. We cannot draw conclusions from the fact that all these specimens are clean-shaven. But I assure you that it would be a strange coincidence to find three men at roughly the same time of day who were so smooth-faced as this. They're like little boys.'

'The melatonin.'

'It makes sense, yes. I couldn't say whether they were capable of sexual arousal or not, or whether their voices had become high-pitched, but they certainly lacked some of the secondary characteristics of adult men.'

'I heard Monsieur Nougayrède on the radio just after he got back from Mexico. His voice sounded like normal.'

'Good, that's worth knowing. Now, I'd like you to see de Harduwijn's pineal, *si vous permettez*.'

'Be my guest.'

'You'll notice that I haven't actually got it here. It's still in his skull: all I've ever seen are a series of CT scans and three X-rays. The fact is that something very strange is going on here. I don't want you to think I am up to any *micmacs*, nor Monsieur Thouement here. What I will show you is genuine.'

He took hold of de Harduwijn's head and deftly set to work with a scalpel, cutting behind the ears, then stripping the scalp from the skull until the bare bone was fully exposed. Thouement plugged a Stryker saw into a socket at the head of the table, and handed it to Arlaten.

Declan had attended several post-mortems in his time, but he had never learned to cope with the unpleasantness. The saw shrieked and screamed as it bit into the hard bone, cutting the skull all round until a deep cap remained ready for removal. It took Arlaten less than a minute to extract the brain, and moments only to slice it lengthwise. With a series of finer slices, he reached the cranial cavity.

'This,' he said, reaching in, 'is the pineal gland.'

He took it out with his tweezers. Declan drew close, squinting at the little cone. It was several sizes larger than the others.

'On the CT scan that I showed you,' Arlaten said, 'the gland was about seven times larger than normal. But I took more than one scan over a period of time. If you like, I can weigh and measure this. But I already know something about it that I have not yet told you.'

'You're obviously a man of mystery.'

'*Au contraire*. I like rational explanations. I do not believe in mysteries. Nevertheless, I'm obliged to tell you that this gland, more than twelve days after Father de Harduwijn's death, is still growing. Perhaps, now that I have removed it from the brain, it will stop. But until now it has been growing steadily, as if it was still alive.'

12

Mexico City

The nurse stayed, sitting on the room's only chair like a statue. He thought of her as a ghost, and pretended he was alone again. In spite of himself, he dozed off, but eventually woke again. He'd managed to drag a catheter from his bladder.

The nurse came across and administered to him, saying nothing. Her fingers were gentle, and once the catheter had been replaced, she smiled at him, one of those cautious Indian smiles that waits for rebuke. He spoke to her softly in Quiché Mayan. Taken aback, she replied hesitantly in the Yucatecan dialect, mixing it with a little Spanish.

'Is you still got discomfort?'

He shook his head. 'It feels fine. I didn't know it was there.'

'They probably take it out tomorrow anyway. You over the worst. Your head will heal. You have a good spirit.'

'How can you tell?'

'I watch you. I'm your nurse since you arrive. My name is Magdalena. They don't know nothing, these doctors. They stitch you up, but they can't heal your spirit. That's why I stay in here when I can, to see that your spirit at peace. That's why she sit here too, so you will have her to come back to. And because she love you.'

'Thank you for watching me, Magdalena. Did they say how I got to be here? All I remember is being in my room at the site. Nothing after that, until now.'

She looked at him gravely, then bent down and put a hand on his head, gently because of the bandages, which fitted the upper part of his head like a cap.

'Is my head bandaged?' he asked.

She nodded and stroked her hand across his scalp.

'It will heal,' she said. 'Bones will knit. Heart will grow calm again. And what you carry inside will ripen.'

'What do you mean, what I carry inside?'

'There is no name. Perhaps the Old Ones had a name. I do not know.'

He wanted to pursue the matter, but he knew that she would say no more. The Old Ones, the ancient Mayas had been invoked, and that was the end of any discussion.

'What happened to my head? I was alone at the dig, then I wake up and find myself here. Did I have some kind of accident?'

She put her hand on his lips. It smelt of burned chillies and *apazote* leaves.

'Wait,' she said. 'I go find her.'

Minutes later, she returned with Antonia. He drew his breath in sharply. Even in the short time she had been out of the room, he had forgotten how very attractive she was. She came to the bed and kissed him on the cheek.

'That's all,' she said. 'You're a sick man. Can't mess about with your hormones.'

'What happened to me, Antonia?'

Her face grew serious. Behind her, the door opened and closed as the nurse went out. She sat on the edge of the bed and took his left hand in hers.

'I know I was at the site,' he said, 'in my room, I think. At least, that's all I remember. Did I go out? Did I have an accident? Did I fall on the pyramid?'

'Not on the pyramid, Leo. In it. In the tomb chamber. And you didn't fall, you were hit.'

It flooded back to him. Not everything, not the accident itself, but the events of the Friday before – the discovery of the hidden chamber, his offer to stay behind while everybody else went to San Cristóbal.

'What are you saying? I was inside the chamber? What the hell was I doing there? Maybe I fell down the stairs and crawled in there. Is that possible?'

She shook her head. Her face was grave. The joy that had been in it earlier had departed.

'No,' she said. 'You couldn't have sustained those injuries, you couldn't have jacked up the entrance slab, or let it down again leaving the jacks on the outside. You didn't fall, Leo – someone hit you. They hit you several times over the head with a weapon of some sort. They tried to kill you, and they probably thought you were dead or dying when they closed the entrance.'

He felt the blood drain from his cheeks. He must have been alone out there for days, bleeding, unconscious, teetering on the edge of death.

'We found you there a few hours after we got back on Tuesday morning. We thought you were dead at first. Thank God we did find you then: I don't think you'd have survived another day.'

She squeezed his hand lightly and he returned the pressure.

'You say someone attacked me,' he said. 'But why? Why would anyone want to kill me?'

She looked uneasy, not sure how much he should be told at this stage.

112

'Look, Leo, it's . . . complicated. Someone . . .' She hesitated, choosing her words, as if to protect him from something, the truth or something worse. 'The tomb was vandalized. Stripped of all its treasures. They managed to remove the lid from the sarcophagus, but it must have slipped: it broke right in half. If there were any offerings inside, they've all gone. All that's left is the skeleton.'

'Who the hell would . . . ? Do the police suspect anybody?'

'The police? *Hijos de chingadas!* They suspect everybody. The whole team. The captain who's in charge of the investigation actually thinks we all flew back to the site, knocked you out, and stole all the treasure. He's put . . .' She hesitated. 'The rest of the team have been sent to Iztacalco Prison.'

'What? He must be completely insane.'

She shook her head. 'It's standard practice here. People don't report crimes because they don't want to be arrested. My father may be able to take care of the captain. But, for the moment, we've all got to stay in Mexico City "For as long as the investigation continues."'

'But it's only an art theft. They're behaving as though it's a murder enquiry.'

He felt her hand tighten round his.

'Leo, I told you this was complicated. They're treating what happened to you as attempted murder. And there's the question of Bill Jessop.'

'Bill? He hasn't been caught trying to slip out of the country with gold ornaments hidden in his overnight bag, has he?'

She shook her head. 'Bill's dead. His body was found a few hours after we re-opened the burial chamber and discovered you.'

113

He said nothing for a while. He'd disliked Jessop, but he would never have wished this on him.

'What happened? Do you know?'

'He was shot. Five times through the heart. The gun hasn't been found. Only . . .' She looked into his eyes. 'Somebody told the police about your quarrel, that you'd dismissed him. Bill was very upset. He talked about nothing else on the flight to San Cristóbal. Nobody really listened to him very much. We'd all been through that sort of thing before, his griping and grousing. Nobody listened. He'd had it coming, we all thought that.'

'You don't think I had anything to do with his murder, do you?'

'No, no, of course I don't. I know you couldn't commit a crime of that kind. But the police think Bill flew straight back to the site and picked a quarrel with you. You shot him and got rid of the gun somewhere in the jungle or down a cenote well. Then you went back to the burial chamber, took all the offerings out, and gave them for safe-keeping to your Indian friends. But something happened and you ended up injured inside the chamber. The police think the Indians betrayed you for the gold. Another theory –'

'I don't need to hear any more theories. Christ Almighty, what sort of Mickey Mouse operation is this?'

'These are Mexican police, Leo; you should know better than to ask. They're not entirely stupid, but with so many foreigners involved, they think they can make some money out of the case, maybe a lot of money. My father can help, but even he has to take care these days.'

'How did Bill get back?'

'Nobody knows exactly. By helicopter, obviously. You knew he could fly one, didn't you?'

'Yes, I seem to remember that. He was very keen on saying he could be a one-man expedition.'

'He must have flown back late on Saturday. We all stayed together after getting back to the city, and we had lunch with each other around two. We broke up after that, but got together that might for dinner. Bill wasn't there. We all thought he was just sleeping it off, but now we think that's when he went back.'

'To tackle me.'

'Yes, to tackle you. He was very screwed up about it. We've tried to persuade the police that it was the other way round, that he attacked you and sealed you into the burial chamber, after clearing out all the offerings. Which means somebody else must have shot him and taken the gold.'

'Not the Indians. They'd have used arrows, not a gun.'

'Unfortunately, the police prefer their version.'

'Unfortunately, it doesn't hold water. The last things I remember happened on Saturday night. I must have been attacked soon after that, maybe late on Saturday night itself or on Sunday morning.'

'In the meantime, love, you cannot leave Mexico, not even Mexico City.'

'Why the hell not?'

'Because your trial starts in a few days' time. If you want to get out of here, you'd better act fast.'

13

Plaza México Bullring
Benito Juárez
Mexico City
Sunday, 28 November

'I don't know why you read that filthy rag, dear. It can't be doing your brainwaves any good.'

Antonia's mother kissed her on both cheeks, stood back, then leaned forward again to wipe away the lipstick she'd left behind. As for Antonia, she just smiled dutifully and said nothing. She'd given up long ago trying to justify her taste in reading matter to either of her parents. She'd taken *La Jornada* since her first day at university; even she thought it too left-wing for her taste at times, but at least it provided a healthy alternative to the bland, government-sanctioned broadsheets like *El Universal* or the cheap and lurid scoops of *La Prensa*.

'Cat got your tongue, dear?'

'No, Mother. I just don't feel like arguing.'

'Quite sensible.' She looked round. Draped in a Chalayan dress, sporting a single gold brooch that could have paid several times over for all the pomp of today's entertainment, and masked by sunglasses big enough to cause a solar eclipse, María Cristina Rocha y Ramírez looked as though she'd be more at home in Paris or Milan. There was a widespread myth that only the very rich can risk wearing jewellery in Mexico City. But in her case it was true. 'I think it's time we started moving,' she said, taking Antonia's upper arm in a firm grip and steering her for the stairs.

On the walls on either side of her, several hands had plastered posters promoting candidates for the coming congress elections. One in green cried '*Arriba y Adelante con Vasconcelos!*', while next to it a red one shouted a simpler slogan, '*Elegan Farías*'. María Cristina spared neither a glance, passing by as one who knows that politics are never decided on the streets, far less by pasting paper on walls. She already knew who would be the next president.

Alongside them were rows of *carteles*, the brightly-coloured posters that announced today's fights. There would be six bulls in today's *corrida*, and three matadors to kill them. Antonia noticed that three of the bulls were from her father's *ganadería*. That would be why her mother was here. That and the fact that the chief matador was Abelardo O'Donojú, a young pretender to the crown of the late great Manolo Martínez, handsome, elegant, and, like most men of his profession, not averse to the attentions of beautiful women.

They passed stalls selling hamburgers, hot dogs, *panuchos*, and *chalupas*, others that carried beer and Coke, and one that sold freshly fermented *pulque*. The yeasty odour mixed somehow with the smells of the milling crowd, mainly men, that followed them as they headed for the stairs.

Once in their box, the stench of unwelcome humanity was blotted out. From their shaded seats, they looked out over a vast amphitheatre. This was the biggest bullring in the world, and today it seemed as though half Mexico City had come to pay their respects to sun and blood. Antonia looked out over the front of their box to see row upon row of tiered seats spill away towards the sand-covered ring at the bottom.

'Actually,' she said, leaning back and half-turning to her mother, 'I only bought *La Jornada* yesterday to see what the smog levels are like.'

'And what are they like?'

'See for yourself.' Antonia gestured skywards. A fine haze filtered the sun's rays. Out in the streets, among the traffic, it was almost impossible to breathe. 'Ozone's around ninety-four, carbon monoxide's touching a hundred –'

'Oh, for heaven's sake, dear, look at all these people. I don't see any corpses yet, do you? You worry too much. Here, have a pastry.'

On the table to one side of the box sat a large white carton from the Pastelería Ideal. In an ice bucket behind it, two bottles of Dom Ruinart defied the heat. A small refrigerator held more champagne, smoked salmon, caviar, blinis, Dalloyau chocolates, and other treats. Antonia looked at her mother, amazed at how thin she managed to stay in spite of her love of fattening foods. As a child, she'd thought her mother a magical being, someone not subject to the rules of ordinary life. In time she'd learned the truth.

'Isn't Father here? It must be quite an honour even for him to have three bulls in the same *corrida*.'

'No, he's much too busy right now. He's been bringing some new cattle down from Texas. All very experimental.'

And it was yet another good excuse not to come to Mexico City, not to see his wife and daughter. Antonia wondered why they both put up with it. She thought of Leo, not knowing if any of it was real.

118

'Are we expecting guests?' she asked.

'Not really. I wanted to have you to myself for a couple of hours. I hope you're free for dinner afterwards. But friends may call in, of course.'

Antonia knew that went without saying. No one who knew the system would dare to avoid calling on her mother during the intervals.

Down below, the visitors had started to leave the *patio de caballos*, and the matadors, the banderilleros, and the picadors had begun to form a little line. The president of the *corrida* took his seat in the box next to theirs, the *aguacils* galloped back and forth, and the procession began. María Cristina broke open the first bottle of champagne and poured glasses for herself and her daughter. She took her seat and put on ordinary glasses in order to see the spectacle better.

There was a knock on the door.

So, that's why she arrived late and didn't see anybody, thought Antonia. The door opened and a sword-handler came in, carrying a heavy *capote de paseo*, the parade cape of his matador.

'With the compliments of Señor O'Donojú. For the graceful Doña Rocha y Ramírez. And his compliments also to the lovely Señorina Rocha y Ramírez.'

Her mother tipped the man and sent him off, while Antonia sat alone seething. Was it not enough that her mother allowed these matadors to offer their indiscreet blandishments to her, but did she have to let them drag her into it too?

'Mother, did he have to mention my name?'

'Yes, I'm sorry about that. I'll have a word with Mr O'Donojú if I get the chance. But all this sending up of capes is merely to lick your father's boots. He's been doing it since last season.'

119

'I suppose he'll dedicate his first bull to you as well.'

'Oh, I don't doubt it. If your father had any sense he'd come down here and take all these compliments himself.' She paused. 'Look, dear, I think Señor O'Donojú has drawn the first bull.'

Below, the *toril* door opened and the bull pushed his way into the ring. A shout went up. They were too far up to see the colours of the rosette that had just been pinned to the bull's flank, but judging by the animal, they must be the colours of the Rocha y Ramírez *ganadería*. Antonia decided to root for the bull. If he was brave enough, he could win an *indulto* and spend the rest of his life on a stud farm. As for the other stud, what was one matador more or less?

'Mother, you know I don't like bullfights. What's all this about?'

'Have one of these pastries, dear. They're quite delicious.'

'No, thanks. I'm trying to slim.'

'Well, some caviar, then. That's very slimming. You'll find blinis and sour cream in there as well.'

But Antonia just sipped her champagne and watched the picadors as they rode in the sun, lancing the bull in the shoulders, slowing down its furious pace. There was already blood on the sand.

'Your father wants you at the ranch. He says he can't look after you so well while you stay in the city.'

'Look after me? Mother, I'm twenty-five years old. I don't need to be looked after.'

'Nonsense. Just because you're brainy doesn't mean you don't need watching. Maybe your brainwaves *have* been addled from living in town.'

'Then yours must be ten times as bad. Not to mention your lungs.'

120

'Antonia, you know perfectly well I never had a brain to speak of. And when I want my lungs cleared I go to Switzerland.'

There was a flurry down below as O'Donojú stood to dedicate the bull formally to the president (it being his first bull of the day), and then, his voice thinned out by distance, to 'The illustrious *caballero*, the much-respected Don Ortiz Rocha y Ramírez of the Hacienda de Nuestra Señora de Guadalupe; and, in his absence today, his gracious wife, La Doña María Cristina, and his daughter, the exquisitely perfumed Señorina Antonia'. His hat, tossed from tier to tier, finally reached their box, and Antonia's mother stood to acknowledge it. Now the man and the bull would fight, one with cape, then cape and sword, the other with horns, to a bloody death.

'Mother, I can't go to the ranch. Not now – you know that. I have work to do here in the city, writing up the dig. I need the library, and I need to be where I can get hold of my colleagues if I need to consult them. In any case, the federal police won't let me set foot outside the district.'

'Oh, that! You know perfectly well that the police can be taken care of. Your father has already paid several large *mordidas* to people he knows. Or perhaps you'd rather not know that.'

'I'd already guessed. I just don't want it taken care of that way. Why can't you and Father understand that not everything can be settled by paying the right people stupid amounts of money?'

'It's how things are done in this country, dear. Do you know how much an ordinary policeman gets paid? How would they live without their *mordidas*?'

'Why can't they just be paid a fair wage?'

María Cristina shrugged. 'I'm sure I don't know, dear.

But how do you think your recent archaeological expedition got its Mexican funding? How do you think anything gets done here?'

'It's still not how I like to operate. The rest of the group are in prison. You know I can't just swan off and leave them behind.'

'You're innocent, aren't you?'

'Of course I am!'

'Then that's all that matters. If your friends are innocent too, they'll be let out in time.'

'Mother, do you have any idea what it's like in those prisons?'

'No, and I don't suppose you do either. Or have you taken up prison visiting in your spare time?'

'They have a reputation, Mother: you know that as well as I do.'

'Well, let's not worry about that. I'm sure Amnesty International or somebody will get round to it in the end. You, on the other hand, are not going to prison. You are going back to the bull-farm, then to the ranch. Your father misses you. He hasn't seen you since last Christmas. Treat this as a break. After all, none of your friends is writing up a report. If you ask me, you drive yourself too hard.'

She reached for the champagne bottle, topped up Antonia's half-empty glass, and poured the rest into her own. A cry went up from the crowd. O'Donojú had just completed a series of slow *verónicas* with a *rebolera*, bringing the bull to its knees and the audience to its feet. He had taken the bull after a single pair of *banderillas*, and was preparing it now for inevitable death. It was a brave animal, charging hard and straight, and O'Donojú knew he could display his skill well on it. He handed his working cape to one of his *banderilleros* and was handed the *muleta* and sword.

Suddenly gripped, María Cristina leaned forward to watch the fight reach its end. The matador performed a series of eight *naturales*, the sword behind the cape catching the sun, biding its time. The bull, turning at the finish of the last of the natural passes, charged again only to be met with a skilfully executed left-handed *pase de pecho*, the horns passing within centimetres of his chest, the cape tenderly sweeping along the bull's body, and the bull, visibly tiring now, its head low and its neck muscles, already weakened by the attentions of the picadors, bringing its horns lower every time, turned and charged directly at its adversary. O'Donojú stood his ground, dropping to his knees for a *derechazo de rodillas*, and the bull still more than strong enough to kill him. He let it go and brought it back again, dominating it with the *muleta*, calculating the beast's run so finely that the horns were grazing his costume and ripping the gold thread from it.

The crowd was on its feet, applauding his performance. The bull was beautiful, courageous, and as dangerous as they get, and it was hard to see how the man could get away without at least a goring. But he stood to the bull again, and with his sword drawn and his feet tight together, enticed it with a flick of the cape. And the bull charged in fast, its nostrils flecked with blood and a sheen of blood across its hump, with the two *banderillas* beating hard at its sides, and its sinewy legs tearing the sand and throwing it up in sightless clumps. And O'Donojú brought the bull to a halt with the *muleta*, until it was at a complete standstill, panting, its small eyes fixed on nothing, blinded now by the cape. Then the *torero* walked away, and his eyes were all the time on the bull and its horns that swayed so slightly above the great, blood-streaked head. Back he walked, putting yards between himself and the bull, and a silence passed among the spectators as one after another realized that he intended to make the kill *recibiendo*. He would not go to the standing bull and kill it while it stood, but he would take it charging, knowing all the time that a lift of the animal's head would be enough to send a horn through his chest with the force of a magnum bullet. And he incited the bull for the kill this time, with his feet together, bending his left knee while he swept the *muleta* towards the animal, sighting along the blade of the sword. And the bull rushed and was passed through by the cape, while the man leaned forward with the sword and pushed down hard and high between the shoulderblades, and the sword went in with a gruesome slowness, making its hard way between muscle and bone, and was not thrown back and forced into the air, and the bull was charging and dying at the same moment, and so it shuddered through all its length and died at last at the matador's feet.

The crowd could not be restrained. A killing like that might be seen only once in five years. They all knew a king was being crowned. They awarded O'Donojú both ears and the tail and a hoof of the bull he had killed, and cheered him ceaselessly as he paraded with his *cuadrilla*, and everywhere people craned their necks to catch sight of him, and stood on top of their seats in all parts of the stadium.

'He'll be along later, dear,' Antonia's mother said, thus dismissing the man who had just risked his life to entertain her. At least Don Ortiz would be pleased that his bull had proved so brave and made it possible for the young bullfighter to achieve such a splendid kill.

'If you don't mind, Mother, I think I've seen enough.' Antonia stood as though to go.

'Sit down,' snapped her mother. 'We still have plenty to talk about.'

'Such as?'

'Such as this man Leo Mallory. I'm told you've been visiting him every day at the ABC. Sometimes twice a day. Even when he was unconscious, you stayed for hours by his bedside. This has been reported to your father, and believe me, he's very angry.'

'Angry? Because I visit someone in hospital?'

'Don't treat me like a fool. Have you been having an affair with this man?'

Antonia wanted to laugh, but found she could not. In her mind she'd been Leo's lover for months now.

'Mother, I hardly know him. He's just the leader of the expedition. A friend, a colleague – nothing more than that.'

'So why do you pay him so much attention?'

'Because no one else can. He has no relatives here. His parents visited, then left without leaving an address. He's been very ill, and he's far from better. Somebody has to look after him.'

'Yes, I'm sure, and it's very loyal of you to say so. But, why you?'

'I told you, he's a friend.'

'You stay up all night at a friend's bedside? Antonia, don't try to do this with me. I have infinitely more experience of the world than you, and none of what you're telling me makes sense. You're in love with this man, or you think you are. Now, I don't know whether you were sleeping with him out there in the jungle or not, but I sure as hell will make sure you see no more of him while he's here.'

'You can't stop me seeing him. That's positively out of the Ark.'

'Is it? Believe me, Antonia, this is purely for your own good. I've spoken with your father about it. He was very clear on the point. If this man has anything more to do with you, he will be very lucky just to wind up in a Mexican prison for the rest of his life. If he pursues you, your father will see that he is killed. And if you insist on pursuing him, your father will have you killed.'

The blood drained from Antonia's cheeks. Down in the ring, another bull was being pursued by men on horses.

At that moment, there was a knock on the door. María Cristina called 'Enter', and a man dressed in a white tunic and white trousers came in. Antonia's mother rose hurriedly to her feet, urging Antonia to do the same.

'Antonia, let me introduce you to my teacher, my spiritual guide. Rafael, this is my daughter, Antonia, the one I told you about.'

Antonia shook hands stiffly and stepped back. The stranger was good-looking, with a degree of self-possession she had seldom encountered in an Indian.

'Rafael will be coming with us for dinner this evening. Isn't that right?'

The man smiled and nodded. In the bullring, the hot sun burned fresh blood into the dark sand.

14

She got to the hospital a little before eleven. It had been a long evening.

After the bullfight, they all – Antonia, her mother, and the mysterious Rafael – spent an hour downing cocktails with Abelardo O'Donojú and his chums at the Camino Real, the city's top hotel, where those who liked to think of themselves as Mexico's elite met in one of its three restaurants, five bars, and single, pulsating nightclub. Unlike many bullfighters she had met, Antonia thought this one looked good in ordinary clothes. He had neat buttocks, and she guessed he worked hard to keep them like that: a prominent backside was every matador's dread.

She watched from a distance as her mother flirted with him, inviting him to the hacienda after the festival of San Luis de Potosí on the first of January. He made up to her, complimenting this and that like a child charmed by easy things seen for the first time, for he knew she was someone to cultivate, and he had the outward means to do it. Antonia did not think him very intelligent, but she could not deny his courage, and she was not totally immune to his good looks, contrived as they may have been.

She overheard an odd remark from Rafael, when he was speaking a little apart with O'Donojú. 'I knew Gaona,' he said, 'when I was a young man. I saw him fight. Today, it was as if he had returned to us.'

Only later did she take in the full pretension of his statement. Rafael looked no more than fifty. How was it possible for him to have seen Rodolfo Gaona in the ring? Or had there been a younger Gaona, of whom she had not heard?

They slipped away from the hotel after about an hour and a half, Antonia and her mother, together with Rafael. María Cristina took them in her Mercedes to the city centre, to the Hostería de Santo Domingo on Belisario Domínguez. This was the city's oldest restaurant, a place where everything was conservative except the prices. The usual table, the same old waiters, the familiar decor, the inflated figures on the menu all evoked an imprisoning world that she had known ever since childhood. All that was different was the company of the teacher, whatever sort of teacher he was.

Antonia had formed the impression that Rafael was some sort of guru, and that her mother had brought him along for the express purpose of lecturing her on whatever it was they might have deemed necessary for her moral guidance. But in the end it did not turn out like that. Rafael showed himself almost indifferent to Antonia, and through the meal made not the slightest effort to woo or impress her. If he was her mother's agent, he did not act it.

They didn't talk about Leo, or honour, or death. Rafael asked if they'd been to the latest exhibition at the Museo del Chopo, seven works by Isidro Sanchez, a young artist from Jalisco. Apparently, one of the exhibits was a case of burned books and broken Mont Blanc pens topped by the slogan *Escribir no vale nada*.

'You don't think that's true?' asked Rafael. His long hair hung down almost to his shoulders. He was an Indian, but he spoke Spanish flawlessly. 'You don't think he's wrong to say that writing is worthless?' And bit by bit he persuaded them both that it was true, that only what lay in the heart mattered.

He was fascinated by Antonia's account of her expedition. She did not say why it had been cut short, but she thought her mother might already have done so. It was clear that the older woman was infatuated with Rafael. Not the sort of sexual infatuation that Antonia had seen more than once in the past, but something more intense, as though he had written something without ink in her heart, and she had come upon it and found it true.

In spite of herself, Antonia came a little under his spell as well. In part it was his physical grace, in part his wit; but she prayed he had no intention of leaving his mark on her heart at such a time. And, strangely, when she left the restaurant, she found her thoughts leaden, and her heart empty.

They'd left the car a couple of blocks away, on a street adjoining the Plaza de Garibaldi, in an area full of seedy nightclubs and bars. They walked there through thick crowds of late-night revellers, Rafael ahead with María Cristina on his arm, Antonia behind, almost tempted to slip off into some dark alleyway in order to make her escape to look for Leo.

The plaza was crowded. Three sides were taken up with huge *cantinas* and a food market where they sold highly spiced soup as an antidote for hangovers. Most of the people thronging the square were drunk or heading that way, strolling, staggering, sitting on the ground and weeping, men and women in all sorts of combinations. They came here to bolt down bowls of soup or cups of cheap black coffee, but mainly to listen to the endless contingent of *mariachi* singers and musicians.

The *mariachis* were mostly dressed in black with silver

ornamentation, their huge *charro* hats barely visible in the tense darkness. Antonia noticed one group sitting on the pavement playing chequers with beer-bottle tops. As she passed, one hurried to his feet and approached her, offering a good price for the best *ranchera* music in town. She laughed and shook her head. Privately, she disliked *ranchera* music, with the possible exceptions of Astrid Hadad and Juan Gabriel.

Then, to her embarrassment, her mother turned and pulled Rafael towards the little group.

'Let's have a song,' she cried out, hustling them to their feet. 'What shall we have? What's that one? *Podría volver* . . . Do you know that one?'

The singer smiled and assured her they did. Someone went and found some more freelance musicians to make up a larger band, then, ignoring the noise and singing all about them, they launched into the song. 'I could return, but my pride won't let me . . . If you want me back, you should have thought twice before you left me.'

María Cristina was in ecstasy, though the band, in fact, was far from good and had never played together before. Rafael seemed tolerantly amused. Antonia hung back, unable to pretend to an enthusiasm she did not feel. A group of tourists, Americans by the look of them, gathered round for a free show.

As the band finished off the song and launched unbidden into a bouncy *huapango*, Antonia felt herself being jostled from behind. At first she thought it was one of the tourists, then she realized someone was trying to snatch her bag. She turned to see a kid, maybe fifteen or sixteen years old, reaching out a scrawny rag-clad arm. She cried out involuntarily, and the boy, realizing he stood no chance now of stealing the bag, turned on his heels and started running.

Rafael had heard the scream and was at Antonia's side in mere seconds. Taking in at a glance that she was all right, he turned his attention to the fleeing thief. He called out in a loud voice: 'Catch him for me, somebody!' Seconds later, the boy fell forward heavily, tripped by a *mariachi* who could smell a reward from a mile away. The musician held the boy down while Rafael approached across the plaza, no hurry in his gait.

'You tried to steal her purse, didn't you?' As he spoke, Rafael bent down and grabbed the prostrate teenager. His face was bleeding, and his hands and arms had been badly hurt in the heavy tumble he'd taken. The boy only stared at him. There was fear in his face, and incomprehension.

Antonia came up behind Rafael.

'Rafael, leave him alone. He didn't do me any harm. And he must have been desperate to try something like that.'

'He tried to commit a crime. You can't excuse that.' He cuffed the boy hard across one cheek. 'You're just a little thief, aren't you? Mm?'

'You're wasting your time,' called someone from the crowd, 'he can't hear you. He's deaf and dumb. He always hangs round here waiting for handouts.'

The boy was Indian, as far as Antonia could tell.

'Let him go, Rafael. He won't do it again.'

'Won't he? This type won't stop their thieving for anything, not unless he's given a proper lesson.'

Suddenly, systematically, he began to beat the boy. Antonia shouted and tried to intervene, but he brushed her aside.

'Go and see to your mother,' he said. 'See she's all right.'

No one in the audience sought to interfere. The boy

131

wasn't one of them, he was an outcast on numerous counts. His race, his disability, and his poverty all made him wholly unwelcome here. There was nothing Antonia could do; Rafael was too strong for her, and too much in command of the situation. He gave the impression that, if he had wanted to, he could have beaten every person in the square, and that no one would have stopped him.

When he had finished, the boy lay on the ground like a piece of raw meat. Rafael had not spared him. There was no blood, except for a stream from his nose that might have been caused by the fall. A woman stepped out of the crowd and bent to the boy, lifting his head. Her clothes and her skin colour said she was American. She looked at Rafael.

'You are one disgusting bastard,' she said.

Rafael seemed not to hear. He looked at the woman and went on looking at her, and as he did so the fight went out of her, and she laid the boy's head down again and stood and returned to the crowd.

Antonia's mother took her arm, drawing her away from the scene.

'You're upset, dear. Don't be upset. It was only an Indian. He'll recover in a day or two. They don't have the same constitution as normal people.'

'You're such a heartless fool, Mother. Can't you see he'll die as a result of that beating? You and Rafael can go wherever you like. I'm going home.'

'It's much too far, dear, and you on your own. The car's just round the corner. I'll drive you home.'

'I'd rather you didn't. Your so-called friend revolts me. I don't want to set eyes on him again.'

'I'll speak to him, dear. Perhaps he was a little hasty. He's a kind man underneath, an understanding man. And full of so much wisdom.'

'Fuck his wisdom. I'll take a taxi.'

'Why don't you buy a car of your own anyway?' her mother asked. 'Or let me give you one.'

Antonia, familiar with this argument, pulled back, gently, but firmly.

'That's just what this city needs,' she said. 'Another motor car.'

When she got to the apartment in the San Ángel district south of the city, her flat-mate Isabel had gone out for the evening with her boyfriend Eduardo, so there was no need for explanations when Antonia slipped out again barely five minutes after going in. She walked to Barranco del Muerto Metro station and took the first train, changing at Tacubaya for Observatorio. It was a short walk from there to Calle Sur 132, where the rear of the ABC was situated. In the dark, its sleek lines and dramatic elevations were etched by bright lights. But at the back there were fewer of these, and large stretches of the building were wreathed by a complicated work of shadows.

Leo was being kept in the North Building, a square block devoted to internal medicine, surgical pathology, and emergency treatment. He was on the third floor in the Intensive Care Unit. Following his return to consciousness, it had been reckoned safe to move him from T7, where he'd been placed after his operation, to 356, an intermediate care room. When Antonia had last set eyes on him, he'd been the only occupant of the corridor in which intermediate care was located. She'd insisted on his being kept under close watch, and had paid to have a trained nurse on duty twenty-four hours a day.

She had also dipped deeper into her trust fund to ensure that an armed policía stood on guard at the rear entrance to the unit. If asked why she thought such a precaution necessary, she'd have mentioned the attack in the dark of the great pyramid, in the room where they'd discovered the sarcophagus set about with gold.

What she refused to admit, even to herself, was that the placing of a guard here in Mexico City, miles from the scene of that incident, was a sort of confirmation that the murder attempt had been directed at Leo specifically, rather than a random attack that might as easily have been directed against any one of them, if they'd been in the same spot when the would-be killer came on the scene. She thought about Bill Jessop a lot. It wasn't that she suspected him of the attempt. It was just that she couldn't get the possibility out of her head.

Although she could have gone through the main entrance on Calle Sur 136, it would only have meant dodging nurses and orderlies all telling her it was outside visiting hours and asking her – very politely, since this was the city's most expensive hospital and she looked like a million pesos – to leave.

Leo's nurse, the Indian woman who called herself Magdalena, had alerted Antonia to the existence of a back door, and had given her a key to let herself in and out with.

She approached the door as usual, key in hand. Sometimes she worried that she might encounter a prowler round here, but common sense told her there was not much to gain from hanging round the rear of an intensive care unit. Of course, if the president had been in residence in the top-floor suite that was permanently reserved for him, a prowler wouldn't have been allowed within ten blocks of this place.

The door should have been locked an hour or two earlier, when the security man made his last rounds. She took the key from her handbag and walked into the little porch. Suddenly she noticed that the light which shone above the door day and night was no longer shining. The only illumination came from inside. She thought that the bulb must have spent itself.

She looked round, studying the shadows briefly, never really at ease in darkness. She thought of the pyramid, and going down into it, that sense of darkness that had no end. This was a dangerous city, she thought, and what she was doing back here involved a certain amount of risk. She could be robbed or raped at knifepoint, she could be stabbed to death, and no one would find her till morning, or for days perhaps.

The door was partly open. She touched it gingerly, and it swung away from her as if its spring was damaged. Looking up, using what light fell from the stairwell, she could see that it was broken, and she felt the beginnings of a true fear tickle her bones, and her mouth opened and closed, and was dry of an instant. She let the door hang as it was and looked ahead of her, up into the cement stairwell, and she noticed that, far up, another light had been extinguished. She guessed it was on the third floor, which was where she was headed. Seeing that, she felt the fear thicken inside her, like a poisoned broth.

She held her breath and started up the stairs. At the main floor landing, she tried the door that led to the internal medicine division, but found it locked. She tried, but her key wouldn't fit the lock. She wanted to call up to the policeman, whose station was a chair on the third-floor landing, but prudence held her back. The night was warm, and inside the hospital heat had been trapped all day and had not yet started to disperse. A trickle of sweat ran down her forehead and dropped on to her nose. She wiped it away absentmindedly and took the next flight of stairs as silently as the one before. She headed directly on up to the third floor.

The policeman was lying on his back against a rear wall. There was not much light, just a dim glow from the ceiling lights beyond the glass door, their brightness brought down for the night. Frightened, she went to the policeman and bent down, realizing only at the last moment that she was standing in a pool of blood, sticky blood that continued pooling as she stood there.

He was beyond help of any kind. His throat had been cut, his jaw looked as if it had been dislocated. He was definitely dead. She ran her hand round his waist until she found his gun. It was still there in its holster, he hadn't had a chance to get it out. Maybe he had known his attacker. Antonia took the gun and slipped it into her pocket, then thought better of that and brought it out again to hold it in her hand openly.

The door leading into the prolonged care unit opened without difficulty, and closed again just as neatly behind her. Antonia was already through, looking for someone who could raise the alarm. But they left the patients sleeping here, and there was no one on duty, no one. It dawned on her that there was a more than even chance that Leo was already dead.

She walked down the soft, beige-carpeted corridor, her heart beating fast. Without her being aware of it, she left a trail of bloody footprints on the light-coloured floor. Her hand was clammy on the butt of the gun, but it didn't shake. She had handled guns before, all sorts of guns, revolvers bigger than this one, out on the ranch. And the policeman wasn't the first dead man she'd seen. There had been little Pedro who snapped his neck while breaking in a *mesteño* brought down from the hills, a horse he was riding with a *bosalea* only, and no saddle.

He'd been her father's *gerente* for seventeen years, and Antonia's closest friend and mentor; his wife still lived on the ranch, on a pension her father had allocated her, her and her five children. And there'd been Manolo, a childhood friend who'd followed the bulls since the age of seven, and who'd been horned by a 30-*arroba* fighting bull during a *corrida de novillos-toros* near Zamora de Hidalgo.

She shook her head free of nightmares and crept further along the corridor, moving like an intruder, not knowing when or where the real intruder might emerge round a corner or through a door. If he was still here, that is, if Leo wasn't already dead. The fear of it was tangible to her, and she had to bite it back down and swallow it in her throat, like bile. The hospital smell which always hung in the corridors like a miasma, filled her nostrils.

She came to a junction of corridors. The one ahead of her made one side of the intermediate care unit. Leo's room was on the left. As she came closer, the door began to open, and she threw herself hard against the wall. A man came out of Leo's room. He didn't look much like a doctor, thought Antonia. She watched as he proceeded down the corridor as far as the next door, turned the handle, and slipped inside.

Antonia chose the same moment to slip into the opposite corridor and get into Leo's room. The instant she was inside she felt the fear double and redouble, and she started to choke. Something lay on the bed, a man with his throat cut, and blood as bright as bull's blood had cascaded over the pure white sheets and down on to the beige carpet that looked like the sand on the Plaza México, and she almost expected to hear thousands of hands applauding and the stamping of booted feet on wooden boards.

She dashed to the dead man, but he wasn't Leo, merely an unlucky stranger, a middle-aged man who must have been moved to Leo's room sometime that day. There was a photograph on the table beside him, a woman of the same age, probably his wife; it too was spattered with blood.

There was a sound behind her. Antonia whirled, the pistol coming up in an instinctive act of defence. The nurse was lying on the ground, Magdalena, the one who'd been with Leo until now. Antonia bent down to help her. She'd been struck sharply on the head by a heavy instrument of some kind, probably the drip stand that lay on its side next to her. Antonia found a pillow in one of the cupboards and eased it under Magdalena's head. As she did so, blood flowed copiously from her wound, and the nurse cried out in pain.

'Where's Leo?' Antonia asked. 'Where did you take him?'

'*Socorro . . . socorro.* I need . . . help.'

'I'll get help soon. But I need to know where Leo is. Doctor Mallory. Do you remember? Which room was he moved to?'

The woman moaned, and a deep shivering passed through her body, and Antonia thought she had lost her. But she was not dead yet, only seeing the first blackness.

'He ask me . . . He ask me has he killed Malry . . . "Is Malry dead?" he ask me, and I stupid, I say, "No, you never kill Malry, you kill Morelos . . ." My patient, he is Mr Morelos, he have heart attack last week.'

She stopped speaking abruptly as another shudder cascaded through her muscles, causing her to arch her back. Her lips were turning blue.

'Which room?' pressed Antonia, knowing she might

have only seconds to avert a further tragedy, that it might already be far too late. 'Which room did they take Doctor Mallory to?'

Magdalena looked up at her, terrified eyes beseeching her for help.

'Three-six-one,' she said. 'He taken there this morning.'

'Did you tell the killer this?'

Magdalena shook her head, but only briefly. Her hand clutched Antonia's, as though she might save herself by that means.

Antonia stood and made her way to the side of the bed, where the alarm button was situated, inches away from the dead Morelos's stiffening fingers. He must have tried to reach it in the seconds before his killer struck. She stabbed it again and again, then turned and made for the door. Magdalena needed professional help, and she was in the right place. There was nothing more Antonia could do.

Coming back into the corridor, she checked that the coast was clear, then dashed to a spot about halfway down. Here, a corridor without doors cut away to the right. Its only function was to provide a short-cut between the two main corridors that made up the intermediate care section. Antonia ran along it, coming to a halt at the far end. Room 361 was directly opposite, but she feared that, if she was seen entering it, it would only serve to alert the killer.

She peeked round the corner. There was no one at the further end. Pistol tight in hand, she crossed the corridor and pushed the door open. From somewhere back where the emergency calls were taken, she could hear footsteps, neither hurrying nor slow. The door closed behind her, and she saw him, sitting up in bed reading. He put down his book and saw her, smiling as he put the book aside. Then he saw the expression on her face and the gun in her hand.

'We have to get out quick,' she said. 'Someone's trying to kill you.'

There was no way of locking the door from the inside, and she didn't have the keys to lock him in, if that was possible.

'I don't understand,' he said. 'Who's trying to kill me?'

'There's no time to explain,' she said. 'I'll help you out of bed.'

He was dressed in a hospital gown with strings at the sides. It wasn't the ideal garb in which to roam about Mexico City late at night, but there was no time to hunt out his own clothes and put them on. She pulled out the needles from two drips and got him to his feet. He looked ridiculous with his spindly legs peeping out below the gown. But his face was so strained with worry that she felt little disposed to laugh.

'I'll explain when we're outside,' she said. 'But first I have to get you out of here.'

The corridor was still empty. Antonia thought she could hear someone coming from the direction of the night desk, not running, not dragging their feet either. She looked to the left, thinking it might lead to the prolonged care unit, and so to the outside: but instead there was a heavy fire door that sealed the corridor off, and when she tried to open it it wouldn't budge a fraction of an inch.

'Quick,' she said, 'we've got to go back the way I came.'

They started for the transverse corridor, but before they got there a man came out of one of the rooms. He had the slim hard looks of a vaquero, as though he'd emerged from long years of tempering, as though he'd been out riding on hard, high desert plains and returned with a look in his eye that spoke of distances to come.

He looked at them and they looked back, and Antonia knew they were all thinking much the same thing. As if in a dream, she saw him fish into his jacket and bring out a heavy pistol, and next thing he was bringing it down and pointing it at Leo, who swayed on legs he hadn't used in a long time, and could do nothing to save himself. There was nowhere to run to, nowhere to hide.

Antonia's arm and hand went into action even before her thoughts had started to catch up. She didn't bother aiming, just pointed and got off three shots in quick succession. The shots sounded like drumbeats, and each one found a mark. The three entry holes blossomed like roses against the man's chest, bright scarlet on his white shirt, while the spent bullets tumbled unseen to embed themselves in the plaster wall behind.

There was a look of surprise on the killer's dark-skinned face, and something like righteous anger in his dark-rimmed eyes. He took a couple of steps further towards them, and started to raise his pistol again. Antonia fired a fresh round that entered his forehead just off centre and came out through the back of his skull with a smashing sound, leaving behind a hole the size of a man's angry fist. The assassin didn't have time to sneeze, he just went back, and his heels lifted from the floor, throwing him down hard. He did not move again.

Antonia glanced at his wretched form, shivered, and grabbed Leo.

'Come on,' she said. 'We're not staying here.'

She put her arm round his waist for support, and they started towards the way out.

15

María Cristina poured two tequilas into long glasses on her mirror-topped bar. She pushed one towards Rafael and kept the other for herself. She wasn't a heavy drinker, and she didn't plan to start now, but all this worry about Antonia was undermining her self-possession.

'Why is it that, even when you try to do the right thing, events seem to conspire to turn everything upside-down? Why is that?'

Rafael sipped his tequila, more out of politeness than anything, and set it aside.

'Perhaps you have been mistaken in defining what you call "the right thing". Perhaps there is no conspiracy of events after all, only a working-out of things as they are destined to work out. Haven't I taught you about this many times? There are seven levels of the heart and ten levels of the soul. If the heart is right, but the soul is not, there will be only discord. Before I leave, I will give you a prayer. It is one my people used in the rainforest. It will bring you harmony of heart and soul.'

She had never doubted his love, his humility, or his compassion. For that and more she'd given him large amounts of money. He'd never asked for it, but he'd spoken often enough of fountains replenishing themselves and the small seeds from which great forests grew, and there was the story of the little boy who'd given him his last meal of refried beans, and today that little boy was a man with whole bean plantations in Chihuahua state. She thought those dark brown eyes could have persuaded her to rip her heart out bleeding. But he didn't want her blood, he wanted her money and her influence to help expand the Mission into all the world.

'Thank you for coming to dinner. I so wanted you to meet Antonia. How did you find her?'

'I thought her charming. And very beautiful. But then I would have expected that in any daughter of yours.'

'Antonia is something unique.' She paused and swallowed a mouthful of the spirit. 'Would you like to meet her again?'

'Very much.'

'Then I'll arrange it. Perhaps just the two of you next time.'

'And your husband?' he asked. 'Have you spoken to him? Did you mention my proposal to him?'

She felt her cheeks redden. She'd hoped he wouldn't mention the subject, not tonight.

'He said . . . Well, he said much what I expected him to. He was quite blunt about it, I'm afraid. I really tried, but . . .' The words trailed away from her. She realized that, really, deep down, she was afraid of him, more afraid of him, perhaps, than she was of Don Ortiz.

'Let me see,' said Rafael. 'Your husband won't have anything to do with Indians, he has no time for shamans or *zahoríns*, he –'

'All that's true, but . . . No, that's almost exactly what he said. He got angry. He wants me to have nothing to do with you. I tried to tell him about you, but he wouldn't listen. He said I was to give you no more money. Master, I'm frightened. My husband is a dangerous man.'

'What about you, María Cristina? What do you want?'

'I want to help you and the Mission. Your research institute, I want to help with that.'

'And in return?'

'I think you already know. Health. Peace of mind. Contentment. A long life.'

He looked into her eyes. They were like shallow pools, he thought, they held nothing but the customary desires and the everyday failings. That was why they came to him, the wealthy dispossessed, the healthy sick, the tired and lame in spirit. He was their only hope in a life that was fast becoming hateful, he promised what the Church could not, what the Jews and Mormons and Jehovah's Witnesses and Seventh Day Adventists and Buddhists and Freemasons and Anglicans and Moonies could not.

'María,' he said, and his voice was pitched lower than she had ever heard it. He lifted his hand and placed it gently against her cheek. Her insides were melting. If God touched her, it would be like this.

'Tell me,' he said, and his hand came round her neck until it held the back of her head. She could feel his breath upon her face, as if he had stepped out of the rainforest just that minute, to be with her. 'Tell me, how would it be if I were to offer you immortality?'

After they'd taken only a few steps, Antonia realized that Leo would never be able to make it back the way she'd come. In the short spell he'd been bed-ridden, his leg muscles had atrophied sufficiently to render him incapable of standing or walking without assistance. The stairs were out of the question. Someone was bound to have called the police by now, and a quick search of the area would find them creeping along some corridor, hunting for the way out.

Leaving him propped against the wall, she ran back to

the room he'd been in. Someone had left a white coat on a hook behind the door. She grabbed it and put it on, then made for the wheelchair in which he'd been moved from his first room and which had been left parked beside the bed.

Everything was still quiet as they hurried down through intensive care, but she caught sight of people running. Two orderlies dressed in white were rushing along on either side of a wheeled stretcher, heading back in the direction of the room where Magdalena lay bleeding to death.

Antonia had come this way often enough to know the twistings and turnings of the corridors well. They reached the main lift without being challenged. As the door opened at the bottom, however, the first thing they caught sight of was about half a dozen policemen from a nearby *comisaría*. Antonia just pushed the wheelchair forward, and as she reached them, she pointed backwards and said, 'Third floor. You'll have to hurry.'

They caught a taxi on Observatorio, and were back at her apartment fifteen minutes later. The driver would remember them if questioned, but she didn't think there'd be much chance of that happening. With any luck, they'd be out of the country by then. She hadn't yet thought where they might go, but the United States was the most likely destination.

'Where's your passport?' she asked, deciding that the sooner the issue was broached the better.

'Passport?' He gave a dry laugh that subsided into a fit of coughing. When he finished, he looked up at her helplessly. 'You want to know where my passport is? The last I saw of it was in Komchen.'

'Komchen?' She got him out of the chair and started

to help him up the stairs. This wasn't going to be easy to explain to Isabel in the morning.

'The city we were exploring out there in the jungle. Remember? That's its name: Komchen. It's on the lid of the sarcophagus.'

'Shouldn't be too hard to get it, then,' she said. 'I'll pop over in the morning.'

'Not hard at all,' he replied. 'But take a heli . . .' He coughed, almost doubling up. He'd need more expert help than she could provide.

'Don't die on me, my love,' she whispered, bending over him as he slumped against the apartment door. He caught her hand quickly, then released it as another spasm of coughing bent his body in two.

She left him crouching there and went down to fetch the wheelchair, which she'd left in the entrance hallway. The light flickered as it always did, and a chilly breeze slipped in from outside. She must have left the main door open. Leaving the wheelchair, she went to the door. Before closing it, she looked out, checking up and down the street. A pack of wild dogs went by, sniffing the air for a scent of food.

On the other side of the road, someone was watching, wrapped in shadow, but Antonia saw nothing and no one. The dogs passed and were swallowed up by darkness. She pulled the door shut and headed back upstairs again, carrying the wheelchair.

Downstairs, the wind disturbed the trees in a mockery of true autumn.

16

Boulevard de Courcelles
Paris
29 November

'You give them names?'

'Why, yes, of course,' said Declan, wondering if doctors had such a thing as a sense of humour. This one had come well recommended, but so far all he'd done was to ask personal questions and make clicking noises with his tongue.

Somewhere, in another room, a choir of little children was rehearsing for a forthcoming Christmas concert.

> *Vive le vent*
> *Vive le vent*
> *Vive le vent d'hiver*
> *Qui s'en va*
> *Sifflant soufflant*
> *Dans les grands sapins verts . . .*

Declan smiled. The tune was 'Jingle Bells', but what a very different animal this was. The children belted it out with gusto, over and over again. If it hadn't been for the doctor and his infernal questions, Declan might have enjoyed himself. He remembered another doctor in Dublin who'd put his headaches down to too little sex. Or had it been too much? If the man had ever met Concepta, he'd have known it was no bloody sex at all.

'Doctor, I don't know about you, but I like to personalize my ailments, make them come alive for me imaginatively. Does that make sense?'

The doctor squinted and coughed. He was Greek, by the name of Apostolos Papadiantis, a liberal ousted by the generals in 1970, part conventional doctor, part homoeopath, a lover of fine wines, to which he attributed health-giving qualities, a churchgoer on the holy days of his seven favourite saints, an occasional smoker of marijuana, a frequenter of cafés, a part-time husband and part-time father, sentimental by nature and much given to introspection.

'And this is why you give your headaches names?' he said.

'You don't think I should?'

'No, it's your privilege, of course. You Irish are very imaginative. Tell me, when you were a child, did you ever have an imaginary friend? Did you give him a name?'

'I had more than one. My own little gang. They all had names, why wouldn't they have? You aren't going to tell me the headaches are old friends come back to life?'

The doctor shifted in his chair and smiled. Declan had been given his name by Arlaten, who thought he was the best general practitioner in Paris. Certainly, he charged enough.

'That would be going too far. But the little boys and girls – I take it there were representatives of both sexes? – the little boys and girls who visited your lonely spirit may have been the medium through which you worked out your conflicts.'

'I don't remember any conflicts.'

'Believe me, you had them. You may have had more

than most, since your unconscious came up with a gang to cope with them. It reminds me a little of multiple personalities.'

'Listen, I didn't come here to be psychoanalysed. I want you to treat my headaches, not my brain. There's nothing wrong with my brain, thank you very much.'

Papadiantis smiled and leaned back in his chair and asked more questions.

'Tell me,' he said at last, 'have you ever been sent for a CT scan?'

'What are you suggesting? That there's an abnormality there, inside the brain? Is that what you think, a clot or a tumour or something?'

Papadiantis shook his head. 'I'm not a prophet, I just prefer to cover all eventualities. I'll make an appointment for you with Poujauran at the Centre Médical Marmottan. It's not far from here, just off the Avenue des Ternes. In the meantime, I'd like you to have a few homoeopathic remedies.'

He reached for his copy of Jouanny's *Therapeutics*, thumbed through it, and made a couple of notes.

'Doctor, I'm not sure about this. I've always steered clear of the unscientific.'

Papadiantis snorted. 'Homoeopathy isn't unscientific. Half the doctors in France use it in one form or another. Trust me. If you've got a tumour in there – which I doubt – we'll have it cut out. In the meantime, these remedies should help. Given time, they may even cure your headaches entirely. Now, I'd like you to take Nux Vomica, five 7C globules twice a day; Venus mercenaria, one unit-dose per week in 30C; and Glonoinum, six times a day in 7C. I'll also prescribe some Sanguinaria canadensis to hold in reserve.'

Hurriedly, his pen skimming across the surface of his

pad, he wrote out the prescription and handed it to Declan.

'You'll get those in almost any pharmacy, but I recommend one run by a friend of mine. If you go back down to the Place des Ternes. One street on is the rue Poncelet. You'll find it a few doors from Le Moule à Gâteau. In fact, you could pop in and buy some of their *chaussons aux pruneaux*.'

'Doctor, do you know anything about the pineal gland?'

'What sort of thing do you want to know? Has somebody suggested that this could be the cause of your headaches?'

'Not really, but . . .'

He explained what he'd seen at the morgue, without giving away any details. Papadiantis nodded sagely, wondering why a policeman would have been brought in to what sounded a purely medical case, however bizarre.

'And you think you may be suffering from a swollen pineal gland too?'

'Not really. I was more interested in the –'

'Because we can determine that very simply through a CT scan.'

'I was told . . .'

He related all that Arlaten had told him, leaving out the details of the autopsies, while Papadiantis nodded. When he came to a finish, the doctor looked at him calmly and put down the pen he'd been holding absentmindedly since writing the prescription.

'That's all I was told,' said Declan. 'I just want to know if it is all, or whether there's more.'

'About the pineal gland?'

Declan nodded.

'Oh, yes,' whispered the doctor, and he looked at

150

Declan with half-closed, serious eyes. In the room next-door, the children's voices rose higher than before, and behind them the sound of simple musical instruments.

> *Vive le vent*
> *Vive le vent*
> *Vive le vent d'hiver . . .*

A cold draught made its way into the doctor's room, and as he spoke, the temperature seemed to drop by several degrees.

L'Hôtel de Marigny Presidential Palace
Paris
Later the same day

'Monsieur Carberry, the president will see you now. But please remember that he has an appointment with an Algerian minister in half an hour. And there is to be a large reception at the Élysée this evening.'

Declan smiled reassuringly, giving the impression that he knew the ropes, which, in his own way, he did. In almost thirty years of marriage to Concepta, he'd attended Dublin's finest receptions, season after season, whoever was in or out of power. He didn't bother to remind the aide that it had been the president who had invited him, not the other way round.

Alain Dutheillet, France's new president, was waiting in a long art-nouveau-style room that had been fitted out as a library. It was one of those libraries no one ever reads in, where men come to talk and smoke cigars, but whose books lie year after year untouched and unread.

As Declan entered, Dutheillet was dictating a letter to a pretty secretary who could have passed as Isabelle Adjani.

Declan suppressed a groan. He'd always wondered where the French built these women, any one of whom would have made the so-called supermodels look dowdy. Perhaps there was a state-sponsored factory on the outskirts of Paris.

'*Je vous prie d'agréer comme toujours l'assurance de mes sentiments dévoués –*'

The president stopped speaking and looked up. Seeing Declan, he held his hand up and smiled. The secretary closed her notepad, took some papers from the table in front of her, and got to her feet.

'*Merci, Monique. Attends-moi dans la chambre verte. Ceci ne prendra pas longtemps.*'

Monique nodded, pushed her hair back with a discreet flick of the wrist, and walked back down the length of the room.

'He's all yours,' she said to Declan in flawless English. 'Give him back to me in reasonable time.'

She slipped out through the door, closing it quietly behind her and leaving on the air a gentle trace of Mitsouko perfume. Or was it Chamade? Declan shook his head and went to join the president.

Alain Dutheillet was young, forty-five or six, athletic and intellectual at the same time. You could tell just by looking at him that he'd been a runner or an oarsman, and that he still fitted in a game of squash or some hard skiing at the weekends. He'd studied philosophy and politics at the École Normale Supérieure at St Cloud, and taught sociology alongside Pascal Lainé at Villetaneuse. When he was thirty he'd published a best-selling novel, an intense *nouveau roman* about life in the suburbs, two years later he'd won an Olympic gold medal in fencing. Declan felt like turning him upside-down and sitting on him till he squeaked.

'Please, take a seat. I've asked Monique to ask for some coffee to be sent in. We get it fresh every week from Verlet, one of their special roasts.' He nodded in the direction of the door through which Monique had vanished. 'Have you ever wondered where they come from?'

Declan nodded. He was devastated. If the French President didn't know, there was no hope in his ever finding out.

'Emmanuelle Béart was in here yesterday,' the president continued. 'She's doing another film with Sautet. I'm invited to the première, of course. Perhaps you'd like to come as well. You could meet her after the performance.'

'I'm not sure policemen and actresses mix too well.'

'Maybe not. But I'm being impolite. I haven't apologized for bringing you here at such an hour. Was it explained to you that I have an important meeting with the Algerian Minister for Home Affairs, and then this wretched reception for their entire delegation?'

He paused and gestured towards French windows behind them.

'Are you happy inside, Monsieur Carberry, or shall we have a stroll in the courtyard?'

'A stroll would be grand,' said Declan, thinking that the weather was not particularly fine. Then he remembered that the Hôtel de Marigny was reserved for foreign visitors and would be as full of bugs as an Eccles cake overfilled with raisins.

Dutheillet picked up a thick folder from the table and led the way into the open air.

The small courtyard was perfectly tended. A fountain designed by Aldrophe threw cascades of water up towards the open sky. The walls on every side were heavily creepered, and at every turn stood pithoi filled with late autumn flowers.

'I've met your brother-in-law several times,' said the president. 'A good man. He's doing good work with the Commission.'

'He did better work when he was Taoiseach. But that's out of the question now.'

'Because of the scandal? But I thought he'd been vindicated.'

'He was. But by the time the verdict was through he'd been out of the loop too long. The seat on the Commission was a sop.'

'Not at all. He does important work for Europe. In some ways I envy him.'

'I haven't heard of him getting visits from Emmanuelle Béart.'

Dutheillet laughed comfortably. 'I'll ask her to call. Or perhaps he'd prefer to meet Juliette Binoche . . .'

Declan smiled tightly. This was bringing a headache on, not to mention a strong desire to strangle the French head of state.

'Why did you ask me here today, Monsieur Dutheillet? I don't expect it was to meet film stars.'

A waiter appeared in one corner and started lifting coffee things on to a round table.

'Let's have our coffee,' suggested Dutheillet.

They sat down while the waiter finished. Dutheillet placed the file he had been carrying on the table.

'C'est tout, monsieur?' the waiter asked

'Oui, merci.'

When the coffee had been poured and *financiers* laid on a plate in front of Declan, the president took a couple of bitter mouthfuls and set down his cup.

'I want to know what you can tell me about Arnaud

Nougayrède. Have there been any further developments?'

Declan told him what he could, which was not much. He embellished the account by reciting details of the investigation as a whole. Above all, he said nothing about CT scans or pineal glands. As far as the president knew, Nougayrède had been murdered in Paris, in what seemed to be a random attack. Both the French Police Nationale and Interpol were in hot pursuit of the killer or killers. Because he knew the story of an accident in the Gorges du Verdon was false, Dutheillet thought he knew the true facts of the case.

When he finished, Declan flashed an anxious smile and took a long drink of coffee, no milk, too much sugar.

'That's about all we know at present, sir,' he said, picking up a *financier*. 'The Police Nationale know nothing more than we do.'

The president said nothing, but continued to look directly at Declan. After half a minute of this treatment, the Irishman started to feel uncomfortable.

'Well,' he said, eating the *financier* in a single bite. 'You seem to have no more questions, so I'll make myself scarce. I know you have pressing engagements.'

He started to his feet, scraping his chair along the rough paving.

'Sit down,' snapped Dutheillet. Declan looked at him, surprised by the sudden harshness in his tone, then sat down again. The taste of the *financier* still clung to the roof of his mouth, but he dared not reach for his coffee cup.

'What exactly do you take me for?' asked the president. 'A total imbecile?'

'Monsieur le Président, I'm not at all sure what you mean.'

'Don't humour me. You know perfectly well what I'm

getting at. I know all there is to know about the other seven bodies. I know how they were killed. All I don't know is who killed them.'

'I understand. I'd been given to believe you wanted to keep up a sort of pretence.'

'That's just for the public. Whatever you do, do not confuse me with the public. The fact is, I want your investigation brought to a halt at once. Any further enquiries into this case will be carried out by the French police. Interpol's help is no longer required.'

'Help? I wasn't aware we were offering help. It may have escaped your notice, but we took on this case because it has several international angles. The victims are from several countries. More than one seems to have a link with Latin America. One, as you know, was this country's foreign minister. His body was found next to an Irish terrorist wanted in more than one country for arms smuggling. How could Interpol not be involved? The situation demanded –'

'I don't think you heard me.' The president's voice, accustomed to command, overrode Declan's without difficulty. The patch of sky above was alive with moving clouds. Faint sounds of traffic came from the streets. 'Let me say it again. Interpol's help is no longer required.'

Declan was tempted to get up and leave, but he wanted the matter resolved first.

'God,' he said, 'you're beyond belief. I remember meeting you years ago when you visited Dublin. You were Minister for Home Affairs or something, and we had dinner together. You were maybe two seats away from myself. I made up my mind then that you were an arrogant bastard, and it wouldn't be honest of me if I said that today's conversation has changed that opinion in any respect.'

'Who the hell do you think you are, coming here with your little memories? Don't you –'

This time Declan's voice got the upper hand.

'Sir, I think you'll find that there are very real limits to what you can and cannot order me to do. If I decide to carry out further investigations in Ireland or Belgium or Mexico, there's absolutely nothing you can do to countermand me. And I think you'll find it's not that easy to stop a legitimate Interpol investigation here in France itself. I don't know what your exact motives were in demanding I back off, but I'd advise you to think twice about them.'

The president let his gaze remain on Declan, and for a moment the Irishman imagined his argument had gone home. But after a protracted pause, Dutheillet spoke again. No arrogance in his tone now, nothing peremptory or caustic.

'Monsieur Carberry,' he said, and his voice was very calm, and his words carefully spaced. 'Tell me, how much do you know about the history of the organization for which you work?'

'As much as I need to, I suppose.'

'I don't imagine you know very much, then.'

Declan shrugged. 'It's not considered essential.'

'I'm sure. But you are, I'm sure, aware that Interpol had its headquarters in Vienna between 1928 and 1945. You will also be aware that the entire operation was taken over by the Nazis in 1938, after they invaded Austria, and that it was very quickly turned into a centre for various police and intelligence operations of the Reich. In 1941, Interpol moved its headquarters to Berlin, to a villa on Kleinen Wannsee, one that had belonged to a Jewish businessman. Did you know this?'

'I'd heard about it, yes.'

'Good.' Dutheillet lifted the file from the table and handed it to Declan. 'Read this,' he said. 'Or as much of it as seems necessary. I believe you read German fluently. I'm afraid I can't let you take it away with you. But take your time. I have to go now, but one of my security people will see you are all right. You can return the file to him when you are finished.'

'Excuse me, but I don't see the relevance of this history lesson to what we've been talking about.'

'You don't? Well, I assure you that by the time you've finished reading this file, you'll know exactly what it's about. The file contains part of an archive of Interpol-related materials that arrived in France during the war, thanks to the Vichy regime. Their existence has been a close secret until now. It can remain a close secret in the event of your close cooperation.'

'And if I don't cooperate?'

'Read the file first, and remember that there's plenty more in safe-keeping. When you have read it, reconsider your attitude towards cooperation. Believe me, Monsieur Carberry, what is in this file alone could destroy Interpol.'

'I don't possibly see how some old files dating back to the 1940s could have the slightest influence on Interpol today.'

'Read them. You'll see that they don't all date back that far. You don't imagine all contact with the Nazis ended when the war came to a close? Now, it's time I was on my way. I can't keep my visitors waiting.'

Dutheillet stood abruptly, bowed slightly in Declan's direction, and glided back towards the main building like a tall ship plying familiar waters.

Declan sat for a while, trying to ingest the conversation, unable to meet even halfway the preposterous allegations that had been handed out by Dutheillet. Finally, he put his hand to the file and opened it.

The first item was a letter signed by the Austrian Secretary-General of Interpol, Oskar Dressler. It was dated 28 August 1940, and was addressed to the new President of the organization. The new man's name was SS-Obergruppenführer Reinhard Heydrich, Heinrich Himmler's closest associate. A terse note attached to the letter in French noted that Heydrich was, at the same time as taking the presidency of Interpol, director of the Reich's Central Security Office, which included the Reich Security Police and its Intelligence Service, the Kripo, and the Gestapo. Another note pointed out that Heydrich had been responsible for calling the Wannsee Conference at which the Final Solution to the 'problem' of European Jewry had been decided on – 'in the office of the International Criminal Police Commission', as the invitation stated.

Declan shivered and turned to the next item. It was a copy of a thin magazine: *Internationale Kriminalpolizei: Einziges offizielles Publikationsorgan der Internationalen Kriminalpolizeilichen Kommission*, the official Interpol journal. The copy was dated 10 June 1943, and its front page sported a large photograph of Dr Ernst Kaltenbrunner, who had just succeeded Heydrich as president, following the latter's assassination by Czech patriots a year earlier. A yellowing note, again in French, listed Kaltenbrunner's war crimes, and recorded the date, October 1946, when he was hanged at Nuremberg.

It was after ten when Declan finished reading. Somewhere inside the palace, there was a sound of lifted voices, and clinking ice in glasses, and laughter, brittle as the ice. Out in the courtyard, all was silence. It was cold, but Declan had refused to retire indoors. Above him, a moon of fourteen days had started to cross the yard with a hard light. He closed the file and handed it to the man, who had been waiting patiently by his side all evening. He was still confused by the contents of the file. But one thing was sure: now he had read it, his life would never be safe again.

17

Mexico City
29 November

Antonia woke to find the room liquid with morning light. She hadn't undressed, her hair was a mess, and every limb in her body ached in its own way. To begin with, she hadn't been able to sleep at all. Scenes from the hospital buzzed through her head like angry wasps, and she turned and twisted as if she'd been stung a dozen times.

She'd given Leo her bed, and made up a place for herself on the sofa near the door. That way, she was able to listen to him, and to be on hand if he took a turn for the worse. Now, looking across the room, she could see that he was sleeping propped up and exhausted against the pillows.

She still had not decided what to do with him. At the hospital, he'd been out of intensive care and immediate danger, but she didn't know how long that might continue to be the case on the outside, without drugs or careful nursing. There were other hospitals, both public and private, but she knew it would be only a matter of hours before his pursuers were aware of his whereabouts again. The man whom she'd killed, the would-be assassin, had almost certainly not been acting on his own initiative.

That meant that whoever was behind this whole thing could have more assassins ready to take up where the other had left off. So a hospital or a clinic was really out of the question.

The alternative was for her to employ a doctor and a couple of nurses, round the clock if need be. She'd have to dip deeper than ever into her trust fund to do it, but any price was worth paying if it kept Leo alive.

The problem was finding a doctor whom she could trust, and who'd agree to go along with her scheme. She thought that if she could get him out of the country, back to Britain, he'd get free medical treatment and not have to worry about killers stalking the wards. But how the hell was she going to achieve that when he didn't even have a passport. Unless . . . She looked at the clock. Six-twenty. At eight o'clock or so, she could ring the British Embassy and try to fix up an appointment with someone senior. Maybe they could issue a duplicate passport just to help him get back home.

She ached her way off the sofa. What if she did manage to get him back to London? What would she do? Would she go with him? Could she stay there? Would he even want her there? She'd loved him for months now, but although he'd seemed to reciprocate her feelings, she couldn't escape the fact that he was a sick man whose thoughts and emotions were severely confused. He might find himself falling in love with the first nurse he woke to see bending over him. Or with her cat, Gomita, so-called because she loved eating rubber bands.

The thought of a nurse tending to Leo brought back to mind the Indian nurse who'd been badly injured the night before. Magdalena had treated Leo well, and she knew he'd grown very fond of her. She crept out of the

162

room and down to the kitchen to find some orange juice and the telephone.

Isabel was seated at the table, helping herself to a plateful of *huevos motuleños*. She looked up as Antonia came into the room.

'You've got egg on your chin,' said Antonia, pointing to the spot.

Isabel grabbed a tissue from the box and dabbed.

'Like some?' she asked. 'There's more in the pan.'

'No thanks. Not at this time of the morning.'

'You look rough.'

'I feel rough.'

'Want to tell me about it?'

Antonia sat down, and quite without warning she found herself in tears. As long as she'd been alone, she'd just got on with things; but the very hint of sympathy in Isabel's voice had set her off.

Isabel had been Antonia's flat-mate for two years. From Jalisco state originally, she'd studied law at the Autonomous University of Guadalajara before making her way to the big city, where she now worked for a leading law firm on Pino Suarez. Antonia called her Mexico's answer to Ally McBeal. She was pretty, energetic, viciously intelligent, and devoted to women's rights. She had everything going for her, but for one thing: she'd defended opponents of the current regime. That meant one thing – her career was going absolutely nowhere.

It took three cups of coffee and the entire box of Kleenex to get Antonia into a fit state for talking. She started with the intention of giving nothing away, and ended with a detailed description of the night's events.

'He's in terrible danger, and I can't even get him out of the country. So long as he's in Mexico, they'll hunt him down.'

'Have you no idea at all who they are, or why they want Leo dead?'

'No.'

'Want another coffee?'

Antonia shook her head. She wanted to look in on Leo to see if he was all right.

'Look, Antonia, I'd like to stay with you both and talk this through a bit more, but I have an important case to defend this morning in the Supreme Court. It's a murder trial, and I have to be there. But I expect an adjournment around ten o'clock. The minute I'm free, I'll go back to my office and see if I can find a way of getting your boyfriend back to England. I'm not so sure about your going with him, but leave that with me. Your real priority is keeping him alive.'

She reached for the pad they kept beside the telephone and scribbled a name and some digits on it.

'Ring this number after I've gone. He's a good doctor, and he's willing to work in borderline cases like this. He's prepared to take risks. Tell him I gave you his number. He'll fix up the rest.'

'I don't know how to thank you.'

'I'll think of a way. In the meantime, welcome to the world of the fugitive.'

'Do you think Leo will be safe here?'

Isabel shrugged. 'He should be. As long as his pursuers don't know he's with you. But I'd try to get him somewhere else by tomorrow. Don't worry, I know how. We'll talk about it this afternoon. For the moment, stay in the apartment, keep your gun with you at all times, and don't answer the telephone.'

'What if it's you?'

'I'll do a double ring three times. You pick up on the fourth.'

Pausing only at the kitchen mirror to fix her hair and lipstick, Isabel kissed Antonia goodbye and hurried out. Antonia sat with her thoughts a while, then picked up the phone.

'ABC Hospital. Can I help you?'

'Yes, could you put me through to intensive care, please.'

'Certainly. Your name, please?'

'Ramírez.'

There was music for about half a minute. It sounded like Prokofiev's *Romeo and Juliet* played by a *mariachi* band. Then a voice broke in.

'Hello, can I help you?'

'Is this intensive care?'

'Yes. Are you enquiring about a patient?'

'Yes. Well, she's also a member of staff. A nurse who worked just down the corridor from you, in intermediate care. Her name's Magdalena, an Indian. I'm sorry, I don't know her second name. She was injured in the hospital last night.'

'What did you say your name was?'

'Ramírez. Antonia Ramírez.'

'Just a moment, Miss Ramírez, I'll see what I can find out.'

The music returned. A minute passed, two minutes. Antonia waited, knowing something was out of place. Then the voice returned, stiff and formal, as befitted a lofty institution like the ABC.

'Miss Ramírez, I'm not sure if I can be of much help to you. The person you mention isn't a patient at the ABC. I understand that she didn't have insurance cover, so, naturally, she would have been transferred to a public hospital. I believe she was taken to either the Centro Médico or the Hospital General. I'd advise you to ring one of them.'

With that she hung up, leaving Antonia staring at the phone. She put the receiver down and fetched the phone book from the shelf.

'Centro Médico. Can I help you?'

This time it took half an hour to get through to the right person at intensive care.

'What did you say her name was?'

'Magdalena. That's what she called herself. I don't know her second name. She was an Indian. It's possible she had an Indian name.'

'But you're not sure?'

'No, I didn't know her well.'

'I see. And you say she was transferred here from the ABC last night. About what time would that have been?'

'I'd guess, about one o'clock. I really can't be more exact than that.'

'OK, let's see. I have no one by that name ... Oh, just a moment. Yes, I see what's happened. Miss, your friend wasn't admitted here. She was pronounced dead on arrival. Her body will have been sent to the central morgue by now. It would be a help if you could go there to make a positive identification. I'm very sorry.'

18

'All you had to do was say "Yes, sir, no, sir, and two bags bloody full".'

Greg Dyson QPM was nearing the end of his five-year term of office as Interpol's day-to-day boss. Once he finished here, he planned to take early retirement, stash his pension away in an offshore trust, and park himself and his digital TV set somewhere on the Costa del Sol.

'You know as well as I do, sir, that, if heads of state or tinpot officials think they can push Interpol around, we're all in real trouble. This is nothing short of blackmail. I could quite easily arrest Dutheillet for perversion of the course of justice.'

'You'll do nothing of the sort, you moron.'

Dyson's manner was exactly what, with hindsight, he might not have wished it to be, the patronizing hectoring of an English officer faced with an Irish rebel.

'I'm merely pointing out . . .' Declan refused to rise to Dyson's bait, but he still felt he had a duty to press his case.

167

'It's not for you to point out. If Alain Dutheillet wants to shut down this investigation or have it taken over entirely by his own police, I won't lift a finger to stop him. This is his country, and he can do as he likes here. Do you have any idea what Interpol owes the French? They set us up with new headquarters after the war, they allowed us to relocate to Lyon when Paris got too small, and they continue to supply us with the bulk of our staff here. We'd find it very hard to work without their support.'

'Sir, so far all the indications are that this is not a French crime, except that it took place on French territory.'

'Which gives the French first call in deciding how the case should be conducted.'

'You aren't at all worried about this incriminating material Dutheillet is threatening to expose?'

Dyson leaned forward across his desk. He liked his desk, its wood and leather, its polish, its heaviness. More than the crest in the centre of his carpet, the desk spoke for what he felt himself to be. He entertained thoughts of buying it and taking it with him into retirement. It was only a few years old, and he hadn't written a single word on it.

'Look, I don't give a damn whether Dutheillet could bring down the United Nations. With an organization this size, scandals are hard to avoid. I learned long ago not to worry about what stories X or Y could tell if they chose to go public. It's far more important to know that they won't go public if we meet their demands. That way nobody gets hurt.'

'Sir, this man is asking us to step back from a major murder investigation that could involve terrorism and possibly drugs. If he goes on to order his own people to sweep the evidence we have so far under the carpet, he'll be guilty of a major obstruction of justice.'

168

There was a good chance that, when Greg Dyson finally lowered the ensign, there'd be a knighthood. There was also the possibility of membership in the French Légion d'honneur. Distinctions like that could help a man find directorships with the sort of companies that pay handsome salaries.

'You'll have to let me be the judge of that, I'm afraid. As from today, you're being transferred to the European Liaison Bureau. I'll submit an official report to the Executive Committee, and I'd be grateful if you would present one to Division II. Let me see a draft before you hand it in. Now, I think that's all. I have some important work to do, so I'd be grateful if you'd excuse me.'

Declan got to his feet. Faced with Dyson's lack of integrity, he felt like marching off to the first newspaper office he could find, and spilling whatever beans he had. But where was the point in that? Innocent people could get hurt as easily as bastards, but only bastards knew how to walk away.

'Dyson,' he said, 'I've been a policeman almost as long as you have, and I've come face to face with some of the biggest shits in creation. But until today I never knew what a real shit looked like or smelled like. Now I know.'

The door closed with a bang, and Greg Dyson sat behind his desk, hands curled into tight balls, neck knotted in frustration. Minutes passed while he absorbed the Irishman's insult and neutralized it. He fingered his MCC tie with his left hand. It gave him none of the reassurance to which he felt entitled. He pushed the button on his intercom.

'Penelope, would you please get Alain Dutheillet for me? Use his private number: you'll find it at the back of my diary.'

*   *   *

Declan sat in his office shoving little white tablets into his mouth. Strangely enough, Dr Papadiantis's prescriptions seemed to be making inroads into his headaches. And if he'd ever needed relief from one, it was now. His head felt like a little chamber in which the French President and the Secretary-General of Interpol had taken up residence for no other purpose than to shout at him. It was like a puppet show, except that they were bashing him, not one another.

He remembered the days after Máiread's death, when the world had stopped and he'd been trapped in the great stillness of it. There'd been days then when the events of a morning had been forgotten by afternoon, and the happenings of an evening had gone from memory by night. All that had kept him going then had been the investigation he'd conducted into her murder, an investigation that had soon turned into a hostage rescue situation. There'd been more deaths after that, but Declan had remained fixed on one thing: to find Máiread's killer and bring him to justice. It had seen him through until the world started moving again, however slowly. After Máiread, it never picked up the speed it had had before.

He picked up the telephone and dialled an outside number. It rang several times before anyone answered.

'Dillon.'

Con Dillon was Ireland's Chief of Police, a former colleague of Declan's, and the man who'd put his name forward for Interpol.

'Con, this is Declan. Can you hear me?'

'Jesus, Declan, I thought you were the Pope's sister. She usually rings me about this time.'

'You're not serious.'

'I am too. Her name's Sister Immaculata. She's in a convent in Naples. Sisters of the Good Shepherd.'

'And you know her?'

'She was in Ireland for several years. This is before the brother was so much as a cardinal. As you know, they work with young offenders and suchlike. She roped me into various things. What can I do for you, Declan?'

'Did you not think I could be ringing just to find out how you are?'

'Yes, and I could be the Pope's sister myself, and a Sister of the Good Shepherd into the bargain.'

'You have to be a virgin, Con. But seeing you're that well connected, maybe you'll ask the Holy Father to put in a word for us where it counts. Now, I have a favour to ask you.'

'Didn't I tell you? Eating snails hasn't changed you at all, Declan. What is it this time?'

'Con, do you think you could give me back my old job?'

Silence, the perfect unhissing silence of the modern digital telephone. Declan wondered if the line was bugged, then decided it didn't matter.

'Would you mind repeating that, Declan?'

'I want my old job back. I'm serious, Con.'

'I see. Well, which old job do you mean? You've had more than one of them.'

'The one I had before I left. Or another one if that's still taken. I want to be the official Garda representative investigating the murder of an Irish citizen, one Liam O'Neill.'

'O'Neill? Is he the one . . . ?'

'Exactly. Look, Con, I've no time to go into all of that. The fact is, I'm in a hell of a difficult situation here. Somebody very high up is trying to shut me down. I shouldn't be at all surprised but that you'll hear about it in a day or two. In the meantime, I've got eight assorted murder victims in the Paris morgue, no suspects, and more flaming headaches than the Pope and his sister put together.'

'So – let me get this right, Declan – what you're after is some sort of carte blanche that'll let you go poking your dirty nose into other people's business. Which, if I know you, means a knock on the door from men in Gestapo overcoats at three in the morning.'

'Well, Con, I mean to please. Will you at least think about it?'

'And why wouldn't I? Give me an hour or two, I'll see what's to be done, so. Do you have a number there I can reach you on? One that isn't bugged.'

A flock of late swallows stuttered and fell, doubling and tripling through the red-glass air of sunset. Declan drove south, away from the city, while the sun vanished in the west towards the Massif Central. It was a short drive of about twenty-five kilometres from Lyon to Vienne, where Declan had a little apartment. Nowadays, wherever he drove, all that waited for him at the end was the dreadful loneliness he'd felt since leaving Dublin. Today it would be worse than ever.

His carphone chirruped. He pressed a button and a speaker sprang into life on the dashboard. A familiar voice interrupted his meditations.

'Allô, Monsieur Carbrie, c'est Alice à l'appareil.'

Alice Bouchardon was a young research assistant from the Analytical Criminal Intelligence Unit. He'd put her in charge of chasing up what few leads they had, in the hope that something might come up for him to get his teeth into. She'd combed laboriously through the files in Automated Search and Archives, made a nuisance of herself with Technical Support, pestered the French National Central Bureau – and all this for a mere 110,000 francs per year and the expectation of a miserly pension. The net result of her labours so far had been zero.

'I have something for you,' she said.

'It's not my birthday.'

'It will be when you hear what I've got.'

'OK, I'm listening.'

'You'll remember that the pathologist found small tattoos behind the earlobes of all the victims. I sent blown-up copies out to several places, and all the replies I've had have been negative. Until this afternoon. One of my correspondents was Professeur Aristide Galouzeau, a classicist at the École Normale Supérieure in the rue d'Ulm. He's been off sick for several weeks, but I heard today he'd got back about a week ago, so I rang him and told him about my query. He rang me back just now. Says he doesn't have a clue what they say, but he knows what they are.'

'Isn't he the clever one? What are they, then?'

'You shouldn't mock. He's been very helpful. He says they're Mayan hieroglyphs. He's certain of that, even though it's not his own field. Apparently he takes a great interest in the decipherment of ancient scripts. For a long time, Mayan was the toughest to crack.'

'All right, we'll take his word for it for the moment. Where do these hieroglyphics come from?'

'Central America. Mexico, Belize, Guatemala, Honduras, El Salvador.'

'That narrows it down a bit, doesn't it?'

'The professor says he'll fax more information over, but he points out that it's mainly stuff from encyclopaedias. He thinks you should speak to an expert. Apparently, there's only one person in Europe who may be able to read our glyphs.'

'And who would that be? Professeur Galouzeau's aunt?'

'I don't think so. It's a man by the name of Mallory, Leo Mallory. Another professor. He teaches at Cambridge University, but Galouzeau says he's in Mexico at the moment. In the jungle somewhere. Halfway inside a pyramid.'

'Indiana Jones?'

'More Tintin, I'd guess.'

'Get me Mallory's mobile number. Jungle or no jungle, we'll root the bugger out.'

'I'll get on to it, sir.'

'And . . . Miss Bouchardon, what are you doing for dinner this evening?'

'Dinner, sir? I . . . I didn't really have any plans as such. Why, sir?'

'I feel like celebrating our first lead. And I need someone to talk to. God knows, you'd probably rather be out at a disco or something, but . . .'

'I hate discos. And I have a thing about older men. I really do.'

'What about geriatrics? Do you think you could spend the evening with a geriatric?'

'You pass. Let me go home and change. Pick me up at my flat at eight. Is that OK?'

'It's terrific. Now see if you can get Jungle Jim on the line.'

19

Mariachi Arriba Jalisco were singing *Esclavo y amo*, a dirge-like love-song punctuated with trumpets. The singer sang of love in a strained voice, striving for effect more than feeling. Someone strummed a guitar. Antonia reached across for the radio and twisted the knob so hard to the left that it snapped off between her fingers. She had never developed much of a liking for *ranchera* music, its over-wrought guitars and trumpets, its handclaps, its ay-yay-yay-yay-yays and bom-bom-bom, bom-bom-bom-boms.

It didn't help that she'd been brought up to it, that it was, in a sense, her heritage. All through her childhood, she'd attended performances by wandering troupes of *mariachi* minstrels, on the Day of the Three Kings, at *novilladas*, on birthdays, weddings, and baptisms. And still she didn't like their music or their big, Pancho Villa hats or their brightly-coloured uniforms. What had happened the night before hadn't increased her love for the sound.

The thought of what had been done to the little thief filled her with compassion and rage. Whoever her mother's friend Rafael was, he needed to be taken down several pegs. And yet she blushed to think how easily she herself had been affected by the man.

She sat unmoving at the table, letting the silence unburden her. The only tears she had shed were tears of anger, not grief, and she wondered if that was right. She had felt guilt beneath the anger, and she knew she could have told someone who she was and who her father was, and so guaranteed payment for Magdalena to be treated. But at what real cost, and to whom? Would she have swapped Leo for Magdalena so gratuitously, even out of love and a certain fineness of conscience?

There was a sudden crash, and as she got to her feet, she heard his voice call her name. Hurrying to the bedroom, she found him on the floor beside the bed, tangled in sheets. He'd tried getting up under his own steam, and fallen, and was unable to get up again.

'Have you hurt yourself?' she asked anxiously, bending down, wondering how on earth she was going to pick him up. Then she saw that that might only be part of her problems. He'd just finished vomiting, his right leg was bleeding, and when she drew the sheet back to see if he was injured, she saw that a pool of urine had formed around his middle.

'Leo, are you hurt?' she asked again, knowing she should remove the flimsy hospital nightgown to check, but embarrassed to do so.

He shook his head tentatively.

'I don't think so,' he said, 'but it's hard to be sure. I'm . . . sorry about your carpet. I just . . . I was more or less on my feet, then I started to feel giddy. That's what made me throw up. The next thing I knew, my legs were giving way. And then I peed myself. What a fucking mess.'

'Don't worry. The carpet's a piece of junk anyway. We'll go down to the mall at Perisur to buy a new one once you're on your feet.'

She knew she would have to ring for a nurse and doctor soon – he couldn't be left to cope with just her in charge. But she couldn't leave him lying here either.

One way or another, it was up to her to get him back on to the bed.

'Leo, do you have any strength in your legs at all?'

He shook his head.

'I have to get you on to the bed.'

'Have you got anything like kitchen steps?'

She nodded.

'If you can clean me up, I'll get on my hands and knees and then use the steps to climb back up.'

'Terrific. I'll be right back.'

In the kitchen she found paper towel, disinfectant, and a bucket. There were towels in the bathroom, and she hunted out a pair of Isabel's pyjamas, which were about the right size.

For the next fifteen minutes, she wiped and scrubbed and laid down towels, before helping him out of the soiled nightgown.

'I have my eyes tight shut,' she said, struggling to untie the tapes at the sides.

'Aren't you curious to feast your eyes on my god-like body?' he asked.

'Which god would that be?'

'Oh, I hadn't thought. Apollo, probably.'

'I was thinking more Cizin,' she replied, referring to 'Old Stinker', the Mayan god of earthquakes and death, usually shown as a dancing skeleton with a cigarette in one hand and a band of disembodied eyes dangling from his death collar.

'Cizin?'

'Cizin. Now, shut up and let me get on with this. Here, take these pyjamas and get them on while I clean up in the kitchen.'

All the time she was mopping up and changing him, she realized that she didn't mind. She'd been brought up to avoid manual work of any kind, unless connected with horses, and any task that involved mess or unpleasantness had been shunned as beneath her dignity. Yet here she was, wiping vomit away, and urine from the body of a man she barely knew, and she didn't mind at all. She smiled secretly to herself, thinking it was good not to mind.

When she returned, he was lying contorted on the floor, struggling to get the pyjama jacket on. She realized it must be two or three sizes too small for him. Without a word, she knelt down and helped him get his free arm into a sleeve, then drew the two edges of the jacket together across his chest.

It was only as she helped him painfully up the steps and into bed that she realized the pyjamas were pink, with fluffy white sheep all over them. The next moment, she noticed that he had an erection. Quickly, she pulled the sheets over him, then burst out laughing to cover her embarrassment.

'I'm sorry,' she said, 'these belong to Isabel. Her room's full of fluffy toys. I'll introduce you to them if you like.'

'I'd rather you introduced me to Isabel.'

'You wouldn't like her. She's a lawyer. Very tough.'

'She sounds just what I need.'

Antonia nodded. 'She said she'd help find a way of getting you back to England. I'm just worried that this business may be out of her depth.'

She helped Leo straighten against the pillows. The bed wasn't really designed to accommodate an invalid, but it would only have to serve until she could find him a secure medical unit, somewhere he could be treated and kept safe simultaneously.

But how safe could safe be? She didn't know who had tried to kill him, that first time in Komchen, and again last night. Unless . . . Her heart felt dead within her suddenly. She remembered her mother's words the day before, spoken in the heat of the bullfight: *If he pursues you, your father will see that he is killed*. Surely not. Not even her father in his portentous anger could have attempted murder for so little. He could be cruel, she knew that; but gentle too. He had always been gentle with her.

'What's wrong, Antonia?'

'Nothing . . . It's just . . . I'm worried about you.'

'You don't have to be. I'll be all right.'

'I wish it were that simple.'

'What do you mean?'

'Someone is trying to kill you, Leo. The sooner we can get you out of Mexico, the better. In the meantime, I have to arrange for some medical care.'

She dabbed his face with a towel she was holding in one hand, then went to the door.

'Antonia?'

'Yes?'

'Can I ask you something?'

'Of course. Fire away.'

'It's just . . . Why are you doing all this for me? I mean, I'm not your responsibility. And if someone's trying to kill me, you're placing yourself in terrible danger just by being around me.'

'I've been in danger before, I can –'

'Look after yourself? I don't doubt it. But we were lucky last night, and you know it. If it happens for a third time, we may both be killed. Are you willing to take that risk for a man you hardly know?'

She felt the light dim inside her. Could he have forgotten? Didn't he know that she took these risks because she loved him? And did this mean that he did not love her after all, that everything he'd said had been under the influence of his condition, or of the drugs he'd been taking?

'But of course I know you. I thought I . . .' She hesitated, feeling her face and neck turn bright red.

It all slipped out of her control. She dropped the things she was carrying, then felt herself crumple up against the doorpost, a little girl in tears, suddenly bereft of all that mattered to her in the world.

He watched her cry, saying nothing until the deep sobs had subsided and been replaced by shallow gulps.

'Antonia,' he said, 'I'm confused.' She didn't answer him, but he knew she could hear him. 'Look at me, Antonia, please.' She partly raised her head.

'I'm confused because my head is full of junk. I don't know what drugs they pumped into me at the hospital, and I can't even begin to guess what effect they've had. All I know is that I'm getting sharper since leaving the hospital.'

'Leo –'

'No, I want to go on. A lot of what happened in there is blurred. I've no memory of being brought there, and only a vague memory of waking up. I think you were there. Somehow, I think you were always there. You'd be sitting by my bed, watching me, and sometimes your eyes would be full of tears. Can that be true? Did I matter that much to you?'

'Leo . . .'

'Don't stop me now. I need to ask this, it's too important to leave. Sometimes you'd bend down and kiss me on the cheek and whisper things to me I could never really hear. You thought I was sleeping, but I knew. Or, at least, I thought I knew. Perhaps it was dreams, perhaps you were never there at all, or did not kiss me. I tried to speak to you, or to signal you, but the words wouldn't come, or I couldn't get my hands to function.

'But there's more, there's more than that. I think somewhere away from all of that, I think you told me you loved me, and I think I said I loved you in return. But all this could be my fantasy, it could be nothing more than memories of dreams. I can't disentangle them, you see. Any man would feel proud to have you visit him in hospital. Maybe my unconscious just got hold of it and allowed it to get out of hand.'

'I don't know why you're asking me all this, Leo.'

She approached him, standing by the side of the bed. She could feel herself tremble intolerably.

'Yes,' he said, 'you do. I want to know if any of this was real. I have to know it.'

'Then you know how I feel too. Why do you think I was crying just now? I need to know what you're thinking. Not when you were drugged in hospital, but now, this moment.'

'I don't know how to say what I feel now.'

But he looked at her, and their eyes met, and it came to him that not all his memories were false. He looked at her like that for a long time, losing words for the moment. She was so beautiful he wished there was no such thing as sleep, so he might have her always in his waking thoughts.

He said it beneath his breath first, *I love you*, and she could not hear him. She sat on the edge of the bed and took his hand in hers and whispered her love to him, and he reached out and held her for the first time, and said he loved her, meaning that there was no life for him outside her, nor for her outside him, and that all that would happen would be the consequence of their love.

They remained in that first embrace minute after minute, defying the world and its betrayals. She removed her dress, and he ran his hands over her body, rousing her. It was the first time a man had touched her like that, truly touched her, like a flame, and she felt herself burn. When she was naked at last, she crept into the bed beside him and helped him remove the absurd pyjamas she'd foisted on him half an hour earlier. He was still too weak to straddle her, but with his help she learned to kneel above him, and he entered her like that, his skin and fingers remembering what he had thought forgotten for ever, and thrust and thrust while his hands moved on her body, never still, and he heard her cry out, moving her hips as she did so, making him come almost at the same moment, and he arched his back and kissed her and told her that he loved her more than the world, and she smiled, putting her dark hair-haloed head upon his chest, and whispered all her love for him to his fast-beating heart.

They lay like that for perhaps an hour, and all the world seemed to have grown still around them. Sometimes there would come sounds from the street, the catch of engines starting, or a voice raised suddenly in anger. Lace curtains hung in the window, and as the morning grew brighter, a pattern of light and shade crept across Antonia's body, as though her skin were being hennaed by unseen fingers.

She rolled over on to her side, and as she did so shrieked. He came bolt upright, but could see nothing. Then she started to rock with laughter.

'What is it, love?' he asked.

'Can't you see?' She pointed gingerly at the floor just past the other side of the bed, and suddenly he caught sight of it, a dark-furred animal with a bushy tail and a small head out of which peered two sad, frightened eyes.

'What the hell is it?' he asked.

'It's Isabel's tayra,' Antonia answered. 'She calls him Pepe after some flamenco singer or other. He's forever getting out of his cage.'

She rolled out of bed and made for the tayra. The little animal seemed on the point of running, but it must have known her smell, for in the end it stood still and let her pick it up. She cradled it in her arms, whispering soothingly to it, and it curled up almost at once across her warm breasts and made a contented noise.

She was heading for the bedroom door when there was a crash as though a truck had overturned outside the window. But the noise was the apartment door being battered down, and the thudding and beating that followed were the footsteps and truncheons of a police squad smashing its way through the flat.

The bedroom door flew open and a pack of policemen in riot gear came hurtling into the room until it seemed too small to hold them all. Their leader made straight for Antonia, who backed away, still holding the tayra in her arms, while it kicked and struggled in an effort to escape.

'What the hell do you think you're doing, crashing in here like this?' she demanded. 'Do you know who I am? I could have you crucified for this.'

'I don't think so,' the leader replied. 'Are you Antonia Rocha y Ramírez?'

'Of course I am. Now, if you'd mind telling me –'

Before she could say another word, the man grabbed the struggling animal and, with a backward flick of his wrist, swung it against the nearest wall, smashing its skull and sending parts of its brain in every direction.

'You're coming with me, miss. Better take a last look at your friend. You'll never see him again. Believe me, that's not an empty promise.'

When Antonia looked, she saw Leo pinned on both sides by burly policemen. A third was pointing a pistol at the back of his head. She cried out in horror, but the leader of the squad already had his arm round her neck and was dragging her naked from the room.

20

El Turuño
The Ganadería of Don Ortiz Rocha y Ramírez
30 November

The vaquero sat his horse in silence, waiting for the smudge on the horizon to grow into the shape of another man astride a horse. In the sky above his head, thick clouds were forming into a thunderhead. Daylight still cut through from somewhere beyond the clouds, a light that turned the dusty plain to shades of honey. The distant rider grew a fraction in height, and his figure shimmered in the warm light.

The vaquero's name was Ruiz Arjona. Perhaps he would not have liked to be called a mere vaquero. He had been *mayoral* of El Turuño for twenty years now and intended to go on for at least another twenty. During Don Ortiz's absence, he ruled the ranch and was master of the bulls, if any man could be said to master them. That morning he'd selected an *encierro* of seven bulls for the *corrida* to mark the festival of Our Lady of Guadalupe in Hermosillo. That had been a long-standing arrangement, one that would be repeated in other towns before the Christmas season was over.

But yesterday the *patrón*, Don Ortiz himself had arrived and ridden up to the high pastures where his Vistahérmosa bulls were grazing. There was to be a small fair at Nuestra Señora de Guadalupe in a week's time, and he'd come out to select the best animals. Ruiz understood that the cocky young contender Abelardo O'Donojú had challenged Morenito Ordoñez to a *mano a mano*, a fight in which each would kill three bulls, one after the other. He grinned, anticipating the newcomer's overthrow. Or better still, a *cornada* right through his upstart belly.

He looked back over his shoulder. The afternoon sun had just caught the white flank of the huge building that made up the bulk of the bull-ranch. It always gave him joy to see it, like a small fortress guarding these vast expanses, a redoubt in the wilderness. It had been home to him most of his life, first under Don Agustin, afterwards under Don Ortiz. It had been whitewashed every year so that it sparkled like a shell washed up on a beach somewhere just out of sight of the sea. Wherever he rode, it would be waiting for him on his return, a permanency on the floor of the *bolsón*, leaping to his view even over long distances.

When he looked round, the dark figure had grown magically. He knew it was Don Ortiz; nobody else rode like that.

The horseman reached him at last, dust-sheeted, white-faced, sitting proudly on the Arabian he'd imported last month from Texas. The horse was called Armillita after the matador, and if it hadn't been covered in dust it would have been ebony from head to foot. Don Ortiz loved that horse, and said it was the best horse he'd ever ridden, maybe the best he'd ever ride. Ruiz was no judge of horses, but even he could see the dignity and rhythm of his master and the horse he rode. In a matter of weeks Don Ortiz and Armillita had learned how to suit one another.

186

Don Ortiz rode up close and lifted his hat to greet his *mayoral*. Had it not been for his seat on the horse and the silver that glinted here and there on his saddle, a stranger might have been forgiven for thinking he was just another vaquero, and a very grimy one at that.

Ruiz reached into his pocket and brought out a strip of cornhusk and a spoonful of *punche*, the rough, stringy tobacco he'd been brought up on. He rolled a cigarette and lit it with an ancient *esclarajo* of flint and steel and scraps of fluff.

'How many times do I have to tell you to get yourself a proper lighter, Ruiz? They sell cheap ones in town. A few pesetas is all.'

The Don would never have bought a lighter for his old friend; to have done so would have insulted him. So Ruiz went on using the contraption he'd inherited from his father and which he would, in all likelihood, pass on to his son.

'I'll take a look next time I'm there, Don Ortiz.' It was what he always said. In any case, he only went into town once a year for the *feria*. 'How were the bulls, señor?'

'They're in good condition. I've had the six best marked out for next week's *fiesta brava*. I don't want any shame, either for us or for the two matadors. Bring them in on Monday. I want them fresh for the ring. Did that fool Casasola make an arrangement yet?'

'Well, he did and he didn't, sir. He says he has the trucks ready to take six bulls and a substitute. It's just a question of the price.'

'How much does he want this time?'

Ruiz shrugged and sucked hard on his cigarette. As though by common agreement, the two men started riding back towards the *ganadería*.

'Says he wants fifteen million pesos.' Ruiz had not yet

learned to figure in the new currency, so all his sums had to be divided by one thousand. Don Ortiz made a quick calculation.

'*¡Hijo de la chingada!* He gets five million. He's not the only trucker in the region.'

'He says you can't treat him like this any longer. He says he's not a *peón*, and you have to pay him a fair price.'

'Go back over there tonight, Ruiz. Explain Señor Casasola's situation to him politely. Take Manuel and Pepe with you. Explain to him who I am. That I demand respect. Remind him I have crushed bigger men than him. And remind him that he should take better care of his daughter. A beautiful girl like that could come to harm. Tell him this with respect. From a neighbour to a neighbour.'

They rode on, making scarcely a sound. Behind them, the sky darkened, and the ghosts of stars appeared on the horizon. Ahead, the windows of the *ganadería* filled one by one with light.

'What about my own daughter, Ruiz? Is there any news?'

'Yes, sir. She and her mother arrived a few hours ago at the hacienda. Enrique rang to say they'd got there safely. He wants to know if you'd like them brought over here.'

Don Ortiz nodded without emotion. 'Tell them to start now. Say I will speak with my wife in the morning.' He considered asking Ruiz to ensure that Antonia's door was locked overnight, fearing she might bolt, but he thought twice about it, knowing his wife would keep a close eye on her.

The two men rode down side by side, passing through a little gully, then exiting to face the *ganadería* once more. The last light had been lit. Down below, a bull bellowed, as though beckoning the night. And a cow, lonely in its pasture, answered through the growing dark.

'Luis brought some letters over. I glanced through them. Nothing urgent, just some youngsters wanting to take part in the next *tienta*. There's one from Diodoro de Quiros, asking if he can have the Miuras bulls for San Luis de Potosí on January first.'

Don Ortiz snorted. 'Only if he pays me what everybody else pays me. How many more favours does the bastard want?'

'And one from the manager of the flamenco singers. He says one of the guitarists has hurt his wrist and can't play. But he says he's found a last-minute replacement, and wants to know if he's acceptable to you.'

'Tell him to go to hell.'

'Perhaps if I mentioned the name of the replacement . . . ?'

The name was that of one of Spain's most eminent musicians, a man who normally played to concerts of thousands, but who would for seven nights be performing to audiences of twenty or thirty at the most, in a series of recitals of *cante jondo*, the 'profound' singing that lies at the heart of flamenco. There would be just two singers, two guitarists, and a single male dancer. Don Ortiz lived for *cante jondo*, and every year at the Feast of Our Lady of Guadalupe he would bring to his *ganadería* a small group of Spanish gipsy musicians and stay up late with a band of select friends listening to songs and recitals and, sometimes, the fullness of all silences.

As they neared the gate of the *ganadería*, Don Ortiz turned in the saddle and looked up at the high ridge that overlooked the ranch buildings, and he saw three horsemen cut against the sky, not moving but standing facing down into the *bolsón*, and he called quietly to

Ruiz, to draw his attention to the riders, not knowing who they might be. But when they turned their heads together, there was no one there, just the horizon of the ridge, where it cut into the paling sky.

21

The prison resembled a bullring, and when they first arrived there, inmates called it La Plaza; in time, however, they learned other names for it. If they survived that long. It was a circular concrete building around a central courtyard of beaten earth. Sometimes it rained, and the earth became mud, and those who could stayed in their cells.

Those were the worst times. The *cárcel* held ten times as many prisoners as it had been built to take. Being forced to spend days in your cell alongside the other inhabitants resulted in violence, often disfiguring, sometimes disabling, and, not infrequently, fatal. Some inmates preferred to stay outside in the courtyard during the downpours, but that was short-sighted. A week or two later, they'd die as a result of their soaking, or develop a weakening cough that left them exposed to the attacks of their fellow-inmates or the warders.

The gaol had originally been built to accommodate the hardest criminals from in and around Mexico City. It was to be a model prison, a sort of panopticon in which inmates could have a degree of freedom while being kept under strict surveillance. Time and circumstance had changed all that. The cells that had once sparkled with new fittings became cracked and dirty and finally squalid. Cockroaches and spiders and lice made their way in through the cracks and never left again. The prisoners multiplied, the bunks were torn out and never replaced. Soon it became a place to dread, so the Ministerio Público began to send a different type of prisoner there: journalists, university teachers, union organizers, Indians – all manner of undesirables were taken there, and very soon it became an important torture centre. People were broken inside its walls, taken past their limits and, if they were lucky, thrown back on to the streets. Others died, in the elusive way that torture victims die, and their bodies were handed back to their families in sealed coffins.

When they first dumped him in his cell, Leo knew he was going to die in the Reclusorio. He hadn't eaten for forty-eight hours now, and he didn't see how he was ever going to eat. They served the food at long tables down in the *periquera*, the circular yard where everything significant in the prison happened. But he'd been put upstairs on level three, as far from the food as he could get. His legs still refused to carry him more than a foot or two before collapsing, and crawling wore him out faster than he could have believed possible.

He'd asked some of the men who shared his cell for help, but they had ignored him, swearing and looking away. In here, you helped yourself: it was the basic rule. He tried to explain that he'd just got out of hospital, that his legs needed exercise, and that he had to have food, that without it he would die; but three of them crossed the room to where he was lying and kicked him until he was almost senseless again. They called

192

him a *gabacho*, and a *bollilo*, and a *pendejo*, and they shouted other things besides, none of which he could understand, for he had never been taught to speak the sort of Spanish they spoke. There were three of them who kicked him, but the others watched dully, and no one raised a hand to interfere. There were twenty-five men in a room designed to hold six. He looked down at his aching, beaten body and knew he was going to die.

During the next day, he remained alone in the cell while the other inmates went down to the *periquera*, where they sat and walked and made deals, or quarrelled or fought. Leo crawled to the window and looked down into the open ring. People were badly injured every day; some were sent to the *enfermería*, most were left to get on with it. You needed money to get admitted to the infirmary, just as you needed money to buy extra food or drugs or a blade to protect yourself with. Leo had no money at all, and no way of getting his hands on any. Without it he would die as surely as though a *cuchillero* had entered the cell and slit his waiting throat from side to side.

He tried to crawl down the stairs, but halfway down the first flight he fell and hurt himself badly, cracking a rib and tearing the skin off one knee. No one volunteered to help him climb up again. When the warders found him on the landing that night after lights out, they beat him and left him there, locked into a no-man's-land from which there seemed to be no escape but death.

He fought against sleep for a while, fearing he might not wake up again. About midnight, the sounds started. Just beneath him, on the second floor, where the Judicial Police had their quarters, men started screaming. Loud voices angrily demanded answers to impossible questions, but were drowned out by the screams. Once, a gunshot rang out, and for a short time there was silence.

'You the gringo?'

His eyes, deprived of rest, would hardly open. He put up one hand to shield them, but the very act of doing so made him feel sick.

'I asked were you the gringo I heard about. Kid they brought in a couple days ago. You sure as hell don't look Mexican. What's your name, son?'

He managed to squint one eye open, and made out, kneeling next to him, a man dressed in jeans and a denim jacket. He had longish hair, and a lit cigarillo hung out of the corner of his mouth. Leo guessed he might be forty-five, fifty years old. It slowly dawned on him that he was speaking English with an American accent.

'Leo,' he said. 'My name's Leo Mallory.'

'Don't try to move, son. You look about done in. Where'd they kick you?'

Leo did his best to show him.

'What you in here for? Not that it matters to those fucks down there.'

Leo struggled to explain, but it proved too complicated, and he found himself struggling for breath.

'Easy, son, take it easy. We can talk later. How long you been in this dump?'

'T . . . two days, I think.'

'You eaten at all since you got in?'

'Nothing . . . to eat . . . Nothing . . . to drink.'

'Hell, they'd let you die of dehydration for the sake of some parking ticket or whatever it was landed you here. OK, wait here till I find you something to eat and drink. Then we'll see about getting you to the infirmary. But don't start getting your hopes up – that place ain't exactly fit for anybody really sick.'

His name was Spalding, Norman J. Spalding, and he came from Deming, New Mexico, where he'd grown up, and where his wife and children were still waiting for him. He had a farm about four miles outside the city, on which he grew milo sorghum for the animal feed trade. Most of his customers lived south of the border, in Chihuahua and Coahuila states.

In his spare time, when he had any, Norman liked to head up into the Black Range on the east side of the Gila National Park, where he'd spend the week-end camping and hunting with a bunch of friends. If his eye was good and there was luck in the air, he'd bag a deer. More often he'd shoot himself a couple of wild turkeys, a gallinule, or a rail, and if he'd knocked back too many beers the night before, he'd go home empty-handed.

Back in early September, he and his family had attended the Curry County Fair over in Clovis. He'd done some deals there, including one with a new wholesale feed outfit down in San Pedro. That weekend he did some hunting, bagging a brace of turkeys and catching sight of a brown bear in the distance. On the Monday, one of his drivers reported in sick, just as he should have been delivering a sample batch of sorghum, and Norman had decided to drive down himself.

It was the thousandth trip he'd made over the border, but on this occasion he'd made a careless mistake. After the fair, he'd gone hunting, taking with him the truck he was now driving. A police patrol pulled him over outside Ciudad Camargo, attracted by his US plates and the possibility of a substantial *mordida* on account of a failed rear light. But when they inspected the truck cabin, they found Norman's Ruger Ranch Rifle and a box of .223 Remington ammunition.

He had his licence, he had the phone number of the sheriff who'd issued it, he had the names of a hundred business contacts through northern Mexico, but none of it carried any weight with the PJDF bullies who had him in their charge. The Mexicans had passed new gun laws a few years before, and they were clamping down on foreigners carrying weapons for which they didn't have Mexican permits.

Most Americans faced a few months in jail and a heavy fine before they could head back home with a heart full with anti-Hispanic sentiments and a firm resolve never to venture south of the Pecos again. The problem wasn't so much the quick trial or the stinging fine the judge invariably imposed as the months spent in prison until judgement could be passed. Some Americans forgot to watch their backs and got badly hurt, others dropped their guard in the latrine or blinked while crossing the *periquera* and got killed. To get out of the penitentiary, first you had to survive.

A lot depended on what prison a man got sent to: Reclusorio Portillo was considered the worst. Human rights organizations up north had cabinets bursting with photographs of the place, which they sent regularly to members of Congress. Firm letters would be exchanged, commissions of enquiry would be sent, and the occasional journalist would put in an appearance, but nothing was ever done to improve conditions.

Spalding watched while Leo ate the food he'd bought him, a thin *pozole* without meat.

'Whoa, that's enough, son,' he sang out, reaching to restrain Leo's hand. 'You'll only start throwing it up. A little at a time is plenty, hot or cold, it don't much matter.'

Leo did throw up the first two portions he took, but he kept on trying and the third stayed down. And the fourth. He started to feel a little bit human again.

'Later, I'll get you down to the infirmary. They won't do much for you, and I don't have enough money to encourage them on to better things. But you look as though you could do with a once-over and a sticking plaster or two. How'd you get the way you are?'

Leo told him as well as he could. When he finished, Norman looked worried.

'I get the feeling somebody's trying to kill you, son.'

Leo laughed and farted simultaneously. The *pozole* was slowly making its way into his system. Never had anything so disgusting seemed so delicious to him.

'Ain't no laughing matter.'

'I'm sorry. The whole thing's just got out of all proportion.'

'Sounds like it. Only one thing puzzles me. If the dude who set you up in the hospital is the same dude who had you attacked out in that jungle city of yours, I'd guess he'd be the same one who had you picked up by the Judicial Police. That makes sense, don't it?'

'Well, yes, of course it does.'

'Then why didn't he have you killed back there in your girlfriend's flat? Why have you sent to this place?'

'I've thought about that. Maybe it diverts attention away from him.'

'Or them. It could be them. Tell me about this girlfriend.'

'It's a bit complicated.'

197

'It's always complicated. Women are complicated creatures. Tell me all the same. And while you're at it, take some more *pozole*.'

Leo sipped the thin broth, and each time he rested he told his new friend what he could about Antonia and his feelings for her, and something of what the doctor had told him about her father.

'But I can't believe . . . This is the twentieth century, almost the twenty-first . . .'

'That was your first mistake. The twentieth century only happened in a few places, and Mexico wasn't one of them. If your sweetheart's pappy don't like you, son, he'll do all he can to get rid of you, and if he's rich enough and connected enough, he'll have you killed. No two ways about it.

'In here, if he means to kill you, he'll send in a *cuchillero*. That's a boy with a blade. You won't know who he is. He could be a kid lying against the wall like he's asleep in the sun, or he could be a warder with his blade hid inside his boot. He'll be waiting for the right moment, and when it comes he'll kill you deader than a snake. You're going to have to watch your back every moment. Either that or find some way of getting money in here and buying yourself protection.'

'I don't think I can manage that.'

Norman looked hard at him.

'That so? Then I reckon you've got no other choice. You're going to have to find a way out of here, and you're going to have to find it sooner rather than later.'

198

22

Declan surveyed the plate of cheeses he had selected from the enormous cheeseboard the waiter had wheeled in front of him a few minutes earlier. A sliver each of Époisses, Cantal, Fourme d'Ambert, Saint-Nectaire, and ripe Vacherin nestled in a circle on the large white plate under his nose. Their yellow and cream colouring was matched perfectly by their flavours that seemed to mix into one flavour. He could not decide where to start.

'Are you sure you won't have some?' he asked.

Alice Bouchardon smiled and shook her head.

'I haven't room, honestly. But I think you've made a very good choice. That Vacherin looks nice.'

'Then have a piece.' He cut his sliver in two and lifted one half across on to her side plate. She raised a hand to protest, then gave in and nodded.

'They seem to know you well in this place,' she said. 'Do you eat here a lot?'

'When I'm in Lyon, yes. Don't you like it?'

'Like it? I've only ever been here once before, when my rich Aunt Lisette came to visit. That was four years ago.'

She was thirty, attractive, and unmarried. Declan wondered why. Perhaps there had been a marriage and it had gone wrong, perhaps she'd found no one to match her high standards. He bent to the table and started to sample the cheeses, starting with the Époisses.

Their first evening together had been a success. They'd dined at a less up-market establishment, where he'd had *falette* and she'd ordered locally-prepared *andouillettes*. 'Yum, yum,' he'd said, eyeing her *andouillettes*, and she'd asked him what on earth that could mean, so he'd explained and she'd given him one of the little sausages to try. He'd done little of the talking that evening, and instead watched her while she ate and retailed stories about herself and her family, or told him about how she'd entered the police force.

Straight out of the lycée, she'd joined the Direction Centrale de la Police Judiciaire, one of the five directorates of the national police. After a few months on general duties, she'd been transferred to the sub-directorate for external liaisons, one of whose functions was to co-ordinate work with Interpol; since she spoke English well and Spanish fluently (courtesy of her mother), she'd been put to work setting up computer databases in those languages. Every time a vacancy came up in Lyon, she applied for it, and after five years a formal transfer was made. That had been five years ago.

He'd driven her home, and watched from the car as she skipped up the steps to her apartment block, turning to wave as she opened the door. Despite himself, he'd felt an adolescent pang of loss as the door closed, and despite himself a second time, he'd spent the days between that meeting and this thinking about her, and how she looked and moved and spoke.

Tonight, despite himself for a third time, he recognized

that she had manoeuvred herself past all his carefully-constructed defences, and wound herself, serpent-like, around his heart. He could scarcely breathe for love of her, he couldn't bear to look at her in case his heart would break.

'Why won't you look at me?' she asked.

'I'm sorry?' he said, lifting his head only a fraction.

'Don't think I haven't noticed. When we were in Le Bouchon aux Vins a few days ago, you couldn't take your eyes off me. This evening, you're all tense and hunched over. You aren't having one of your dreadful headaches, are you?'

'No, no, not at all. The little tablets are doing their work well.' He felt himself reddening, realizing he must have stared at her more than he'd intended. He was twenty years her senior, for God's sake. A widower whose unstirred lust had suddenly become visible in the anxious way he looked at women.

'I'm glad to hear that. But you aren't yourself this evening.'

He'd never have told her otherwise, but the embarrassment drove him to it. Keeping his eyes firmly fixed on the centre of the little table, he began to relate the details of his meeting with President Dutheillet, the threats he had made, and the climb-down by Secretary-General Dyson.

'I can't believe he did that,' Alice said angrily. *Merde*. The bastard goes on all the time about the integrity of the Commission. We're always being exhorted to work in the knowledge that Interpol's standards are above reproach. Now this. I'm disgusted.'

'He's frightened. Dutheillet could do a lot of damage. He could wreck important operations for months, if not years.'

He looked up at last and caught sight of her face. An angel with premonitions of a fall.

'The files Dutheillet showed you – were they that bad?'

He nodded. 'It's hard to be sure, but I think a lot of that material could be profoundly damaging. And he may have more. It isn't really a question of what's true and what isn't. If even some of that stuff gets into the hands of the tabloid press, Interpol's reputation could suffer irreparable harm.'

Alice looked at him, at the bags under his eyes, the lines on his forehead, the sadness that sat on his face like a thin veil. She wondered what on earth it was she saw in him; and then she looked into his eyes and wondered why it had taken her so long.

'Back in the early eighties,' she said, 'there was some trouble here over "Jewish files" that Interpol was supposed to have in its possession. That was when headquarters were out at St Cloud. Before my time.'

'What sort of files were they supposed to be?'

'They used to put a criminal's religion on his record sheets. That enabled the Gestapo to compile lists of Jews they wanted to round up. Some people think that files of names were still kept by the Commission as late as the eighties.'

'Do you think they were?'

'I didn't. But if what you say is true . . .'

'It *may* be true. Some of it certainly is. After the war years, it gets more conjectural. A lot of ex-Nazis and collaborators managed to bury themselves in organizations like Interpol. How much influence they had, or how long it continued is hard to guess. But it scarcely matters. The minute those files are leaked . . .'

'What are you going to do?'

'Do?'

'Are you going to let the case drop, just as they want you to?'

'I don't see what choice I have.'

'But you don't want to.'

He nodded slowly. 'What do you think? It's a multiple murder, it has connections to God knows what. I can't just let it go. But if Dutheillet doesn't wreck us first, that bastard Dyson will kick me out and close the whole thing down anyway.'

'How determined are you to get to the bottom of this case?'

'Totally determined. I've got eight bodies in the morgue. There's a possible terrorist link, maybe a neo-fascist connection. But I can't go over Dyson's head.'

'Then we find a way of blocking him. Or even better, blocking Dutheillet.'

He smiled. 'And just how on earth would you plan to go about that?'

'You're such a dreadful *ingénu*, Declan. Haven't you any idea how things work? I don't mean in Ireland, I mean in the world at large.'

Their hands were only inches apart, in the centre of the table. Alice let her fingertips graze the top of his.

'To be honest,' he said, 'I don't think it makes any difference. Dutheillet's way out of my league. He's a world player, he isn't going to sit around and wait for a little squirt like me to frighten him.'

Alice laughed and leaned forward to kiss him on the nose.

'You are so loveable,' she said. 'I wouldn't have you any other way. But you're too innocent for your own good. You're a high-ranking Interpol official, you have a password that gives you access to all the databases, all the files you'd ever want to look at. You've got me to manage them. Believe me, Declan, Dutheillet is well within your league. You can scare him witless and put an end to all this nonsense about Nazi files.'

'But he's the French President. I can't use Interpol information to bring him down. That really would spell the end for the Commission.'

'I'm not suggesting you bring him down. That would be counterproductive. All you have to do is make him see that publishing his files would be a fatal mistake for someone in his position.'

Declan thought hard. What Alice was proposing was illegal. But he could see that it might prove the only way to prevent a greater illegality.

'What about Dyson?' he said. 'You don't plan to dig up dirt on him as well, do you?'

'Only if it's really necessary. We can try getting some sort of statement out of Dutheillet, saying he'd like your investigation to continue. That ought to pacify Dyson.'

'Let's hope so.'

He fell silent and looked at her without the awkwardness he'd felt before. Her initiative and determination were quite astonishing. He wondered if she would agree to come with him to Mexico. After all, she spoke the language fluently, and she'd probably be a match for the most corrupt Mexican policeman.

'What would happen if I started digging about in your past, monsieur? Would I unearth any dark secrets?'

'I told you before, Alice, I'm Irish. We don't have dark secrets, we have holy wells and Guinness.'

'I'm sure you do.' She reached across and filched a slice of Cantal, which she slipped straight into her mouth.

'You're a hypocrite,' he said.

'Yes, but hypocrisy is only a hobby for the French. You Irish – *vous en faites tout un plat*!'

'A what?'

'Oh, you make a song and dance about it. You need to relax. Get it out of your Celtic systems. Why don't you tell me your deepest secrets?'

He grinned, and took some cheese, and slipped another piece within her mouth, and his fingers as he did so rested on her lower lip, and he thought that the darkest secret he had was what he felt for her.

'Well, there's nothing to tell, honestly. I was married to a good woman whom I didn't love. I had a daughter whom I loved like nothing else on earth. They're both dead. It's what happens.'

'Did you never have a lover?'

He looked at her, and for a moment everything teetered. He could have lied, he felt impelled to lie. But he could not have lived with the lie, or looked her in the face again.

'One,' he said, 'just one.'

So he began, late in life, to speak of himself with honesty. She listened, taking his hand gently in hers. By the time he came to an end, they were closing the restaurant.

'May I drive you home?' he asked.

'If it's not out of your way.'

He drove her home through dark streets, while memories played through his brain.

'What about yourself?' he asked. 'You've never been married?'

She laughed. 'Only in my dreams. But there have been boyfriends. And two long-term lovers.'

She told him a little about them. At first, she made

light of both love and its absence, and he did not press her or ask for details. But quickly the accent shifted, and she was talking, not of love or men who had failed her, but of disappointment and loneliness and fear, without using any of those words.

'Would you like to come up?' she asked when they were sitting at the kerb in front of her apartment building. 'We never had coffee.'

'You make good coffee?'

'My father . . .' Her voice trailed away.

'Your father taught you how to make coffee?'

She nodded. 'He owns a coffee shop in the eighth arrondissement. Makes his own blends, grinds all the beans. He sends me a couple of packets every month. Want to try some?'

'This beats "Come up and see my etchings", doesn't it?'

'Etchings?' She looked bemused. 'Why should I have etchings?'

He laughed and squeezed her hand. There was a long pause. The windows of the car had misted up, shutting them inside the small shell.

'Declan,' she said, and her voice was very small and hesitant. 'I want to know where to go from here. I mean, this isn't like going out on a date with someone. You're my boss. I don't want to get things wrong. But I think something is happening between us, and I want to know whether I should just walk away from it or . . . I don't know.'

He didn't answer at once. Everything hinged on what he said, and he knew that he really didn't have the words. Instead, he fell back on the obvious.

'Alice, I'm . . . nearly twice your age.'

'That's not true. You're just twenty years older than me.'

206

'Well, twenty years, then. If I . . . If we . . . When I'd be sixty, you'd still only be forty.'

'Lucky you.'

'Lucky me, yes. But what about you? You'd be losing out on so much. I could drop dead of a heart attack and leave you stranded. I could get prostate cancer and die, and where'd you be then?'

'The same place I am now. Declan, I'll ask you a simple question. I just want a truthful answer, that's all. Just promise me that.'

'Of course.'

'Do you love me?'

It was like a blow in his stomach. She couldn't have been more direct.

'Alice . . .'

'Answer me, yes or no.'

'I . . .' He looked at her, barely visible but for the light of a street lamp that fell on her face from the side. 'I love you more than anything,' he said.

She said nothing, but she put her hand to his cheek and rubbed it. His skin was stubbly, but warm and masculine.

'If this was an American movie,' she said, 'I'd have to say, "I love you too".'

'Don't you?'

'Of course I do. But not in that silly movie way. I love you. I can't explain it yet; maybe I'll never be able to. But that's how it is. Do you want to come in?'

He bent forward and kissed her softly on the lips.

'Not tonight, Alice. It's too soon for me. But next time.'

'And when will that be?'

'Soon. Very soon, I promise. In the meantime, we both have work to do in the morning.'

'What about tomorrow night?'
'I like my coffee black.'
'I think I can manage that.'
She opened the door.
'*À demain*,' she said, and vanished into the darkness.

23

The *cuchillero* made his presence felt within minutes of Leo's being booted out of the infirmary. 'There no so much wrong with you,' the doctor said. He was a middle-aged man in a dirty white lab coat, wearing a two-day stubble and long dry hair that was turning yellow instead of white. There were puddles of blood on the floor. On a bench in one corner a drug addict lay shivering, poisoned by adulterated cocaine. Another man had died during the night. A smell of vomit hung over everything. It fought with cooking smells, and sweat, and urine.

'You crazy or something?' The bulky shape of Norman Spalding hung close in on the doctor. 'The kid's sick. Real sick.'

'He no look sick to me.'

'Listen, José, where the hell did you learn medicine? In some field? Because even I know when somebody looks ill. You keep this kid in here, or you'll have another stiff on your conscience.'

'You wasting you time. I no have a conscience. What fucking use a conscience in a place like this? Eh?'

The doctor – if he was a doctor – chuckled.

'I can get more money,' said Norman. 'How much to keep him in the *enfermería*?'

'More than you can pay.'

'Why's that?'

The doctor shrugged. 'Get the fuck out,' he said. 'Or I tell a guard to make you.'

Norman went on arguing, but it was water off a grubby duck's back. The duck had lived in this pond longer than anyone could remember: he wasn't going to start making concessions now, not when he had his own neck to watch out for. He'd just go on quacking till a park warden came along and cleared the pond of interlopers.

'I don't think you should go back to your own cell,' Norman said to Leo. 'For one thing, there are too many stairs to climb, and for another you don't know anyone in there. I'll pay the guard on my floor to have you transferred to my cell. There are a couple of good boys in there. They'll help me keep an eye on you.'

All the way to the cell, Leo could feel eyes boring into him. Norman helped steady him, but he made it look as far as possible as though Leo was walking independently. Weakness was one thing no one could afford to display in here.

They'd almost reached the cell when something caught Norman's attention.

'Bend down,' he whispered to Leo. 'Make it look like you're tying your shoelace.'

They bent down together.

'OK, just look to the right. See the kid with the red bandana round his head?'

Leo nodded.

'Don't look at him again. Avoid looking at him at all costs. He is your man, believe me.'

'How do you know?'

'He has a knife: I caught sight of it just now, while he was moving it from one pocket to another. And he was watching you. I don't mean the way these *peóns* look at you. I mean the way an assassin looks at his victim. Weighing you up, feeling like God, cutting you with his eyes.'

They straightened and walked on to the cell. Leo did not turn round, and did not see the *cuchillero* again.

For the rest of that day, Norman negotiated until he found a blade that Leo could use. It was an old switchblade with a missing spring and flecks of rust all over; but it had been sharpened well, and used with determination, it would kill a man as well as a brand-new knife.

'You've got to remember, this comes between you and being killed. Let it drop, and your opponent will finish you off. Hesitate about stabbing him to the heart, and he'll cut your throat from side to side.' Norman lectured Leo about survival all that late afternoon, while suspicious eyes watched them round the cell.

'I'm going to ask Ramón to teach you how to use this baby. He doesn't know who you are. He doesn't care.'

'He knows I need to be protected.'

'Because you're weak, son. That's all he knows. People like you come in here every day. They just don't all get fitted up with one of these babies, is all.'

Ramón was a kid from a *barrio* in the north of the city. This was not his first time in prison. Leo guessed his age to be around twelve. The Spanish he spoke was very difficult for Leo to understand, but he conveyed all he needed by simple demonstration.

'Hold you han' low, *cuarte*, no, no, no like that, he gonna get you here, in the side. Hold it like this, *sí*, *sí*, that's right, then move it quick like this. No, faster, you

211

mus' go faster. You gotta hit the heart, see, or the throat. Nothing else will kill him before he kill you. Now, stand back, see how near you get.'

By the time Ramón had finished, Leo's forearms were hatched with shallow gashes, almost as though a Moroccan bride had tattooed him with henna. Ramón had taught him all he could, but it was up to him what happened next.

The next day before breakfast, the guards cleared everyone out of the cells early. This they did from time to time, for no particular reason, as far as anyone could see. Leo shuffled out of his cell and down the stairs, discreetly supported by Norman. He was thinking about Antonia. She had not been much out of his thoughts since waking up here.

Now that he had made love to her, his thoughts were sharper and more desperate. He could smell and feel her if he but shut his eyes, her flesh was etched on his mind, warm and vivid as a *ganadero*'s brand. He wondered if her father had been responsible for his arrest, whether he was paying the *cuchillero* with the red bandana. In that case, what had happened to her? He asked himself whether she might not have been hustled off to a women's prison like his own. Would her father do that to her for the sake of honour, of *pundonor*? Or remove her tongue and imprison her at home for ever?

Once everyone had lined up in the yard, the guards did the count. They did it the same way they did it every morning, taking their time, reading each name out alphabetically. If they really wanted to hurt the prisoners for some reason, they could stretch it out to three hours, four if they put their minds to it. Everybody had to stand out in the *periquera*, and breakfast was not served until it was over. This morning, it took an average two hours.

And all this time the morning sun blazed down, turning the air to dust. The stench of pollution came up on a wind from the city.

Those two hours were like two years to Leo. His legs still had barely enough strength to hold him, and his back found the strain of remaining still in one position all but intolerable. If it hadn't been for Norman and his *cuates*, he'd have collapsed in the first ten minutes. Even so, he still had to use his legs, otherwise inertia would set in and he'd never be able to stand again.

When the roll-call was done, the trestles were set out, and breakfast, and someone began to slop *pozole* into shallow bowls. The prisoners broke ranks and fell on the waiting tables. There were seven tables in all: privileged persons were allowed to sit on hard benches at the top two. The others held the bowls and the *pozole* urns for everyone else. A couple of orderlies stood behind each one, ladling out the thin soup.

'Stay with us,' said Norman, 'and take it easy. Anyone tries to jostle you, anyone tries to steal your food, let us handle that.'

Leo was handed a bowl and spoon. They hardly looked as though they'd been cleaned since they were last used. The *pozole* tasted not just thin, but nasty. The lump of bread that came with it was stale, and had been made from the poorest quality wheat. Leo bit into it regardless, determined to regain his strength, however much it took.

He and Norman and three others worked their way in silence through the pressing crowd. Some inmates scowled darkly as they passed, most simply ignored them. Slowly, they made their way back to the wall, to make one direction less in which to look.

Leo looked skywards. At regular intervals around the

perimeter of the prison stocky watchtowers gave notice of the impossibility of escape. In each one he could make out the figures of guards, and he caught the glint of rifle barrels as they flickered in the sun.

He didn't see what happened next. Someone jostled his right elbow, and he looked down and round. A group of men, two blacks, an Indian, and a Hispanic boy wearing a black T-shirt with a faded Rolling Stones logo, had cut in on Leo's protectors. He saw the kid in the T-shirt lean close in and whisper in one of the men's ears, and the next moment the man broke away from the group and shuffled quickly away, wriggling back out into the *periquera*. When Leo looked again, the others had gone too. Only Norman was still there, looking grim and ready for a showdown. But there was no chance of that. Norman wasn't their target, he was just in their way.

Two men cut in between him and Leo, then started to jostle him fast. He raised his voice, arguing with them, cajoling, pleading, hectoring in quick succession. His companions had slipped back into the limbo from which they had materialized, Leo was already several feet away, stumbling in a hopeless effort to break away from the bodies pressing him in.

Norman kept on struggling to regain nearness to Leo, but all the time he was moved in the opposite direction, towards the centre of the ring. His soup spilled over his top and trousers until the bowl was empty. He caught sight of Leo being dragged back, then the kid in the red bandana, a little away from him. The kid wasn't doing anything, he was just watching and waiting, letting things unfold. He wasn't going anywhere, and he was frightened of no one.

Leo couldn't see Norman, or any of the others. There was no one round him whom he knew, and he realized

214

this hadn't been routine. Someone wanted him on his own. Looking behind him, he could see that he was being forced into one of the ground-floor toilets. A few light-bulbs struggled to provide illumination from behind wire baskets. But even with his eyes closed, he'd have known exactly where he was. A violent smell made up of stale faeces and pungent urine filled the whole room. There were no cubicles, just a series of holes in the ground, each one caked with layers of ordure that had accumulated over the years. Most of the urinals had been smashed and left desolate, and as a result the floor was covered in a permanent film of urine. All the flies in the world had gathered there to feed. They would rise up in a cloud in one place and settle in another. Leo felt giddy. The walls seemed to sway around him, and he felt about to collapse in a heap in the middle of it all.

Half a dozen men were squatting wearily over the latrines. No one fell asleep in here, or spent their time day-dreaming. As he entered, one of the men accompanying Leo snapped his fingers. The squatters looked up and guessed at once what was happening. They yanked their trousers up and ran outside, averting their eyes from Leo and his companions.

Moments later, his escorts went outside, leaving Leo alone with the flies in the stinking room. His stomach heaved, and he had to fight down the retching that threatened to rush up into his throat. The urine was making his eyes sting, and the slick floor tried to drag his legs apart. He knew he was about to be attacked, probably killed.

Against all his instincts, he moved away from the door, down into further shadow and an unbearable stench. There were more flies here than ever, deep, dark patches of them that lived their whole lives here. The door became a rectangle of light in which gilded figures moved to and fro like the marionettes in a shadow play. One of them would detach itself in a moment, he thought, one of them would be his killer.

On the outside, someone began to beat his feet rhythmically against the hard floor. The rhythm moved slowly and with grace, laying down a percussive pattern that was taken up in a while by two hands clapping. And then, at long last, a man's voice, out of the reaches of a very deep despair, a voice soaked with the darkest pain of humanity, stretching out the words of a *solea* until they seemed to fashion themselves into something more than mere words.

Con un puñal la maté . . .

It was a song Aguteras had made popular. But here it was more than a song.

Con un puñal la maté . . . With a dagger I killed her . . .

Leo hung back against the wall. Were his killer and the singer one and the same? he wondered. But no, that was unlikely. The singing and the proud stamping of men's feet on the prison floor would continue while he was being hunted and dispatched. He thought of Antonia, wishing there were some way he could apologize for all that had happened, and for all the trouble he had brought her into.

A shadow detached itself from the other shadows. Someone had entered the room. Leo was sweating. His back was covered by a slick film of sweat, his groin was uncomfortable with it. The *cuchillero* made no sound. He moved round the edge of the room, like a tiger that has just entered his cage and detects a rival prowling on his territory. He didn't sniff – who in his right mind would have dared even breathe in that place? – but he knew Leo was down there in the shadows waiting for him, so he just waited for his eyes to adjust to the half-light. He'd done this before, many times, he could afford to take it easy. He'd seen too many killings botched by haste. Haste and poor judgement. He prided himself on suffering from neither defect.

The flies buzzed angrily, rising and falling lazily in a world of their own. Rats scurried along the walls: huge rats, black-coated rats, sleek-bodied rats, bright-eyed rats. And outside the song continued, the singer's voice rising and falling in the long *cante jondo*. Hands clapped staccato, boots set the rhythm.

'*¿Quién te mandó?*' Leo asked. 'Who sent you?'

But the assassin said nothing. He had not been paid to speak, just to see to it that Leo did not leave the Reclusorio alive.

Leo shifted a few feet to the right, swivelling to keep his eyes on the boy. As he did so, he caught the glint of something sharp and bright in the killer's hand, the naked blade coming awake as if it had eyes and was stalking him. The boy could not have been more than nineteen. He carried himself well, he was graceful, sure and nimble on his feet, and he was already at the top of his profession. Not many lasted as long as he had lasted. He lifted the knife gently, lowered it, raised it again, executing an arc whose centre was a strip of sunlight that fell directly into the pit of the toilet. He did this, not from braggadocio, but simply because it gave him pleasure to see the knife move so smoothly between his supple fingers.

Leo started to move towards the door, not because he thought he could escape that way, but in the faint hope of getting his back to the light, thereby forcing the boy to come at him eyes blinded. But the boy had not stayed alive so long by letting himself be tricked so easily. He entered the doorway and stood in it, waiting for Leo

217

to approach him; in the sunlight behind, the arabesque rhythms of the dance continued unabated.

Leo left the knife in his trouser pocket. He knew it was there, he knew he could have it in his hands in seconds; but some instinct told him to keep it hidden until the last moment. Norman had started a rumour that Leo had no money for a blade. Perhaps the boy believed that. If so, it would make him careless.

'¿Quién te mandó, chico?' he called out, thinking to taunt the *cuchillero* into impatient action. 'Did they remember to wipe your bottom? From the stench in here, I think you wet your pants as well.'

The boy said nothing, but he moved in towards Leo now, as though impatient to get this over. He wasn't being paid to bicker, just to kill. He rolled once on the balls of his feet, then darted forward, lifting and dropping the knife in the momentum of his run. The blade slashed down across Leo's chest, leaving a six-inch gash. Leo staggered back, knocked breathless by the force of the blow, hitting the wall and slumping to his knees. Within seconds, his chest was covered with blood. The boy turned and charged again, and Leo made a vain effort to evade him, but the knife drove across his upper arm, opening a deep wound that filled with blood before bleeding fast on to the urine-soaked floor. While he tried to recover from this blow, the boy came back and hit him again, bending down and striking with the naked blade across his belly, knocking him sideways so that he fell clumsily on to the floor. The boy stood over him, enjoying the power that the knife bestowed on him, toying with him, taunting him.

Leo scrambled for purchase among the filth of the latrine, twisting to get away from the stinging blade. He was very clear-headed now. He sensed that his legs had little strength left with which to keep him upright. The wounds made him feel weak and nauseated, and he started to wish it was over, and that one more stroke of the assassin's knife would put him out of his misery.

Outside, the pace of the music quickened to a *bulería*. The clapping and the stamping speeded up. The *cuchillero* felt himself inspired with the dignity of his labour, like a matador who goes in to make a clean kill with a single stroke of the *estoque*. He smiled as Leo pushed himself up and turned to face him again. The next few cuts would be deeper, and the one after would be mortal. Leo looked at him grimly.

'Who sent you?' he asked.

For answer, the boy started to run. Leo steeled himself. It was all or nothing now.

He'd played enough rugby at school to know what he should have done before this. Just before the killer reached him, Leo threw himself at him in a flying tackle that tore the boy's legs right from under him. He heard the *cuchillero* hit the floor with a crack, saw the knife fly from his hand and go skidding across the liquid surface of the floor until it lay within inches of an open latrine.

Leo limped over and with a little kick sent the knife the rest of the way into the hole, where it bobbed momentarily on a bed of stools before vanishing entirely.

The boy was trying to right himself, but his shoulder had been badly hurt, possibly dislocated.

'*¡Carajo!*' he shouted.

Leo knelt down beside him. This close, he looked even younger and more vulnerable than ever. Back in England, back in some neat and tidy little town full of Women's Institutes and lollipop men outside every school, he'd have known what to do. But they didn't teach you in a Women's Institute or a grammar school or Cambridge

University what action to take when bleeding to death in a stinking, disease-riddled latrine. So he put England and green fields and civilized behaviour out of his mind, and did the only thing he could do if he was to stay alive. He took the knife from his trouser pocket, and he put the blade against the boy's smooth throat, and he pulled it with all the strength left in him until his hands were thick with blood. When it was done, and the boy still, Leo looked towards the entrance, bathed in the brightest of lights.

'Sing about this,' he whispered. 'Sing about this.'

He stood and walked unsteadily towards the light.

24

Ganadería El Turuño
2 December

The long line of vaqueros rode strung out against the wide horizon, their capes belling at times, turning their silhouettes into the outlines of some strange, otherworldly creatures. Below them, the night filled with the sound of cattle, fighting bulls being moved down from the high pastures to the paddocks behind the house. There would barely be enough room for them all, but they were fortunate in having sent so many mature bulls out to die in the festive season. The bulls they were bringing in from the pastures were of all ages and all dispositions, *mansos* who would curl up and die sooner than raise their horns in anger, and *toros bravos*, who would kill at the first opportunity. All were covered by a cloud of dust that they'd brought with them from the heights; but at the head of the drove the dust vanished as the bulls stepped on to meadowland.

Ruiz Arjona stood in his stirrups, watching the vaqueros count the bulls down and through the fences. A scattering of castrated animals, the *cabestros*, led the bulls into their new homes. These were the last of the herd now, bulls from the furthest pastures. All carried Don Ortiz's *hierro* on their right flanks. The cowboys shouted softly and whistled or clapped, the bulls bellowed; and in the distance, cows lowed in a paddock, aware of the coming of the bulls.

It all seemed orderly, and as calm as on hundreds of similar evenings in Ruiz's life; but beneath the surface something fearful was lurking. He turned to the horseman beside him. Luis Miguel Sanchez was Don Ortiz's *conocedor*, the one man on the ranch who knew all there was to know, not just about bulls in general, but about all the bulls who lived there.

'What do you think?' he asked.

'They're nervous,' said Luis Miguel. 'The killings have unsettled them.'

Over the past few days, someone – or it might have been several persons – had gone in among the bulls at pasture, slipping past the vaqueros on guard duty, and cut the throats of several animals. Others had been injured so badly they had to be put down. It was an unprecedented matter, something that sent a chill to the heart of anyone who heard of it, for no *ganadería* had ever been made the object of such attacks.

The local police had swept the area several times, but found no strangers, no one suspicious. There was talk of bad blood between Don Ortiz and several of his neighbours, most recently the owner of a truck company, a man called Casasola. But no one was willing to talk openly of any of this, and it seemed outrageous to imagine anyone local taking such an enormous risk, for however great a slight. An inspector had had a quiet word with Casasola, and had left satisfied he was not involved.

The long evening sun laid an ochre sheen on the horns of the hungry beasts as they approached the upper paddock. Tonight, armed guards would patrol the area in pairs. They'd been given orders to shoot any intruders on sight.

At the far side of the paddock, Don Ortiz sat astride Armillito, his black Arabian. He watched the brown and black bulls thread themselves between the hastily-erected partitions that had been put up to accommodate them. His heart felt heavy, and his mind worked relentlessly on the killings in an effort to understand what they meant, and who might want to cause him harm. To understand, above all, why one bull, a Miura named Islera, should have had its heart cut out and placed bloodless on the ground beside it.

El Turuño
7.15 p.m.

'No, I will not go.' Antonia tried desperately to stand her ground in the face of her mother's insistence. 'That horrid man will be there. I don't want to see him again.'

'He wants to see you, Antonia. Apparently, he was greatly taken with you when you met in Mexico City.'

'Taken?'

'He found you very attractive, darling. Most men do. It's your great talent. Unfortunately, your recent behaviour has made it virtually certain that you'll never leave the hacienda again. And don't ask me to plead with your father. It's entirely your fault you've got yourself into this mess.'

'My fault? Jesus Christ, Mother. A bunch of goons burst into my apartment, they grab Leo, and they bundle me into a car and drive me up here – and you have the gall to say it's all my fault?'

María Cristina brought her hand back and slapped Antonia hard across the left cheek.

223

They were in the *cuarto de estar*, an old room built by Don Ortiz's great-grandfather. On all four walls hung the mounted heads of bulls, some dating back to the last century, the bravest bulls, the worthiest of this honour. There were paintings of bulls and horses, photographs of one *ganadero* after another, shaking the hands of a succession of bullfighters, bronze models of famous bulls, and all the implements of the ring, *garrochas, banderillas, varas, estoques, descabellos*.

Antonia had always hated the room. From early on, she'd thought it wrong to call it a living room, not merely because everything in it spoke to her of death, but because no one could comfortably live in a room so weighed down with memorials and trophies.

'You'll keep your opinions to yourself, Antonia. You aren't in Mexico City now, among your smart friends. This is your father's kingdom: you'd do well to remember that. Out here your father has complete freedom of action. If he decides to have you killed, no one will come out here asking questions.'

'I've done nothing to merit being killed. What sort of monsters are you even to think of it?'

'For someone with brains, you're not very clever, Antonia. Out here, the only code is honour. You've broken that code.'

'Fuck the code!'

María Cristina's hand went up again, descending in a short arc towards Antonia's cheek. But this time Antonia caught her wrist and forced her arm back.

'I said fuck the code, Mother. How could my own father pay a gunman to kill a man I cared for? How could he have me followed to my apartment and have me dragged naked into the street and brought here by force?'

'You know the answer to all those questions. You drove

224

him too far, and this is what you get. Don't blame anyone but yourself for this.'

'Then why don't you explain why my own mother can do what she likes in Mexico City? You have affairs, but he doesn't send men after you with guns, and he doesn't shame you by having you dragged naked from your bed. Why don't you explain that to me, Mother? I have a right to know. Why do you get such a special deal?'

María Cristina finally succeeded in breaking free of Antonia's grasp. For a moment, Antonia thought she was going to hit her again, or spit in her face; but instead she sank back on to one of the seven or eight sofas that made up most of the room's furniture.

She sat quietly for a few moments, as though composing a retort to her daughter's accusations, then let herself sink back into the sofa.

Antonia looked at her, wondering precisely what hold it was her mother had over Don Ortiz. He, with his pride and twisted honour, had less power than he laid claim to. He had buttons that could be pushed, levers that could be pulled. And whatever they were, her mother knew them and had used them all her married life to her advantage.

'Wherever he is, I want him out, Mother. Do you understand? I don't care what it takes, and I don't care what happens to me as a result. But Leo has done nothing to deserve any of this. You know that as well as I do. He has to go free. He has to be allowed to go home.'

Her mother looked up at her with eyes like pools of pain. She was shaking her head, and her mascara had run, and her hands were shaking so much she had to squeeze them together into little fists of rage and shame. It was no longer a moral problem, or a question of honour, simply one of what was possible and what was not.

'It's too late,' she whispered. 'Do you understand me? Too late.'

25

Rue Mazenod
7th Arrondissement
Lyon

'Your father produces very good coffee. Best I've had since coming to France.'

'All he does is blend it. He buys the best beans he can afford, the rest is down to experience. But he's talking about giving it all up. The price of coffee has become crazy, and you can't always get the varieties you want.'

Declan savoured the last of his cup.

'What age is he?'

Alice shrugged. 'A bit older than you, maybe five years. My mother would be the same if she were alive.'

They were sitting side by side on a sofa in Alice's apartment where she'd recently served him a dish of *oeufs en meurette*. The lights were soft, and the room was warm. Every now and again, the oil heater banged, as though bringing messages from beyond the grave. Then it would fall silent, and they would sink a little further into a silence of their own.

'You said you had something to show me,' Declan said.

She was wearing a long black dress that fitted her too well. His fingers itched to untie the long silk scarf she had fastened round her neck. He kept telling himself to focus his thoughts on Ireland, Gaelic football, and the glorious uprising of 1916, but nothing could compete in distraction with the slope of her breasts beneath the dress.

'If you could manage to take your eyes off my delicately moulded chest, I'd like you to look at these.'

She stood and went to a cupboard on the other side of the room. From it she took a battered briefcase, and from this she removed about six pink files. Declan took his breath in sharply. Pink files were not only sensitive, they were strictly out of bounds to anyone below his level. Removing them from headquarters was a serious offence, one punishable with between five and ten years in gaol.

'How the hell did you get your mitts on these?'

She shrugged. 'That's not for you to worry about. The main thing is, I got them. Here, take a closer look.'

She passed them to him. Within seconds his protests had been swallowed up in astonishment at what he was reading.

He read his way through in sequence, taking his time, leaving nothing unturned or unexamined. Beside him, Alice sipped her coffee and ate her way slowly through a box of madeleines. Finally he laid the last file on top of the heap. An hour had passed. His coffee was cold. The room felt like ice to him, though it was still warm. She did not ask him for his thoughts. She'd seen the files, she knew what was in them. And she too felt the ice creeping from them, as though summer had turned to winter in a day.

'Janey Mack!' he said. 'These things are dynamite.'

'Yes,' she answered. She wanted him suddenly, and her body cried out, yes. 'That's the general idea,' she continued. 'Anything less he could afford to ride out. That would expose us to serious risk.'

He shook his head. 'Not any more than these. The moment he gets wind of them, we're exposed to more risk than you can imagine. If we go so far as to use them, there won't be any going back. Dutheillet will always know. We would have to watch our backs for the rest of our lives.'

She slipped a little closer to him, knowing he was aware of her, feeling his warmth touch hers, wanting above all things to touch and comfort him. Her hand brushed against his, then moved away again. They were like scared children caught in the middle of something vast and perverse, and like children they needed words of comfort, and sweet things to eat, and soft beds to sleep in.

'It depends on how careful we are,' she said. 'We have to arrange things so that, if anything should happen to either of us, it will trigger off precisely the course of events that Dutheillet wants to avoid. We have to make him our most zealous protector. If necessary, we have to get his wife on our side. From all I've heard, she has a more level head than his. They have to know that if harm of any sort comes to us, they'll be the next to suffer.'

'And if he doesn't use sense?'

'Believe me, I've been thinking this through. He'd be a fool not to.'

Her hand found his and squeezed around it tightly. He looked into her face and knew she wanted him, and he knew within himself that his whole life would be pointless now without her. If he kissed her, it would be more than a passing gesture.

'I meant what I said the other night. I love you.'

'I never doubted that,' she said, and reached out and pulled him to her. He put his arms round her and started to kiss her, his breath suspended in his throat as though

229

for ever, and as she kissed him in return, he gave up his breath to her and felt hers enter him, her breath and all of her with it, and he knew there would be no going back, ever.

Ganadería El Turuño

Don Ortiz had changed for the flamenco performance that was to take place later that evening, after dinner. He'd watched the last bull brought in to safety, and seen to it himself that the guards were in place, well armed, and alert. They'd be changed at midnight, and again at dawn.

If he was to be honest, he wasn't in the mood for that night's *juerga*, which would be the first in a week-long fiesta for the *hacendado* and his guests. But cancelling had been out of the question. The state governor would be there, along with the bishop, mayor, and police chief of Ciudad Camargo, the *alcaldes* of Las Mesteñas and Jaco, and a sprinkling of *aficionados* who had come up from Mexico City, as they did every year. Don Ortiz's private fiesta was an event looked forward to eagerly, if only because invitations were so hard to come by.

He sat immobile behind the huge inlaid mahogany desk he'd inherited from his grandfather. The walls of the study were lined with books, shelf upon shelf of them, all bound in leather. Most had to do with the science of bullfighting, *la tauromaquia*, but above them, stuttering along on shelves of painted silk-cottonwood, stood stern rows of books on theology, written and printed by the Jesuits in the days of Diego de Landa. A bookcase almost as tall as the room held dusty volumes of scientific learning that had been imported from Spain in the eighteenth and nineteenth centuries.

230

Don Ortiz had opened none of these, nor even fingered their spines. He was the least lettered of a long line, having spurned higher education for a spell of military service and a life among bulls and horses. He'd been all the more delighted, then, to have fathered a daughter whose academic performance from school to university had been a source of pride for her whole family. He had never thought his liberality would lead to this, never thought her capable of such treachery, of such moral deformity. Until now.

He rose and walked to the wall on his right, where a mirror hung that had been passed down from his great-grandfather. They had all used it as a looking-glass, every male member of the family since then. He thought of them, of his father and grandfather whom he remembered, of his great-grandfather whom he knew only through portraits and some photographs. They had been good-looking men, all of them, strong-boned, straight-backed, with the stern mouths and noses of their hidalgo ancestors. He looked at himself and scarcely recognized the man that looked back at him, the greying hair, the hollow cheeks. It was as though a bloodline had been lost to the world for ever.

He gulped down what was left of the brandy in the glass he was holding, and stood for a moment like that, almost without direction, then threw the glass hard away from him, to shatter on a bust of Porfirio Díaz. Until now. It shamed him beyond imagining that his own daughter should have been found naked in bed with a man of no station and no honour. Well, her seducer had been dealt with by now, and Antonia herself was back under some sort of control. This evening he'd explain to her just what that meant, just what her future was to be into old age and the grave. If she fought him, so much as showed defiance in her eyes, he would have no mercy, not even if it meant his having to kill her himself. Honour could not be treated as a thing of no merit. It was the core of all that mattered: the family, the community, the nation.

Bare knuckles drummed lightly on the door. Don Ortiz braced himself, then bellowed '¡Pase!'

She entered, and for an instant he was caught unawares, for he had truly thought that she was eight or nine years old again, innocent, virginal, his perfect child, and he a doting father whose only wish was to please her. The woman who entered wore make-up and had eyes of silver, and she looked at him as though from a great distance.

'You asked to see me,' she said.

She did not call him father. When the door closed, she went on standing just inside it, like a *peón* come to beg an increase in wages.

'I am still your father,' he said. 'You will give me my name at least.'

She looked at him calmly for a few moments more.

'You don't treat me like a father. Unless you treat me like one, you do not deserve the name.'

He took a step towards her, his arm raised, all anger running through him. It was his intention to hit her, but as he approached she neither flinched nor stepped away. Had she done so, he would have beaten her until he grew tired of it, but her mute denial of his strength was enough to make him lower his hand. Without a word, he went back to the desk and sat down.

'Sit in that chair,' he ordered. 'I don't want to have to look up at you while I talk.'

She sat and stared across the room at him. Her gaze did not falter or break away, and he knew that, like a poorly-broken horse, she could still kick out. But he would break her before the night was done.

'Where is Leo Mallory?' she asked, hoping to probe his defences before he had a chance to make an attack.

'Mallory is none of your business. Consider him as dead. It'll do you no good to pursue this any further.'

'Is that true? Have you had him killed? Did your people kill him back there in my apartment?'

He shrugged. 'I don't know where he was killed. It doesn't matter.'

'It matters to me. We would have been married if there'd been a chance.'

'Then you'd be a widow tonight instead of tainted goods. Do you have any idea just how serious is the crime you've committed?'

'Crime?' She half-rose to her feet. 'I've committed no crime. Leo committed none.'

'He stole my family's honour. I don't have to spell it out for you, you were brought up to understand. Without honour, we are nothing. A family's honour resides in its women. Your behaviour has destroyed the honour of a noble house.'

'You're out of touch, *Papá*. Maybe the world just moves too quickly for someone like you, but I assure you, it does move. In civilized countries, people aren't judged according to mediaeval codes of honour. Look around you. Look at this room, these books, that stupid bust of Díaz. You're trying to shut the modern world out, just the way your father shut it out, and his father before him.'

'Don't you dare insult my father.'

'I've no intention to. Listen – if you hadn't interfered when you did, none of this would have happened. All the time I was at university, from the day I left our hacienda until a few days ago, I played the part you wanted me to play. I was a good girl. If boys asked me out on a date, I told them I was busy, or I had to wash my hair. I told lies until it was pathetic, and I acquired a reputation I would rather not mention to your face. Believe me, *Papá*, men came after me. I am very beautiful, there's no point in pretending to false modesty. Men like how I look, they want to kiss me, and they want to get me into bed.

'I had none of that for years, and it wasn't always easy, because some of the men were good-looking, and some were very smart, and there were times when all I longed for was to be loved. Above all I wanted to be loved physically. But I did nothing. I acted cool towards men. I never let anyone get close to me. I was the dutiful daughter you wanted me to be.

'Then I met Leo Mallory. He wasn't like other men I had known. He was better-looking, and smarter, and he looked at me like nobody else had looked at me. Even then I played games with him, I pretended I was involved with someone else so he'd be put off. Then somebody attacked him. Some goon sent by you, some moron you'd paid to kill him or disable him.

'They brought him back to hospital, and I watched over him every minute I could, and in spite of myself I fell in love with him, so much it scared me to be near him. And when he came to I discovered he loved me as well. He was in bed and he was helpless, we'd done nothing but hold hands, but you couldn't leave it at that, you sent another assassin, only this time I shot him and I got Leo out of the hospital.'

'Antonia, I —' Don Ortiz tried feebly to interrupt the flow of her narrative, but she was running now with the force of it, and he could not stop her.

'I took him home that night, thinking I could keep him safe. He was bleeding and frightened, but I managed to settle him down, and I watched him all night long. Even though, *Papá*, it never so much as crossed my mind that we could be lovers. And then he woke, and something happened between us, something a man like you could never understand, for which you have all my pity. That was when we stopped imagining and became lovers in the true sense.'

'I don't wish to hear any more of this.'

'You have no choice. You chose to be part of this, now you can pay attention to what it means. According to you, my sleeping with Leo was a sin. My all-devouring, God-offending sin. That's why you sent your creeps again, to kill Leo. No more sin, no more dishonour. Which is why I have to spend the rest of my life like a leper.'

She stopped speaking, catching her breath on the last words. A horrible silence filled the room. She waited for a storm, knowing her father's anger and what it could do.

But he did not mount into a rage. He sat staring at her, and the look on his face was one of disbelief more than anger.

'I sent no one to kill him at the pyramid,' he said. 'I sent no one to the hospital. Only the men at your apartment. Do you understand? Someone else wanted to kill him. Someone else wanted him dead.'

'Then they should be grateful to you for doing their work for them.'

He shook his head slowly.

'He may not be dead. He's in the Reclusorio Portillo. If he has survived, I can get him out again in a matter of hours.'

'And will you do that? Will you get him out?'

She noticed that his right hand trembled visibly, even when he laid it on top of the desk to rest it.

'On one condition only,' he said.

235

'What is that?'

'That you swear a solemn oath never to see him again. That he returns to England and never comes back to Mexico. That his name is never again mentioned in this house. Those are my terms. I have only to lift this telephone and he walks free.'

'If he is still alive.'

'If he is still alive, yes. Now, do I have your promise?'

She nodded. 'Yes,' she said. 'You have my promise.'

'Very good. Now, leave me while I make this call. You don't need to know who I'm ringing, or what sort of agreement I come to with him. Come back in five minutes, and I'll tell you if he is still alive or not.'

'I'd like to know . . .'

'It's a private matter. There are palms to be greased, money to be paid to the right people. I'd really prefer it if you were not party to any of that. It is bad enough for you to be morally bankrupt; I would not have you become further sullied by seeming to connive in something you know to be illegal.'

She left the room unhappily, and her father picked up the telephone. He knew what he had to do. He had heard from her own lips a confession of her guilt, he had listened to her make a promise he knew she had no intention of keeping. To her, all that mattered was the Englishman, a man who could never be tolerated in respectable society, let alone within the Rocha y Ramírez family. Don Ortiz had no intention of leaving temptation in her way.

A voice came on the line.

'Pablo,' replied Don Ortiz. 'This is Ortiz. Is the Englishman still alive?'

'When I saw him last, yes. Why do you ask?'

'I don't need him alive any longer. See to it that he has

236

an accident. But make sure not to leave the body, in case the British consul comes poking his nose in.'

'Don't worry, Don Ortiz. It will be as though he never existed.'

'Let me know when it's done. Good night.'

Rue Mazenod
Lyon

He lay sleepless on his side, looking at her, unable to take his eyes off her. She was lying on her back, naked, perfectly still, engrossed by something in her sleep. He had discovered that, if he touched her lightly, she would reach out blindly for him and try to pull him to her. And that, he'd found, would lead to intimacies that ended in yet more energetic coupling. She possessed what seemed to be an inexhaustible passion and an energy that knew no limits. He, unfortunately, was possessed of the usual limitations of maleness and middle age. If only he could sleep, he'd wake beside her in the morning and bend over to kiss her breasts, bringing her awake into his embrace. But sleep had deserted him tonight.

It wasn't just that he'd entered into something very important in his life, that he'd found love finally at an age when other men sought for solace in peepshows and the Viagra bottle. It was the other thing, the uneasiness he felt about where this investigation was leading him. He wished he'd never asked Alice to probe into the president's past, wished he'd never seen the files she'd discovered.

What had started as a murder enquiry was rapidly taking on the shape and dimensions of a political scandal, one that could rock the establishment, not just in France, but in a dozen other countries. He felt himself in danger, and wished he could put the genie back into the bottle. But that was the rub. Innocent people, people as guiltless as the girl sleeping beside him, had suffered and died needlessly. If he didn't do something about that, what was he? If he didn't try to exact some sort of justice, what right did he have to draw a salary and give orders, or arrest and imprison lesser criminals?

He switched off the light before closing his eyes and summoning up the gods of sleep. They came slowly, shy presences that seemed to emerge from a jungle deep within his mind. They were naked and pale, and their eyes were blind. He could hear drums beating somewhere in the heart of the jungle, far beyond the nearest trees. However close they came, the figures remained indistinct. He felt himself begin to move, as if he was already in a dream, and one figure came closer than the others and brought its face close to his, and for an instant he thought he saw it grow clear and familiar.

Suddenly there was a screech, then another screech, somewhere out of sight, as though a bird was crying high in the treetops. His eyes came open and he realized it was the telephone. Alice was twisting away from the sound. He reached out his hand and picked up the receiver. A man's voice spoke, gravelly, like ground coffee. Declan thought it was Alice's father. He passed the handset to her, and she took it, rubbing sleep from her eyes.

'I think it's your father,' he said.

She frowned. 'Something must be wrong.'

She spoke sleepily into the receiver.

'Allô, Papa? C'est Alice.'

The man's voice spoke again, and Alice turned, thrusting the receiver back into Declan's hand.

'It's for you,' she said, and turned back, vainly trying to regain sleep.

'Yes,' Declan said. 'Who is this?'

'Monsieur Carberry. I think you should get over to your office as quickly as possible. It's extremely urgent.'

'What's wrong? Has something come up?'

'I can't explain. But you have to get here now.'

The line went dead. Declan looked at the receiver stupidly for a moment, then laid it to rest on the base.

'I have to go to the office,' he said. 'You stay here. Try to get back to sleep.'

She reached round for him and kissed him softly before sinking back to the mattress again.

'Have fun,' she said, yawning. 'I'll make some coffee when you come back.'

26

She came back into the room just as Don Ortiz put down the telephone. He looked her up and down. He could see that she was trembling, as though cold. Her skin was flat and pale, like an Englishwoman's skin, as though generations had leached out of her.

'Well, child,' he said, 'aren't you grateful?'

'Grateful?' Her eyes narrowed, and for a moment he thought she would come at him. 'Grateful that I have a father who can do such things? Grateful I have a mother who's never lifted a finger to stop you? Or maybe I should be grateful that I will have to spend the rest of my life alone.'

'Not alone, Antonia. I've spoken with your mother about this, and she's persuaded me to be merciful. There's no reason for you to remain alone.'

Antonia snapped her eyes shut, and opened them again. For a moment, everything seemed unreal.

'I don't understand.'

Don Ortiz hesitated only moments.

'You will meet him soon at dinner. Don't judge him at once, take your time. He has agreed to the match on his part already, so there will be no need for a lengthy courtship. Your mother and I have given our consent, both on our behalf and on yours. But he will prefer to hear that from your own lips, of course.'

'¿Papá? Papá, what are you saying? You're making me frightened. What is this? What are you talking about?'

'Why must you be so obtuse? I'm talking plainly enough. Young lady, you've left yourself with no choice. You can accept the marriage I've arranged for you, or you can suffer the consequences of your actions.'

She looked at him in horror.

'An arranged marriage? Just . . . who am I . . . supposed to marry?'

'You've met him before, he is no stranger. His name is Don Pédro Alvarez. You last met when you were sixteen, at the hacienda. Do you remember? I do believe he danced with you more than once that night.'

Remember? The thought went through Antonia like a hot knife. How could she have forgotten? This Don Pédro was one of their neighbours to the north, up past La Morita, on the Llano de Los Caballos Mesteños, a *hacendado* whose family, like theirs, had bred horses on their ranch for generations. His precise age was unknown to Antonia, but she knew he was at least seventy, a toad-like little man of no morals, little intelligence, and a famous lack of a sense of humour.

How could she have forgotten the last time they'd met? There had been a ball, and he, to be polite, or so she'd supposed, had indeed danced with her two or three times, wheezing as he scraped across the floor, spitting his gossip on to her face. Foolishly, she'd mentioned the horse her father had given her for her birthday a month earlier, and he'd insisted on being shown the animal then and there. She'd taken him out to the stable, and in the horse-filled silence, he'd pinned her against a wall and tried to rape her.

Actually, he hadn't raped her. It had, in its way, been worse than that. Holding her against the wall with a

241

strength that she'd found remarkable in such a wizened creature, he had worked his hand up inside her skirt and slipped it inside her pants, tearing the elastic. She'd cried and pleaded, but she might as well have sung the national anthem backwards for all the good it did. He crooked his fingers into her labia and moved them back and forth without care or attention, hurting her badly. Then, as abruptly as he'd started his attack, he'd backed off, taking his hand away and holding her less firmly.

'As dry as sandpaper,' he muttered. 'No use to me, no use at all. Come back when you lose your virginity, eh? Otherwise, don't waste my time.'

He'd unzipped his trousers then, and taken out his small, erect penis, and forced her to masturbate him. It happened quickly. He came with little warning, spurting over her dress. He'd sunk back with a tiny moan, and she'd used the opportunity to make her escape.

She'd gone back into the house by a side door, passing through the courtyard on her way to the *casa chica*. She'd almost got to her room, when a door opened and Carmela appeared. Carmela was the housekeeper, a pious woman who'd seen off two husbands and lost three children at birth. She took one look at Antonia, saw the panties dangling from her hand, and summed up the situation immediately.

'This way,' she said, leading Antonia at full speed to her bedroom. There, she'd helped clean her up while Antonia told her hesitatingly what had happened. Carmela listened, but not with great attention. She'd heard stories like this often enough before.

'He didn't . . . Did he put his thing inside you?' she asked.

'No, he . . .' Antonia explained what he had made her do.

'Then you're still a virgin. That's a blessing, at least.'

'Carmela, I must tell my father. He must see that Don Pédro is punished.'

Horror-struck, Carmela put her hand over Antonia's mouth.

'Do nothing of the sort. Don't even think of it, *mi querida*. You don't understand these men. Your father will not punish Don Pédro. It would not be honourable for him to say so much as a word of rebuke to him. Instead, he will hold you responsible for everything. He will say you led Don Pédro on, that you forced him to have sex with you.'

'But he can't say that, it's a complete lie. I –'

'Child, don't you know what country you're living in? This isn't New York, you can't just walk into a police station and accuse a man of rape. If Don Pédro was a poor man, certainly; then you might succeed. But you still would find yourself treated as a whore. Here, a woman is nothing but what a man makes her, especially a rich man like Don Pédro. If she loses her honour, she's as good as nothing. And without honour, without *pundonor*, a man may rape her or beat her or even kill her, and no one will be found to criticize him.'

Carmela had cleaned her and put her to bed, then gone back to the ball to offer Antonia's apologies for the headache that forced her to remain absent from the rest of that gathering. Now she felt another headache mounting.

'How can you, Father? How can you possibly think of marrying me to a man like that. He's old and loathsome. I'd sooner kill myself than let him lay a hand on me.'

Don Ortiz stared at her as though he really had no comprehension of her difficulty.

'You will let him lay as many hands on you as he

wishes. You know he has never had a child, but he wants that more than anything. A boy child to be his heir, even at this late date. Give him that, and I swear he will leave you alone afterwards.'

'You expect me to have his child? How can you . . . ?'

'How? Are you so stupid that I have to explain the smallest thing to you? Do I have to tell you who Don Pédro Alvarez is? How many acres of the best ranchland he possesses? How many head of horses? How much real estate in Mexico City? When you and he marry, he will change his will. If you have a male child, he will inherit everything, and he will become my heir as well. He will change his name to Rocha y Ramírez. Don Pédro has given me his solemn word on this.'

She felt shame and anger and disgust struggle in her for pre-eminence.

'Is this my caring father?' she shouted. 'You used to kiss me when you thought I was asleep. You brought me presents. You wiped my forehead dry when I was ill. And now you say you're willing to sell me to a scrap of a man in return for more of what you already have too much of. Don't waste your breath or your time any longer. I'd rather stay here at the *ganadería* like my Aunt Consuela. You can cut my tongue out if you please, or mutilate me any other way. But I will not live with that man, not if you offer me every bull and every horse and every precious thing you have.'

He looked at her, very still. He was tired, but a long night stretched ahead of him.

'There will be no hacienda,' he said. 'No life of regrets and contemplation. If you do not marry Don Pédro Alvarez, if you do not open your whoring legs and let him plant a son in you, as it is every woman's duty to do, then you are no daughter of mine for ever. I swear

I will see you die rather than bear the disgrace you have brought on this house. Tell me, have you heard of the Campo de Caballos Muertos?'

She nodded. Though she had never visited it, it had preyed on her thoughts since childhood. The field lay a mile to the east of the hacienda. Some time in the past, when her father had been a much younger man, someone had dug a pit there. And every time a horse died that could not be sent to the butcher, it would be dragged out there on the back of a small truck, and its body tipped into the pit and covered with quicklime. It was the most final place she had ever heard spoken of, and in the winter the coldest.

'Very well. If you refuse to marry Don Pédro and bear his child, then I will take you myself to the Field of Dead Horses, and I will walk back from it alone. That is my solemn promise to you, and I shall not break it.' He paused, letting his words sink in. 'Now, it's time for you to get ready. They will be serving dinner in half an hour. Your mother will take you in and seat you with your future husband.'

A breeze passed like a slow breath through the paddocks where the bulls stood packed together in the darkness. The animals were ill at ease. On the horizon, a horned moon was rising, as if in homage to the great beasts, goring the sky with a luminous motion. It let little light fall to the fields below. But if the eye adjusted, shadows could be seen creeping towards the first fence. Scattered along the perimeter, the guards saw and heard nothing.

A light went on in an upper window of the *finca*. Downstairs, the finishing touches were being put to the meal.

Declan headed straight for the night security office. Lights were on in different parts of the building, where staff worked through the night, liaising with police in other countries.

The duty sergeant recognized him.

'What brings you here so late, Monsieur Carberry?'

'I had a phone call. Didn't you ring and ask me to come in to the office?'

'No, sir. I haven't made any calls out this evening.'

'Someone said there was something up, that I should come in.'

The sergeant shook his head again. 'Maybe it was someone else, sir. Just a moment, I'll check with the other security staff.'

One by one he contacted them on their portable phones, and one by one they said they knew nothing about an emergency concerning Declan Carberry.

'Let's get down to your office, Mr Carberry, take a little look,' the sergeant said. Leaving his assistant in charge of the security unit, he took a phone from the rack and some keys from a keysafe, and followed Declan into the corridor.

Declan went to unlock his office door, but no sooner had he touched it than it swung open almost of its own accord. He stepped inside. The duty sergeant followed nervously.

At first glance, it seemed that nothing had been touched or stolen, nothing, however trivial, moved or broken. Declan checked his desk. Nothing on it had been disturbed. He crossed to his filing cabinet; it was still locked.

246

'I don't understand this,' he said. 'I was told that something was up. What do you think I should do?'

'What exactly did he say, this caller?' asked the sergeant.

'Say? He . . . said I should get to my office right away, that something had happened. I suppose he meant this room. Or maybe headquarters in general.'

'I think we should get out of here,' said the sergeant. 'It could be just a prank, but it seems an odd one. Perhaps they just wanted to get you out of wherever you were. Where were you, incidentally? At home?'

Declan shook his head. 'With a friend.'

He saw the sergeant glance involuntarily at the clock.

'Just a friend, sir? Or someone connected to Interpol?'

'There's a connection, yes.'

'Then I think we should phone this person and warn them to be on the lookout.'

'Yes, we should. I –'

At that moment, his eye happened to fall on the fax machine in one corner. A sheet of paper sat on the in-tray.

He crossed the room and picked it up. It was just an ordinary A4 sheet. There were no words on it, no indication at the top to show who had sent it. There was just a single image. Declan looked at it for several seconds, then crumpled the paper in his hand.

'Sir? What is it, sir?'

Declan looked round as though he had only just become aware of the man's presence.

'It's a drawing of a triangle,' he said. And then it dawned on him. 'No, that's wrong,' he said. 'It's not a triangle. It's a pyramid.'

27

There were about fifty people at the dinner. Most of them planned to go home once it was over, without attending the performance. Others who regarded themselves as members of the *afición*, would stay until the early hours of the morning in the expectation of music that would reach their souls, if they had any. For the most part, they would watch Don Ortiz and take their cues from him, applaud when he applauded, grow pensive when he did. That was their true *afición*, the love of power and money and influence. Don Ortiz knew them all well, knew their greed and ambition as well as he knew his own, and gave them what they wanted in return for what they had to give.

The state governor was, naturally, the guest of honour. He did not attend every year, since his diary was a full one. But come election time next year, and he would mount a series of *corridas* across the state, to which entrance would be free. The bulls would be supplied by Don Ortiz, the *espadas* and their *cuadrillas* would perform free of charge (in return for later favours outside the ring), the butchers would distribute the meat of the vanquished bulls to the poor, and everywhere there would be posters of Don Esteban Torres, smiling beneath the Mexican flag.

This evening he paid off his future debt by whispering

in the ears of a banker, a building contractor, and a young American venture capitalist that Don Ortiz Rocha y Ramírez had his confidence, and hinting that a union between the Don's lands and those of his neighbour, Don Pédro Alvarez, was imminent.

When the dinner ended, Don Ortiz called, as he did every year, on his brother, Bishop Paco Rocha y Ramírez, to deliver a short address followed by a blessing. The bishop, a short man of about sixty, was the regional establishment's favourite man of the cloth. They brought their babies to him to be baptized, they sent their children at the proper age for confirmation, he solemnized their marriages and he opened the gates of heaven for them.

'"Thou shalt take up this proverb against the king of Babylon, and say, How hath the oppressor ceased! The golden city ceased!"' He paused dramatically, pursing his already tightened lips for further effect.

From the opposite end of the table, Rafael watched him with an amused expression on his face. He had finally been invited to the *ganadería*, at María Cristina's insistence.

'How many golden cities have come and gone like apparitions?' the bishop went on. 'How many men have perished in pursuit of them? We have all been taught that our ancestors, the *Conquistadores*, came to these shores in search of gold, and that they found it in abundance. Some who came later wanted fresh gold for themselves, and they set off in all directions, following rumour and legend.

'Who has not heard of Alvár Núñez Cabeza de Vaca, and the black slave Esteban, or of Francisco Vásquez de Coronado, and their fruitless search for the Seven Golden Cities of Cíbola – Las Siete Ciudades Doradas de Cíbola? How many hunted for the golden land of Eldorado, and its great cities Manoa and Omagua? Spaniards and Portuguese, Germans and English – they all came as treasure-seekers, and they all came to the end of their journeys empty-handed. Others sought after Quivira, the lost City of the Caesars, and yet others spent their lives in pursuit of Otro Méiico and Otro Peru.

'Did they waste their time? Were their lives squandered needlessly? Yes, if we speak of gold, yes, if all we care for are riches beyond belief. But look on any map and see where their explorations took them, see how their footsteps opened up this new world of ours. They found no cities of gold, no towers of rubies, no fallen Babylon among the trees of the hidden jungle. But after them came the priests and the friars who built the first churches and the first monasteries in the heart of savagery.

'Those were our ancestors, true-hearted men who flinched at nothing, heroes who opened the way for the Gospel of Jesus Christ among heathen Indians. And what are we today? Are we still worthy of those trailblazers, who went before us into darkness and brought out, not gold but the souls of men? Who cared nothing for riches, yet brought the greatest gift of all, the gift of eternal life.'

Everyone knew that the bishop owned silver mines at Pachuca and Zacatecas as his ancestors had done; and an iron ore mine at Durango; and copper mines at Cananea and La Caridad. Fewer knew of his coffee and sugarcane plantations on the eastern slopes of the Sierra Madre Oriental. And almost no one but his brother and María Cristina knew of the slums he owned in Mexico City, whose inhabitants sought, not for the gift of eternal life, but for the strength to go on living from one hard day to the next.

His lustrous voice went on. No one really noticed very

much; they had not come here to listen to a sermon. They had eaten well, and for the men there would be cigars and whisky and *tequila* soon, and for the *aficionados* hours of music.

Antonia might as well have been in another world. Side by side with her presumed fiancé, she strove to distance herself as far as possible from everything. No more than a dozen words had passed between them. She'd made her mind up to kill herself, and she knew that neither her father nor her mother nor Don Pédro could take it away from her. She'd be sure to do it openly, so no one could deny it, and there would be no bishop to drone at her funeral, and they'd be forced to bury her out of sight somewhere, perhaps in the Campos de Caballos Muertos.

She remembered her own lost city, and the gold they'd uncovered there. Was it the reason for all this? She looked up and saw that someone was looking at her. Rafael, her mother's friend and guru. What had brought him here? she wondered.

'Today, just as then,' the bishop said, bringing his oration to a conclusion, 'there are men among us who spread tales of cities of gold. The new Eldorados, the new Cities of Cíbola. But how different these cities are from those of old. The communists preach a mythical land of equality and harmony in which all true virtue is overturned, where slave rules over master and worker over boss. The liberals tell of a series of golden cities: the City of Abortion, and the City of Contraception, the City of Homosexuality, and the City of Feminism. They call on good Catholics to abandon their homes and go to these cities, that are no more than the Cities of the Plain, that God destroyed, Sodom and Gomorrah.'

María Cristina sat with her hands clasped on her lap.

She was tense, knowing what might happen after dinner. But she'd given herself up to what Rafael called 'the flow of instinct'. Life would work out well, and they all be freed of the shadows that crowded in on them. She wished the bishop would shut up. And, she having wished it, he did.

It was a custom of the house that, between dinner and the entertainment, Don Ortiz would sit in his study to receive those of his friends who wished to speak with him on matters of business or other urgency. Deals would be struck, money would sometimes pass hands, alliances would be formed or reaffirmed. Powerful though they were as a group, most of his visitors would come to him as suppliants. Members of the *afición* would wait till late morning, since they would stay over after the music.

It was nearing the end of the first session when María Cristina entered. She looked a little tired, and on her silk dress a small red stain showed where she had spilled some chilli sauce. She closed the door behind her.

'Is there anyone left?' asked Don Ortiz.

'Just one.'

'Well, perhaps you could leave us for a while, and call on me after that. Assuming you have something to speak to me about.'

'No, I don't want to speak to you about anything in particular.'

'Because I refuse to talk about Antonia. Do you understand? That matter is closed. She understands her obligations, and the consequences if she fails to meet them. That's all there is to it.'

'I won't argue with you. I'm sick of arguing. But . . . do you think she was ever a good girl? I remember, when she was small, you thought the world of her.'

He looked at her, letting her remain standing as though she were not his wife but just another woman tricked out in red, seeking favours.

'He raped her, you know. Did you know that?' he asked.

'Raped her? What do you mean? Her boyfriend?'

'No, not the boyfriend. Don Pédro. Are you a total fool, woman, that you didn't know about it?'

'I heard nothing. When . . . ?'

He told her what he knew. It was not everything. No one would have risked telling him everything.

'And you never . . . ?'

He looked through her. 'I kept it to myself. I had my reasons. They seemed good to me then. Not so good now.'

'Rafael wants to speak with you,' she said. 'I've come to ask you to see him.'

'Isn't it enough that I gave in and invited him here? An Indian in my house, at my table, for no other reason than that you asked for him.'

'You don't understand. Rafael is not just any Indian. He is immensely rich and immensely powerful. You know that, of course. But I don't think you know the full extent of either his wealth or his power. He has a proposal to make to you. A favour to ask from you, and something in return that he believes you will not reject.'

'He should have written to me.'

'This is something he has to speak about face to face. Don't let your prejudices ruin things for you. Let me bring him in.'

'Since he's here. But tell him to be quick. The *cante jondo* will be starting soon.'

She went to the door and summoned Rafael inside.

Though she wanted to stay, she thought better of it. Her presence might antagonize Don Ortiz; and she knew her teacher could handle this without her help.

'Don Ortiz. I'm so pleased to have a chance to speak with you at last.'

'Señor Rafael, please don't think me rude, but you really should know that you're here in my house only under sufferance. My wife pleaded to have you here, and in the end I gave in to her. But, frankly, I neither approve of you nor trust you. Above all, I don't like to have Indians laying claim to some sort of equality with me. You may call me a racist if you like, but you will not make me change my opinion of your people.'

Rafael showed no sign of anger.

'I haven't come to change anything,' he said. 'What you think of me or my people is of no concern to me. For my part, I would not consider you my equal, even if all the mountains became dust and the seas dried up and you learned to walk like a human being.'

'*¡Chinga tu madre!* You'd better –'

'Don Ortiz, I've not come here to argue with you or exchange insults. I have the greatest personal admiration for you. Your dear wife has told me much about you, how great a man you are, how you have triumphed over adversity to achieve all you have achieved. She has also told me that you are not content, that you wish to accomplish much, much more than this. I congratulate you. Most men of your age have abandoned ambition; they seek to hold what they have, they dig their heels in, they retrench. Whereas you seek fresh horizons. I've come here to tell you that you can rely on my assistance in achieving your goals. All I can do for you, I will gladly do.'

'I don't need your help. Who the hell do you think

you are, pretending you can be of help to someone in my position?'

'You're right. I am only a shaman, a *zahorín*, a humble man born of generations of humble men. My abilities are of an entirely different order to yours. But . . .' He looked directly at Don Ortiz, seeking to capture his attention and his intelligence by his eyes.

The Don, long accustomed to facing down his adversaries, found to his consternation that it wouldn't work with this man. For the first time in his life, he blinked and looked down.

'Don Ortiz, you don't know who I am. I come to you this evening as a supplicant, but the truth is that I am vastly richer than you and vastly more powerful. You can lift a finger to have a man killed anywhere in Mexico. I can have him killed within hours in any country of the world. You have bishops and small-town mayors under your sway. I number cardinals and presidents among my adherents. Believe me, Don Ortiz, I can make you rich beyond your sweetest dreams. I can give you power you have never imagined you could possess.'

The look on Rafael's face was not that of a fanatic. He really knew that all he said was true, like a businessman offering a share in a straight venture. Don Ortiz felt a profound unease seize hold of him.

'And in return? You didn't come here out of the kindness of your heart, offering me all these things for free, without expectations, did you? Do you think I'll join your cult, sit at your feet and drink in your words of wisdom, spread your message among bullfighters and horse-breeders?'

Rafael laughed.

'None of that, I assure you. I would welcome you to my community, of course. Men like yourself are always especially welcome. But something tells me that is not likely to be your true inclination. In which case, there is only one thing I want from you.'

'And that is?'

'Your daughter Antonia's hand in marriage.'

28

Reclusorio Preventivo Portillo

At night, the prison crouched in the darkness like a spider about to spring. People in the *barrio* could see its towers and barbed wire illuminated against the night sky. To them, it was a silent place, the source of all their myths and stories, the theatre for their night fears, the stilt-legged spider at the heart of their dreams.

Leo huddled in his cell, as though glued there by fear. Following the knife fight, he'd been stitched and bandaged at the infirmary, then sent back out to fend for himself, knowing his life depended on how many dollar bills remained in Norman Spalding's hidden cache.

In the cell, frightened men moaned or cried out in their sleep. Beyond its bars, other night-time cries punctuated the silence. Men were being raped, by guards or stronger inmates. It had little to do with homosexual need, just a despair that made some men force themselves on others. There was no love here, just stark strength and an overwhelming desire to dominate.

Leo snatched what little sleep he could, crouching in a corner, waking every few minutes to look around him. In order to calm himself, he sang little songs to no one in particular, 'I'm H-A-P-P-Y', 'Rudolph the Red-Nosed Reindeer', and 'Tom Pearce, Tom Pearce, lend me thy grey mare', which his uncle Charlie had taught him when he was twelve, during a visit to Harrogate. He went on mental expeditions to England and France and Italy, places where he'd known happiness, or at least contentment. And when all this faded, he let himself think of Antonia. He sang to her in his head, a song without words, for a lost love who had deserted even his dreams.

Norman slept a few feet away, his presence reassuring. He'd been here long enough to learn how to sleep in more than snatches. It was more dangerous, but it gave him the extra energy that drove him through each day. His friends were scattered through the cell. Everywhere, people slept, or squatted, or stood at the bars. Those who could get drugs used them at night. Those who could not cried tears like the damned.

Leo fell into a light sleep at last, his first proper sleep of the night. At first there were no dreams, then something changed and he was in a place without vision, a place where there were only voices. Antonia's voice, in a mockery of itself, in a man's tones, singing songs he'd never heard. Then a shuffling of pebbles broken by a man's voice, an Indian voice singing in Quiché Mayan, an old song that he did not understand. The song ended, and a different voice began to whisper, beguiling him to open his eyes.

He opened them and came hurrying out of the dream into full wakefulness. Something had brought him awake, something not the voice. He squinted to see in the semi-darkness. Near him there were shadows that had not been there before, moving near Norman's sleeping body. Leo snatched himself up and cried out in Spanish, '¡Atrás, atrás!'

The shadows flickered and moved away suddenly, as though vanishing into the floor. Leo hurried over.

258

'Norman, wake up. Somebody was messing round here, I think we should get the others.'

Hearing no response, he shook Norman by the shoulder. Still nothing. Then his hand slipped from his friend's shoulder, forward towards his chest. That was when he realized there was blood everywhere, that Norman's throat had been cut from side to side. That was when Leo realized that he was utterly alone and minutes away from death.

La Ganadería

Don Ortiz stared at Rafael, wondering how he could have made such a request so calmly. It was then that he recovered his spirit, or something of it. He could have killed the rascal then, shot him or knifed him or kicked or bludgeoned him to death at the back of the house, where the dogs lay in their kennels. To marry his daughter to an Indian medicine man with inflated ideas of himself was utterly absurd. It wasn't that he valued her, but that the shame of such a marriage would put a stain on his family for ever. He found it impossible to find the words to answer such an outrageous request.

'I do not ask this thing casually, Don Ortiz, believe me. I have not come here without profound self-examination. I have the deepest respect for you and for your family.'

'If that's the case, then why have you come here with such a shameful request?'

'Shameful? I don't consider it shameful. You are descended from Conquistadors. My ancestors were Mayan kings. There is royal blood in my veins, and the blood of gods. If I close my eyes, I can hear the voices of Hunab Ku and his son Itzamná, lord of the heavens, of Kinich

Ahau and Ah Puch, all the gods of my fathers trembling inside me.

'It is the gods of my people who have guided me to your door. I come as your equal, even if you do not recognize me as such. I advise you not to mock my gods, señor – they inhabited this country long before your forefathers first set foot on its shores. Don't imagine that, because you can't see them, they are not still there, hiding in the rocks and pools.'

He paused. From another room, the plucked notes of a guitar came to them. The performance would start in a few minutes, and nothing would force Don Ortiz to miss it, not even a judgement affecting his own daughter's fate.

'Don Ortiz, you must treat me fairly. I have dreamed of your daughter all my life. She is tied to my destiny as a god is tied to the earth and stones of the land to which he belongs.'

'Your destiny? What exactly do you mean by that?'

'It is written in the stars that Antonia and I shall be man and wife. Please don't try to resist this. The gods see everything we do. If you say "Yes", they will bless you with all you have ever desired.'

'And "No"? What if I say "No"?'

Rafael did not move, but his eyes blinked once and followed Don Ortiz's until they held them, and there was a deep chill in their pupils that grew until it seemed a ball of ice.

'You will suffer.'

'You mean you will do me harm?'

'Not you personally. But, yes, I will do you harm until you grant me your daughter's hand.'

'Then I shall never grant it. Get out. Take your gods and your Indian baggage, and never come here again. And be sure of one thing: I shall see Antonia dead sooner than have her marry you.'

Rafael held his gaze for a few moments more.

'Very well,' he said. 'You have spoken. When you are ready to see reason, ring me. I will be waiting for you.'

Don Ortiz stood at the window of his study, looking directly out on to the hardtop drive that ran from the house to the main gate. He watched the tail-lights of Rafael's Range Rover as it negotiated the turns, bobbing and weaving among shadows until it was out of sight. Had he been out of doors, Don Ortiz would have spat in the car's general direction. He was still shaking with rage, rage that sought revenge but did not yet know exactly how to find it.

There was a soft noise as someone entered the room. He whirled round, ready to bawl out an unsuspecting servant. Instead, he saw María Cristina hovering in the doorway.

'They're waiting for you downstairs,' she said. 'The musicians have been ready for some time. They'd like you to join them.'

'Shut the door,' he said.

Knowing what was coming, she pushed the door shut and turned to face him.

'Did he tell you why he came here?' Don Ortiz asked. She nodded.

'And you said nothing to me of it?'

'I thought it better you should hear of it from his own lips. He can be very persuasive. I thought he might persuade you.'

'You were willing to go through with such a farce? To give your daughter to a savage?'

'He is not a savage. But even a savage would be

better than a geriatric with no teeth, no brains, and no balls.'

'The geriatric has land.'

She took a step forward.

'Don't you understand anything?' she asked. 'The geriatric will be dead by tomorrow if Rafael hears of your little arrangement. *Mi querida* – because you are a dangerous man, you sometimes forget that there are others as dangerous as you and more. Believe me, Rafael is one of those. If you've crossed him tonight, don't waste your time on this concert. Just go to bed and get down on your knees and pray he will give you a second chance.'

'I think you have been reading too many books. We'll talk about this tomorrow. Now, it's time for the *cante jondo*. Try not to fall asleep: it's embarrassing when you do that. And tell Antonia before she goes to bed that I've fixed a wedding date with the bishop. She's to be married to Don Pédro the day after tomorrow, in the cathedral at Ciudad Camargo.'

Out on the plains, the wind passed as winds pass, and the moon hooked and hooked the darkness to itself. In his cell at the *Reclusorio*, Leo Mallory sat awake beside a pool of thickening blood. In one corner of the cell, two men had begun to perform a slow *martinete*, a lamentation for God knows who or what. One sang while the other tapped his feet and clapped. In Komchen, Leo's city among the clouds, something indistinct shuffled from the jungle towards the moon-capped pyramid. An ocean away, in his office in Lyon, Declan Carberry put the phone down softly. His heart was beating uncontrollably. Not many miles away, in Vienne where he had his apartment, all was dark. The Pyramide du Cirque, an ancient structure built over the old Roman circus, glistened in the street lights and the headlights of passing cars. Back in Mexico, a single car drove steady as an arrow until it was well out of sight of the *ganadería* of El Turuño. Suddenly, its brake lights went on and it drew to a halt nowhere in particular. Outside, the wind blew across the open countryside.

Don Ortiz took his seat at last. There was silence for a little while, then the performers took the stage. Two men dressed in black approached the front, the *cantaor* and the *bailaor*. At the rear, the guitarist took his seat. There was no microphone, no speakers, just the acoustics of the long, dim room in which they sat.

The dancer announced the first *cante*.

'We shall begin with a *toná* followed by an accompanied *seguiriya*.'

The singer closed his eyes, and in the room no one spoke and no one cleared their throat, and in the silence a deeper silence formed, and the singer raised his voice at last, like a woman on a wave-beaten rock calling for her demon lover. The deep song had begun.

The dancer's feet began to move, cracking hard on the wooden surface of the stage, and he began to clap. And when it was time the guitar answered them both, and the music rose and fell through *soleás*, *cañas*, and *martinetes*, until the voice of the singer was united with the voice of his inner demon, the *duende* that lurked at all times inside him, waiting for its time of revelation.

> *Ay, por los siete dolores que paso mi Dios*
> *Mas dolores paso yo por tu amor,*
> *que por los siete dolores que paso mi Dios.*

Antonia sat in a place of honour, without moving, and

as the room filled with music, tears ran unchecked down her cheeks.

I have undergone more sorrows for your love,
than for the seven sorrows that my God has undergone.

Outside, in the kitchens and the stables, they had already tied up or killed the servants and the vaqueros. They had killed all the horses, and had started work on the bulls. In order to preserve as much silence as possible, they used portable bolt-guns that sent steel bolts through the heads of the cattle. Without space in which to run or use their horns, the bulls could do nothing to save themselves. One by one, their killers toppled them. They fell in the dust or on top of one another, and as they dropped a ripple of fear ran through those that were left, and a wave of moaning broke across their heads, again and again, while in the room the singer sang of his heart's pain and Antonia's tears fell unheeded on her dress like drops of sweet blood on a bull's forehead.

Lyon

He didn't bother going back to her apartment. She wouldn't be there, he knew it as certainly as he knew the crescendos of fear and loss. His car screeched round corners heedless of regulation.

On the southern edge of Vienne the Romans built a pyramid sixty-five feet in height as the centrepiece to their chariot racetrack. Modern inhabitants know it as the Pyramide du Cirque.

He knew he should not have come when he saw the blue lights flashing in the distance. He wanted to go back to Alice and tell her all was well, but there was no time for that. Her voice followed him everywhere. She whispered her love for him as though she was right there beside him in the passenger seat.

A traffic cop waved him back with impatient motions of his hand. Declan lowered his window and flashed his Interpol card. The cop waved him on. He parked in the only available space, between a police car and an ambulance.

It's all right, Alice, he whispered. *I'm here now. You're all right.*

Past the blue lights was the darkness of the pyramid itself, dwarfing everything in its presence. He walked to its foot, where a group of policemen and paramedics were gathered.

'I'm sorry, sir, but this is police business,' said one of the policemen, taking his elbow to guide him away.

Again, he displayed his card. The policeman stood aside, and Declan walked through.

There was just one body this time. He'd guessed that much. He didn't need to pull the blanket back: her naked arm lay outside, with a silver bracelet he'd given her a day or two earlier.

'Her name is Bouchardon,' he said, speaking to no one in particular. 'Alice Bouchardon.'

Several of the officials gathered round the body turned and looked at him, wondering what had brought him there. He scarcely saw them. He bent down and pulled the blanket away from her head. Her face was untouched, still sleeping as he had seen it not so very long ago. He bent and kissed her lips, brushing away the hands that tried to pull him back. And when he could kiss her no longer, he reached out with one hand and closed her eyelids for ever.

'Alice Bouchardon,' he said, getting to his feet. 'Remember her name.'

29

He remembered seeing a film starring Bill Murray and Andie MacDowell. *Groundhog Day*, it was called. In it, Murray had woken morning after morning to find himself trapped in the same day. The day and the people in it never varied, only his own attempts to break free.

Leo felt like that now, like someone struggling to tear himself away from a nightmare that ran, day after day, along exactly the same tracks.

He'd been here before, held down by the stiff white sheets of a hospital bed, sore in places, numb in others, unable to see more than a patch of blank ceiling, like a dead or a dying man.

He arched his back in the grip of a sudden pain that clamped his muscles together. There were still men who crucified themselves alive down here, he thought, men who inflicted an ancient barbarism on a new faith. They would lie upon their crosses in the heat of midday while their accomplices, gathered about like vultures, pounded cold nails into warm flesh with hammers of cheap American steel. Once pierced hand and foot, and lashed like wrecked mariners to a raft of planks, they would be hoisted aloft and adulated there by the crowd while their sweat mixed with their blood.

He pictured them, *toreros* for the Almighty, wounded by the horns of the divine bull, God's invincible *toro bravo*, hanging mutely in the sun-baked air like the wasted carcasses of dogs; and he wondered if that wasn't what had happened to him, if he hadn't been cut and pierced for the sake of some jade god with bright, obsidian eyes, whose unpronounceable name and indefinable features remained hidden from him and would remain so hidden for ever until death. And he felt that death, however invoked, was very close to him now, and that he could not hide from it much longer, as he might have tried to hide from a *cuchillero* or a *filero* with a naked blade and eyes of blood.

'How are y'all this morning, Doctor Mallory? You ready to talk to me yet?'

It was an American voice. He hadn't reckoned on hearing an American voice. He was tempted to lie without moving, to keep his eyes shut in an effort to keep down the nausea that threatened to erupt every time he so much as moved an eyelid.

'Doctor Mallory, I know y'all had a bad time down there in that filthy gaol in Mexico' – he pronounced the name 'Mehico' – 'and I know y'all damn near to got yourself killed. But that's behind you now. Trust me, son, you can open your eyes.'

Something about the voice reminded him of old Norman, Norman who'd been filleted in the prison. Maybe he could trust the speaker after all, maybe he could open his eyes and see what kind of world it was he'd wound up in this time.

The room was a white-painted hospital room almost the same as the one he'd been in at the ABC, the bed was the same sort of bed, the machines were the same sort of machines. But the resemblance to *Groundhog Day* ended there. The white-coated figure looking benignly down on him bore no resemblance whatever to the doctor who'd treated him before, the Mexican who'd first warned him of Antonia's father.

The American held out a hand.

'Name's Grady. Doctor Jim Grady. I'm glad to see you looking better. You came in here in one hell of a state.'

'Where am I?'

'This is the Parkland Hospital, son. You're in Dallas.'

'Is that Dallas as in Dallas, Texas.'

'Unh, unh. What other Dallas is there?'

'I was hoping maybe Dallas, England.'

The doctor shook his head, amused.

'We ain't built that one yet, but when we do, you'll be the first to be invited. You'all were sent to San Antonio first, when they took you across the border, but they just patched you up a bit and sent you on here on account of we've got the best facilities in the south-west, second to none. We've done what we can, son; but it's gonna be a while. What you need is rest. Time to let your wounds heal.'

'Rest? But I –'

'Forget it, whatever it is. Most things in life'll wait if you give them the chance.'

'But Antonia . . .'

'Women too, son. If she's any good, she'll wait, believe me.'

'She doesn't have a choice. I've got to get to her. Her father may kill her.'

Grady looked pensive. 'She Mexican?'

Leo nodded.

'Looks like you might have yourself some trouble there. I just don't recommend trying to tackle it long as y'all still find yourself in this state. Now, if you don't mind, I have someone outside who's been waiting to speak to you for a few days. You think you're up to seeing him?'

'Who is he?' asked Leo, suspicious suddenly. His troubles hadn't left him behind, evidently. And what the hell was he doing in Dallas of all places?

'He's some sort of policeman, far as I can figure out.'

'Mexican?' Leo's heart raced uncomfortably.

The doctor shook his head. He was a tall man with rounded shoulders, accustomed to stooping over sick-beds.

'Irish. Name's Carberry. He says he's with something called Interpol. You ever hear of that?'

'Yes.'

'I'll be damned.'

'What does he want with me?'

'He brought you across the border, I believe. Took you out of that prison down there. Believe me, son, you were like to have died back there if he hadn't come for you.'

Leo hesitated a moment. He knew he had no choice. Whoever this Carberry was, it looked like he had complete control at present.

'Send him in,' he said.

Grady puffed up his pillows and helped him find a comfortable position against them. That was when Leo first became aware that he was hurting all over.

'You were cut up badly back there. But I've seen worse. You'll heal in time. You've got a reason to live, don't you? You got a girl waiting for you on the other side of the river. Ain't that so?'

'I'm not so sure. It's one of the things that worries me. But why don't you send this man Gooseberry in and let me see what it is he wants with me?'

Leo had no expectations of his Irish visitor; but the moment he set eyes on Declan's face, all thought of

269

wisecracking fell away from him. The Irishman had suffered, and more than once, and not that long ago, he thought.

'Doctor Mallory?'

'So they tell me. I haven't looked in a mirror recently. I was told your name's Carberry and that you're a policeman.'

'That's right. Do you mind if I sit down?'

'No trouble at all.'

Declan helped himself to a chair and drew it up close to the bed.

'I can come back another time,' he said. 'Tonight. Or tomorrow.'

'I'll be all right. I've only just woken up, and I don't feel like going back again for a while.'

'Are they giving you drugs?'

'I expect so, yes. They tell me I was badly wounded. I don't remember much about it.'

'You were near death's door when I found you. I couldn't believe it when you made it this far.'

'Why didn't you just take me to a hospital in Mexico City?'

'I did, but I couldn't leave you there, not after all that had happened to you. They patched you up for the journey, and I flew you out that afternoon. San Antonio, then on to Dallas. You're OK now, nobody's coming after you in here.'

'How come they let you take me out? I was on a murder charge.'

'That was the first thing I looked into. They didn't have a leg to stand on. I made a few protests in the right places. Got your friends out of their prison as well. Damn one of them was being kept in prison for any good reason.'

'You sound like an influential man. Why are you interested in my case in the first place?'

Declan did his best to explain.

'When I heard you'd been attacked, that there'd been a murder, that someone had tried to kill you more than once, I had a gut reaction. There's a link between your situation and the murders I'm investigating back in France.'

'Link? What sort of link?'

'I wish I knew. But I haven't been a policeman all this time without learning to see connections between things. I think you're my key, if only I knew which way to turn you.'

'A lot of people have been trying to turn me. I'd just as happily be left alone.'

'Me too.'

Declan's whole life now was a single act, a suppression of feeling that threatened to overwhelm him in his entirety. As far as possible, he spent no time alone, and when he did he blotted it all out with drink or drugs. They didn't take him far. Every road he walked down led to her. She was crushing the soul out of him. It had been such a short love, yet she had entered every pore and cell of him till he felt he would die of her.

'I've got something here to show you,' he said. 'Just some photographs. Could you look at them for me?'

'Whatever you say.'

Declan took out the blow-ups of the tattoos they had found on the bodies in Paris. He passed them across the bed.

Leo let the photographs drift through his fingers one by one. They did not appear to excite his interest very much.

'What can I tell you about these?' he asked, letting the last piece of card fall to his lap.

'Well, what I'd like to know is – do they mean anything to you? A man in Paris said you'd be the person, that you'd whistle a meaning for them out of thin air.'

'Did he indeed? Who was he?'

Declan explained.

'I've never heard of him. But I suppose he was right. I can give you meanings for each pair, but I'm not sure they'd add up to anything as a string of text. Did they follow any particular order when you found them?'

'That's hard to say. But they were very definitely in pairs.'

'Fair enough. I might have guessed that anyway.'

'Listen, can you explain to me in words of one syllable just what they are?'

'What they are? That's simple enough. They're Mayan glyphs. Glyphs as in hieroglyphs.'

'Like the Egyptians?'

'Just the same, but a lot harder to decipher. Each one represents a word or a syllable or a name – they were carved in long stone inscriptions by the ancient Maya. You have eight out of the nine names of the Nine Gods of Darkness. Each one appears alongside a date. Where on earth did you find them? I can't see why a policeman would cross the Atlantic and get me out of gaol just for me to tell him names he could find in any textbook.'

'What about this?'

Declan rummaged in his inside pocket and drew out another rectangle. He handed it to Leo. His hand shook as he did so.

'This was found under similar circumstances,' he said. The glyph had been inscribed on an amulet tied round Alice's neck.

Leo glanced at it. This time, his reaction was more definite. This was the Xiknalkan glyph, the flying serpent whose appearance in the skies would signal the end of the present world, the end, perhaps, of Time itself.

'I think you'd better tell me all you can,' Leo said.

Declan placed the photograph on the pile and told him everything.

30

Several times he tried to make contact with Antonia. There was a telephone at his disposal, a fragile shell of white plastic into which he poured his heart twice a day for a week. Enquiries gave him Don Ortiz's official number, and every morning and every evening Leo rang the hacienda, and every time he got through he asked to speak to her, but the phone was cut off without a word of explanation. The better he felt in himself, the more certain he grew in his heart that she must be dead. He reckoned that he didn't have the kind of resources a man would need to go in pursuit of her. Wealth, and strength of body, and a crazy kind of willpower that isn't handed out to most Cambridge academics, or to most people of any kind.

Declan went to the ranch himself in order to question Don Ortiz who, he considered, probably knew something about the attacks on Leo; but he too was met with a blank wall, albeit a more polite one. When he asked to speak to Antonia, he was told she was no longer at the hacienda, that her family did not know her whereabouts. But no one looked him in the eye when they said that, and he was sure they were lying.

'I don't think they were telling the truth,' he said back in Dallas, 'but either way, I don't think you'll have an easy time of it trying to run her down.'

'How did her father strike you? I was told he was ruthless. A killer, perhaps.'

Declan nodded. He'd formed much the same impression. He knew he'd have to ask questions about Don Ortiz in places where he'd be unwelcome. And after Don Ortiz, questions about the late French Foreign Minister and his visit to Mexico.

'I heard one thing,' he said. 'I stayed the night in a little place called Carillo. It reminded me of somewhere out in Galway or Clare, a one-street town where the pub and the undertaker's are in the same house. There was a small church, and the priest asked me to spend the night with him. He was a young man, and when he found out I was Irish he was all over me. There'd been some Irish nuns in the neighbourhood a few years earlier, and they'd made a fine impression on your man.

'We talked about all sorts of things, and I discovered he was a bit of a radical, very keen on helping the Indians, that sort of thing. His English was great, though devil the chance he had of making much use of it out there. Well, the two of us downed a few glasses of *vino tinto*, toasted our ancestors, and talked. He did me good, that priest, I opened my heart to him and he didn't say a word of rebuke, can you imagine that? He even told me a few of his own sorrows in return.

'It was nearly time for putting out the lights and making our way up the wooden hill, when I happened to ask him about the man I'd come to see, Don Ortiz. I told him no details of the crimes, of course, for I had no right to cast suspicion on what was very likely to be a totally innocent man. But I fished for information. He told me a little, none of it good. And he mentioned something that had happened recently. It seems the *hacendado* also runs a bull-ranch about fifty miles away. It's one of the

275

biggest and best in Mexico: he supplies all the big plazas, his bulls are famous.

'But a couple of weeks ago, when you were still in prison, a handful of men went in to the ranch there one night and killed every last bull they set eyes on. He told me he went up to see for himself, that when he got there the rear pastures were covered with carcasses, as though giant cockroaches had crept in and died there. They'd used the sort of guns that are used in slaughterhouses, that send a bolt through the animal's skull. And some they'd cut their throats, so there was blood everywhere, you could never wash it from your boots afterwards.

'When Don Ortiz was given the news that morning, he was a broken man. The financial blow on its own must have been crippling, not to mention the near impossibility of ever building up an operation like that again. It's all to do with stock and breeding. He can never breed the bloodlines clear again. Of course, he has money in his other ranch, in his horses, and in any number of ventures I've not been able to identify as yet.'

Leo looked at him in bewilderment.

'Who would have done a thing like that to him?' he asked.

'A business rival? It's possible, though if word got out . . .' He hesitated. 'The priest mentioned a name. I tried to get more from him, but he clammed up. The name was Rafael. Does that mean anything to you? Ever heard of him?'

Leo shook his head.

'If you do, let me know.'

Leo made a good recovery, as all his doctors had predicted. There were scars he would carry all his life, long, ugly cicatrices that mapped his body strangely. It was not the same body as the one he'd carried into the jungle when he first set out on his expedition. Every time he bathed, every time he made love to a woman, there would be these vivid reminders of imprisonment and mortality.

Declan, meanwhile, went back down to Mexico City, where the other members of the expedition were still resting and waiting, having been released earlier on his insistence. He questioned them, but came away each time having learned nothing new. Some wanted to go home, others wished they could get back to the jungle site that housed their lost city. Diane Krauss had found a Mexican boyfriend, no one knew how, and had moved in with him to a small apartment in Chapultepec Morales.

Mount Popocatépetl erupted, sending a film of black ash forty miles north-west as far as the city. A plume of sulphurous ash sat above it, ominously predicting an eruption to come, but all seismic activity had ceased for the time being. Declan heard of the eruption while watching television in the bar of his hotel. He heard nothing, however, concerning the small eruptions of Tolimán, Atitlán, and San Pédro, the three volcanoes that fringe the southern shore of Lake Atitlán in Guatemala. And, though there were rumblings right down the Cordillera Volcánica, and in the volcanoes that make up the island of Ometepe in Lake Nicaragua, they were so faint that only departments of seismography in a handful of universities had wind of them; no news services learned of all this, and none reported anything unusual. Declan had his suit cleaned in a little *tintorería* just off the Zócalo. He learned the Spanish for 'pollution' and 'dust', and was charged a moderate sum. That night, the sun went down in a bath of blood.

In Dallas, Leo fretted. He had a telephone, but he was running out of people to ring. No one ever answered his parents' phone, it was as if they had slipped off the face of the earth, taking a direction he could not hope to follow. He spoke to colleagues in England and in certain American universities, in the hope that he might yet salvage the expedition, returning to the site with a fresh team next season. The fact that a major find had been made should have motivated people, got them queuing up behind him to get things moving and to overcome whatever barriers the Mexican authorities might try to put in his way.

At night he dreamt of pyramids stretched out across a grey horizon, pyramids whose temples blotted out the moon and whose stones ran red with the blood of innocent victims. He saw them tumbled all across the steep steps, men with their heads severed from their bodies, women with their breasts exposed and their hearts tipped sideways on to their arms. And he saw smoke rising from the temples, long spirals of smoke that floated across the jungle. Several times he seemed to wake to find himself in a dark inner chamber where someone was breathing next to him, and gold shimmered, and the serpent star Xiknalkan crept naked across rough stone from dawn to dawn.

One morning he rang Gwen, the departmental secretary at Cambridge, a terse woman of middle age, middle rank, and middle opinions who nevertheless ran her band of pusillanimous academics and boisterous students with an efficiency that always demanded admiration.

She set about Leo with a will, now sympathizing, now berating. They wanted him back in Cambridge as soon as possible, had he found time to finish his paper for the sixth annual conference of the British MesoAmerican Society, was he badly hurt, one of his postgraduate students desperately wanted to speak to him, what was the weather like where he was, they'd had freezing weather, some parts of the country had been cut off for a week, Professor Metcalf desperately needed his comments on the proposals for a change in the syllabus, his college urgently wanted to know if he would need his rooms for the coming term, she had a pile of mail that had been building up over the weeks for him, should she send it on together with whatever mail was waiting for him at college?

He asked about colleagues, students and old friends, and found the distance that had opened up between himself and his old life a crazy, crippling thing. For some reason, this made him cling with renewed vigour to his new life, whatever course it now took.

His medical insurance company started to play up, saying they'd paid out enough and that his claim merited no further payments. But Parkland Hospital employed some clever people to deal with precisely this sort of problem. They showed Leo how to fill out the right forms, how to compose the right letters, and how to identify the right people. In the end, a few judicious phone calls solved the problem: he could stay at Parkland until he was given a clean bill of health.

'How long?' he pestered his doctor for the seventeenth time that day.

'I told you, it's like string, depends where you cut.'

This was a new doctor, some sort of specialist they'd sent in to make an assessment. He was examining Leo's notes through half-moon glasses. These latter gave him a quiet academic look that was at odds with his loud checked shirt, blow-dried blond hair, and enormous cigar. Sam Bevins never lit the cigar on hospital premises, but he sucked it hard and was impervious to angry looks.

'Make a guess. I have to get out of this place.'

'Me too. Let's see your chart.' He made as if to consult it, tapping it here and there with his cigar.

'Could be a week. Could be two. Why are you so eager to be on your way?'

'I have a life to live. Just say the word and I'll be out of here.'

'Well, I ain't going to give the word today. You haven't made a full recovery, nothing like. I'd reckon on your being here another couple of weeks.'

'Can I have a computer, then? I want to get some work done.'

They lent him an i-Mac, and within half an hour he'd started downloading files from his own computer in Cambridge. The next few days went by with great speed, and he began to think he could stay in bed as long as they wanted. He started accessing the Internet, logging on to a number of academic forums he'd been involved with over the past year or two. Suddenly jolted out of an unnatural passivity, he began sending e-mails in every possible direction, contributing to unfinished debates, and downloading new translations of glyph texts that had been posted in the past few months.

That first evening, in order to wind down, he started browsing Websites. He spent a while at Amazon Books, charging a few titles to his account, then checked out sites on medicine, extradition treaties, and pyramids. There was little of interest anywhere, and he was preparing to close down when he recalled something Carberry had mentioned, a name, Rafael or Raphael, someone who might slaughter bulls, who might perhaps murder in the name of rivalry.

He went to Alta Vista and keyed in the British spelling, Raphael, since it was what he was most used to. As expected, dozens of sites were listed, perhaps hundreds. There was a St Raphael Community, a Hotel Excelsior at the French resort of St-Raphaël, Raphael, King of the Zodiac, and Raphael's MIDI Karaoke Page. Even Raphael the painter had his site, and no doubt the Pre-Raphaelites had theirs. But there was nothing here that hinted at dark deeds on the cattle ranches of Mexico.

He tried the Spanish spelling instead, Rafael. It was more logical, after all. More listings appeared, and he scanned them quickly, discarding most of them as he went, glancing at one or two before moving on to the list again: San Rafael Downtown Farmers Market, the Rafael Martez Brass Institute, Magic Rafael, the Rafael Development Corporation. He sighed and thought of dinner. There were sounds of its preparation in the distance. The Rafael's came at him like a tide and died softly on the shore.

What made him single it out, he never really knew. Some fatal instinct, some premonition, some psychic link that joined the two men like a bloodless umbilical cord? Or just dumb luck?

Rafael: Teacher and Guide the site-name read. Leo remembered something Antonia had mentioned in passing, that her mother was in the habit of visiting a guru of some kind, a native Indian shaman who screwed her for money and repaid in platitudes.

He clicked once and the site opened. Bit by bit, the components of an elaborate picture fitted themselves on to the screen. The picture was moving, rotating steadily like a vortex. It went spinning round, colours mixing with colours, shapes with shapes until Leo felt dizzy. And then, slowly, it came to a halt, and Leo found himself looking directly into a man's face. It was not just any face, but a face born of tribulation and greed.

Leo could not tear his eyes away, much as he wanted to do so.

He clicked on the centre of the picture, and the face dissolved. In its place was an elaborately-designed page of text. Leo read slowly, scrolling down with his mouse.

When we attend school, we have teachers. And later, at college or university or army training school, there are yet more teachers to guide us on our way, to instruct us in new things, and to remind us of the old. Yet most of us come away from our studies dissatisfied, filled with a sense that, if only this teacher had been more intelligent, or that one more in tune with his subject, they might have taught us better. We try to teach things to ourselves and learn that isn't any better.

Real teachers, teachers who can take us to the heart of a subject are rare. Rarer still are those who can instruct us in the truths of life itself. And rarest of all are those – perhaps one in every generation – who can inform us of what lies beyond ordinary life, and instruct us in the truths of immortality.

In recent years, many have sought the teacher of the age, but only a chosen handful have succeeded in finding the lonely path that leads to his door. He is among men, but known to none but those who truly love him and who see in him their guide and their redeemer. The world is full of traps for the unwary, and its cities are overflowing with false Messiahs and deceitful prophets. Do not be deceived. Only one man in this age has passed through the gates of life and returned. Only one man possesses the key to that doorway, only one teacher can instruct us in the realities of this life and the afterlife . . .

Easily tired, Leo stopped reading and downloaded the rest of the Website to his hard disk. It sounded as if he had stumbled on the right man. But the right man for what, he wondered?

Next morning, a little sack of mail arrived for him. His heart sank at the thought of how much work might be lurking inside the Federal Mail bag they handed him; but the moment he saw the contents, with their endless college circulars, interdepartmental mailings, and scribbled notes from students and colleagues he felt a sudden sense of connection. It was almost like being home again.

The box was almost the last thing, clinging to the bottom of the package like a grey limpet. Made of stout card, it had been firmly taped on all sides. The tell-tale trails of staples were visible beneath the tape. Leo turned it over. It was addressed to him at his department, the inscription executed in fine, legible handwriting. On the back were the name and address of the sender: *Mgr! Luis de Sepúlveda, Îles de la petite terre, Guadeloupe, Leeward Islands.*

Inside he found a handwritten letter, an ancient, folded map, and some sheets of paper of about the same date, sewn together and bound in a narrow modern binding of the finest leather. Tucked away at the bottom of the box, he found an airline ticket offering first-class return passage from any airport in the world to Guadeloupe.

He stared at the ticket for a long time, and thought hard about the destination. He had never been to Guadeloupe, and, to the best of his knowledge, knew no one who lived there. But there could be no mistake. The ticket had been made out in his name.

31

Îles de la petite terre
Guadeloupe
21 December

He'd dreamt of places like this, but never woken to anything that even came close. He'd got up that morning, still tired from his flight, and thrown back his shutters to see a veil of pure white sand, and sea lapping it, in all the shades of blue and green, as though the feathers of every kind of bird had been cast into the water and their colours leached into it.

His muscles still ached abominably, and his scars still burned where their stitches had recently been removed; but something about the island was already soothing him and telling him the pain didn't matter. It was a sort of paradise, and with every minute he spent there he felt its healing properties work their way inside him.

Leo had arrived the night before. He'd flown from Dallas to Miami and then down to Guadeloupe the previous day. At Guadeloupe airport he'd been met by a small black man with a warm smile that turned out to be the only answer he would ever give to Leo's questions. His escort had driven through Pointe-à-Pitre and on down the coast to a small fishing village called St François.

There, a motor-boat had been waiting to take them out to the island where Leo's host lived.

On his arrival, Leo was shown straight to the small bungalow which was to be his. A light supper was prepared on the veranda, and soon it was time for bed. His host had not put in an appearance by then, and Leo gave up on the chance of seeing him until the next day.

He found breakfast laid out for him on the table on the veranda. Just one setting, as for supper. He had expected to find at least a note to say when his host planned to visit him, or to find instructions as to what he was expected to do; but he could see nothing of that description. The food was delicious, mostly fresh fruit and a variety of breads. A lot of it would have been brought in from somewhere off the island, probably St François or Pointe-à-Pitre. The island he was on seemed too small and uninhabited to sustain much in the way of agriculture.

Hot coffee was kept at a constant temperature on an electric plate. Glancing at it, Leo realized that he had scarcely noticed the many refinements of the quarters he occupied: electric lights, a refrigerator, a heated shower, a television, a telephone – all powered, he guessed, from some generator on the island.

As he ate, his slight impatience ebbed away. He watched the waves crashing gently on the shore, and the tall palms feathering in a soft breeze. Wherever he looked, he could see that the island was a place made to relax in, as though God had stepped in during its creation and granted it a special status among the places of the earth.

After breakfast, he lay down for a while and fell into a light doze. A few times he awoke, but quickly the doze became real sleep; each time he re-entered it, it became a little deeper until, for the first time in weeks, he slept soundly, without nightmares. When he finally awoke, his wounds were still marked on his skin, but they seemed less harsh, as though sleep had softened them. Sleep would have been a balm had it not been for the constant thought of Antonia, and the growing knowledge that he might never see her again, or hear her, or sleep beside her.

Someone, anticipating his needs, had placed a pair of white bathing trunks on a rail in the bathroom. He undressed and slipped them on, then ran out to the beach. Moments later, he was swimming with all his strength out to sea. At first the raw salt stung his wounds dreadfully, almost forcing him to turn back. But he fought on through the pain until it subsided and was replaced by a sense of fullness, as though the scars had fed on the salt.

It was only as the pain receded and he allowed himself to take proper note of his surroundings that he realized he might be taking a very real risk swimming so far out. No one knew he was out here, and should anything go wrong, he'd be unable to summon help. Treading water, he looked back, and his heart missed several beats when, for half a minute, he could not make out the island at all. The *Îles de la petite terre* are small islets on the very edge of the Guadeloupe group, and beyond them lies the open and frequently perilous sea.

Struggle as he might, he could see no sign of land in any direction, and all at once he grew uncertain as to the way he had come. He became frightened that he might not have left himself enough strength to swim all the way back again, even if he could find his way.

Then he saw a hill he had noticed earlier, or just a small rise, topped by a modest wooden structure like a shrine. It bobbed into sight, then out again, but he took a bearing on it and fixed it when it appeared for a second time.

He started to crawl back, fighting against the high ocean waves. Time and again he thought he was about to die. His body was still in poor shape, and his muscles set up a cry that all they wanted to do was throw up their hands and give up the struggle. He shouted down their voices inside his skull, and crawled and kicked his way towards a more visible shore. Once, lifting his head to see better, he saw a man's figure etched on the shoreline, someone dressed in black, who seemed to watch him intently as he fought his way to safety.

He staggered out of the water, coughing and spluttering, and collapsed on his knees in the spume, as though he had come to the beach by way of pilgrimage. Instead of kissing the ground, however, he started to throw up, then fell on to the foreshore, still straining. He was barely conscious of someone taking hold of him solicitously, and of a man's voice raised in French, summoning assistance.

He came to on the bed in the bungalow. *Groundhog Day* again. Frightened, he tried to call out and at the same time raise himself to a sitting position, but a gentle hand pressed him back and the voice he'd heard earlier told him to rest. The realization swept over him of how foolish he'd been, and his stomach felt suddenly empty.

He opened his eyes again and tried to focus them. This time he managed to move himself higher on to the pillow. An old man dressed in black was sitting on a chair near the bed. On his lap he held a straw hat, a ragged old thing full of holes. He was watching Leo closely, running his eyes concernedly along the wounds that covered his body.

'These seem fresh,' he said.

Leo judged him to be a very old man, ninety or perhaps more. That judgement was based mainly on the face, which was made up almost entirely of lines, among which the most striking were those around the eyes, lines of humour rather than pain. The old man was frail but unstooped, and his eyes were the brightest blue, as though he had just fished them from the warm waters outside. The eyes radiated warmth, and in a matter of moments Leo felt at ease.

'I did not know about this,' the old man said, letting a long-boned hand sweep the length of Leo's body. 'They seem very angry, very inflamed; but that will be the salt mostly, and the heat. I don't recommend you return to the sea without first covering yourself in oil of some kind. If you want to swim, there is a freshwater pool at the main house. By the way, my name is Luis de Sepúlveda. I am your host. You must forgive me if I don't speak such good English.'

In fact, he spoke it very well. Leo added that to the other mysteries surrounding the priest.

'I'm sorry to have given you such a fright. It was stupid of me,' he said. 'Completely reckless.'

The priest looked indulgently into his eyes.

'Tell me how you came by those wounds,' he said. He made no apologies for thus invading Leo's privacy. There was something simple about him, Leo realized; or perhaps not simple, but he could not readily find another word. Not then, at least. Later, in the heart of the jungle, in that deep darkness, it would occur to him. Holy.

Leo spoke readily enough about the wounds. But one thing led to another, and the rest of the day passed in an account of what had happened to him in Mexico. When he finished, the old man seemed very pensive.

'I have tired you out,' he said, rising. 'Next time, you should just tell me to leave.' He went to the door. 'We shall talk again at dinner. Now, I think you owe yourself a little sleep. And no more swimming, please.'

*   *   *

The black servant arrived for Leo shortly before seven o'clock. It was dark by then, but the path between the bungalow and the main building, up a steep slope and to the right, was brightly lit. Low lights like small earth-bound moons ran along neatly-trimmed grass verges. Above them, the sky was a chocolate-box crammed with lights.

As they approached the longest wall of the main build-ing, a lit window drew Leo's attention. Beyond it lay a softly-illuminated room, on whose far wall hung an enormous mirror. As Leo watched, a woman came into the room, a tall woman of perhaps thirty, dark-haired, simply- but well-dressed. She stepped to the window and looked out once on the night before closing wooden shutters.

There was little opportunity for Leo to see the house at first. Glimpses of undecorated white walls, some large vases filled with simple flowers, a plainly-carved wooden statue of the Virgin, and above it what seemed to be a dove's wing, set alone.

The meal was served in a long dining room deceptively furnished in the simplest of styles. Leo saw right away that the furnishings, for all that they seemed pared down, were of the very highest quality. The dining table and chairs alone probably cost as much as Leo's bungalow. On the wall overlooking the top chair was a single painting: a child might have pronounced on the name of the artist, though the specific painting was not so easily identified.

The priest entered, still dressed in the long soutane he had worn earlier. It still had no collar, but the old man had brushed his hair and shaved.

'I'm sorry if I'm a little late,' he said apologetically. 'You must think me a very perfunctory host.'

'Not from where I'm sitting,' insisted Leo. 'I find myself

in a place that might quite reasonably be described as paradise, my ticket paid for, my accommodation *gratis*. If that's perfunctory, I'd hate to see you taking trouble.'

They sat to table at once.

'You'll see that we don't observe all the niceties of civilization here. You'll be accustomed to High Table, of course. Passing the port in the right direction. Chit-chat in the Senior Common Room beforehand. Trying not to fall asleep afterwards. Which college are you a Fellow of?'

'King's.'

'I've eaten there. I was Rawlinson's guest. Before your time.'

'By quite a few years, I'd think.'

'I'm quite an old man.'

Leo's eyes rose again to the painting on the wall behind the old man. He was no expert, but he'd guess this was early, a few years before *Guernica*.

The priest caught his gaze.

'He gave it to me himself,' he said. 'He'd just moved in to the new studio at Boisgeloup. It's a portrait of Marie-Thérèse Walter. She'd have been, what? Eighteen, nineteen? I met her one evening over dinner and quite fell in love with her. I must have been twenty-five or six. He'd have been fifty-something.'

So, not 'early' after all, thought Leo. He was glad he hadn't said anything.

'Why would a priest –'

At that moment, a young woman entered carrying a polished wooden bowl. She was not the woman Leo had glimpsed through the window earlier. As he watched, she served up the first course, which the priest said was turtle eggs cooked in red wine. The girl vanished. Conversation hesitated while Leo got to grips with the eggs.

'I've never tried turtle eggs before,' he said.

'Then take your time. You'll find them delicious. We're quite fortunate: the turtles come every year to a beach on the north of the island in order to lay their eggs. We take what we need and make sure the remainder are well protected from predators. Those that we don't eat fresh we freeze.'

Leo bit into one.

'Delicious,' he said.

There was renewed silence for a while as they ate. The eggs tasted rich and winey, with a salty edge, like gannet's eggs cooked in samphire.

'My name is Luis de Sepúlveda. I hold the honorary ecclesiastical title of Monsignor, but it means nothing, I am just an ordinary priest. This is my parish, this little island. Its proper name is St Juste. I first set foot on it eighty years ago. It was almost barren then, but my father built a little hut down by the beach. He bought the island first as a refuge, then the other islands of the group in order to protect it from being encroached on by commerce or tourism.'

He ate the last of his eggs and mopped up the remaining moisture with a piece of French bread, then gestured to Leo to do the same. The bread was delicious, as though it had just come from the oven.

'Does my name mean anything to you?'

Leo pondered for a moment. The eggs had left a creamy taste in his mouth.

'You wrote a paper on Mayan artefacts of the Xe horizon. It was in the *Journal of Meso-American Studies* some time ago.'

'Over twenty years. There have been a few others.'

'I read it when I was researching for my Ph. D. I seem to remember it was quite an impressive paper. And I remember wondering then just who you were. I've never seen you at a conference or –'

The old man shook his head.

'I am past all that,' he said. 'But I pursue my studies as well as I can. I have been following your researches closely. Everything I've seen of your work so far has impressed me. I'm eager to learn more about the city you've just been excavating. Perhaps we can spend a little time speaking about it after dinner.'

Leo felt flustered. He'd brought no notes, no materials. But the paper he'd read had been the product of a sharp, enquiring brain, a brain that, so far as he could tell, had suffered no deterioration in the twenty years that had followed.

'I'd be glad to,' he said. 'But I can't believe you brought me all the way here just for that. The report will be published in due course.'

'I am over ninety years old, Doctor Mallory. "Due course" to me as often as not means "Never". But you're perfectly right: I didn't inconvenience you to this extent merely to satisfy my curiosity about your recent dig. I have a rather more serious purpose. I wish to put a proposal to you, a proposal of employment, if you like – though I hope it may be seen as more than that.'

'Employment? I don't understand. I have my post at Cambridge. This island –'

'The employment would not be on this island. Please do not be misled, Doctor Mallory. I am a priest, and so I live a very simple life and attend to the needs of my tiny parish. But even priests have families, even priests inherit money. I inherited more than a little. I am a very wealthy man, wealthier, I think, than King's College or the Cambridge Department of Archaeology.'

'But I have students to teach, seminars –'

'I don't want you here, Doctor. I want to finance an expedition with you as its leader. An archaeological expedition of the utmost importance. I hope you will at least give my proposal some consideration.'

'But, I . . . What sort of expedition do you mean?'

'The usual sort of expedition. I want you to find a city for me. A Mayan city that has been lost in the deepest jungle for centuries now.'

Leo laughed, partly from relief, partly from a sense of how preposterous this sounded.

'You expect me to set off into some uncharted tract of jungle and come out the other side with photographs of a lost city?'

'You will have a map. And an eye-witness account of how to find what you seek.'

'And do you expect me to find anything there? Gold, perhaps?'

There was a long pause. The girl came in and removed their bowls. A wine stain spread slowly across one corner of Leo's napkin. Picasso's portrait smiled at him enigmatically.

The priest shook his head. 'No,' he said, 'not gold. I have more than enough of that already. You are to look for something else. You are to return with the secret of eternal life.'

32

If it had not been for the priest, and if it had not been for all he later learned of him, Leo might have turned his back on the expedition then. Lives might have been saved, and more than just lives. But if Leo had turned him down, the priest would have gone elsewhere. He had the money, he could have hired whole departments. But who in his right mind would have turned down the priest's proposal anyway? It took Leo moments to make up his mind, and a couple of days to own up to it.

When the dinner things had been cleared away, they took the last of the wine and their glasses and retired to a room just behind the one they'd dined in. The walls of this second room were covered with Picassos. There were pieces representative of every period, and in every medium in which the artist had worked: oils, collages, etchings, aquatints, lithographs, and, on plinths, plaster heads from Boisgeloup and ceramics from Vallauris.

Leo sipped his wine and set the glass down on a table by his chair.

'This is extraordinary wine,' he said.

De Sepúlveda nodded and took a sip from his own glass.

'Romanée-Conti. One of the rarest wines you can buy. This bottle came from the La Romanée-Conti vineyard itself. It's a tiny vineyard, just four and a half acres, one of the smallest Appellation Contrôlées in the whole of France. It produces maybe five thousand bottles a year. Most wine drinkers never see a bottle, let alone drink some.'

'You're wasting it on me. I'm no wine expert.'

De Sepúlveda smiled. 'Are you enjoying it?'

Leo nodded.

'Then it hasn't been wasted.'

Leo took another mouthful, carefully rolling the smooth wine round his mouth. He looked round the walls.

'I'm not sure I believe this room,' he said. 'Are they really all . . . ?'

'My father started the collection,' said de Sepúlveda. 'After he died I still paid visits to Picasso's studios, at least once a year. Mostly I bought, always from him directly; sometimes he would make a present of a canvas or a ceramic. Do you like painting?'

Leo stammered out what little he knew of art in general or in particular. Of his love of the Symbolists and his fascination for de Chirico.

'Your family must have been very rich,' he said, 'to have bought all these.'

The old man shook his head.

'Well, not so very rich, perhaps. Not then, at least. My father had a good eye. He recognized young painters and bought their work at good prices. Soutine, Gris, the Delauneys when they were in Madrid, Modigliani, and some less-known names: Marcoussis, Gleizes, Jean Metzinger. The rest of the family collection is kept in Madrid. I sold about one third of it ten years ago. It fetched several million dollars. The income allows me to live here very comfortably and to indulge my interests.'

'You don't have a church to look after? Or can priests retire?'

'Of course we can retire, though not all of us do so. However, I hold no official position with the Church. Let's just say that the Vatican and I don't entirely see eye to eye.'

He poured rum into small elegant glasses.

'This is Appleton's Special,' he said. 'Al' de way from Jamayca.' He spoke in a perfect imitation of a Jamaican accent. 'I spent two years there. I've lived in more countries than you can imagine. Over twenty years of my life were passed in Mexico, most of them in Chiapas. I first visited the city you have just been excavating forty years ago.'

'Komchen?'

'We never discovered its name. You must remember our knowledge of the glyphs was minimal back then.'

'How did you . . . ? I'm sorry, I don't understand. You say you found the city. But there are no reports of a discovery from that period.'

'You won't find any. Those we kept were destroyed soon afterwards.'

'Afterwards?'

'After the decision to keep its existence a secret. To say nothing to anyone about what we had found.'

'I still don't understand. You were an archaeologist?'

The priest shook his head. 'Only an amateur. I've made progress since then, but I've always been an amateur. Nevertheless, in 1952 I set up a society for the study of Mayan history in San Cristóbal. We gave it the grand title of the Association for Mayan History and Archaeology. Membership grew rapidly, mostly schoolteachers and bank clerks with nothing better to do on a Saturday afternoon but travel out to the local sites. We went mostly to Palenque, and quite often to Bonampak, which had only been discovered a few years earlier. Then someone said we should do our own excavating.

'We had an offer of help from a professor at the university, a man called Francisco Gomez, the brother of Enrique, you may have heard of them.'

'Of course. I've read all Francisco's books on Palenque. But I've never heard anything about your Association.'

'Well, it didn't last very long. Francisco was quite eminent by then, of course, but he always needed field workers, preferably volunteers who would embark on digs without pay. He used to take groups of us out at weekends, up into the Lacandón Forest. There were old Indian legends that suggested the existence of other cities in the area. You're probably aware of them. Most of them led us nowhere, but one . . . Well, I think you came upon Komchen by the same methods.'

'It was almost by accident. One of our group stumbled across a giant head. Once we started looking, we found more and more of the city beneath the overgrowth.'

'Yes, it was very overgrown in my day as well. Anyway, we spent about a year there, mostly clearing the forest away from the central pyramid. We'd no idea there was anything underneath the pyramid, of course. All our excavation work was quite superficial. But we knew it was a major discovery, we were immensely proud of what we'd achieved.'

In the distance, waves broke on the empty shore, as though the world out there in the darkness had become a conch through which the rolling of the sea could be heard.

'What happened?' Leo asked.

'To our city?' De Sepúlveda gave a half-smile. 'We abandoned it. We let the forest grow around it again.'

'But . . . I don't understand. Why would you want to do such a thing?'

'We didn't want to. But our Association was entirely controlled by the Church. Such things were more common then. I applied to the Bishop of San Cristóbal for funds, and he supplied them quite willingly. He always wished to appear a generous patron of the arts and sciences, and I won't deny that he did a lot of good with his benefactions. In our case, however, his involvement turned out to be disastrous.

'Those were the days before Pope John XXIII and Vatican II. Some prelates had real power and knew how to use it. I'd taken Bishop Bienvenida at face value: a bit conservative, especially in matters of Church doctrine, politically reactionary – as practically all our bishops were in those days – but a genuine *padrino*, capable of great generosity, a man of learning and taste.

'On the contrary, he turned out to be the most benighted old bigot I've ever known. Listening to him talk at times, it was as if the old-style Inquisition had never ended. He'd thought our Association was a sort of Sunday afternoon club devoted to discussion of the Conquistadors and how they'd brought the Gospel to the savages of this continent. When I told him we'd found an entire Mayan city, complete with idols and temples and God knows what other hidden treasures, he hit the roof. He turned on me as though I'd just threatened to burn his cathedral down. To this day I can see his face: he went purple from the neck up, and I was genuinely frightened that he'd choke to death or have a stroke.

'Unfortunately, he went on for another thirty years, in spite of all the reforms in the Church. In the meantime, he closed us down. He didn't just withdraw his own funding, he made sure nobody else gave us a penny or ever

298

would. A few of our members were more independent and thought they could treat a Mexican bishop like an Anglican vicar. They all lived to regret it. The school-teachers were dismissed from their posts, the bank clerks were posted to parts of the country no one had ever heard of, and never came back, and the one or two businessmen who might have thought themselves immune from his influence quickly found their customers falling away. Within six months they'd all shut up shop and gone elsewhere.'

The priest's words were followed by silence, as if to emphasize the vastness of the bishop's domain, the extent of one man's power. Leo thought about Antonia's father, and about the mysterious figure called Rafael, who was rumoured to have inflicted so much damage on him. He wondered if de Sepúlveda knew of them.

'What about you?' he asked. 'You had money, didn't you?'

'You're right. I could have financed several expeditions. But I was a priest. In those days, I was dedicated to my vocation, I believed the Church hierarchy was to be obeyed. Bishops, cardinals, and Popes were close to God, and their slightest whims were to be obeyed. I could no more have disobeyed Bienvenida than turned my heart against God Himself. Try to understand. It was a different world.'

'Not so very different, perhaps. People still long for authority. They want prophets and gurus and teachers, someone to follow, someone to obey.'

De Sepúlveda nodded. 'In the end I came to see things differently. But it seemed too late to re-open the dig. I was getting old, I was no longer in Mexico. It all savoured too much of the past. Except . . .' He paused. 'I could not quite break myself away from my studies. There were questions to which I wanted answers. And the answers were being given in the translations of Maya inscriptions that started to appear. But that wasn't all. There was something else, something only I knew about. I sent you a copy of a map. Did you get it?'

Leo nodded.

'It has no particular value on its own,' said the priest. 'It's part of a set drawn in 1561 by an ancestor of mine, Joaquín de Sigüenza y Góngora. He was an *oidor*, one of the four judges appointed to sit on the Audiencia of Guatemala in 1559. It was one of his jobs to travel through the region of Chiapas, collecting information on the condition of the Indians and how far the local *encomenderos* were observing the New Laws of 1542.

'My ancestor was a conscientious man. He left a memoir in which he gives full details of his travels, his struggles with those responsible for mistreating the Indians in defiance of royal decree, and his attempts to record the various towns and settlements he passed through. He made maps like the one I sent you, very detailed maps that show, not just the Spanish settlements, but the Aztec and Mayan villages and – what is much more interesting – their ruins.'

'How come I've never heard of this account?'

'The memoir and the maps were originally intended to be sent directly to King Philip. I have the letter that Don Joaquín wrote to accompany them. Needless to say, they were never forwarded. Don Joaquín made a lot of enemies among the *encomenderos*, and his report was never made public. Of course, there were details about some of his activities in letters and other documents. The family always knew the basic facts of his life, but no more.

'It was only a few years ago that all this changed. My

brother Alonso died. Until then I'd been little more than a wealthy priest. Suddenly, I found myself in possession of what seems like unlimited wealth. It's given me certain freedoms, certain powers of influence.

'From all sorts of indications, I was certain that a copy of Don Joaquín's *Relación* had remained intact, that it must be buried somewhere in the Spanish or Mexican archives. I employed researchers in both countries, and they dug their way through every library and every record office they could find. In the end it proved very simple. In his last years, Don Joaquín was closely associated with the Franciscans in Guatemala. He'd always admired the friars because they treated the Indians well, and his closest friend was Fray Gerónimo de San Francisco.

'One of my researchers found Joaquín's report in the Franciscan archives of Guatemala City. There was a note accompanying it, saying that the *Relación* was to be sent to Spain, for the attention of His Imperial Majesty. Instead, it had remained buried in those archives down through the centuries, waiting for someone to stumble on it again.'

He got up and crossed to a table on which sat a highly-polished box of mahogany. From it he took a book bound in embossed leather, and a sheaf of other papers, stained and dried with age.

'He wrote about the city in the last chapter of his report. There's an accompanying map, similar in style to the one I sent you. Take them to bed with you tonight. Read what you can. Joaquín's style isn't always easy, and his handwriting leaves much to be desired. But he does his best to tell his story directly. He won't try to mislead you.'

Leo took the book and maps. They felt dry in his hands, and brittle. An odour came from them, damp and cold, and some ancient perfume.

De Sepúlveda seemed relieved to be rid of his charges. He stood in the doorway, seeing Leo out into the tropical night.

'Some say he is still alive,' he said.

'I'm sorry? Who's still alive?' Leo asked.

'Joaquín de Sigüenza y Góngora, of course. There is a tradition in my family to that effect. They say that when he came back from his last expedition he was greatly changed. He had found something in the depths of the jungle, something that made him different to other men. My own father told me this, and he in turn had heard it from his own father. That when Don Joaquín left the jungle, he left it with the secret of eternal life. That he never died. That he is still alive.'

Leo felt the book nestling in his arms. For a moment, he had thought he felt it move, as though it had acquired life.

'I'm glad to know of it,' he said. He started down the steps.

'Doctor Mallory . . .'

'Yes?'

'I wish you good night. Sleep well and wake refreshed.'

Leo thanked him and continued on his way. But he was sure the priest had been about to say something quite different.

33

He did not attempt to read the *Relación* that night. Too many thoughts, too many speculations crammed his head. He lay awake in visible darkness, dreaming without sleep. There was no need to close his eyes. Pictures came to him out of nowhere, like waters lapping an ancient pier, eating it away stanchion by stanchion. He saw a tract of dense rainforest run away from him, dark and green, its floor covered with fallen, moss-eaten logs, and out of nowhere masses of web-spinning spiders, each one the size of a man's head, covered the undergrowth and spread themselves high up into the canopy of treetops. Cobwebs as big as curtains began to obscure the light where it fell from above, until the path ahead was no more than a long tunnel gripped by long legs and scuttling bodies.

He shuddered and opened his eyes. A moon had risen and was filling the untouched sky with light. He got out of bed and walked on to the terrace. Sea and beach were bathed in the same white light, an earthly substance. High above the moon, a satellite passed, a detached thing, belonging to neither sky nor earth. Leo imagined a man in the robes of an *oidor*, walking through forest, his hand at a horse's high rein. He seemed weary and alone; by his side, a long sword swung as he walked.

He closed his eyes, and in an instant he saw something else, a city of stone set among trees. At first he thought it must be a ruin, Komchen or Palenque or Chichén Itzá, but when he studied it more closely, its streets and houses seemed perfect, its doorways and windows betrayed no signs of decay. An old man, his body decked with feathers, sidled along an alleyway. Blood dripped from a knife. A serpent glided between fallen stones, insinuating its brightly-coloured coils through the cavities of eyes and mouths. Nearby, a child walked along a precipice and fell, eyes wide open, staring at the sun. Leo opened his eyes and heard the surf roar against rocks half a mile along the beach.

Ganadería El Turuño

Antonia sat on the edge of her bed, trembling. The night outside was freezing, and there seemed to lie nothing but emptiness and the eternal cold between her and any hope of safety. She could not bear the thought of so much emptiness, but she had to get out, and soon.

In the days immediately following the slaughter of his bulls, her father had gone half-insane. Everyone had stayed out of his way, even María Cristina and Ruiz Arjona. Antonia had insisted on their calling her father's doctor; but when the man drove up to the ranch he was met by a hail of bullets and had to drive straight off again. He sent packets of tablets after that, and they'd be left in Don Ortiz's bedroom at every opportunity. But in the morning the maid would find them floating in the toilet bowl. The Don and his rage were one, and he would be no more parted from it than from his own heart.

He'd roamed the *ganadería* with a pistol permanently in his belt, looking with glazed eyes for someone to kill. All he'd wanted had been revenge, hot or cold, he didn't care. During that period, Antonia had taken refuge with her

Aunt Consuela, living in the small bungalow she occupied at the back of the ranch. Her mother had taken the first plane out of Chihuahua for Mexico City, and once there she'd gone to ground, neither making nor receiving telephone calls. A professional bodyguard watched over her day and night. He was armed to the teeth, a lonely man with no true affiliations, an Englishman who'd served long years with the SAS. He had little wings tattooed on his shoulder, like a butterfly, and María Cristina thought he was cute. Rafael rang a few times, but she ignored his calls and desperately hoped he would turn his grotesque attentions elsewhere. She was displeased that he had become so obsessed with her daughter, that he would slaughter for her, or offer unimaginable amounts of money to make her his.

Don Ortiz had spent about a week in the worst madness, without undressing or washing, sleeping or eating. From time to time, Antonia had seen him riding past, slumped in his saddle, or walking with his feet dragging, and if she saw his face it was almost unrecognizable to her, and she'd drawn out of his way, watching him go past from whatever hiding-place she could make for herself.

Later, Ruiz had told her that if her father had stumbled on her in that state, he would certainly have killed her with a blow or a gunshot. He had grown convinced that the person responsible for the tragedy was Rafael, and he drew a direct line between Rafael and Antonia. In reality, he knew next to nothing of Rafael or the power of his attraction to his daughter, an attraction so great he would gladly have seen all his other dominions perish for its sake.

One afternoon, when about two weeks had passed, she took advantage of her father's absence from the *ganadería* in order to visit the main house. She found the servants there all jumpy. Several had left during the previous fortnight, and those who stayed on were the unfortunates who had nowhere else to go and stuck it out in the hope things would turn round. Had it not been for Ruiz, his devotion to Don Ortiz, and his love for the *ganadería*, things would have been infinitely worse. He saw to it that wages were paid, victuals laid in, meals produced, horses groomed and fed, bringing in supplies from the *hacienda* for the purpose. He also made sure that a constant armed guard was kept over Antonia.

She asked if she could return to the *hacienda*, but was told that Don Ortiz had left explicit orders to the contrary. Then she asked if she could ring her mother, and Ruiz gave permission. Five times she tried, with no success. Her guard sat in the far corner of the room, bored and careless. She had no confidence in him. When she put the phone down for the last time, Carmela, the housekeeper, approached her and, speaking in a low voice, told her that a man had rung the hacienda several times a day for the past week and more, always asking for her by name; his calls had never been put through, but he had persisted in ringing until about three days ago. Had he left his name? asked Antonia, feeling her heart beat, feeling it pound like the hoofs of frightened bulls within the tight confines of her chest.

'Not at first,' said Carmela. 'But the last time he did. He said his name was Leo. And he left a telephone number.'

The beach was bone-white and hot, and utterly free of footprints or other markings. Small sea creatures clung to it, some sucking moisture from its depths, some already dying in the harsh sunshine. Leo felt like Robinson Crusoe. No signs of human habitation were visible from where he stood. He looked back along the way he'd come. A line of coconut and royal palms stood between him and the bungalow, and none of the other buildings were visible from this far back. He walked hard on down the beach, scanning it for footprints or for whatever flotsam and jetsam might have been washed up by the last tide.

He looked out to sea. It seemed as though Matisse, haunted by a dream of Tangier, had painted it, sweep after sweep, in a collage of blues and greens: flecks of turquoise and teal, swirls of celadon and ultramarine. Bright pools of gentian and cyan marked, far out, the outline of a coral reef. And the sky pressed down, closer and closer, cerulean touched here and there with the thinnest streaks of white, like gauze.

He looked behind him again, along the ragged line of footprints that his feet had left in the wet sand. All the time, he thought of Antonia, and the impossibility of contacting her so long as she was kept at her father's home. If de Sepúlveda's project was to take him back to Mexico, and if he were to find a way to track her down and rescue her, he was more than willing to take whatever risks that might involve.

He came at last to a point where the beach ended. Heavy rocks had tumbled from a height just above into the sea, forming a long needle that ran out for two hundred yards or more into the nuzzling waves.

His first thought was to climb over the rocks to the other side, in order to pick up the beach where it continued, as he presumed it must. As he started to scramble over, however, his eye was caught by a path that twisted its way out of sight into the hill above. Little fat balls of melon cactus decorated the edges of the path, their spines caught by clumps of wool, serving notice that this must be a goat-track between the beach and the interior of the island.

The hill looked to be neither too steep nor too rough for him to risk a climb before lunch. As soon as he started his ascent, he was sure the little track was man-made, cut through the hill to provide a means of access for more than goats. Fifteen minutes later, he was less certain. The narrow trail cut elegantly through clumps of tangled undergrowth, growing steeper and more difficult every few yards. He was about to call it a day and turn back when he noticed that he was not, after all, so very far from the crest of the hill. His nostrils were filled with the scent of a million winter-flowering plants, and his skin burned with the heat of the lifting sun.

As the path started to flatten out, he looked up and saw something he would never forget, that nothing would have led him to forget in this place.

Towering above him to a height of sixty feet or more, was a Mayan pyramid, or, if not that exactly, the very image of one. He stood staring at it, unable to take it in at first. It was painted red, exactly as the original pyramids had been, and the temple that sat on its shoulders was multicoloured.

He hurried up the remaining stretch of goat-path, emerging through a clump of purple bougainvillea on to a broad sward of grass and flowers. Right ahead of him, steps rose up the face of the pyramid to the temple. A broad avenue of manchineel trees led him to their foot.

For the first time since starting out on his walk, he felt alone and unprotected. A cold breeze made his light shirt feel inadequate. He did not expect to find an entrance to the pyramid at ground level, and after only a few minutes' hesitation, started up the steps. It was not a long climb, but the higher he went, the colder and more exposed he felt. Wherever he looked ahead of him, he could see only the blood-red outer surface of the pyramid. He wondered

308

what it was for. Did it serve de Sepúlveda as a monument, a shrine, a chapel, or perhaps a tomb? If so, to whom was it dedicated, and who was buried in it?

The last step was a broad one, offering no choice to the climber but to start back down again or enter the gaudily-painted temple through its single narrow door. He hesitated only momentarily.

High up in the temple's sides, a few pierced windows let in light. The result was a dimness that exposed wide areas of the walls while leaving others in half-shadow or total darkness. It took his eyes a minute or two to adjust to the strange light, and longer to allow the darkness to fit him to itself.

He was in a large rectangular room with a high ceiling and a single door that lay behind him. He could not at first make out what took up so much of the wall ahead of him. It seemed out of all proportion to the room and everything else in it, shadowy and unshadowed, and he could make no sense of it at first, neither its head, that vanished into the shadows near the ceiling, nor its feet, that seemed locked within a spectacular darkness on the floor. He saw feathers, bright with all imaginable colours, and a man's face contorted in pain, and hands stretched out and somehow mutilated, all on a scale above the human. And his eyes adjusted further to the shadowiness of everything, the room and its purple silence, the rising and dipping light, and the slow brooding of the dappled dark.

What he saw at last took his breath away, then and every time he thought about it in the long days afterwards. Most of the wall was occupied by a cross, and on it hung the tortured figure of a Mayan chief, nailed to it hand and feet, wearing full ceremonial costume, a vast back-frame from which feathers radiated in the shape of an enormous fan, green and red and yellow, the tail feathers of all manner of tropical birds, above all the sacred *quetzal* feathers. On his feet he wore jaguar sandals, and on his back there hung a jaguar robe, stained with his own blood. The huge Christ figure seemed to rear up against the humiliation and pain of the cross, as though trapped in a desperate attempt to break away, held there as much by the weight of his own feathers as by the nails that pinned him to the unbearable wood. He could neither fly nor submit, and in his face Leo looked in vain for the slightest hint of a wounded saviour.

Immediately beneath this extraordinary crucifix stood a low, white-clothed altar, atop which stood the vessels necessary to the celebration of the Mass. None of these seemed at all unusual. Someone had brought flowers and placed them in two vases, one at either end of the altar table: hibiscus, abutilon, protea, lilies, and bright red bromeliads.

Leo's attention passed to the other walls. His eyesight was adjusting quickly to the strange half-light. On every wall he found fixed a series of paintings and sculptural pieces, almost in the manner of an art gallery. But it became quickly apparent as he walked among them that they had been placed there in order to convey a higher significance than that suggested by mere works of art.

One of the first things he came upon was a print he recognized as the work of the German artist George Grosz. It showed another crucifix, in which the emaciated figure of Christ wore a First World War gas mask and military boots. It and two other prints had been the occasion for a great controversy and a public trial of the artist not many years before the Nazis came to power.

Near it stood a sculpture, almost certainly the work of Jacob Epstein, portraying the crucified Christ as a tormented Jew dressed in prayer shawl and *tefillin*. And a painting by Stanley Spencer showed naked men and young girls making love in the shadow of the crucifix.

He continued to walk slowly round the room, now shocked, now outraged, now fascinated by the images. It was an extraordinary collection of the banal and the exalted. The theme – if there was one – was the search for a Christ who could serve the ruptured world of the twentieth century. All images led, as though by design, to that more-than-lifesize figure on the central crucifix, feathered, broken, cut with knives, a king come to dance for his own execution. Leo wondered what the troubled priest's theology must be; but it was not hard to guess why he had experienced a falling-out with the Church.

No one came. He sat in the perfect silence of that dim place, caught up by his own thoughts. It was only then that it sank in on him just who de Sepúlveda thought himself to be. 'That when Don Joaquín left the jungle, he left it with the secret of eternal life. That he never died. That he is still alive.'

Thinking to leave at last, he approached the altar again, to take a last look at the winged angel held by nails above it. As he looked away and prepared to turn, he happened to look down. He had guessed by the presence of the fresh flowers that someone must have already said Mass that morning. Now he saw further evidence of that event: a streak of red flanked by red blotches ran diagonally across the altarcloth. He touched it to find it still wet. Stepping back, he looked down and saw that the floor was covered in old stains, dating back who could say how long. He ran a damp finger through the fresh stain on the cloth and put it to his lips. Not wine, certainly; this tasted much more like blood. He knew what blood tasted like:

he'd licked off more than enough of his own in recent weeks.

He went back out into the sunlight. Nothing had changed, except that the sun was an hour or more higher in the sky. He felt a shiver pass through him. What he had seen inside the little temple was both grotesque and sincere. In a sense, it was a museum to the victims of persecution. The most powerful painting had been that of a Jew, bent down and carrying the burden of Auschwitz on his back, denied entry to a heaven ruled by Christ and his saints.

Realizing he might be expected back at the main house, he hurried down the goat-path. He reached the beach, panting. There was a long, uncomplicated run ahead of him. Pausing to get his breath back after the descent, he bent down, hands on knees. Then, straightening, he followed the long line of his own footprints where they vanished in the direction he had come from. Neatly incised in the sand beside them as far back as he could see was a second set of footprints. He looked more closely. Two naked feet, narrower and shorter than his own. Not de Sepúlveda's feet, he thought. He looked again. They were almost certainly a woman's. He looked all round. Whoever it was had followed him, and had either returned to the little settlement by another route unknown to him, or was still here, watching him.

He stepped on to the beach, feeling the hot sand graze his soles. In his mind's eye, he could see a tall, dark-haired woman coming towards him, her naked feet leaving their imprints etched in the wet sand as though she were Man Friday and he a shipwrecked sailor looking for rest.

34

The door slammed even before she heard it open. The crash was followed at once by the pounding of her father's feet on the wooden floor, and then a heavy thud as her bedroom door was flung open.

He stood in the opening, glaring down at her like madness itself. His eyes were red, his hair tangled, his face unshaven. He seemed to have lost five or six stone in as many days, without losing any of his stature. He had not changed his clothes in weeks, and it looked as though he had not slept in all that time. His shoes were muddy, and his jacket and trousers were streaked heavily with blood.

Torn from sleep by his furious entrance, Antonia cried out and pulled herself as far away from him as the confines of the little room allowed. His voice was like a hammer that beat at her incessantly. He was incoherent, railing at her like a drunk, and for a long time she could make out no sense or direction in any of it, and only wanted it to subside and go away.

The ranting did subside, but it did not go away. Don Ortiz had not come to her room merely to shout at her. When his storm finally expended itself, he stood looking down on her, his breath wheezing in and out, his chest heaving.

'*Aquí tiene*,' he said, holding something out between

two fingers. She tried to make it out, and saw it was a sheet of white paper, folded in two. One side had been written on. A letter from her mother, perhaps. Antonia raised herself on one elbow and held out her hand for the paper. He stepped closer and let her take it from him. She held it for a moment, then it fell on to the sheets.

'Take it!' he bellowed. 'Take it and read it and see what your whoring and loose living have brought us to. You haven't just shamed me, you've ruined me, ruined our family.'

'What's this about, Father? What on earth are you talking about?'

'Don't play the innocent with me, you little bitch. I know exactly what you've been up to down there in Mexico City, you and your precious pimping mother. There's no point in denying it, it's all there in his letter, in black and white so even a numskull like me can catch his drift.'

'I don't know anything about a letter.'

'Don't worry. By the time I've finished with you, you'll know all there is to know about everything. I'll ram his letter up your tight little cunt: maybe you'll be able to read it more easily that way. Maybe you can read it to your cheap whore of a mother while he screws you both.'

She snatched the paper from where it had fallen and began to read. It was addressed to her father and dated the day before. The signature was simple: 'Rafael'.

Con el mayor respeto, Don Ortiz,
On every lip I hear talk of the great disaster that has overwhelmed you, of the terrible slaughter that was made among your bulls. When I first heard this dreadful news, I felt sure God had visited you with one of the plagues of ancient Egypt, or that your sins

had reached out for you and toppled you, leaving you alive to savour your defeat. I thought of our last talk, and your obduracy, and I remembered the many times God has seen fit to take an interest in my affairs. Last night He spoke to me again in sleep, and today I am writing this humble letter to you in the hope that I may help you in bringing your great treasure to safety after this terrible shipwreck.

When God speaks to me, He does not do so out of mighty winds or from the mouths of volcanoes or in the burning of forest fires. I leave such things to lesser prophets, whose followers expect greater things of them. God's voice, when He speaks to me, is never more than a whisper, barely audible above the clamour of the world. I have to enter deep into myself in order to hear it, but there can be no mistaking when I do. I am a shaman, a man of Nature, a seer and a listener. I am a *zahorín*, a *to'o'hil*, and the Nohoch Tata of my people.

When God spoke to me last night, He told me that I must fulfil my destiny. He spoke your daughter's name, and confirmed what I have known for this long time now, that she and none other is eternally proclaimed my heavenly consort, the goddess who will inhabit all the spaces my mind leaves vacant, upon whose body I shall beget the last of those that will die and the first of them that will not die . . .

She stopped reading and flung the letter hard on to the bed.

'What the hell has any of this to do with me? It's just a load of nonsense, really.'

'Is it? Is that what you think? As far as I can see, you and your precious shaman are the only ones who

315

know just what's going on round here. I don't doubt he's already had more than enough practice begetting God knows what bastards on your filthy little body. He thinks you're some sort of goddess, he gives you all sorts of fancy Mayan names – but when it comes to me, I'm just some stupid wart on your backside. Shall I tell you what this Rafael thinks of me? He says he can replace all the bulls I've lost. All the fucking bulls he had killed. Just like that. He can take them away, and he can give them back with a flick of his finger. All I have to do is agree to your marrying him. That's all. If I do, if I give you away in public while Cardinal Montaño does the business, he'll restock the *ganadería* entirely at his own expense. It will cost him millions upon millions of pesos, but he will not do it for me. He will do it for you. That's how important you are to him. He'd give anything just to get you, and he'd destroy anything of mine in the process.'

She sat upright in the bed, holding the clothes up to her chin, for she was naked under the covers.

'Father, I honestly don't know what any of this is about. The man is probably mad. I've only met him once, with Mother, over dinner. I didn't like him then, and I gave him no encouragement of any kind. I've certainly never slept with him, and I haven't the slightest wish to do so. If you've made up your mind to kill him, that's fine by me. I couldn't care less. As long as it makes you happy –'

'Happy? What the fuck would you know about what makes me happy? This isn't about making me happy. Nothing can do that. If you'd any brains, you'd understand that. This is about getting even. Nothing would give me greater pleasure than ramming a *pica* up his arse and seeing it come out of his skull. But I can't do that, apparently, I can't even pay to have it done. I've asked around. I've called in a lot of old favours, and all I've found out is that this animal is untouchable. He wouldn't be more untouchable if he was the Pope himself. I can't get near him, not even halfway. So that leaves me with no choice. Do you understand?'

The tone in his voice was harsher than ever, flavoured with every sort of bitterness. Antonia shook her head, cowering against the headboard.

'It's very simple,' he said. 'If I can't kill him, I'll just have to kill you. That will hurt him enough, and it will give me the satisfaction of clearing this family of the stain you've brought to it. Come on, we've talked enough. I want to get this over. Once you're dead, he'll leave me alone.'

He reached down and took a clump of bed linen in his hand and tore it from her with all his strength, leaving her shaking on the bed, naked and defenceless. She caught sight of the revolver in his belt, and the knife on the other side.

'Not here,' she shouted, 'don't kill me here,' not knowing where or how she wanted to be killed. She felt like a child, stripped bare, powerless to fight back.

He grabbed her by the hair and forced her to her feet.

'Outside,' he ordered.

'I have to dress.'

'You won't need clothes where you're going.'

He continued to drag her, slapping her and beating her around the head, then hitting her breasts and her stomach so that she staggered and could barely walk.

When they got outside, she saw a group of men and women standing nearby, watching. She called out hoarsely, pleading to them for help, but one by one they turned their faces away. Even in his present condition, Don Ortiz owned them.

He bundled her into a Cherokee and drove off without pausing. Hardened mud and stones flew up in every direction. Chickens that had been pecking among the ruts scattered, their feathers in disarray. The vehicle pushed out from the courtyard on to a twisting track that took them through the old pastures and up among the dark, stony fields beyond, where nothing grew.

The weather had turned cold, and up above threatening clouds were stacked in a poisoned sky, and black birds whirled themselves in a dark fandango, and as they drove further up the track and rose thus, coming through an old *arroyo*, on to flat country where the sky and earth entangled, Antonia saw that the turning birds were vultures.

Line's from a poem by Lorca passed through her head, and she knew as she recited them in that silence that she was already dead, that nothing, neither man nor nature, could exclude the inevitability of her death.

> *Compadre, quiero morir*
> *decentemente en mi cama.*
> *De acero, si puede ser,*
> *con las sábanas de holanda.*

Not decently in bed, she thought, beneath Holland sheets, but in the back of a stony field beneath the wings of scavengers, on a black day without rain.

She knew by now where they were headed: to the Campo de Caballos Muertos, where he had threatened before to kill her. Except that, as they approached, it was not the same wretched field she remembered, with its single pit for the disposal of dead horses under lime, but something much grimmer and darker than that.

Overnight, it seemed, the place had been transformed from an occasional necropolis for horses to what was more or less a production line for the interment of the *ganadería's* bulls. At least twenty fresh pits had been opened, some of which were already full with cremated remains. Instead of quicklime, they were burning the carcasses at the highest heat they could generate. Don Ortiz had tried to sell off as much as possible of his herd as meat, but wherever he went, he found that Rafael had been there first. A few local dealers had taken a handful of dead *novillos* off his hands, but the rest had either laughed in his face or shut their doors in fear.

Over the pits wooden derricks had been erected to enable the men to manoeuvre the corpses over the fires beneath. Everywhere, the bloated corpses of dead bulls lay awaiting treatment. Trucks brought up new ones every hour or so. Men dressed in black with bandanas tied over their faces and thick leather gloves on their hands, squatted over the field, hacking the corpses limb from limb. Most went into the incinerators, others were thrown into quicklime pits that were rapidly filled and covered. The field was thick with buzzing flies, gigantic black creatures that had come here from a nearby swamp. They hovered over the corpses, or lay on them, fat and bloated, like miniature gods of death and decay, sucking life out of the bodies of the dead.

Don Ortiz stopped the truck in the middle of the field and switched off the engine. He leaped out and ordered everyone to leave. The men, staring through the windscreen, could see Antonia, but none of them raised a finger to help her. They were about as low as men could get, scraping a peseta here and a handful of beans somewhere else. Like whipped dogs or jackals, they left the carrion field, heads bowed, feet dragging in the mud and dried blood.

The stench that filled the cab was overpowering. Antonia gagged and felt her stomach heave. Moments later, she was sick. She opened the door to escape the smell of vomit, only to find herself breathing in yet more of the foul air and tainted smoke that covered everything. The next second she felt herself flattened against the bonnet of the Cherokee.

'This is where it ends,' her father shouted down at her, while holding her hard by the neck. She was coughing and choking now, scarcely able to breathe in the poisonous air surrounding them. Her father took a bright blue bandana from his pocket and slipped it over his head, tightening it with one hand at the back.

'There's no point in killing me,' Antonia shouted. 'It won't bring your bulls back. I'll marry him if that's what you want. You can have new bulls and be rid of me.'

'Better to be rid of you entirely. This will hurt him. I'll make sure it will.'

He grabbed a coil of rope from the Cherokee, then reached in again and came out with a Polaroid camera which he slung round his neck. Like a crazed tourist, he proceeded to frogmarch Antonia across the field, her naked feet torn by the scabby ground. They arrived at a large pit filled almost to the top with quicklime. On the ground in front of it lay the huge carcass of a black fighting bull. He threw her down on top of its bloated, flyblown body and tied her with the rope to two legs. Stepping back, he photographed her as she lay. The photograph that emerged moments later seemed to satisfy him.

'I want him to see,' he said. 'He must see everything. How I took the thing he wanted most from him.'

'Don't you have the slightest feeling for me? I'm your daughter, not your enemy. Get your revenge some other way.'

'This is the only way.'

He picked up an axe that lay near the carcass.

'I'll help you get close to him. I'll kill him myself, if you want.'

'I may kill him someday. But first I want him to experience the bitterness of total loss. Limb by limb he'll see his goddess reduced to dead flesh. I'll cut out your heart and send it to him in a box. Maybe he'll see visions. Maybe he'll hear the voice of God.'

Lifting the axe up in both hands, he stepped towards Antonia.

As he did so, a shadow fell over him. He didn't notice it at first, but Antonia, turning her face away from him, caught the edge of it and turned back. Behind Don Ortiz someone was sitting astride a tall black horse. They must have come up to him slowly, making no sound.

'Father,' she shouted, 'there's someone behind you.'

He laughed, then noticed the shadow. Putting the axe down carefully, he turned. As he did so, Antonia recognized the rider. Her Aunt Consuela, still wearing her nightdress, had ridden to the Campo de Caballos Muertos. Her long hair was tied behind her and fell down to the horse's flanks. It was her father's favourite horse, the black stallion called Armillita. Antonia wondered how her aunt had succeeded in bringing such a finely-tuned animal into this place of rotting carcasses and fire.

Consuela said nothing. She could not speak, not even in a whisper. But in her right hand she held a gun, a long revolver she had kept in a drawer for weary, pointless years, never really thinking that she might have a purpose for it. The look on her face told Don Ortiz that she had found a use at last. He tried to reach the gun he kept in his belt, but she shot him in the stomach and he gave way at once, falling to his knees in front of her.

She got down from the horse, stroking and caressing it all the time, and came round to where Don Ortiz lay in the mud, gazing with astonishment at his wounded stomach. She shot him again, this time in the upper thigh.

His right hand moved for his gun, but she anticipated him, reaching over to lift it from his belt. As she did so, he made a wild grab for her, scared beyond measure.

'You stupid woman, you'll pay for this!' he screamed. She pulled back easily from his grasp and shot him again, this time in the penis, and again and again in the same place, until he was completely emasculated. While he lay sobbing and screaming, Consuela walked across to Antonia. She smiled at her, and stroked her long hair, and untied the ropes that bound her to the bull.

When Antonia was on her feet again, Consuela went to the horse and took something from the saddle-bag. It was a change of clothing, jeans and a shirt, snatched from a drawer in Antonia's room. Antonia dressed, and the two women embraced, weeping. On the ground, Antonia's father groaned loudly and asked to be put out of his agony. Consuela handed the gun to Antonia, who took one look at it and handed it back, shaking her head.

Consuela took the gun and put it in her pocket. Then, steering Antonia to the Cherokee, she embraced her again and put her behind the steering wheel. From the other saddle-bag she took a roll of pesos and handed them to Antonia. It was not a lot of money, but it would get her to Mexico City.

They kissed, then Antonia put her foot down and drove off on to a track that would take her to the main road. As she changed gear, she heard a crisp shot behind her. Then a final roll of smoke and she was able to breathe clean air again.

35

She was there at lunch, no doubt of it, there couldn't have been two women like her on an island this size. De Sepúlveda introduced them right away.

'This is Marie-Louise Malavoy, a very close friend of mine. I'm sorry not to have introduced you before, but Marie-Louise has been a little unwell.'

She was anything from thirty-five to forty, Leo guessed. When she smiled, she seemed even younger. She possessed that quality of femininity that is purely, absolutely French. It presented itself, not just in her exquisite looks, but in the sureness of her smile, the manner of her speech, and, above all, the grace with which she moved and was still.

As lunch progressed, Leo became aware of Marie-Louise less as a beautiful French woman who had stepped from the latest Sautet film, and more as an intelligent, crafted, and animated woman who seemed to possess a poise and a wisdom beyond her years.

'Have you finished reading the *Relación* yet?' de Sepúlveda asked.

'I haven't even started it,' Leo confessed. 'I don't feel quite ready.'

'That's all right. You can blame your reluctance on the island.'

'The island? Oh, I see. You think it's making me lazy. All this sand, this blue sea . . .'

'In a sense, yes,' said the priest. 'Here, have more *ouassous*.'

He passed the plate holding a mound of lightly-spiced crawfish, and Leo helped himself to some with *chow-chow* and *taro*.

'I think there's more to it than that,' ventured Marie-Louise, 'more than just sun and sand, all the tourist clichés. Tens of thousands of visitors come to the Caribbean every year, but very few are touched. Even fewer come here, to this island, and are touched by its magic.'

Leo nodded. 'It is magical, isn't it?'

She looked at him gravely, as one might look at an earnest child who has missed the point.

'Not in the way I think you mean, no,' she said. 'The island is very beautiful, of course, and very remote, and very still. Anyone could find a little of what you loosely call magic here. If you stay long enough, you will find that this place conceals more beauty than you could ever imagine. But that isn't what I mean. You must understand that very few are ever given permission to visit this island. Those who do set foot here have a rare opportunity. La Petite Terre is a place of strange influences. You will read the *Relación* when you are ready, not before. The island will tell you when it is time.'

'Have some *camarones*,' said the priest. He was dressed in black as before. Leo noticed that a tattoo circled his wrist, made up of delicate emerald flowers. His eyes were soft and kindly, but Leo was not fooled into thinking that de Sepúlveda was a simple or an emotional man. He sensed behind the smiles a steady intellect and wealth of experience, not all of it benign. Thinking of what he had seen in the pyramid chapel that morning, he found himself unable to guess what way the priest's mind worked.

'Do you mind if I ask why you left the Church?' he asked, caught a little unawares by his own question.

'I never said that I left it,' said the monsignor. 'Just that the Vatican and I do not always see eye to eye. There are issues on which we are in harmony, others . . .'

He smiled and sipped from the wine glass beside him. The lunch, like dinner the night before, would have graced the tables of any Michelin-starred restaurant.

'You still celebrate Mass?'

'I have never ceased to do so.'

'So it isn't really a religious disagreement.'

The priest smiled and shrugged his shoulders.

'You are talking about boundaries. And all talk of boundaries is doomed to end in frustration. Let me simplify matters for you. My first clash with the Church occurred in the seventies. I had a parish in Chiapas, a little place forty miles from Tuxtla, called Santa Marta. My parishioners were all Indians, farming their own land in a large clearing extracted from part of the Lacandón Forest. The land had been theirs by right from the time of the New Laws. They were poor people, very poor, but I believe they were content. They grew enough food to fill their bellies, and their other needs were minimal. I did what I could to provide them with health care. They attended Mass. There was very little crime. And I believe there was a measure of happiness. Some young people came from Caritas and set up a centre to teach the women crafts, and we started to sell their work and to generate a little extra income.'

Leo listened, not without interest. He'd always been impressed by the Indians he met, by their powers of endurance and penetration. He knew how the story would end. It was an old story. More priests told it than de Sepúlveda, it ran through more forests and more ruined villages than the Gospel narrative.

'In 1976, a logging company moved into the region and started felling trees. They began to encroach on our land, but when we protested they employed a host of legal tricks to delay our case. The following year, they brought bulldozers in and started clearing Indian villages. Some of the young men had acquired a few weapons, some knives and bows and arrows, nothing more deadly. They attacked the loggers, who sent in men armed with guns. Over one hundred Indians were hunted down and shot.

'I gathered about fifty of the survivors together, and we travelled with the young people from Caritas as far as the state capital of Tuxtla. We mounted a protest about the killings outside the governor's mansion, and everyone was arrested. Because I was a priest, I was let out almost at once. I went to see my bishop. He was eating at the time, a meal very like this one, but he had me brought in. When I told him my story, he became very angry and ordered me back to my parish, where I was to ensure that the Indians abided by whatever instructions they were given by the forces of law and order. As for those in prison, they would be excommunicated as a warning to the rest. I cannot tell you how I left that house, what manner of thoughts I had about God.

'By the time I got back to my village, the logging company had all but wiped out the community I'd lived with. He simply . . .' He hesitated. 'Within six months, the Indians of that region were either dead or scattered to the winds. Many ended up in Tuxtla or San Cristóbal, the women as prostitutes, the men as toilet cleaners or worse. Not many years later, my bishop was elevated to the rank of cardinal. I was sent to another parish in a *barrio* of Mexico City. But I had already seen the Devil's face. I was not to be deceived again.'

'Is that why you've collected so many portrayals of the Devil? Is that why you hang them in your temple?'

De Sepúlveda did not blink. 'Is that what you think they are? Devils?'

'I'm not quite sure. But they seem that way to me. Gas masks. Terror. Depravity.'

'Are those only the Devil's realm? My paintings are of something quite different. You should look more closely next time. Not like a tourist in the Louvre. Marie-Louise here will show you. I have sought for the true face of Christ. Not some puling blond-haired godling, but Christ without love or dreams or pity, Christ in a soldier's helmet, caught in barbed wire, Christ with his back against a wall, waiting for a firing squad.'

He explained his philosophy with the fervour of first love. Lunch drew on, less a meal now than an opportunity for a sermon. No one ate with a heart. Coffee came with rich imported chocolates, and they went on talking. Little by little, Leo began to understand.

'Why the blood?' he asked. 'The altar was covered in it.'

De Sepúlveda smiled.

'What did you think?' he asked. 'That I carry out human sacrifice? Like the Aztecs, perhaps?'

Leo shook his head, but his eyes admitted his suspicion.

'The blood is that of cockerels. Many religions in this region use it in their rituals. *Vodoun* in Haiti. *Candomblé*. It's a custom that came from Africa. But you'll also be aware that many of the Mayan *costumbres* also shed blood in this way.

'When I celebrate Mass, I do so with real blood. If wine

327

can be transformed to a man's blood by the utterance of a few words, I can perform the same magic over the blood of a cock. Perhaps your Anglican tastes would not approve. But we aren't in a village church in Surrey. This is the Caribbean. Our gods are different gods.'

Leo got to his feet.

'I'm sorry,' he said, 'but I have to go. I need to find out more about this lost city of yours.' At the door he turned. 'You said the bishop became a cardinal. What happened to the logging company? Did it prosper?'

The priest looked at him oddly.

'Why do you ask?' he said.

'You referred to the logging company as "he" at one point. Was that a mistake?'

De Sepúlveda shook his head.

'Just a slip of the tongue,' he said. 'One man was at the head of the enterprise. I held him responsible for everything that happened. I still do. The terrible thing was that he was an Indian himself.

'When I first approached him in the hope he might show some mercy, I thought there was a real chance that he might understand. But he just laughed at me. I have never forgotten that. Or the fact that he was an Indian, that he claimed descent from the Mayan kings.'

'What was his name?'

'His name? He was called Rafael. I don't suppose you've ever heard of him.'

36

Carta de Don Joaquín de Sigüenza y Góngora a su Majestad Felipe II, Rey de Espagna, con la breve y sumaria relación de él sobre los indios y los siete ciudades de Chiapas. Valladolid de Comayagua, La Fiesta de Nuestra Señora de los Remedios, 1561.

A letter sent by Don Joaquín de Sigüenza y Góngora, *Oidor* of the Audiencia of Guatemala (Audiencia de los Confines), formerly *Oidor* of the Audiencia of Mexico, author of the *Historia de los indios de Nueva España*, to the Very High and Most Potent and Invincible Lord, Don Felipe, August Emperor and King of Spain, Our Lord, to accompany his brief account of the Indians of the region known as Chiapas, and the seven cities in the past inhabited by them, in some of which there is gold, and in some silver, and in one what is neither gold nor silver, but greater than both, as shall be found in the narrative.

Very High and Most Powerful Prince, Very Catholic and Invincible Emperor, King and Lord. Having now completed the accompanying report, as your majesty commanded me, I send it to you with my sincere greetings. I regret that circumstances make it inadvisable for me to send it by the usual mails. All that passes between Spain and the Audiencias, likewise all that returns from New Spain homewards is subject to the authority of the *oidores*.

Others too have access to the posts, among them the *corregidores*, the *alcaldes mayores*, the *visitadores*, and the *juezes de residencia*, and see all that they wish to see. My report, as you shall see for yourself, contains much that should remain concealed from all eyes but yours. Wherefore, I have determined that it should reach your royal hands by means other than those ordinarily employed. I do assure you of my abiding love and gratitude.

Most Catholic Lord, may God Our Lord preserve and augment the life and very royal person and powerful state of Your Caesarean Majesty with increase of much greater Kingdoms and Lordships, as your royal heart may desire. From the city of Valladolid de Comayagua[1] of this New Spain of the Ocean Sea on the 8th of September, the Festival of Our Lady of Remedies, 1561. Most Powerful Lord, Your Caesarean Majesty's very humble servant and vassal who kisses the royal hands and feet of Your Majesty.

Don Joaquín de Sigüenza y Góngora

Relación de Don Joaquín de Sigüenza y Góngora acerca de los Indios de Chiapas, y en otras provincias sus comarcanas, los mayeques, y los macehualtin, con un diario de su viaje 1559–61, y un parecer sobre los ciudades indígenas.

I must before all else relate a little of my own past, and of how I am come to this position, that my Lord

---

[1] For the benefit of the modern reader, Valladolid de Santa Maria de Comayagua was founded in 1537 as the Spanish capital of Honduras province. It is today known simply as Comayagua.

may know what manner of man I am, how worthy of trust, and how suitable of belief. My father, Juan Ginés de Sigüenza y Góngora, was known in his day as a man of letters and learning, and was a popular figure at the courts of Ferdinand and Isabella and of Philip the Handsome, who are in glory. He taught me my books as a child, but my mother, Louisa, who belonged to a noble family of Seville, saw to it that I understood the arts of a gentleman. She taught me to ride and to hunt, and she saw to it that I had teachers in fencing, dancing, and music. Nevertheless, it was my father's spirit that ruled me always and led me to my present career.

I was born in the year of Our Lord 1520, in the reign of King Charles, the illustrious father of our present king. When I reached the age of twenty-five, my father, thinking I might be about to become a wastrel, sent me from our home town of Córdoba to the town of Salamanca, in which place I was enrolled to study law, with the aim that I should become a *letrado* and, in due course, a judge or an administrator. All went well with me at the university, and I took my bachelor's degree in the year 1548.

My father escorted me to Granada, then the supreme court of Southern Castile, and before long I found myself practising before the Audiencia there. Within the year I took to myself a wife, the Doña Joanna, who in time bore me five children and grew nearest my heart of all persons . . .

In the year 1555, I was appointed by royal order to serve as one of the four *oidores* of the Audiencia of Santo Domingo on the island of Española. I, Joanna and our children left with the March fleet, sailing from the port of San Lúcar de Barrameda, and arriving some two months later. Of that journey, I can only say that nothing would induce me to undergo such suffering again. We slept on the bare boards and ate hardtack and salt beef, with nothing to wash it down but half a measure of water a day, and all this in the most oppressive heat, which left all of us passengers, including most particularly my wife and children, in an enfeebled condition. Our two youngest boys, Fernández and Francisco succumbed, together with their baby sister Isabella, and were buried at sea . . .

After three years in Santo Domingo, I was posted to the Audiencia of Mexico, where I arrived in the spring of 1558. Two days after our arrival at the port of Veracruz, my dear wife fell sick of a fever known in those parts as *cámaras*, from which few recover. Her death followed swiftly, and she was buried in a little cemetery there which is maintained by a community of Franciscan friars. May God sustain her living image in His eternal present until I rejoin her. This was my first encounter with the Holy Fathers, a sad enough meeting, yet one of much consequence for my later understanding of the Indian and his situation.

During the year I spent at this Audiencia, I was assigned by it to make *cuentas* and *visitas* to several towns throughout New Spain, where I interviewed everyone in an official capacity and exposed much corruption and ill-dealing. It was at this time that I first became concerned for the plight of the Indians, and the indignities and hardships they endure under the system of *encomienda*. I was much encouraged in this concern by various religious, among them Fray

Jacinto de San Francisco and Fray Domingo de la Anunciación . . .

Such was the success of these *visitas* that a request was made by the Bishop of Chiapas in the Province of Guatemala, Fray Tomás Casilla, that I should spend some time in that region in the quality of *visitador*, above all to inspect the Indian settlements and to interview members of their nobility. I therefore took up residence in the city of Santiago de los Caballeros,[2] leaving my children in the care of their nurse in Mexico.

In Santiago I met numerous *caciques* and *principales*, among them lords of the second, third, and fourth rank. Among these latter I met one young man named Zuazo, a Mayan of rank and one whom I considered worthy of trust, he having been recommended to me by Fray Tomás. This Zuazo accompanied me in my travels among his people and provided me with much information concerning their customs and laws.

Together with my servants and an armed guard, he and I travelled the length and breadth of Chiapas province, visiting the *barrios* and *calpullis* of the Maya. I made assessment of their conditions, and received depositions from their elders regarding their treatment at the hands of the Spanish landowners. In the course of these travels, we made frequent detours in order to inspect the ruins of cities that had once been occupied by the Maya in the days of their greatness, and everywhere we

---

[2] Santiago de los Caballeros de Guatemala was founded in 1527 and later twice destroyed. It is now known as Antigua Guatemala.

went we observed the most remarkable buildings and streets, much of them deeply overgrown by the forest that covers much of that country.

When over a year had passed, I penned my report and lodged it with the Audiencia, and at the same time made application for leave, it being my plan to return forthwith to Mexico to be with my children. In the meantime, however, I had found the leisure to talk at great length with my friend Zuazo, and found him to be a source of much knowledge and wisdom concerning the beliefs and history of his people. It seemed to me not undesirable to set down a record of all he told me, that I might perhaps combine these things into a history of the Maya and a discourse on their religion. In this I was much encouraged by Fray Jacinto and Fray Domingo, who had often thought of preparing just such a chronicle themselves.

After we had spent some months together in this endeavour, my friend Zuazo confided in me that he had in his possession some of the secret books of his people in which are recorded their priestly codes and arcane matters. These were, he said, written in the same ciphers that I had seen employed for inscriptions at their cities, and which I was told signified no more than a record of dates and royal events.

He was at first reluctant to give me sight of these books, among which he said there was a copy of the sacred text known as *Popol Vuh*, which, so I had heard, was used by the Quiché lords in their divinations of the future. But I worked slowly upon his confidence, reassuring him that I shall pass on none of this knowledge to others unless he should consent. And he, knowing me in truth a well-wisher of his people, and thinking it prudent that I should be well advised of their deepest principles, accepted in the end to teach me these 'Speeches of the Ancients', such as he had by him.

Several months passed after this fashion, and I began to think that I should resign my position as *oidor*, for I truly wanted nothing better than to acquaint myself with these legends and set them down in writing for the benefit of the learned and the religious both. However, I was one day most surprised when Zuazo took me aside to say that we had exhausted all the books in his possession and that he could obtain no more. For some time after this, I was most despondent, for I had begun to depend upon our sessions for my mental stimulation, and I had, indeed, begun to learn the Mayan language in the form he spoke it.

This proved, however, to be a mere setback. After many days of reflection and, I doubt not, consultation with those of his fellow-tribesmen in whom he intended to confide, he asked me to accompany him to a place where we could talk in private. He told me that it was rumoured among his people that a city existed deep in the forest where the old books and the old traditions continued to be kept. It had a special reputation as a city of conjurers, where men feared to go except in times of extreme peril, and it was on account of that fear that it remained forgotten by all but a few. He, however, though he had not been there in person and knew no one who had, possessed a map that would lead us to it in a matter of weeks.

I confess that I was at first sceptical that such a

place existed, then fearful that it would prove to be a very real danger not only to our bodies, but to our souls. I had sworn silence, otherwise I should have spoken to one of the Holy Fathers and obtained his opinion on the wisdom of proceeding.

In the end, Zuazo made up my mind for me by speaking of the potion the elders of that city prepared, the peculiar property of which was to grant eternal life to those who are worthy of it.

With Zuazo's help I prepared an expedition, saying we wished to visit certain settlements about the fringes of the forest. In private I spoke with Fray Jacinto, confiding in him our true goal. He said nothing, but agreed to accompany us in the hope that many souls might be saved for Christ in the very heart of heathendom . . .

We departed with the utmost secrecy on the seventeenth of November 1560. Our party was composed as previously of fourteen armed men under the command of Captain Alonso de la Torre, my Spanish servants, Juan Monzón and Andrés Ramos, my faithful secretary, García de Benavente, thirty Indian bearers, my Indian informant, Zuazo, Fray Jacinto, Fray Domingo, several of their Indian converts, and myself. In addition to their swords, the military force was armed with harquebuses, crossbows, and pikes, and all wore well-polished cuirasses and helmets. Captain de la Torre carried a pennant he had had made in Valladolid, this being blue and white with a red cross at its centre, bearing on it the motto: *Amici, sequamor crucem, et si nos fidem habemus, vere in hoc signo vincemus*. He was a man of many battles, both here and in the Old World. Despite his motto, I noticed that he kept himself apart from the priests, and attended Mass reluctantly.

The Indians were *macehualtin* of the Quiché Maya and had been hand-chosen by Zuazo, that we might the better depend on them. They wore only loin-cloths and *mantas* woven from maguey fibre, and, of course, they went unarmed. Our group went heavily provisioned, yet such was the nature of our journey that we had to trust to Providence that, should we stray far from cultivated land, we might supply ourselves from the trees and bushes of the forest into which we aimed to penetrate.

Lest anyone in the city of Santiago guess our true direction, and come enquiring after information or send spies to follow us, we set off on a false path to the west, which way we followed for some ten miles before heading due north, deeper into the high country of the Sierra Madre. The region that we entered has been little explored by Christians, and we were at all times anxious lest we be observed and attacked by Indians not as yet pacified and baptized into the true faith, of whom Zuazo told me there were still many.

On our second day we passed a town of stone houses that has been named Mixco Viejo, and was until some years past the capital of a people known as the Pocomam. We found several great buildings set up on flattened hilltops, or on spurs surrounded by deep ravines. There were well-paved squares and preserved temples, but the place had an air of hopeless desolation, and as we passed by I sensed the ghosts of those who had inhabited it, as though our coming had stirred them up. Just outside the city we found many beehives, with much wax and honey, the hives being very like those of my native Spain, though smaller in size. We saw nothing of the keepers who tend these bees, but passed through groves of *jarale* trees on which the creatures feed.

We found hares and rabbits in that country, and most nights we feasted well on them. Our Indians ate of a bread made from the root known as *yucca*, which they scrape and crush until a sort of flour be made of it, which they bake in ovens of clay erected for the purpose. When hot it is passable food, but once cold it has a bitter taste and can no longer be endured.

The volcanoes and high peaks of the Sierra were far behind us, and ahead of us lay the last Spanish town, a little place called Cobán, that was founded by that most holy and peaceable of men, Father Bartolomé de las Casas some twenty years past. It rains heavily in that region, and by the time we passed through we were thoroughly wet and miserable. A beautiful flower called an orchid grows in the valley, and the Indians often plucked them and put them in their hair for the delight of it. Nor could I find it in my heart to rebuke them for their simple love of nature.

A little before Cobán is reached, and somewhat to the west of it, we came to a river known as the Chixoy, and here we made camp for more than a week while our Indians felled cedar trees and cut and burned them to make long boats which they call *cayucos*, and which we know as canoes. They are not comfortable boats in which to ride, but they served us well and took us to our next destination.

After a long descent through the mountains, the river enters into a series of bends until it comes to the mouth of another river, reaching it from the north, which I was told is called by the Indians Etz'nab Muluc or Knife Water, and which was christened by Fray Jacinto the Pasión, for our Lord's passion and death that day.

A little before this river mouth, upon the right bank, there is an array of ruins that were, I believe, once set up to be a place of worship or sacrifice to the Indians. For there are to be found there many altars of great size, each large enough to take a man, for that, I understand, was the nature of their sacrifice, as it continues to be today whenever there is opportunity. I named the site the Altar of Sacrifices. We did not camp there, because our Indians said there were restless ghosts all around us.

But in the morning we returned there, so that we could cross the river at that spot and so climb to the left bank. Here the trees of the forest came to the very edge, so that we were no sooner landed than we found ourselves within the darkness, and in a very short time came into deep forest, where the sun's light penetrated very little, by reason of the great height of the trees and the canopy their upper branches made more than one hundred feet above the ground.

We entered this dark and dreadful place, not knowing if we should come out alive. Not many yards from the spot where we entered, we found a great head, a man's head that had been carved many centuries ago. The Indians took it for an idol, and might have worshipped it, had not Fray Jacinto and Fray Domingo brought them back to their senses and led them in prayer. The soldiers for the most part stood aloof from this, but I could see that they were to a man terrified by the world we had come into.

Our forward progress was much hindered by the heavy undergrowth that clutched at our legs at every step. We were haunted by the cries of the great many barbarous birds and animals that inhabit the forest. Some of the birds have the most beautiful plumage. I saw one with a bright scarlet breast, a green cloak, and a remarkably long tail feather, also of green, that Zuazo told me is known as a *quetzal* and is sacred to his people. In the long past, he said, their kings would wear its feathers in their crowns.

On the third day we were checked by a small but fast-flowing river, that came down out of the uplands. Zuazo insisted that we had to cross, and so we made every effort to do so, swimming against a torrent that threatened at times to rip us away. One man indeed, hampered by his armour, was sucked under and drowned, his body being dragged downstream too quickly for any of us to retrieve it.

The forest at night is filled with fearful sounds, for it is then that the animals do most of their hunting. We would seek out clearings or cut them to our satisfaction, in which we could light fires and so ward off the attentions of the forest's predators, above all the jaguar, whose roar was often heard as he stalked the jungle.

We had to exercise great vigilance at all times, for there are giant snakes and spiders, and even plants whose sting is fatal, and yet others who, though they may be powerless to kill, will render a man unconscious for a spell or cause him to become sick so that he cannot walk and has to be carried on a litter. Several were thus afflicted within the first day of our being in the forest, and each day after that another would succumb, some in a small way, others that were brought close to death.

We proceeded in this way for three days, by which time some of the men had started to grow restless. Their captain laid upon them the heaviness of their duty to me, but in private he confided that he feared the outbreak of rebellion should we not soon reach our destination.

It was here that we stumbled upon a large village of Indians, all of them naked savages who had remained thus far deprived of all the uses of civilization, for they neither built with stone nor cut with iron. They spoke a Mayan tongue which they called Ixil, and our Indians understood them with a little effort. We stayed two nights in their huts, during which time Fray Jacinto and Fray Domingo preached the Gospel to them and baptized the entire village, though there were some that seemed reluctant to know Our Saviour.

Before we left, Fray Domingo said that he would stay in that place, together with the Indians he had brought, in order to instruct the savages further in their new faith, and to show them how they might build a church right there in the forest, to God's greater glory and the honour of the Church and the glorification of Spain. We were all sad to leave behind that kind and holy man, but our mission would not allow us to linger beyond the span we had already waited. Among those who remained with him were several Mayan converts who had been stone masons previously, and who had been instructed in the methods of constructing a Christian church.

Once beyond the village, we were in deep forest again. We had tried to find out from the Indians of the village whether they knew of the city we sought, but to our enquiries they answered always the same: 'We know of nothing like that'. For two days more we continued on our way, crossing a series of small streams that ran athwart our path. On the third day, one of our company fell ill of a fever, from which he died some days later.

On that same day the first of the attacks began. A hail of long arrows came through the trees on our left, striking several of our party and killing four, three Indians and one Spaniard. Others, myself included, were wounded. Captain de la Torre organized his men into circles, while shouting to the Indians to lie flat. This time, when more arrows came, they were answered by a mix of harquebus balls and cross bow quarrels. Things went thus for several minutes, with the two sides exchanging fire rapidly, yet our adversaries remained invisible to us throughout. Then, as quickly and as silently as they had come, the Indians vanished back into the forest.

We buried our dead and pressed on. All that night a double guard was posted, but no one came. Since the soldiers would not entrust weapons of any sort into the hands of our Indians, they remained powerless to help us or themselves in the event of a skirmish.

A second encounter followed the next day with like result. Only the thought of gold, whispered into their ears by Captain de la Torre, kept the men at their posts and willing to walk on.

Each day after that more of our party died, but we could not tell how many of the enemy succumbed to our fire. A few times we sent out volunteers to scout the area and see if we might not come upon some sort of camp or bivouac; but for all the trace of them we could find, we might as well have been fighting shadows.

Seeing, perhaps, that the Indians in our charge carried no weapons, our opponents concentrated their fire upon the soldiers, and after a matter of four or five days, the number of fighting men still with us had been reduced to eleven. All of those remaining were wounded, and their ammunition was almost gone.

I could do nothing to prevent what happened next. Fray Jacinto had been killed, an arrow through his neck, along with my two servants. My secretary remained alive, and of the Indians Zuazo and seventeen others. That night, with so little authority to hold them in check, the Spaniards rose up and slaughtered the remaining Indians, as though they held them in some way responsible for the attacks. Since Zuazo was considered under my special protection, his life was spared. However, I swore silently that, should we ever return to civilization, I would hold those responsible for the slayings culpable in law.

We had just decided to risk going back the way we had come, when one of our party found a carved pillar the height of a man, standing, as it were, like a marker signifying some sort of border. And when Zuazo examined this pillar he declared it to be the boundary stone of the city called Kaminalhuyú, the City of Eternal Life.

Against our best instincts, we proceeded further, and on the following day our faltering steps brought us to an enormous clearing. There before us stood Kaminalhuyú, a city of white stone, more magnificent than any place I have ever seen. Seven great pyramids rose to the heavens, each endowed with four mighty stairways that led to the temple at the summit. There were public squares and parks where they played a game with a ball, public buildings, and street after street of ordinary houses and shops. Some parts of the city were in ruin, others dilapidated, yet the whole spectacle I beheld that day astonished me beyond measure, for I had seen nowhere in Spain and nowhere on my travels to rival it.

A party of Indians approached us from a building on our left. These were, as far as we could tell, different in their dress and general appearance to the ones who had previously attacked us. Although some of them were armed, they kept their weapons by their sides and made no movement that might be deemed aggressive. Zuazo approached them, and although he had much difficulty in making himself understood, he managed in the end to communicate something of our purpose to them.

He came to me in the end and said that they had forbidden us to enter the city. I asked if I alone might enter, and he returned to them to ask this. No sooner had he opened his mouth this second time than one of the armed men, who was carrying a great club like an axe, took his weapon in both hands and split my poor friend open from head to belly, causing all his entrails to fall upon the ground.

We turned and ran, and for seven days and seven nights we continued in this fashion, fleeing from our persecutors. When we at last left the forest, only Captain Torres, García de Benavente, my secretary, four soldiers, and myself remained of our original party. Two more died before we returned at last to Santiago de los Caballeros, on the nineteenth of January.

This is the truth concerning the expedition of Don Joaquín de Sigüenza y Góngora to the lost city of Kaminalhuyú, in the region known as Petén. More than this is not needful at present. May God preserve His servants and give them eternal life through His Son Jesus Christ. Amen.

Leo put the manuscript down. His head was spinning from trying to take in all the details of Don Joaquín's narrative. It was all plausible, he thought, and he could already picture the first part of the expedition's route as far as their entry to the forest.

He rubbed his eyes and leaned back in his chair. He wondered if Don Joaquín had known the true meaning of the name of his city. Kaminalhuyú. Perhaps it was a City of Eternal Life. Perhaps the secret of immortality had been preserved there. But its name meant something very different. Kaminalhuyú was Mayan for Hill of the Dead.

37

A pall of black smoke hung over the city like a vulture. Antonia took one look at it and shivered. The three volcanoes that ring the southern flank of Lake Atitlán had erupted two days earlier, and a steady stream of smoke and hot ash had been carried north-east since then. The capital, fifty miles away, had suffered badly. Black ash was piled up everywhere, and every day brought more. Those who could afford to leave until the volcanoes settled down again had already done so. Everybody else, tied by work or family or finances, struggled to get by. Some did better than others. The hospitals were full of asthmatics choking up black phlegm. There was talk of evacuating babies and small children. The best thing was to stay indoors, preferably in rooms with air-conditioning. If you had a room.

Antonia hauled her bag off the bus at the Terminal de Autobuses Extraurbanos. Like everybody else, the first thing she did on stepping down was to tie a scarf tightly round her mouth. God knows what it's like down at Atitlán, she thought, if it's like this here. She'd visited the place once, in her teens, spending a week with her mother relaxing on the lake. She remembered it as a beautiful place, with a sky that, in winter, could seem as clear as ice. It was said that the Tzutuhils hid their treasure in the lake when the Spanish arrived. By now, any gold that lay on the lake bed must be covered with lava inches thick.

She pulled the scarf over her nose. Several boys rushed towards her, clamouring to take her bag, but she brushed them aside. Her mind was on other things.

Fleeing after her father's murder, she'd paused at the *ganadería* only long enough to collect some clothes and stuff them in the bag she was now carrying. Consuela's money had been barely enough to get her to Mexico City by bus, a long journey that had sapped her strength. Single women her age seldom travelled on public transport, and she'd found herself the object of unwelcome attention from several men before her journey was done.

Her first instinct on arriving in the city had been to go to her mother's place and throw herself on her mercy. Without Don Ortiz to bully her, María Cristina could turn out to be a reasonable, if selfish, woman. She would certainly not want to see her daughter harmed, much less arrested and imprisoned for murder. In any case, Antonia had no intention of telling her or anyone else the real sequence of events that day at the *ganadería*. Neither she nor Consuela must be suspected of the Don's death, even for a moment. Everyone knew he already had bitter enemies: why bring his family into it?

But second thoughts brought Antonia up sharply. Her mother might be talked round to treating her well and even helping her put her old life together. But she was inextricably linked to this man Rafael, and Antonia wouldn't have put it past her to try some trick in order to marry her off to him. After the letter her father had shown her, and thinking over some of his

347

remarks about Rafael, Antonia wanted to keep as great a distance between herself and him as possible. If necessary, she thought, she'd leave Mexico and take up residence elsewhere merely to be out of his reach. If, she thought sickeningly, it was possible to get out of his reach.

Instead of heading for her mother's apartment in Chapultepec, she used her last pesos for the tedious Metro journey from Autobuses de Norte to San Ángel, where her old apartment was situated. She rang the bell, but there was no reply. Glancing at her watch, she sat down and waited for Isabel to get back from work.

Coming on her like that, a crumpled heap on the doorstep, Isabel was astonished past measure at the change in her old friend. Since Antonia's disappearance, she'd been frantically hunting for her everywhere, only to be firmly rebuffed by the authorities and finally warned off by some serious people working with the police. It was like a miracle, Antonia back again, thin, but otherwise not hurt. She brought her in and started making a meal at once.

An hour later, having heard it all spill out of Antonia's lips, she had lost her appetite. More than that, revolving her friend's story in her mind, she thought she had lost her innocence.

'You can't stay here in Mexico City,' she said. 'This Rafael sounds very powerful. He'll find you here before anywhere else.'

'Where can I go? I have to stay here. I need to find Leo, if he's still alive. The last I know is he was in Portillo prison.'

'I can make enquiries for you there. Stay here tonight, then we'll work out what you should do next.'

Isabel stayed off work the following day in order to help find out what had happened to Leo. She spoke to someone in the Reclusorio and was told that Leo had been released some weeks earlier and handed over to Interpol. Interpol's local office had no record of a Leo Mallory, but they did know that one of their European officials, Declan Carberry, had visited Portillo prison on the day Leo had been released. A call to Paris confirmed Carberry's existence. Antonia made a call to Lyon, taken by the Commander himself. He told her that Leo had been taken to a hospital in Dallas, and before he hung up asked her to get in touch again, since there were questions he needed to ask her.

'About your father,' he'd said. 'And a man called Rafael.'

She'd said nothing, not knowing what to say.

Dallas had been confused. Someone thought Leo had gone to the Caribbean, someone else that he was in Cambridge. She rang Cambridge and was told that he was in Guatemala City putting together an expedition. She'd hung up and told Isabel she was taking the first bus to Guatemala.

'Why don't you fly? I can let you have as much money as you want. More, if you need it.'

'Thanks, but I . . . What I mean . . . I will need to borrow some money from you. But I don't think I should fly anywhere. If Rafael has people looking for me, the airport here is one of the first places they'll try. Plus, I need to get a new passport, preferably under a false name.'

'And some plastic surgery to go with it. Don't worry, I'll draw some money from the bank in the morning. The passport may be more difficult. Where's your existing one?'

'In the back of a drawer in my office at the university.'

'I'll try to get it. Maybe I can do a straight swap.'

'Be careful. They may have someone watching my office.'

Two days later, Antonia woke to find a well-used Argentinian passport on her breakfast tray. It had an entry stamp for Mexico dated one month previously, and carried a photograph of her with her hair dyed blonde, the colour it was now.

'Why don't you ring him before you leave?' Isabel asked, more than once. 'Let him know you're on your way. Hell, you don't want to arrive and find he's gone.'

'I want to see what happens when I walk in. I want to see his face. He didn't ring me after getting out of prison. Maybe he doesn't want to see me again. I don't want him putting on some act on the telephone, then us both having to go through some sort of routine, acting like lovers, when all he wants is to get as far away from me as possible.'

'Guatemala City's just a bus ride away. You don't know he didn't ring you. You don't imagine they'd have put the call through, do you?'

'Maybe you're right. All the same, I want to do this my way. I want to see his face.'

Now, standing alone on the Avenida de Ferrocarii, she thought of the possibility of rejection. What if he really did betray his lack of feeling in a single look? Where would she go from here? Would she be driven somehow back and back to Rafael? Unable to face a walk through the smog, she managed to find a taxi. It was a short drive to the Museo de Arqueología y Etnología, halfway between the zoo and the national racecourse. But horse-racing had been cancelled, and the nearby bullring was silent, its floor as black as the bulls that fought and died there.

The museum was not only open but busy. It was worth

the price of a ticket just to get inside and breathe good air. Antonia went to the desk and gave her name. Her real name, not the one she'd whispered to the passport policeman who'd walked through her bus the night before.

'I'm looking for a Doctor Mallory,' she said. 'I think he may be here organizing an expedition.'

'Mallory? Oh, yes, the English professor. Of course. If you go through that door on your left and along the corridor, I think he's with his group in the Kaminalhuyú Room. Have you got an appointment with him?'

'In a way, yes.'

'Shall I ring through for you?' the receptionist asked, picking up the handset of her telephone.

Antonia shook her head. 'No, thanks. I'd rather surprise him. If you don't mind.'

The receptionist sniffed. She didn't much care for blondes, least of all artificial ones.

Antonia followed the directions she'd been given. The door was marked with a small brass plate. She pushed it open.

They were sitting round a table, talking animatedly. She knew most of them, recognized them straight away. Leo was at the top end. Seeing her enter, he stood.

'Yes?' he said. 'Can I help you?'

The look on his face was blank. There was no recognition in his eyes, she might as well have been a stranger. She felt her heart clatter disagreeably and suddenly wanted to be sick, as if her lungs had been stuffed full of ashes. The ashes of her father's bulls, the ashes of old volcanoes. She smiled and opened her mouth, trying to speak, but the words she wanted would not come, not even his name, not even her own name.

And then she saw his face change and his eyes fill with

351

her, and she remembered she had dyed her hair and had walked into the room unannounced, like a stranger. And when she caught herself and looked again, he was coming towards her.

He stood in front of her, still unable to believe his eyes.

'I rang,' he said. 'Every night for weeks.'

'I know,' she said. 'Carmela told me afterwards. But you were gone when I tried to ring. It doesn't matter now. He can't keep us apart now.'

He caught her as she fainted, and helped her to a chair, and when he looked up again the room was empty and filled with silence.

38

At certain hours of the day or night, at sudden moments when his eyes were half-closed or his thoughts half-asleep, her absence would wound him like a knife. The brevity of their relationship should have meant – or so he told himself – that her memory might fade as quickly as it had come. But he found no truth in that in practice; indeed, the more days passed, the more intense his memory of her, and the deeper the wound.

At other times, all Declan's thoughts were focused on the single objective of bringing Alice's killer or killers to book. To that end, he had pulled every string available to him in order to set up a special squad to investigate the Louvre killings. Ignoring Nougayrède and the warning notices that had been posted all round him, Declan concentrated on the other victims. The Irish police made a specific request for a full investigation into Liam O'Neill's death, and the Belgians wanted a proper enquiry into the murder of Father Justus de Harduwijn. The Germans had been less cooperative about Habermayer, the neo-Nazi, and it hadn't taken long for Declan to find out that they were trying to keep his death hush-hush, for fear that news of it might spark off some sort of internecine

353

fighting among right-wing factions, or between fascists and their opponents.

One of the men chosen by Declan for his team was a German, Hans Dietrich Liebig, who had served previously with the Bundeskriminalamt in Wiesbaden. Declan had selected him just because he needed a German, any German, in the group; but Liebig turned out to have a hidden asset. He'd worked with the BKA's Terrorism section for several years, where he'd been responsible for setting up a division that handled right-wing crime. He was an expert on the Freiheitliche Deutsche Arbeiter Partei, and had been a keen observer of Habermayer himself. Once he entered the investigation, it began to get personal.

Within minutes of Liebig's coming on board, the German police entered an official request for Interpol to handle Habermayer's death 'and any consequences arising therefrom'.

One day very near the start of the team's existence, Declan spent an afternoon with Sophie Dutheillet, the president's wife. In her early fifties, Sophie was everything an older French woman could want to be. Dutheillet had married her for her looks, and these she still had in abundance, along with about two hundred silk and velvet scarves, eighty cocktail dresses, one hundred evening dresses, seventeen pairs of black court shoes, and an account at the La Perla store at number one Via Montenapoleone in Milan, which she visited every spring.

The moment she sat down, he could see she was clever, much cleverer than her husband. She too had written books, including several studies devoted to the philosopher Derrida, whom she claimed to be able to understand. Declan only had to look at her to realize that she probably could. She had, he could tell, taken counsel about his visit, and about himself.

'I have agreed to say nothing to my husband about this visit, Monsieur Carberry; but that is only on the understanding that you do not threaten him in any way, that you do not try to manipulate him through me.'

She wore a long black cashmere dress with a single silver brooch and a subtly-coloured velvet scarf by Georgina von Etzdorf. Her hair had been cut short and skilfully coloured, not to conceal the grey, but to mute it. Declan found her intimidating, but it was rumoured she exercised a powerful influence over her husband, so he made up his mind to persevere. In the end, however, she did almost everything for him.

'Put your files down over there,' she said the moment he entered. 'I won't need to look at them.'

'Why not? They could be anything . . .'

She shook her head. 'Not quite anything. You're not the first to come here carrying a handful of files. I've had all sorts of people. You'd be quite surprised. Prostitutes. Journalists. The boss of an oil consortium. And several politicians, of course. French deputies. MEPs. Even a European Commissioner. They all wanted the same thing, as if there was only ever one thing that mattered.'

'You haven't seen what's in these files.'

'I don't particularly want to. I'll gladly take your word for their contents. I don't expect you have anything that will surprise me. Mind you, you do have the distinction of being the first Interpol official to turn up here. Perhaps that signifies something.'

'You're taking this all very philosophically.'

'I've had a lifetime's practice. By the way, your left shoelace is undone.'

With that tiny remark she sought to put him firmly in his place. He ignored it.

'Madame Dutheillet, you have the reputation of being an intelligent woman; so please allow me to explain very simply why I'm here. Your husband is currently obstructing my investigation into a series of murders. He's doing so in order to cover up for one of his colleagues, or perhaps to cover up a wide-ranging plot or conspiracy. I don't really know, and at the moment I don't particularly care. My concern is with my investigation, wherever it may lead me.'

'Then why don't you go to my husband? Explain all this to him.'

'I've already done so, as you probably know. I'd gladly do so again, but he won't see me for one thing, and for another, I think he innocently believes he has information he can use to exercise influence over Interpol. If I showed him these files, he might become – shall I say, careless? And, besides, I'm not sure you would want him to see them.'

'You're perfectly right. He has much better things to do than read through some grubby letters or semi-literate diaries put together for the purpose of blackmailing him.'

He examined her as she talked. Her elegance and assurance were not contrived. She had none of the brittle bad taste of an American woman her age, all lifted face and silicone-enhanced breasts. She was neither wholly natural nor a plastic surgeon's creation, and he admired her for it. But watching her made him think of Alice, and the thought of Alice diminished the First Lady in every way.

'I had hoped you might just talk with him. Late one evening, perhaps, when he's feeling mellow after a glass of wine. You're an intelligent woman, you will know just what to say. Point out to him that he risks being arraigned on a charge of obstruction of justice. And remember that this is not a case of fraud or tax evasion: it is one of murder.'

'Yes, I know perfectly well. You don't imagine I let you come here without first checking up on you. I know all about your severed heads and plucked-out hearts. I don't know how you can bear to work in such a grisly profession.'

'Someone has to, ma'am.'

'I'm sure. But necessity is no qualification for moral superiority. You may have your murders and your drug-running to deal with – and I wish you the best of luck in pursuing all of them – but my husband has been entrusted with the running of a country. And not just any country, but one of the most technically advanced and commercially competitive in the world. He makes decisions every day that affect the lives of thousands, even millions. Don't think he does any of this lightly. Or that he acts without integrity. On the contrary, he takes everything he does very seriously indeed, and he has a right to become impatient when some whining functionary from the Irish bogs has the temerity to tell him what he should and should not do. As if you even understood the most elementary facts about modern political ethics.'

'Quite right, ma'am. We're a nation of poets, not philosophers.'

'You're flippant too, I see. That's no matter. I hope I managed to get my point across. Your interests, however important, have to be placed in the context of the broader interests of France and its international relations. And the simple truth is that, whatever dirt you've managed to dig up on my husband, he has the means of putting it back in the ground. The French press is bound by very tight privacy laws. I understand that one of your assistants has already suffered a fatal accident. I'd hate to think there might be others.'

Declan stood. Inwardly, he was seething at her manner and the arrogance of her little lecture, but he strove to preserve outward calm.

'I take the point of everything you've said,' he declared. 'But I'm afraid you're mistaken about one thing. None of these files contains what you call "dirt" about your husband. I have plenty of that, of course, but I don't see what possible interest it could hold for you. If you'd care to take a look, I think you'll find that everything in these files concerns you, not him. I'll leave them with you, if you don't mind. These are all copies, of course. The originals are so far out of your reach, they might as well be on Mars. And I think you should be told that if another of my assistants dies or is injured in the course of this investigation, at least one of these files will be made public, probably in Canada, where the laws of privacy are not so strict. I may not be able to destroy you or your thug of a husband, Madame Dutheillet – but I assure you I am more than capable of hurting you, and hurting you very badly. Now, if you'll excuse me, I have several murders to investigate. And I'm sure you've got a hard day's philosophizing ahead of you.'

With Dutheillet thus muzzled, it was possible to put Nougayrède back into the picture. The first question Declan wanted an answer to was 'Where did Nougayrède spend the last couple of days before he was officially reported missing?' He sent one of his best men, a French-Canadian called Jean-Hugues Gallimard, direct to Mexico City.

'And while you're there,' he said, 'see what you can find out about this woman.' He gave him what details he had of Antonia Rocha y Ramírez. He felt sorry for Leo Mallory and hoped he could do something for him.

Outside, the day turned pale as the sun dropped slowly from the air. Declan looked down from his high office window and thought of Alice.

His door opened. Rob Barlow, his English computer expert, was standing, waiting to be asked in.

'Don't stand on ceremony, Rob. Just come on in. You look as if something's up.'

Barlow nodded. He was used to being tossed into a little room somewhere and forgotten, but this investigation was proving more hands-on and interactive than he could have imagined.

'We've just received an e-mail from the Italian carabinieri,' he said.

'I didn't know the Italians had joined the world of cyberspace.'

'Some of them have. They have very pretty Websites. Have you ever been to Rome, sir?'

'Rome? Of course. My late wife was desperate for Rome. I used to take her there every few years. It was the Vatican, of course, that was the draw. That and the Holy Father. She attended more audiences with one Pope and another than was good for her. I used to tour the city while she was inside.'

'That's handy, then, sir. I can't make sense of this message myself.'

'What's it say?'

'Well, sir. Is there a pyramid in Rome at all?'

Declan felt as though his heart began to bleed. He thought quickly, then understood.

'Yes,' he said. 'It's the pyramid of Caius Cestius. It was

built a few years before Christ. You'll find it built into a mediaeval wall outside the Porta San Paolo.'

'Is it very big, sir?'

'No, not very. About thirty metres high . . . You're not going to tell me –'

'Someone rang the carabinieri this morning. Told them to go inside, into the tomb chamber. It was . . . the report says it was filled with hearts. As far as they can tell so far, all human.'

'No bodies?' Declan felt as though he had lost control of his tongue.

Barlow shook his head. 'No, sir. But there's one thing. Apparently, each of the hearts has a label tied to it, and each label has a name printed on it. Or written on, I'm not sure, I don't think it says.'

'It doesn't matter. I take it there've been no bodies reported elsewhere.'

'Not yet.'

'Do the Italians know this is connected to our case?'

'I don't think so, sir. It was just a routine report.'

'Ah, yes. You're quite right there. In the choice of your words. "Routine". Well, Mr Barlow, you'd better book me on to the first flight to Rome. It's time I had another look at the Pope.'

39

McDonald Annexe
Department of Archaeology
Downing Street
University of Cambridge

Winter in Cambridge never changed, thought Gwen Radcliffe as she looked outside prior to locking up. Always damp, always cold, always ready to undermine what little health she had left. Noxious vapours – what her late mother had called miasms – slipped off the river at early evening and crept unhindered through the city. Tomorrow morning, dons, students, and solid citizens alike would wake to coughs and running noses, flooded lungs and searing throats. Almost surrounded by fen country, the city was badly situated in the first place. Gwen swished the curtains together and turned back with a sigh to the room.

Twenty-three years she'd worked here, she thought, and now she was about to retire. Early retirement, perhaps, but final enough for her. Tomorrow would be her last day. She surveyed what had been her domain most days of her working life. The fish swam in their never-ending circles, the clock ticked, the photocopier hummed. Nothing had changed very much, she thought. But tomorrow everything would change, and a young girl would sit where she had sat, and download files from the new computer, and set up something called Websites, and flirt with young Dr Halabi, all things she'd never been able to do. Hers had been the virtues of hot tea and biscuits, neat shorthand, and a fast typing speed. Tomorrow's secretary could speak straight to the computer and it would type out everything three or four times faster than the best human hand.

Footsteps sounded in the corridor. Startled, she looked round. There shouldn't be anyone here at this time, not in the annexe. Unless Professor Popper had got himself lost again. He'd have kept her on, she thought. Except that he'd been due for retirement himself for the past eight years. The rest of the staff had gone home long ago, or should have done: she was only here this late in order to wallow in a little nostalgia and pack some things before her departure.

The door opened and closed. A breath of damp air came in from the corridor. Gwen looked round. It was not Professor Popper. It was no one she knew.

The stranger looked entirely foreign, with slicked-back black hair and eyes as dark as baby olives. He reminded her of a bullfighter she'd seen once in Torremolinos, young and arrogant and still as he watched the bulls paw the ground before each onslaught. This man was older, fifty or so, though he looked as fit and as cunning as that young man all those years ago.

'Mrs Radcliffe?'

She stepped forwards. Something made her feel jittery. Her nerves hadn't been right since the dog died. Denis. He'd been run over by a Fiat Uno on Cherry Hinton Road.

'I'm afraid we're closed . . .'

But he asked for her by name.

362

'I hoped you were Mrs Radcliffe.'

'Well, I am, but . . . You'll have to come back tomorrow, I'm just closing the office. The department's already closed.'

'No, that's all right. You don't have to worry.' He came several steps closer. 'It's you I came to see.'

'Me? Oh, you mean about my retirement? Couldn't it wait until tomorrow after all? I'm not really up to filling in forms just yet. But tomorrow, certainly. Why don't you come to my house then?'

'I don't have time. And this won't take a moment. All I want is information about one of your staff members. Doctor Mallory.'

'Information?' She found herself leaning against the desk for support. He had such poise and bearing. She had to look up at him. His long black overcoat, that seemed to be made of cashmere, glistened with moisture from the air outside.

'I understand he rang you from Texas, from a hospital in Dallas.'

'I don't see how –'

'You sent him a package, as a result of which he checked out of the hospital and flew south, I'm not sure where to. I also understand that a large sum of money reached this department to pay for teaching cover during his continued absence over a period of at least a year. And that the money in question was accompanied by a much larger sum which is to be spent –'

'Look, sir, I don't know where you heard all of this, but it's private information. I'm not in a position to disclose anything to you or anyone else about it. Not without authorization from the Board of Studies. Are you from the press?'

'Do I look like a journalist?' He let the coat fall back. Underneath, he wore a black silk suit.

'I don't know, but that doesn't change things.'

'Well, it does in a way. A journalist wouldn't do what I'm about to do. Oh, by the way, I've taken the liberty of locking up from inside. The building's quite empty: I've checked. It's just the two of us.'

'I'm going to call the police if you don't leave here at once.'

He nodded towards the telephone.

'Please,' he said.

She felt nausea pass through her, for he seemed too confident to be sent away. She picked up the receiver. The line was dead.

'Who are you?' she asked.

'Let's just say that I'm very interested in Doctor Mallory and what he's up to. He must be on a dig, and you must have some idea where that is.'

She shook her head fiercely.

'That's top secret,' she said, blundering into his trap. 'No one knows where he's gone besides Professor Norman and . . .'

'Yourself.'

'I didn't say that.'

'No, but it's obvious someone has to communicate with his expedition from time to time. I did think of speaking with Professor Norman, but it seems he's gone to a conference in the Czech Republic.'

'He'll be back next week,' she suggested, thinking that by then she'd be gone and her successor could handle this.

'Too late. I need answers to my questions now. Surely you can tell me where Leo Mallory is now.'

'I've told you, that is confidential. He made a point of asking us to keep his whereabouts secret. There are risks that treasure-hunters may try to get in ahead of him and spoil the dig.'

'Really? He expects to find treasure, then? Did he say anything else?'

'Please, I honestly can't say more.'

'Of course you can. You just have to be helped. Look, why don't we both sit down over here?'

Gwen cast a look at the clock. It was half-past six already.

'I don't have time to sit down.'

That was when he showed her the first photograph. Her world went topsy-turvy after that.

'Where'd you get that?'

He'd shown her a photograph of her niece Ellen. Ellen's parents – Gwen's sister and her husband – had died in a car crash seven years ago, leaving their small child to be taken care of and finally adopted by her aunt. Ellen was now fifteen and the centre of Gwen Radcliffe's existence.

The second photograph, a Polaroid, showed Ellen terrified and naked, strapped to a kitchen chair. A thin gag went round her mouth, and her eyes bulged with fear. They lived a little out of town, in a bungalow next to Teversham Fen. It was a quiet place, with few visitors. Ellen was a pupil at St Bede's, and every day after school she cycled back from Cherry Hinton to Church End, then on to Teversham, a journey of little more than ten minutes unless the roads were packed. She'd have been back a couple of hours now, and should have been getting tea ready. Perhaps it was there on the table, where she could see it awaiting her aunt's return, ham sandwiches and cake and sausage rolls fresh from the little shop she went to in Cherry Hinton. A good girl, very loving, very dutiful.

'Try to calm down,' he said, watching her hyperventilate. She'd been prone to panic attacks ever since Bob and

Rosie's crash, almost as though she'd been in the car herself.

'How . . . can I . . . calm down?!' she shouted, catching her breath on the words as though snagging a cardigan on brambles.

'Take deep breaths and think how important it is for you to remain in control of yourself.'

'Have you . . . Have you hurt her in . . . any way?'

'That depends what you mean. She has been raped, first by myself, then by a friend of mine who is with her even as we speak. She was a virgin, you'll be pleased to discover. Admirable in such an attractive child.'

She spat at him then, not caring what he might do to her. He only wiped the spittle away.

'Try not to irritate me,' he said. 'Your niece's well-being depends on it. Now, let me explain. I have a mobile phone in my pocket. My friend has another one. If I ring him, he will hurt your niece. If necessary, he will kill her. It's up to you.'

'Please, for God's sake leave her alone. She's done nothing to harm you.'

'Where did Leo Mallory go when he left Texas?'

She leapt for his lifeline at once.

'Some place . . . In the Caribbean, some island.'

'Do you remember a name?'

She shook her head.

'I don't mean for the island. He must have stayed with someone there.'

'I . . . I don't remember. Oh, please, don't harm her. I can't remember. There was an envelope: I sent it on to him, to Doctor Mallory.'

'Was it de Sepúlveda?'

She hesitated, digging deep into her memory.

'It might have been. I really can't be sure.'

'But a Spanish name?'

'Yes, I think so. I posted it on. I didn't really look.'

'Very well. Relax. You're doing well. You'll be with your niece shortly. All I want to know is, where is Doctor Mallory now?'

'Oh, God: I can't tell you because I don't know. He's in Guatemala, and anything goes to the Archaeological Museum there. I can let you have the address. But he said nothing about their dig. In fact, I think he said he hadn't even found it yet.'

'You're sure that's all you know?'

'It's all, I swear.'

'Did he have any maps? Do you have maps here that he might have used?'

'For his last dig, yes; but not for this. I honestly can't help you further.'

He looked at her for several seconds. The heating had gone off a little while earlier, and it was beginning to grow bitterly cold in the room.

'I believe you,' he said. He reached inside his jacket and took out a phone, on which he keyed in a set of numbers. It rang for seconds at the other end, then a man's voice answered.

'Augusto? Kill the girl. Use your knife. Wait for me there.'

'Nooooooo!' the secretary screamed. 'I told you everything. You said you wouldn't hurt her.'

'Don't worry, he'll be quick. He'll cut her throat. In the bathroom, probably. I'll take you over there now. He'll be quick with you too, don't worry.'

40

Iles de la petite terre

The Piper Aztec hovered breathlessly on the blue air like a dragonfly. Heat shimmered all along its forty-foot wingspan. With a whisper, it dropped like a white insect, down towards the little archipelago beneath, white sand and blue sea, the tiny islands spread like drops of wax.

Marie-Louise looked up, squinting against the sunlight. She could hear the plane, but strain as she might, she could see nothing. No aircraft normally came this way at this hour, but the occasional tourist charter made an appearance and passed out of sight again en route for somewhere more exotic, with bars and music and fast dancing.

She turned her attention back to the letter she was writing. A friend had once told her that e-mail and a telephone would transform her life, but she'd just smiled and kept on writing letters by hand. What would be the point, she asked herself, of living in a place like this if you had to tailor your lifestyle to that of people who lived in the middle of Manhattan? That's why she'd agreed to join Luis out here, giving up her job as a corporate lawyer with one of France's largest perfume houses. She'd never regretted the move, not even when Luis was at his most demanding and foolish. And she'd never have stood for all that if she hadn't loved him as she did. That had been strange too, she thought, finding real love so late in life, and with a priest.

The engine noise grew louder. She looked up, squinting again, and this time made out a black speck low down towards the horizon. This time she did not take her eyes away. The black speck grew rapidly in size, and suddenly it was a long white insect flying low across the blue water in her direction. She stood and went to the railing. The Aztec hit the water, its communications tower bobbing as the pilot slackened the throttle and the little plane fought for an easy position against the waves. Slowly, it came to a standstill, its white wings casting a shadow across the water.

A seaplane was a rare visitor to the island. Marie-Louise watched while someone got a dinghy into the water and climbed aboard. Two minutes later, a man stepped out into the surf. He drew the dinghy with him up on to the dry sand and dropped it there.

She picked up the phone and rang Luis. He was at work in his studio, and normally she would not have disturbed him for anything. He ignored the ringing at first, but persistence finally paid off.

'Yes?' He sounded like ten generations of annoyed creative artists rolled into one.

'Luis, a seaplane has just landed off Soufrière beach. Someone's brought a dinghy ashore.'

Visitors to the island were few and well controlled.

'Could you make out a name on the seaplane?'

Rather than come in by boat, some visitors chartered a seaplane from the little airport on Pointe-à-Pitre, from a French-Canadian pilot called Jacques Vauclin. Vauclin flew a couple of Grumman Ducks that had seen better days and better passengers. He had only one good eye, a fact he kept well hidden from the civil aviation inspectors at Basse Terre. Luis trusted him because he flew with a small plastic figure of the Virgin in the cockpit.

'Not Vauclin. In fact, I don't think there was any sort of logo or wording on the fuselage.'

'Very well. Whoever it is, tell him I'm too busy to be disturbed. Fob him off. Tell him whatever you like.'

'And if he isn't willing to take that for an answer?'

'Ring François. He'll know what to do.'

'It may not be that easy. What if he's armed?'

There was a silence at the other end, then the priest put the phone down.

The man on the beach was no longer to be seen. Marie-Louise squinted, trying to displace shadows and tidy rocks away with her bare eyes, but he was nowhere to be seen. She went back to the phone and dialled '4', François' number.

François was responsible for security on the island. He'd served with the 44th Infantry Regiment based in Orléans, which was the usual cover for soldiers belonging to France's Direction Générale de la Sécurité Extérieure. Now aged forty, he'd been working for de Sepúlveda for seven years, single-handedly guaranteeing his personal safety and that of his island.

There was no reply. She put down the receiver and frowned. Normally, François kept to his quarters at this time of day. He liked to keep to a strict routine, so his employers could find him at any time. Marie-Louise shrugged, thinking he must have heard the seaplane come in as well, and that he must have gone out to meet anyone landing from it.

She left her bungalow and took a familiar turn to her right. Luis might have to be disturbed after all. They'd have to do something to improve security, she thought. François was good, but there was only one of him. And at forty, he wasn't as sharp as he should be. Give him another ten years . . .

She turned the corner between the generator room and the foodstore, and was brought up short by a man approaching her with long strides from the direction of the main complex. He must have found and climbed the stairs that led straight up from the beach.

He stopped and gave her a 100-watt smile. It should have lit up his face, but somehow it had the opposite effect.

'I'm sorry to surprise you,' he said, 'but there was no chance to call in advance.'

'You'll have to leave. This is a private island. Visitors aren't welcome.'

'Really? But if I'm not mistaken, you've just had a visitor.'

He wore a white suit, expensive by the look of it, she thought, Armani probably. She guessed his age at around fifty. His slim figure, his slicked-back hair and coal-black eyes disturbed her both sexually and morally. She found herself wanting him to come to her, and yet she knew he was death in some form or other.

'We choose our visitors. We invite them ourselves. It's none of your business who we ask to join us.'

'Perhaps not.' The smile faded, as though power was drained from it for other purposes. 'But I'm here now, and I've travelled a long way to get here. I think you should tell your boyfriend I'm here. Or is he too engrossed in prayer to care?'

She felt a chill pass through her. The stranger's familiar manner was threatening. She wondered what had happened to François.

'You're worried about François,' he said. 'There's no need. He's perfectly all right. As long as he doesn't try to interfere, he'll come to no harm.'

'What have you done with him?'

'Nothing. Now, let's not waste any more time.'

He drew a gun from his pocket, a small silver pistol that shone in the sun.

'Who are you?' she asked.

'Didn't he tell you?'

'He told me nothing. Is he expecting you?'

'I'm the face in his mirror. We're old friends, he and I, but we happened to go different ways. Nothing unusual in that, is there?'

'Why didn't you . . . ?'

But he gestured to her with the gun, and she led him to a flight of wooden steps that wound their way gently up a dry hillside between the tiny houses of the colony. She was weak with fear. Her insides seemed to have shrivelled at sight of the weapon he held. There would be no point in trying to trick him, she understood that.

'Your name is Rafael, isn't it?' she asked as they climbed.

'I see he talks of me.'

'Not very much, as a matter of fact. You're something he wants to forget.'

'I don't believe he can do that. After all, he made me what I am.'

She turned and looked at him. His skin seemed almost untouched by age.

'We make ourselves,' she said. 'You're no more what he wanted to create than the monster was Frankenstein's choice. You made yourself.'

They continued up the hill in silence. At the top, Luis'

studio, originally designed by Le Corbusier for his father, to be built in Spain, stood against the skyline, white and significant. Next to it stood the museum, built in white marble in the Doric style, in deliberate contrast to its neighbour.

Luis was at work on a large canvas, painting in perfect light. A Christ-figure lay bleeding on a white beach that closely resembled the one below. In the sky above him, angels flew like seabirds, their white garments billowing in the air like feathers. The painter did not at first seem to be aware of the arrival of visitors. His hand continued to sweep across the canvas. The eyes of Christ were mournful and deep, and Luis was busily trying to paint a touch of hope into them.

They watched him for a while, saying nothing. In the end, it was Luis who broke the silence.

'Come closer, Rafael,' he said. 'I can't see you from here.'

He stopped painting and put his brushes and cloths down on a small, paint-spattered table behind him. Rafael came closer, prodding Marie-Louise with his pistol.

'Oh, for God's sake, Rafael, put the gun away. There's no need to over-dramatize. I'm hardly likely to attack you, nor is Marie-Louise; and I expect you have François tied up somewhere else.'

Rafael smiled indulgently, then stepped behind Luis, gun still in hand. He scrutinized the half-finished painting like a prospective customer in a gallery.

'You haven't changed much, old friend,' he remarked.

'Why should I change? I'm not in search of anything. I have my themes, just as Monet had his water-lilies. I paint on eternal subjects, Rafael. Why should I change because fashion alters a little here and there?'

'You could move on as I moved on.'

'What should I move on to? To heresy, perhaps? Like you?'

Rafael shook his head, though Luis could not see him.

'No more heresy,' he said, 'at least no more than you already believe in. You taught me yourself to question all things.'

Luis turned at last and looked his killer in the face. He had no doubt in that moment that he would die, that Rafael could not bear to leave him alive.

'My dear Rafael,' he murmured. 'You talk of movement, yet you change so little yourself. You seek eternal life, but what you mean is permanent changelessness. To live without outer signs of having lived. Like being pickled, but without the flavour.' He smiled as if at his own joke, then gestured to one side.

'Let's go over there so we can sit and talk in comfort. My old legs will not support standing for as long as yours.'

There were chairs and a small table covered with tubes of paint and brushes. Without waiting for Rafael to say yes, Luis crossed to the table, taking Marie-Louise with him. Rafael followed slowly. He slipped the gun back into his pocket before sitting down.

'I've heard rumours about this island,' he said.

'Really? I'm sure they can't be very interesting. Nothing much ever happens here.'

'Is that so? Well, I've heard that this little island contains more great modern paintings than half the world's galleries of modern art combined.'

'Really?' said Luis. 'I do not listen to rumours as a rule. Nor should you. I seem to remember teaching you that many years ago.'

'I scarcely remember what you taught me now. So many things have changed. In the case of rumours, I think persistent ones deserve at least some attention. If there should be any truth in what I've heard . . . I'd be honoured if you allowed me to see some of your collection.'

'I didn't know you were such an art lover.'

Rafael shook his head. 'Not an art lover, perhaps, if you mean someone truly dedicated. But curious, I think I might call myself that. And speaking of curiosity, I would so like to see your pyramid and temple. I had just a glimpse of them from the plane on my way in.'

Luis looked at him coolly.

'What possible interest could such things have for the likes of you?'

'I'm surprised you should ask. You know very well what interest I have in the old gods.'

'There are no old gods here. The temple you saw was built to honour Christ, not Kukulcán.'

'That position could be reversed.'

'Only in your mind, Rafael. You still haven't understood the most basic principles I tried to teach you.'

'On the contrary, I understand them too well. But you were never my only teacher. When I learned to enter my own heart in a trance, like a shaman, it was never Christ that spoke to me. Only the old gods came to answer my questions. They still come now, and they teach me things beyond your imagination.'

'I'm sorry to hear that.'

'It was you who taught me to listen to my heart.'

'Your heart, yes. In God's time, you would have heard a different voice. But you chose to listen to your self. That is the source of the voices you hear.'

'Call them what you please, my voices offer me far more than your Christ ever offered me.'

'Do they? Can you be so sure? You've been listening to devils, Rafael. Or perhaps to the Devil himself. The Bible –'

'The Bible promises eternal life to those who die, but it gives no guarantees. My voices instruct me in the path to true immortality. I shall gain eternal life in this world, and never face death. What can you offer that is superior to that? Some hymns, some incense, and the biggest gamble of all?'

'There's no point in my trying to argue this with you. If you don't understand by now, nothing I say will change your mind. Assuming you did not come here to be taught further by me, perhaps you can tell me why you came here. Then I can tell you there is nothing I can do to help you, and you can be on your way.'

Rafael looked round the room. Light, filtered through cunningly designed windows, stunned the sight. On the walls hung portraits of Marie-Louise, some head-and-shoulders, some full nudes. The light was in all of them, as though Luis had painted with it, or as if the sitter had been made of light.

'I want some information,' he said. 'It will not hurt you to give it to me. But if you refuse, I shall make it very painful for you.'

'Are you threatening me?'

'Yes. And if you know anything about me, you will know I carry out my threats. I want to know where Leo Mallory is, and where he is headed. You have maps: I would like copies of them, please. And you know where the girl is. Antonia. Let me have what I ask for, and I'll leave you in peace. Otherwise . . .' He hesitated only momentarily, but the shift in his posture and the look in his eye were enough to hint at a dark crevice opening beneath their feet. 'Otherwise, I shall destroy this island and everyone on it.'

41

Chixoy/Salinas River
Lacandón Forest
Guatemala
1 February

The river shimmered like a panel of deep green glass stretched to infinity, reflecting in every eddy and every current the curtains of jade- and loden-coloured leaves that hemmed it in on both sides. They were running freely now, on a strong current that pulled the rafts along like toys. Leo stood in the prow of the leading craft, watching the right-hand bank carefully for the first sign of what they were aiming for. The wooden deck was permanently awash, but the raft was capable of pushing water out again as fast as it came in.

There were two rafts, nineteen-foot Whitewater River rigid inflatables, one green, one orange. Leo had bought them secondhand from a Utah-based adventure tour company that ran whitewater rafting expeditions on the Usumacinta River. Word had gone north about the volcanic eruptions, and tourists were cancelling their trips every day now. There'd been another eruption, this time Santiaguito, just south of Quezaltenango. The village of Llanos de Pinal had been wiped out.

One raft carried four expedition members, the other

three, together with supplies. The latter had been kept to a minimum: after all, the inflatables would only be taking them part of the way. Once in the forest, they'd be carrying their own equipment and supplies.

The rafts had rigid aluminium hulls to which inflatable flotation collars had been attached along the top of the gunwale. They were virtually unsinkable, whether by rocks or water. Their inboard petrol engines drove them hard down the twisting lane of water, throwing up great plumes of white water in their wake.

'We should be getting there soon,' said Leo, slipping one arm around Antonia's waist. Barney Kavanagh stood on his other side. He'd been in these parts before, on a prolonged visit to some of the less-well-known Mayan sites, including the cluster west of Sayaxché.

'Hopeless trying to outsmart it,' Barney said. 'There's a sharp bend, and you're on it. Did I mention the rocks?'

'You did.'

'The shallows?'

'Yes.'

'The fifty-foot spiders on rubber strings?'

'Frequently.'

Antonia turned and kissed Leo on the lips. He kissed her back, then turned his gaze back to the riverbank. They'd been kissing on and off for days now, ever since her arrival in Guatemala. There'd been no opportunity to sleep together again, but neither of them cared about that. It was being together that mattered, it was knowing at every moment where the other was. One would not stray from the other more than a matter of yards, nor would they be out of one another's sight for more than a few minutes at a time.

They'd talked a little, enough to know that it wasn't yet time to talk. One morning, soon after they set off, he'd absentmindedly removed his shirt when she was watching, and the sight of his scars had chilled her through and through. She would not speak of her father, or of Rafael, or how very close she had come to madness.

The expedition had left Guatemala City two days earlier, flying by helicopter as far as San Cristóbal Verapaz, a one-horse town just north of the Chixoy Dam. The plan was to follow the route of Don Joaquín as closely as possible. Unfortunately, the Chixoy River was no longer the powerful waterway it had been in his day. The dam had all but choked it, making navigation difficult for a great part of its course. Running in a deep valley between the Sierra los Cuchumatanes to the west and the Sierra de Chamá on the east, it eventually re-established itself from dozens of mountain streams. After Flor de Cacao, it created the border with Mexico, hurrying in a series of tight loops down towards its final meeting with the Usumacinta that would take it to the sea.

They weren't going that far, at least not in the rafts. Don Joaquín's lost city lay somewhere in the dark heart of the Lacandón forest, overgrown by centuries of jungle. Leo glanced up to the thick wall of trees on his left. Somewhere in there, he thought. This close, the idea of dark pyramids and the secret of eternal life seemed less absurd than it had done on a Caribbean beach. In there, behind the leaves, there would be no sunshine. A man could walk for ever in circles and never come out again. Cut it, burn it, map it – the jungle always won in the end.

With Antonia's arrival, most of the original team had joined up. They'd all been living in Mexico City without passports, but a call to Luis de Sepúlveda had secured travel documents and enough money to buy them all first-class air tickets to Guatemala. Diane Krauss had dumped her Mexican boyfriend and headed home instead, having vowed to give up archaeology and take up a career as a TV anchorwoman instead. The rest, excited by the project, had signed on under conditions of the greatest secrecy, as dictated by de Sepúlveda.

Bob Maddox had been given a blank cheque to procure fresh photographic equipment – his own had been 'confiscated' by the Mexican police and was unlikely to turn up again short of a presidential decree. Steve Sabloff had bought an Apple G3 Powerbook 300 and a host of peripherals, including a modem capable of linking to communications satellites. For energy, he'd bought up all of Guatemala City's stock of Powerbook batteries, all fully charged. He wanted to produce a computer simulation of their route, updating it daily as they cut their way through the jungle, plotting in rivers and any other landmarks to check against Don Joaquín's map and account.

In the raft behind, the Minnesota twins, Dorothy and Dorothea Filbert, swayed in perfect unison. They were dressed in black as usual, in *huipils*, *refajos*, and *rebozos* they'd had woven specially before leaving. The weavers had demanded *muchos dólares* before taking on such a strange job, so far removed from the weaving in blue, red, green, and other bright colours, to which they were so accustomed. In a large aluminium box by their side, they carried all manner of strange devices, from endoscopes to digital cameras to listening equipment capable of mapping an unseen room just by reading an echo, rather like a boat's sonar.

They turned a bend and there it was, a shallow beach of shingle and rocks above which some undergrowth had been cleared away. Just beyond, Leo could make out the opening where the Rio Pasión entered the Chixoy. The site was far from conspicuous. There were no pyramids, no acropolises, no game courts – none of the in-your-face architecture of the great sites. They might have missed it through a moment's carelessness.

The next minutes were filled with hard, fast paddling to turn the rafts and guide them to the right bank. With a flurry of bumping and grinding, they caught the beach just as Leo thought they were about to be swept past. Everyone disembarked, and they drew the rafts halfway up the beach. They weighed in at over 700 pounds each, not to mention supplies and equipment.

On the riverbank were two thatched huts, both in a state of collapse, built to accommodate a team of archaeologists who had investigated the site many years earlier. Behind them, the jungle pressed in hard. They climbed up to the land above the bank and began to cut their way through a wall of lianas and palm fronds. Barney had been here six or seven years before, and knew roughly what to look for, and where to look.

Altar de los Sacrificios was a little-studied, often-pillaged archaeological site that held very little of interest for sightseers. Scattered groups of stelae decorated with reliefs of gods and rulers were almost the only remaining signs of ancient habitation. Fallen monuments lay all over the site, covered in undergrowth, with the jungle thick about them, their time-blackened stone crumbling, their fronts cracking, their inscriptions fading to nothing.

They came to a ridge on top of which a grove of corozo palms lifted their branches to the sky. In the middle of the grove stood a large altar, a wheel of stone some six feet across, covered in bright green moss.

They'd been pottering about for ten minutes or more

before anyone noticed anything out of the ordinary. It was Antonia who sensed it first.

'I think we're being watched,' she said, taking Leo's hand tightly in hers.

'Probably a jaguar back there in the trees, wondering if we'll make good dinners.' But even as he spoke, Leo felt a cold veil fold itself over his limbs.

'No, not an animal,' she said. 'Someone's out there. Someone's watching us.'

Even as she spoke, a figure detached itself from the trees and began to walk towards them. As he neared them, Leo saw he was an Indian, almost certainly Kekchi Maya, a man of perhaps forty or fifty years, dressed in nothing but a loincloth. He carried a bundle on his back and a long machete at his waist. No one said a word as he approached. He seemed to be coming, not from the forest, but from the past, a Maya warrior come to reclaim his land.

No one spoke, and no one moved in his direction. Unerringly, he headed straight towards Leo. When he was a few paces away, he stopped and looked Leo up and down.

'Are you Leo?' he asked. He spoke in English, with what seemed to be an American accent.

Leo nodded.

'My name is George,' the Indian said. He stretched out a hand. 'I'm pleased to meet you.'

'I . . .' Words failed Leo. He wasn't used to Indians coming out of the trees and addressing him in flawless English.

'Surprised to see me?'

'Well, I . . .' Leo felt like a stuffy Victorian traveller, unsure how to answer this strange-looking foreigner, simply because he did not know the proper form.

'Didn't Luis tell you I was going to meet you here?'

'Luis? I don't think . . . No, he didn't say anything about our being met.'

'It doesn't matter. You got here on time.'

'On time? I don't understand.'

'I'm your guide. For part of the way. And your mentor in jungle lore.'

'Luis sent you?'

'Didn't I say so? No, perhaps not. Does that trouble you?'

'It does in a way. This is a secret expedition. I'm worried that someone can just come up to us and proclaim himself our guide. How do I know Luis sent you and not someone else?'

Within moments, a letter was produced from somewhere. It was an old letter, faded in places and torn in others, but it carried Luis de Sepúlveda's signature and it testified to George's probity and skill in eloquent and convincing Spanish. It also gave his real name, Rokché.

'How come, George?' asked Leo. 'And how come you speak such good English?'

'Can we sit down while we talk? And how about some coffee? I take it you have some on board.'

Leo laughed, and called the others over to meet their guide. The twins set about making a pot of strong coffee.

'We've only got powdered milk,' Antonia apologized.

'As long as it's Coffee-mate.'

Somebody found the little camp stools and set them up in a semi-circle.

'I am bushed,' proclaimed George, whistling as he sank on to the first stool. 'Standing about all day waiting on you folks, I'm near collapse.'

'Does anyone ever refer to you as "George of the Jungle"?' asked Leo.

'All the time. Ever since the movie reached the art houses of Guatemala. I'm a big fan. Actually, I was christened George back in the old days, when I was a Christian. I got in with some *evangélicos*, Southern Baptists with a mission base out here in Petén. They have a couple of schools in Flores and another in Sayaxché. I started in the school, then I got Jesus when I was sixteen. I became a good Indian. They had high hopes of me, thought I'd grow up to be a preacher, a missionary to the Maya. That was the plan.'

Leo looked at him, smiling, his torso lightly touched with sweat, his long hair tumbling behind his neck and caught in a knot. The machete in his belt had been long used. He didn't look like any missionary he'd ever seen.

'Guess it didn't work out,' said Barney.

'Hell, no. It's a long story. When I was eighteen, my church decided it was time I had some further education. I'd been the top pupil in the school, and every year there was a scholarship to study at their private university in Mexico. It's a small place in Tuxtla Gutiérrez, name of Jim Hawkins College, after some televangelist or other. I stayed there a few years, but while I was there I got involved with Luis de Sepúlveda. I heard about his work with the Indians in Santa Marta and started visiting. He changed my ways of thinking. Maybe it wasn't too hard. I was never a very convinced Christian.'

'What are you now? A Catholic?' asked Antonia.

'No more than Luis, I think. I believe in the gods, that's all.'

'The Mayan gods?'

'Are there any others?'

'Well, perhaps in –'

George shook his head. 'We are in Petén,' he said. 'We

are about to enter the deep forest. There are no other gods here but the gods of my ancestors.'

Dorothy – or it might have been Dorothea – approached with the steaming coffee pot. Cups were handed round, and the coffee poured almost ceremoniously.

'There are some cakes,' said Antonia. She opened a box of *torrijas* that she'd bought in San Cristóbal Verapaz before embarking on the raft.

George put his hand in and brought it out again with a sticky honey cake between his fingers. 'Yum yum,' he said.

'Yum yum?'

'Ancient Mayan incantation. Makes the gods of the stomach feel happy.'

'Were you forced to leave university?' Antonia asked.

He nodded. 'I just got to feeling uneasy with the place. A lot of the professors were missionaries more than academics. It wasn't a proper university, and it wasn't what I needed. That's where Luis stepped in. He paid for me to go to Harvard. I majored in politics, then I went to law school. That's what I am, as a matter of fact. A lawyer.'

'We're being taken into the middle of the jungle by a lawyer?' exclaimed Bob Maddox, who'd been taking photographs of the site and the team until now.

'You don't think I know the forest?'

Bob laughed. 'I don't know. But I do know that by the time we reach this place, you'll have more lawsuits going than a piranha has teeth.'

'I'm a good lawyer. I only defend people who have no money. As you can imagine, I have a lot of clients. When I need to make a little money, I slap on the war-paint and take some tourists a mile or two into the rainforest. We spend the night, they think they've come close to

God or nature or something, and they give me a lot of money.'

'You think that's what this is?' Leo said. 'A quick jaunt into the woods?'

George looked at him, and for once the smile left his features and he became serious. Slowly, he shook his head.

'No,' he said, 'that's not what I think. I've never been as deep into the forest as we will be going. This quick jaunt may prove more dangerous than you imagine. Some of us may die. If any of you are tourists, this is the time to say so. There will be no shame for anyone in going back. But remember – once we are in the forest, it may be too late to leave, too late to find your way back here again. This is the time to leave if you plan on doing so.'

Leo said nothing in reply. Nor did any of the others. A few minutes passed, during which no one moved or spoke. George nodded. He drained the coffee from his cup.

'Good coffee,' he said.

They spent the afternoon examining whatever memorials they could find, and recording any inscriptions. There was a faint possibility that Altar de los Sacrificios had some sort of relationship with the city they were looking for, and an even fainter one that it would reveal information about it. The inscription on the main altar gave little away. Some dates, some names, no more. But Antonia sensed it, they all sensed it, that hundreds, perhaps thousands had died here by the knife, their arched backs held fast to the altar wheel to expose their chests.

'We're wasting our time here,' she said a couple of hours later. She'd found only one item of interest in the very few inscriptions they had come up with, and no one else had stumbled across anything in the least bit meaningful. Anything that might have provided a clue had probably already been pilfered and sold at the street market over at Sayaxché.

Except for one thing. On a stela lying near the circular altar, Antonia had found one short inscription, broken off. It gave a date that corresponded to 1 March 790, and a name, Ah Cacau, 'Lord of Kaminalhuyú, which is the City of the Balams'.

'The City of the Jaguars,' said Leo, leaning over her shoulder as she deciphered the words.

She pushed herself up and squatted on her haunches in front of the stela.

'Not necessarily,' she said. '*Balam* has more than one reading. It can be a cat or a jaguar, a *hach balam*, or it can mean "sorcerer". Kaminalhuyú could very well be the City of the Sorcerers.'

Leo looked at his watch. There was still some time before sunset, long enough to make the river crossing and find a place to camp in the forest before nightfall. On the other hand, they could camp here for the night and cross first thing in the morning.

'What do you think?' he asked George. 'Should we spend the night here?'

'As opposed to?'

'The other bank. It's just trees over there. It may take a while to find somewhere suitable for our first camp.'

The light was fading. A macaw flew screeching across the river. In the forest, an ant shrike called. Above the altar, a huge ceiba tree rose above its partners, and caught on its giant crown a scarlet veil thrown by the sinking sun.

George looked at Leo strangely.

'Let me worry about that,' he said. 'I don't think this is such a good place to spend the night.'

'Too damp?'

The Indian shook his head. In the forest behind him, a host of tinamous cried out, their calls sad and mournful.

'The gods have never left here,' he said. 'I can feel them round me. And the ghosts of the dead. They are here for ever. The air is thick with them. I would not spend the night here for a million dollars, not even if the most beautiful woman in the world invited me.'

42

They sat on the steps of the pyramid and looked out across a purple sea. Luis, as always in recent days, was tired by the climb, and his heavy breathing was audible above the sound of crickets and the distant crash of breakers on rocks immediately beneath. Marie-Louise had as yet said nothing about it to him, but she knew it would soon be time to do so. He could build a new chapel in the little settlement, where it would be easier for everyone to reach.

The priest sat still, taking in the view and the stillness and the warmth and the whirring of insects as though this was the first time he had ever come here, so high above everything. He felt absurdly like a tourist, a day-tripper who snatches a glimpse of something he does not begin to understand.

'Why do you want the girl?' he asked. 'What on earth for?'

'Antonia? You've heard of her, then?'

'Yes. Leo talked about her when he was here. You know that, of course, or you would not be here. As for Antonia, he didn't know if she was alive or dead. He'd tried to contact her, but with no success. One thing he did know, that you were chasing her. But not why, he didn't understand why.'

'She's a very attractive woman. Wasn't that reason enough?'

'Not for you. I told him so. You have your choice of women, you have your personal charisma: you do not need to pursue or even advertise. Or am I missing something?'

'You're missing everything. Just like your friend Leo. Because he loves her in his bourgeois way, and lusts after her in a purely physical fashion, he thinks my love and my passion must be just the same. And in that he is seriously mistaken, as are you. I'm disappointed in you: I thought your love for Marie-Louise was more than it seemed. Evidently not.'

'You know nothing about it. And you've told me nothing that might excuse your pursuit of Antonia.'

Rafael looked at him as though their roles had been reversed, and he was the elderly teacher putting a difficult pupil in his place.

'I'm surprised that you can't guess,' he said. 'After all, you were the one to introduce me to the books of the ancient Maya, to the sayings of the Old Ones. Have you forgotten what it says in there, that when it is time for the old gods to return, the present World Cycle will end in a conflagration that will be followed by a new world?'

'You don't believe –'

'One of the figures who is destined to return to life in the last days is the hero Tecún Umán. And there are texts that say he will be accompanied by his wife, Nana María Tecún. They will return to the world, and they will live for ever to rule over men, bringing peace and harmony to the world.'

Luis shivered in spite of the heat. He could hear the words of an old Quiché prayer humming in his ears.

Capitán del reino Quiché
Tecún Umán . . .

390

Ay, Dios Mundo . . .
Nana María Tecún . . .

He knew where all this was leading, and he despaired. The Maya had divided time into cycles, some long, some short, all carefully calibrated through detailed astronomical calculations. The last cycle – the last *baktun* – had begun in 1618 and was due to end in their lifetime: on 21 December 2012, to be precise.

'I knew when I saw her that Antonia was Nana María Tecún, and that she was destined to be mine. Not for a lifetime, but for all time. Can you understand now why I am so desperate to find her? If you know anything of her whereabouts, and if you have the slightest pity for me or for yourself, tell me what you know.'

'I wouldn't tell you to turn round if she was standing behind you. As for this nonsense about new ages and eternal life –'

'Nonsense?' Rafael tried to sneer, but Luis could see at once that his words had piqued him. 'You think my voices are nonsense, is that it? That they tell me nonsense?'

'I don't know, I –'

'You don't know, but that doesn't stop you mocking. I never mocked the nonsense you believed in when I was with you. Did I? But you're not content with that. You're no different to all those other priests, the ones you think you're better than.'

'Rafael . . .' Marie-Louise put her hand on his shoulder. 'Why don't we go up to the temple? It's what we came to see.'

He looked at her angrily, then regained his composure in a flash.

'The temple? Yes, of course. Will Luis be able to climb to the top?'

'He can wait here. I'll show you round, you won't miss anything.' She turned to the priest. 'He won't miss anything, will he, dear?'

Luis forced himself to smile. He was grateful for the respite her suggestion offered him. Not just a physical respite, but a mental one. He nodded.

'You understand it all very well, my dear. He couldn't wish for a better guide than you.'

Marie-Louise took Rafael's hand and lifted him from his seat, as if they were old friends. They went like that together up the steps of the little pyramid, like children away from home for the first time. Above them, the door of the temple gaped, dark and forbidding. All about it the figures of winged serpents coiled and twisted themselves.

Candles burned inside. They were changed once a day by François. Protected from the prevailing wind, they never guttered or went out.

Marie-Louise led him inside. He inspected everything in silence and at great length. Time had no meaning for him. He contemplated the Jesus figures, and the dead and dying soldiers, and the Holocaust victims, saying nothing, playing his part as the dutiful voyeur.

'Is that true?' Marie-Louise asked. Her voice echoed in the high-ceilinged space. 'What you said about the girl, Antonia. Do you really believe you and she are destined for one another?'

'Do you not believe in destiny?' he rejoined. 'Or has he driven all that sort of thing out of your head?'

'In destiny, yes. But in ancient gods reborn, in worlds ending and coming to life again . . .'

'The end of the world will be symbolic. But it will bring with it a genuine change in men's fortunes. Antonia and I will rule over that change.'

392

'With what? You lead a small sect. You have a certain amount of wealth. That's all.'

He looked at her, half-hidden in the gloom, and pale.

'Is it?'

Above him, the feathered Christ hung over the altar like a strange bird with crystal wings. He looked up at him, trying to see the hidden eyes.

'You don't know what I have,' he said. 'Or what I will have. My small sect, as you call it, is more powerful than you can imagine. Don't judge us by our numbers.'

'What else is there to judge the power of a religion by?'

'Its true influence. Men crave all sorts of things, and the various religions try to satisfy them in whatever way they can. But telling someone he will enjoy all the good things of the world in some never-never land isn't enough. I offer them more than that. I offer eternal life itself. Not in the hereafter, but in this world. I have already learned how to extend a man's life by as much as twenty years by altering his pineal gland. That alone has convinced dozens to join my cause.'

'But it's hardly enough,' said a voice from behind him. Out of breath again, Father Luis stood in the entrance to the temple, his figure starkly etched against the pure white brilliance of the sky.

'They will die eventually,' he went on. 'And what then? They will have cheated death by a few years at the most. What of it? Good medicine, a good diet will achieve much the same more easily.'

'That's not what my people are looking for. The mass of them, perhaps – they come along because they want to hear the shamanistic wisdom of the ancient Mayas, or because they've heard I am a healer and can cure their cancers with plants from the rainforest, or because I fascinate them in some other way. Such people come and go. Some become dedicated followers and are elevated to my inner circle. But they are not my true elite. They keep the organization going, that's all.'

'Who are your elite?'

Rafael smiled. In spite of himself, he felt a need to boast. Meeting Father Luis again after so many years had awakened unexpected needs in him. He felt himself a teenager again, overawed by the power of the Church and devoted to a priesthood which he hoped one day to join.

'Much like your elite,' he said.

'My elite?' Luis laughed. 'I don't have such a thing.'

'I'm sorry, I was forgetting how you've severed links with the Church. The Catholic Church has always fostered an elite among its members. Kings, emperors, presidents, all the way down to mayors and local bigwigs. Look at the way anybody who is anybody in the community tries to join one of the *cofradías*. And look how church organizations like Opus Dei go out deliberately to recruit the most powerful and influential people. What was it their founder said?'

'"Fishes must be caught by their head."'

'Precisely. It's an old trick. Control the elite and the rest will take care of themselves.'

'And you have such an elite?' The priest's voice caught as he spoke, for even as he did so he realized that Rafael was talking in deadly earnest. He looked at Marie-Louise, and he could tell that she too had sensed the confidence in Rafael's voice.

'Of course. You would be surprised if I told you some of their names. Here and in Europe, a few in the United States. My little circle grows quickly, though. Rich men know one another and move in one another's company.

394

Politicians, diplomats, church leaders, judges do the same. Once you have recruited one, it's not so hard to recruit another.'

Luis looked at his dying Christ and sighed.

'Most politicians have a sensitive nose for bullshit,' he said. 'Your shamanistic mumbo-jumbo surely doesn't go down well in hard-headed circles like that.'

'It's not my mumbo-jumbo, as you call it, that does the trick. You're probably right. Powerful people aren't looking for platitudes, however well dressed. But precisely because they are powerful and rich and overfed, they wish to keep their power and riches and indulgences. Two chief things stand between them and the continuing possession of what they hold most dear: illness and death. I have shown them that I can cure their illnesses. Now I'm ready to give them eternal life. All I need now is your map.'

Father Luis felt as though someone had punched him hard in the stomach.

'Map?' he whispered. 'What map?'

'Oh, come on, you don't have to put on such an act. You invite Leo Mallory here and you finance him to go on an expedition in Guatemala. Have you forgotten all the times we used to speculate together about Kaminalhuyú, the fabled city of eternal life? All you had to do, you said, was to find the papers of some distant ancestor, and the rest would fall into place. You'd lead an expedition into the rainforest, so you said, and come out immortal.'

'There is no such map.'

'Then what did Mallory take with him?'

'He suggested the site. He came to me for help in financing the trip. Universities don't have that sort of money nowadays.'

'Luis, I don't have the patience to stand around listening

to this sort of thing. If you can't furnish me with what I need to find Mallory and his crew, then you're of no further use to me.'

'Does everyone have to be judged by what use they may prove to you?'

Rafael advanced on the priest, pushing him hard in the chest so that he staggered backwards. Marie-Louise ran across, but Rafael simply knocked her aside. He pushed Luis again, and again, each time pressing him closer to the entrance. Moments later, they were facing one another within inches of the steep steps that led down to ground level. Seventy steps in all, a fearful fall.

'We can share this secret,' Rafael urged. 'It's not your exclusive property. It belongs to mankind.'

'Then mankind shall have it. You, at least, shall not.'

Rafael pushed again, and this time the blow sent Luis tumbling back, spinning with such force that his body bounced on the steps and went on tumbling with no loss of momentum until it reached the bottom at last and lay still like a rag doll. Streaks of blood covered the steps where he had touched them. Within seconds, flies began to cover the blood with their black bodies and shimmering wings.

Behind Rafael, Marie-Louise stood staring at the sea below, and the rocks and the sky. It was as if someone had taken a sharp instrument and cut her heart out from her body and thrown it far, far away.

Rafael opened the throttle, and the seaplane moved forward, picking up speed, sending water in great sprays into the colourless air. He pulled back tightly, and the nose lifted, pulling the plane behind it, up out of the water. The Aztec climbed rapidly before levelling out suddenly at one thousand feet.

Before climbing further and heading back towards Guadeloupe, he banked steeply in order to fly once over the island he had just left. Looking down, he saw vast billowings of smoke, and beneath them the brightest of bright flames, red and orange and yellow. It was as if the entire island had caught fire. First the buildings had started burning, but the flames had spread quickly to the dry grass and undergrowth and trees. Everything down there that could burn was burning: Picassos and Braques, Modiglianis and Balthuses, the abstract figures of de Chirico and the white writing of Mark Tobey, Christ and Quetzlcoatl, Krishna and Mary and the lost kings of Mayapan, the seven golden cities of Cibola and the dead gods of Emal and Izamal. He thought on the words of the *Chilam Balam:* 'Destroyed was the town of Emal the Great, and Izamal', and the words that followed those: 'Where there descended the Queen, the Virgin, the Holy Person.'

He dipped his wings and lifted into the smoke-filled air. On the seat beside him lay all he needed to find what he'd been looking for all his adult life.

43

From the Diary of Leo Mallory

3 February
*The jungle is all about us now. I can sense it in every direction,
growing, breathing, watching, as if it's alive in more than a
vegetal way. You feel at times that it moves and then grows
still, as though it's stalking you. The forest is made up of more
than just trees, more than ferns and creepers. Above all, it's the
constant dark and the constant heat. We can scarcely breathe at
times, so great is the humidity. The canopy above our heads is
so thick, the sun is virtually incapable of penetrating it. A little
dull light gets through, but by the time it's been filtered by layer
after layer of heavy leaves all we get down here is a soporific
twilight in which we stumble about like drunks from root to
root, hoping to avoid injury. I've found myself falling asleep
at the most inappropriate moments. We're all sleep-walkers in
here, with the exception of George. He forges ahead untired
and untiring, cutting a swathe through the creepers with his
machete.*

*We take it in turns to follow him, cutting out a wider path
for those behind. His sense of direction is uncanny. At the end
of the day, Barney gets out his global positioning system kit and
checks our position from coordinates beamed back from space.
He checks and double-checks, but we're never more than a few
yards away from where I think we should be.*

Don Joaquín's map is useless, as I thought it would be. It will only make sense if we come across any of the landmarks he has placed on it, something I'm far from confident about. George says it doesn't matter, he'll get us there anyway. I've asked him if he knows anything about Don Joaquín's lost city, but he claims not. I suggested that he'd been there more than once, that he knows exactly where he's headed, and that all the sniffing about and listening and bending down to examine bent twigs is just a façade. He shrugged and said there are no trails where we're going, not even in men's minds.

'Aren't there any Indians in the forest?' I asked.

'Perhaps,' he said, and I saw his normally straight gaze slope away from me and enter the trees behind me, where I could not follow him. He sees things in the forest none of the rest of us can see. It's like being with a cat or a dog, the way they sometimes stop and stare, and you know they can detect something you're blissfully unaware of. He has that uncanny feel of a cat, of being complete within his skin. 'Perhaps,' he said a second time, and I turned this time and followed his gaze, but all I could see was a density of trees, with shadows woven in and out of them like dark cloth.

Everyone is jumpy. It's as though the jungle has awakened something primitive in each of us. A primitive fear, but God knows what of.

Partly, I suspect, it has to do with the sheer scale of everything. The forest doesn't deal in half measures. It grows and grows as though there was no time left. I can almost see it growing even as I write. And it grows into such extraordinary shapes and in so many forms. I've read that even a small parcel of rainforest can contain species that exist nowhere else on the planet. Such abandon seems almost profligate, as if someone was trying to squander all their resources on one place at one time. And yet, no matter how far we walk, there's no let-up in anything.

4 February

In its way, the forest is bigger and more full of life than the biggest city. There is too much of everything. There's a constant background buzz of insects that gets to sound like a deafening roar if you let it. It never stops, not by day, not by night, until I want to scream 'Stop!'. The trees are covered in moss and lichens, their branches are decorated with orchids and bromeliads, butterflies cluster in little glades like yellow, red, and blue carpets, and clouds of bats flitter and squeak like devils from some Mayan hell. There are vampire bats among them, with sharp teeth. Dorothy and Dorothea were bitten in their sleep last night, and now they sport small wounds on their necks and faces. George has rubbed something on them. He says it will encourage healing and deter future visits. I do not ask him what else is waiting behind the trees.

Vampire bat bites are not the worst. We are plagued by mosquitoes, by sand flies, inch-long ants whose bite can bring on a fever, hornets whose nests hang in the bushes almost everywhere, and, worst of all, the ubiquitous sweat bees, horrid little things that crawl all over the body. They infest our nostrils, they drill their way into our ear channels, they even succeed in getting under our eyelids, sucking for salt. At least they have no stings. Botflies lay their eggs on your skin, and if you don't get rid of them the maggots will hatch and burrow their way underneath, emerging forty days later as larval flies ready to pupate. Bob has found several on his legs. My problem is ticks. They seem to like me, and once they sink their mouths into your flesh, they're very hard to extricate. We all itch except George. He claims Indian skin is impervious to pests, but I think he has secret herbal formulas that he rubs on his skin when the rest of us aren't looking.

He knows the names of everything, in English, Spanish, and Mayan. I only have to point and he'll nod and squint and reel off the creature's name, bird or mammal, rodent or reptile, tree or flower, in an instant. I've no way of knowing whether he's right or wrong, of course; but he conveys such an impression of self-assuredness that I'm inclined to take everything he says at face value. For all I know, he's just a spy sent by de Sepúlveda to keep an eye on us. If he knows the forest as well as he claims, he could lose us or delay us at will, and we'd be none the wiser.

We crossed the Lacandón River at noon. It cuts off the Lacandón highlands from the lowlands of the Petén, and we all had a sense of crossing a boundary of some sort. Or an interdiction. The actual process of getting from one side to the other was more arduous than we'd anticipated. The river was in full spate, and several times we nearly lost items of equipment to the stream. We created a bridge with two ropes for ourselves, which George set in place. He swims very strongly, and seems already less the lawyer and more the woodsman, all muscle and instinct. Our equipment had to go on a wooden raft which we strapped together from the branches of a ramón tree – the sort that carries breadnuts, which the spider monkeys love.

It was late afternoon by the time everything was over. We were all wet and shivering, and sat huddled round a fire that never seemed to grow. Behind us in the darkness, a margay or an ocelot set up a banshee cry that went on for over an hour.

I'm worried about Antonia. She has told me almost nothing about what happened to her at the ranch. I explained to her about how I'd telephoned from Dallas, time after time, but how on each occasion I'd been rebuffed. She just smiled and held my hand and said it didn't matter now. In one way, she's exactly as I remember her from Komchen and Mexico City; but in another she has undergone some tremendous change. Very often, when we're walking, she'll fall behind, and when I come on her again, I find her sad and withdrawn.

When she turned up at the museum, I hardly noticed anything at first, I was just so out of my mind to see her at all. But when I think about it now, she was pale and drawn, like

401

a shadow of herself. She tells me her father is dead and her mother God knows where, but she does not say how. Her secrets spill out, garbled and torn, in sleep, and when she wakes in the firelight I pull her close to me and whisper to her until she sleeps. She calls out something about her father, but I do not understand. I can feel her drifting steadily away from me, but I'm powerless to stop her, as though she's on a river, falling down steep rapids, and I'm trying to hold on to her hand.

5 February

Today we walked through a cathedral of orchids. We were trudging along as usual, our minds occupied with nothing but expectation of the next break, when suddenly Bob looked up and called out. What we saw took our breath away: in every direction, the trees were covered in orchids of every possible colour. Here and there, thin shafts of sunlight pierced the leaves, lending the orchid petals a little of their brightness. They were high up, and we walked under them as though beneath a tall ceiling, gently, as though afraid of disturbing something fragile and remote. Not even George knew the names of all of them. I recognized a large expanse of monja blanca *orchids, white as snow along a tunnel of* chicozapotes. *The smell was pungent, turning the forest briefly into a perfume house. I picked some for Antonia and set them in her hair to lift her spirits, but she shows no signs of pulling back.*

She spoke to me tonight about the visit Rafael made to her father's bull-ranch before Christmas. I'd already heard most of the details from Declan Carberry. But something else happened that night, I'm sure of it, something she won't talk about. I tell her I love her and that we'll marry when we're through with this expedition, and she smiles and tells me she loves me too; but I think she is feeling something else, something she keeps hidden from me, and I fear it may destroy us in the end.

6 February

The weather changed today, quite early in the morning. Heavy rain began to fall, and is still falling hours later. We're sheltered down here, of course, and we all wear rain ponchos, but it's still uncomfortable to have leaves throwing water down on you every step you take. I keep thinking of the Lacandón River, and the Usumacinta to the east, how swollen they must be, and completely uncrossable. If this weather continues, there is no way out of the forest except to continue forward as we are.

The same day, midnight

There were sounds in the forest earlier tonight. Not the usual sounds, the crying of birds or animals, the chirruping of crickets, all of that. This was more human, or so it seemed. A regular scraping sound, very remote, and something that might have been a steady drumbeat, heavily muffled and far away. I asked George if there are Indians in this part of the forest. He shook his head and looked out beyond the dying campfire to where a haze of fireflies burned like tinder.

7 February

This morning we came across a margay kitten. It must have been abandoned by the mother a few days ago, and was in a very weak and dehydrated state when we found it. Perhaps the mother was killed or caught somewhere and didn't make it back. Margays tend to have one cub per litter, so this poor little fellow didn't have any brothers or sisters. We fed him on dried milk mixed with water, and weren't too sure at first if it would work. But he showed signs of responding within minutes, and in an hour he was running around like any normal kitten. George was for moving on and leaving him to fend for himself, but the kitten wouldn't leave us, and none of us could face the idea of dumping him. Dorothy and Dorothea have adopted him and named him Marvin, after Marvin Gaye. I had thought Antonia

403

might offer, but she held back. Then I remembered the tayra, the little pet that had belonged to Antonia's flat-mate, and her refusal didn't seem so strange after all.

Not all the wildlife is so amenable to kind words and milk. There are jaguars out there, the largest cats on the American continent, six feet long and capable of killing a man with a snap of their jaw. Vampire bats with infected bites. Coral snakes. God knows how many species of spider. They hang wherever we walk, monsters some of them, suspended across huge webs like something out of your worst nightmare. The webs are often stretched right across the path, and in the dusk it's not hard to walk right into one. Bird-eating spiders are the largest, quite as large as dinner-plates, but fortunately their bite isn't particularly harmful to humans. They hunt at night, so everyone makes sure his tent is zipped tight. Some of the smaller species are deadly and to be avoided at all costs. I don't have a phobia, but I find them loathsome, and I steer as wide a path from them as I can.

It continues to rain, but in here the temperature is higher than ever, and humidity has risen out of all proportion. What seems like ash is coming down through the trees, and we think the wind has shifted and is bringing material from one of the erupting volcanoes in this direction. We take more frequent breaks, and dream about fans and air-conditioning and ice-cold Coca-Cola direct from a machine. We've been replenishing our water supply from little streams that cut across our path from time to time; but these are fewer in number now, so we must be careful not to drink too much, when all any of us would like to do is take a long swig and empty the bottle.

'What made you give up a normal legal practice?' I asked George this evening. We were sitting round the fire, trying to get warm. He'd been showing me how to extract chicle from a sapodilla tree. I think it will take a little work to make into *chewing gum. We brought back some fruit, however, which was much appreciated.*

'What's normal legal practice?' he asked. 'I had offers to join some big law firms in New York and Boston, and when I came back down here, I could have made a lot of money working for the government. But the government here kills people, and most of those it kills are Indians like myself. Most of the lawyers in this country are Ladinos, and only a few of them care enough about los Indíos to challenge the government or its agencies in court. Lawyers like that don't last long. They disappear, they're tortured, their bodies turn up at the roadside, just more victims of a civil war that's been going on for forty years. Not even the Irish hate one another like the Guatemalans.'

'But I still —'

'Look, in a situation like this, where one dictator follows another, where death squads carry out the meanest of orders, where whole villages are massacred just so some state department or business can get hold of their land, you can't have a normal legal practice. You can't have it because there's no law, no justice, least of all for Indians like me. So I practise a different sort of law. Sometimes my clients pay me, sometimes they don't.'

'But to give up what you might have had. That takes courage.'

I could not see him well in the darkness, but I saw him look at me with a look of such sadness that I could not continue gazing at him.

'Not courage,' he said finally. 'I am not a brave man. Every day I'm frightened because I know they'll come for me eventually. It is not courage.'

'Then what?'

'I . . .' He hesitated. 'I had a family. I married soon after getting back from Harvard. I'd met my wife there, Helen — she'd just finished a degree in Spanish. We got married in

405

the States and came back here. I started working with a little law firm in Flores, she did translation work. We didn't have a lot of money, but we were very happy. It wasn't long before we had children, two girls, twins called Helen and Helena.

'Before coming to Guatemala, Helen belonged to a North American human rights organization that concentrated on Central America, and when she settled here she continued to be involved with them, sending back reports and so on. I tried to warn her about it, several people did, but she probably felt invulnerable. Who was going to lay hands on a United States citizen? She forgot who she was married to. One day I . . . came home to find she'd been raped. Repeatedly. The children had been beaten to death with a gun. Helen was out of her mind. She didn't recognize me, couldn't remember who she was. In the end, I sent her back to the States, to her parents. They said they'd look after her, but they couldn't. She's still up there, in a mental institution in Utah. It's a long way for me to travel. Now do you understand?'

There were sounds in the forest again tonight. The same steady notes, not near, not far away. Antonia and I lay in our tent listening until the early hours. She will not make love to me. But when she's asleep, she rolls to my side and reaches out for me unconsciously, and she will only be still when I hold her. What happened up there?

I'm writing this near dawn. The tent is stifling, but we have no means of cooling it down. We lie together naked, covered in sweat. Morning will bring no relief.

8 February

The jungle seems quieter today, as though the great heat has enervated everything. A jaguar was hunting near us. It growled a few times, sending Marvin scuttling for cover in Dorothy's rucksack.

We came to a small dip that had somehow become a muddy pool. Everyone stripped to their underclothes, and we went in one at a time, and rolled in the mud, coming out with the stuff caked all over. It was the most refreshing thing in days. When I looked at us all afterwards, I thought we looked like a gang of savages, and then I reflected on where we are.

George spent the noon break cutting himself a bow and making arrows. He says he will look for a coral snake or a fer-de-lance to provide poison for his arrowheads. I asked him if any of this was necessary, but he would not answer me. He has asked us all to call him by his proper name, his Indian name, Rokché. The forest is changing him. I think perhaps it is changing us all.

9 February
We woke this morning to find that Barney was gone, along with all his equipment, including the global positioning system and the radio. We have no way of tracking our direction now, and no way of communicating with anyone to come and get us out of here should that prove necessary. Some of our medical equipment is gone as well, and two packs of dehydrated food.

It's noon, and we've scoured the area round last night's camp, but there's no sign of Barney anywhere. George says he has found tracks.

'Not one person,' he said. 'Four, maybe five.'

He took me to one side and showed me something he'd found near the tracks. It was Barney's mosquito net. It had been torn and tossed aside, whether deliberately or by accident, it's hard to say.

The net was dirty, and only the permethrin in which it had been soaked seemed to be keeping insects away. I didn't notice the large stain in the centre. George drew my attention to it. A dark brown stain about twenty inches by ten.

'Blood,' said George.

407

I looked at him, not wanting him to say what he was about to say.

'Human blood,' he said. And he was silent for a long time after that.

44

The Bell LongRanger shaved the treetops like a heron skimming a green lake. In whichever direction the pilot looked, he could see nothing but forest. Above him, dark clouds scudded through a darker sky. They were a mixture of water and ash, and when they opened it was not rain that fell, but a thin, dirty grey mud that had already drowned hundreds in the west. Beneath them, a thin layer of ash moved on the wind, spotting the little helicopter with dark volcanic smears.

Rafael eased back on the throttle. This was his seventh run, and still nothing. He knew what he was looking for, and he knew roughly where he expected to find it, but instead he could see nothing but the endless green of the forest, broken from time to time by a tree taller by a head than its companions, or by the startled flight of roosting birds frightened by the helicopter's passing.

Behind him in the cabin sat the five men who made up his private archaeological expedition. His co-pilot, Diego O'Malley, sat beside him, scouring the treescape below with powerful binoculars. They were all members of Sacbe or the White Road, the religious brotherhood of which Rafael was the Nohoch Tata, the Great Father. They were all sworn to absolute secrecy and had come with their master, not to further Meso-American archaeology, but to help him find a lost Maya city and the secret of eternal life. In furtherance of that objective, there was nothing they would not do.

Rafael had been certain that there would be some sign of the city visible above the trees. Don Joaquín had written of a large pyramid. In Rafael's experience, the taller pyramids tended to be higher than the forest roof, and it was generally easy to spot them from the air. Sometimes they escaped observation because their shape had changed so much over the centuries. One had been found recently that was used for many years by the airline pilots as a marker, thinking it was a hill.

The plan had been to locate the city from the air, then hand over to O'Malley while the others were winched down to the forest floor at the nearest clearing. But it was beginning to look as though they might have to enter the forest at one end or the other and hack their way through. For any other prize, Rafael would have been content to let someone else do the hacking; but for this, he wanted to be there every minute until the city was found, and then to be the first to uncover its secret.

The engine coughed. Rafael glanced at the dials spread in front of him. Everything seemed fine. He turned to Diego.

'What was that?'

The co-pilot shrugged. 'Some impurity in the petrol, I'd guess. I'll speak to Pédro when I get back. I've suspected him of selling us adulterated fuel for some time.'

There was a second cough, heavier than the first. Rafael caught sight of a needle swinging up and back again. It was attached to a filter that controlled air intake to the engine. A sudden shudder passed through the little aircraft.

'I didn't like that,' said Rafael.

'Me neither.'

410

'How far to a safe landing-place?'

'The nearest is a village called Nueva Huitiupán. We could be there in twenty minutes. But if this gets any –'

The word was taken from him by another cough, upon which the engine died. The 'copter immediately began to drop. It was a single-engine model, with no reserve power.

'Keep it under control! Keep it under control!' shouted Diego.

'There's no response from any of the controls. Hang on!'

'Keep the nose up.'

'I'm trying, but it won't respond.'

Next thing, the helicopter dipped and began to plunge nose down towards the trees.

'Pull back! Pull back!'

'Before we hit, get off an SOS!'

Diego leaned across, trying to make contact with the button that would automatically send out a distress call. But the helicopter was spinning now as it went into the final seconds of its dive. He was thrown back into his seat, then bounced forward. There were cries from the cabin. None of the passengers had been belted in when the drop started.

Rafael flipped a switch in front of him.

'Mayday . . .' he started. But the next second they were coming into the trees, and the high branches were swallowing them up. Birds flew skywards in every direction, trees shattered and split, the canopy of leaves and branches caught them for a moment, then sagged and began to give way.

'Mayday,' Rafael shouted as the rotors and tail crumpled and the egg of the helicopter's body sank faster and faster into the trees, coming to rest about halfway down, swinging precariously in the stout branches of a ceiba tree.

There was a howling of monkeys, and on the ground a great uproar as animals rushed to get out of the way of the commotion up above. Tapirs rushed alongside jaguarundis, kinkajous raced coati-mundis, agoutis and pacas and peccaries left whatever they were doing and ran, grunting and crying at the tops of their voices.

And then, quite as quickly as it all began, the howling and screaming faded and there was a most awful silence through the forest, as far as anyone could hear. The helicopter bumped a little lower and was still again. And into the hole that had been made in the forest fabric there fell a slow dropping of ash, like snow. The very same ash that had worked its way into the LongRanger's engine, that had travelled all the way from the volcanoes of Lake Atitlán, carried on a long wind.

45

Rome had been wet, the Pope – seen from a great distance in Nervi's 12,000-seat Audience Chamber – had seemed tired and under strain, the Tiber had been muddy, the Bocca della Verità had been silent, the Colosseum had been encased in scaffolding, half the museums had been closed for refurbishment, the Tritone fountain had been dry, and he had been gripped by one of the fiercest headaches of his life – by that and an overwhelming burden of grief for the loss of Alice. The pyramid of Caius Cestius had been dark and damp, and the hearts of these latest victims – eight in all – had offered no clues.

All the names on the labels attached to the hearts were Italian, and so far not one of them had matched up to anything on the country's various missing-person lists. It was as if eight people with ordinary names had fallen into a black hole, and nobody had noticed their absence, or cared enough to notify anyone. Perhaps, Declan reflected, they had been sad, lonely people, the sort of people nobody really misses when they are gone, because nobody really noticed them when they were there.

413

He'd spent days travelling back and forwards between the headquarters of Italy's various police forces, and an afternoon looking at the excised hearts in Rome's central morgue. The hearts had amounted to nothing. Certainly, they showed no indication of a probable cause of death. But he'd spoken with the pathologist, a soft-mannered Neapolitan called Umberto Rossellini, and asked him to run tests for indole alkaloids.

'I'm sorry?' Rossellini scrunched up his nose when he was perplexed. All he knew of Irish policemen had been gleaned from the Italian translation of Flann O'Brien's unsettling classic, and here was a real one behaving with the same baffling surrealism as his literary models.

'I'm only repeating what I've heard,' said Declan. 'You should look for traces of aspidospermine, quebrachamine, quebrachine, gelsemine and sempervirine. And you could keep an eye out for some methyl aesuletin and monomethyl ester of emodin. Also a couple of drugs from the Amazon called *ebene* and *yopo*.'

Rossellini had rung him the next day to confirm that he'd found significant amounts of all these in the hearts, and several related substances, all of which had their origin in Central American plants. Declan had told him what he could in explanation of the mystery.

He'd spent his last morning walking among ruins, communing with his ghosts. Everywhere he looked he saw fallen pillars and ruined doorways, carvings worn down by age and pollution, the busts of gods and emperors, and the walls of abandoned temples. Alice went with him everywhere. He could feel her hand in his, and whenever he escaped the constant hum of the traffic, she whispered softly in his ear.

*   *   *

414

'Come in,' said Declan without looking up from his desk.

Rob Barlow came in, the clever Englishman who got things to happen on the computer.

'I have something for you, sir. I think you'll find it interesting.'

'See if you can find something to sit on.'

Rob looked round in desperation. Declan leaned across to a chair that was stacked high with files, skimmed some off the top and handed them to his subordinate. The Englishman removed the rest and sat down.

'If you'd get properly on-line, sir. Just give the word, and I'll do the rest. All these files can be scanned into your database and . . .'

'I have an affinity for paper, Mr Barlow. Robbie. When I die, they'll take all these files and make a big coffin out of them.'

'They won't keep the worms out, sir. Whereas, if I were to scan you into the mainframe down the corridor, you'd be there for ever. People could open your file ten thousand years from now, and out you'd pop as big as life.'

'I've no intention of popping out in ten or twenty thousand years' time. And if you imagine any of your software's going to work on the sort of computers they'll be using by then –'

'God, you Irish are such cross-patches. No wonder you can't get on with one another.'

'Spare me the lecture, Rob. I'm not in the mood. I'm the boss, I have a headache, and I have no time for chit-chat.'

'*Mea culpa*. What about this, then? Hans and I have been working our way through files relating to the neo-Nazi, Habermayer. As you can guess, the Germans have him tucked away in more databases than Glenn Hoddle has past lives. Here's a recent photograph of him and his darling Helga.'

Barlow dropped a large sheet of shiny paper on to Declan's desk.

'Is that true?' asked Declan. 'Is she really called Helga?'

'Top to toe, sir.'

'And she still won't talk?'

He looked down at the photograph. The man staring back at him was blond, in his late thirties, going to seed. His eyes seemed like pickled onions, and he had a tooth missing on the left of his mouth.

'Not a word, sir. The German police have tried everything, but she's keeping quiet. They say she's frightened of something, but they can't find out what.'

'Presumably whoever killed her *liebling* Jürgen. What else have you got?'

'Habermayer ran an art gallery in Stuttgart.'

'He doesn't seem the type.'

'Here's another photograph.'

A second sheet landed in front of Declan. This one showed a very different Jürgen, dressed in an Armani suit, his hair well cut, his missing tooth in place.

'When was this taken?'

'Not so long ago. Something happened in the past three or four years to make Jürgen the man he was before he got the chop. But let's concentrate on the gallery for the moment. It's called the Galerie Moderner Kunst, otherwise the Habermayer Galerie, on Dollernstrasse in the Altstadt. Not a very prosperous concern, but from time to time Habermayer secures a young artist of promise and things go well for a while.

'However, the gallery is really a front. Habermayer has served three prison sentences for art theft, and he's

416

thought to have been involved with numerous other heists, mainly as a middle-man. At one time he had a nice little thing going with a priest, of all things, man by the name of de Sepúlveda.'

'Don't tell me. Mexican. Or Guatemalan. Or . . .'

'Spanish, as a matter of fact, sir. But he spent a lot of time in Guatemala. Seems he's very wealthy. He lives on an island in the Caribbean. And he collects modern art in a big way. There was a time when Habermayer was supplying him with works by modern masters. No fakes, nothing like that. The real thing. Until de Sepúlveda found out that Habermayer's sources weren't as clean as he claimed and that some of his paintings weren't really Habermayer's to dispose of.'

'And de Sepúlveda was where when this was going on?'

'Guatemala, I think. But at that time he had a private gallery in Spain. He moved it out to the Caribbean later.'

'Right. Well, thank you, Rob. We've got another Central American connection. It's something to go on.'

'There's more than that, sir. There's a funny coincidence. You remember asking me to look up this bloke Rafael when I had a moment, as a sort of favour for your friend Mallory.'

'Yes, I remember. Did anything ever come of that?'

'Well, it did. But that isn't the odd thing. The thing is that your Mr Rafael was at one time a close associate of this Father de Sepúlveda.'

Declan sat back in his seat. 'That is a coincidence. Have you tried making contact with this priest?'

'Yes, but . . . The fact is, sir, de Sepúlveda is dead. He was killed in a fire on his island a few days ago. I just got confirmation this morning.'

'Jesus. We've been slow, haven't we, Rob? All this effort, and all the time it was staring us in the face.'

'What's that?'

'We need to go after this man Rafael. You were going to tell me that he and Habermayer were in contact, weren't you?'

'Yes, sir.'

'And anyone else?'

'I think with all of them, sir.'

'Would you believe that? OK, Mr Barlow. Show me what you've dug up on Rafael. I think it's time we found out just who he really is.'

46

Lacandón Forest
11 February

Rokché moved through the forest as though it had always been his habitat, as though he had never left it from birth until now. He belonged to it as much as the fiercest jaguar or the mildest anteater. George, the *civilizado* who had accompanied him throughout his life until now, had been locked securely away in a basement area of his mind, alive but barely kicking. He tasted things again as he hadn't tasted them in years, smelt and heard and understood in ways he had almost forgotten. Every few minutes he paused to pick out a single sound from among the clatter of animal noises that surrounded them. Every trail, every broken twig, every crushed leaf and broken flower was scrutinized for what it could tell him.

But not even Rokché was sure what direction they were travelling in. The expedition had relied so totally on the geo-positioning equipment that no one had thought to bring so much as a single compass with them. Until now it had seemed so unnecessary.

In a vain attempt to orient them, he'd climbed to the top of the highest tree he could find, but all he'd found up there had been a solid ceiling of cloud and ash, beneath which there stretched for mile upon unvarying mile a green ocean on which nothing sailed. He'd come down inwardly despondent, smiling to reassure the others, knowing all the while they were hopelessly lost. They'd listened in silence while he told them he'd seen enough of the sun to get his bearings; but the truth was, there were no bearings in this place and never would be.

The forest continued to change the deeper they progressed into it. Rokché found himself unnerved by these changes, and found himself changing to accommodate them. He spoke less, and he found his memory of the world outside blurring and giving way to an instinct born of the forest. Nothing in here was as it should have been. The colours, the sounds, the dimensions all shifted and took on different meanings. They were deep into Mexico by now, he thought; but that didn't matter. This was a world without conventional boundaries, without anthems or presidents or national aspirations.

The forest darkened day by day, brooding all round them like a living creature, breathing, sleeping, waking, howling, whispering, coupling, breeding, watching, watching, watching. Even the most innocent-seeming passages could hold traps for the unwary. Every step, every handhold had to be made with exquisite care for fear of disturbing a poisonous insect or a deadly frog. Not even the trees were safe. One day, as Leo was about to cut through some vines that hung from a large tree, Rokché grabbed his arm and pulled him back.

'That's a *hura* tree,' he said. 'See the water coming off it? That has sap in it, from higher up. If that gets on your face it'll blind you. We'll have to take the long way round.'

Several times they crossed the paths of deadly snakes, corals and fer-de-lances, and once, coiled in a low bush, a poisonous green palm viper. They passed a sleeping anaconda, fifteen feet long, powerful enough to strangle a young sheep. By night, tarantulas padded silently across the jungle floor, hunting mice and fallen birds. Their long, hair-encrusted legs would graze a sleeper's face and be gone before he woke.

They found what was left of Barney two days after his disappearance. All that morning, they had been walking down a gentle slope that had brought them towards noon to a swift-flowing, amber-coloured stream in which pieces of ash swam as if in the aftermath of a forest fire. Just beyond the stream, the land began to rise again, and they had gone little more than one hundred yards when the trees opened to reveal a small clearing.

In fact, they heard the clearing before entering it. It was filled with the buzzing of flies, as though every fly in the forest had arrived there for a convention. When they entered it what little light there was showed clouds of black insects circling everywhere. In particular, they clustered about an object that stood roughly in the centre of the clearing.

Leo took several steps forward. The object was a plain wooden cross about four feet in height, atop which someone had placed a spherical object. It was around this sphere that the flies buzzed, spinning black beads that had become fused together into a shifting mass of foulness, blackflies, botflies, sandflies, all knitted together like a living balaclava helmet.

While the others held back, Leo took a few more steps towards the cross. He scarcely heard Rokché as the Indian joined him. The image of a balaclava had given him a fair idea of what lay underneath the carapace of flies.

'Do you think . . . ?'

Rokché did not answer. He was scanning the trees on all sides of the clearing. His right hand took hold of the bow he'd slung over his shoulder, while his left picked out an arrow from the dozen or so he'd made. The arrows had been dipped in the venom of an Arrow-Poison Frog that Rokché had captured with great care and roasted. His care had been essential: the toxin produced by a single frog was so powerful that just four ten-millionths of an ounce would be enough to kill a man.

They reached the cross. The circular object resembled a bee's hive, swarming with thousands of flying and crawling creatures. Leo reached into his shoulder-bag and brought out a half-full spray-bottle of Maxpel, an insect repellent made up of ninety-five per cent diethyl toluamide.

'This doesn't always work,' he said, unscrewing the top. 'But most insects don't like it.'

He sprayed it liberally on the sphere, and slowly the flies started to fall away, now in ones and twos, now in clusters, until only a hardy rearguard remained. By then Leo's worst fears had been confirmed. He staggered back, retching, then fell to his knees and was sick. Rokché did not react. He was more interested in the forest than the head.

Things rot quickly in the jungle, and what was left of Barney was quite unrecognizable. It was only possible to make an identification because his killers had adorned the head with a thin gold chain that he had worn round his neck while alive.

There was no sign of the body anywhere in the clearing. Rokché was on edge, and said he wanted to leave the open area as quickly as possible. He was certain they were being watched.

Wrapping Barney's head in one of his shirts, they vacated the clearing, pursued by a cloud of persistent flies.

'We can't carry this with us,' said Dorothy. She and Dorothea had been Barney's best friends, and this confirmation of their fears had left them bereft and confused.

'Can't we bury him here?' suggested Dorothea.

No one disagreed. There were plenty of shovels among the archaeological equipment. Rokché instructed them to dig deeply, otherwise the first scavenger to come along would have the head for dinner.

'Was he a Catholic or Protestant or what? Does anybody know?' asked Antonia.

Out in the jungle, it seemed a pointless question. But Antonia had been brought up to be punctilious about these things.

'Does it matter?' asked Steve Sabloff, whose Anglican upbringing had taught him to be indifferent to such nuances.

'I think it does. I think we should at least say a prayer for him.'

Rokché fashioned a small cross from two pieces of mahogany roughly cut from a fallen tree and placed it near the head. Leo wrote Barney's name and dates of birth and death on a piece of card and put it into a small plastic wallet, which he attached to the cross. Antonia recited a Spanish prayer, the words issuing out of childhood memory into the stifling forest air, *Oh Corazón amabilisimo de Jesús! Puerta celestial por donde llegamos a Dios y el viene a nosotros, dignaos de estar latente en nuestros deseos y amorosos suspiros . . .*

When she finished there was a short silence. Someone whispered the Lord's Prayer. Another silence, then Rokché chanted a Mayan prayer. He did not offer to translate it: it was his private communication with the dead and the Lords of Night who had taken him to themselves. All the time he prayed, he watched the forest darkness.

423

They carried on.

'Where do you think the cross came from?' Steve asked of no one in particular. He meant the large cross on which Barney's head had been found. They had left it where it stood.

'Someone may have been here before us. Missionaries perhaps,' Dorothy suggested.

'I don't give much for our chances of finding them alive.' Leo went on walking, knowing there was little point in turning back.

Half an hour later, they found the answer to Steve's question. In a second clearing, partly overgrown, and fallen into heavy ruin, stood a small stone building that must at one time have been a Christian church. Closer examination showed it to be, not the work of modern missionaries, but almost certainly the structure Fray Domingo and his Indian converts had stayed on to build.

They lingered long enough to take a few photographs. What remained of the building was heavily overgrown by vines and lichens, and any sort of excavation would have taken weeks. The style of the building was conventional, and from what little they could see, it was possible to work out which end was which. Assuming that Fray Domingo and his converts had known which way the east lay, they were suddenly presented with the first clear indication in days as to the points of the compass.

Just outside the east end of the church they found a number of gravestones, covered almost beyond recognition by thick layers of moss and wound about by thorns. They cleaned the largest, and found on it the name of Fray Domingo, and a date, 1563. The priest had lasted three years. Had the church been completed by then, wondered Leo, or was it left unfinished? Only a proper excavation would ever supply an answer.

More confident of their direction now, they pushed on. The forest closed in again, as thick and impenetrable as ever. At sundown, flocks of *chachalacas* called to one another from the treetops with a regular beat that reminded Antonia of a metronome. They made camp, hanging their hammocks as closely together as possible. Sitting by the fire, no one found it easy to keep up much of a conversation. The day had been dominated by the discovery of Barney's head, but it was not a subject that anyone found it possible to approach.

Antonia seemed very down. Reciting the prayer to the Sacred Heart had unwittingly unlocked waves of memory from her childhood and adolescence, when she used to murmur it fervently in church and out. Now, abandoned by Jesus and lost in the forest, she felt herself teeter on the edge of a private precipice.

'Are you all right?' asked Leo. They had just eaten, and bedtime was not far off.

She said nothing. The fire lit her face with a redness out of a lost era, when the forest was inhabited by shamans and sorcerers.

'We need to talk,' he said. 'But not here.'

He took her hand, and she let herself be drawn to her feet. Nobody said a word to bring them back as they slipped away into the shadows. It was hard to know where the greater risk lay: by the fire or in the dark.

'We can't go on like this,' said Leo. 'Whatever happened to you in Mexico, don't let it come between us.'

'You aren't my husband, you can't tell me what to do.'

'I love you, Antonia. If I could marry you here and now, I would. But I wouldn't tell you what to do.'

He felt her try to pull away from him.

'You say you love me, but what's the use of that?' she asked.

'It's of no use, no use whatever. Love doesn't have a use. Not to me, at any rate.'

'It only complicates things.'

'What does it complicate?'

'I don't know. I don't care. All I know is, life used to be a lot simpler than this.'

'The forest complicates nothing.'

'I don't mean the forest . . .'

'What then?'

Suddenly, she threw herself into his arms, sobbing as though her heart would break. She sobbed from fear, her fear above all that he would die out here with her, and from pity for Barney, whom she had scarcely known, and from anger at her father's death. And with that thought she began to talk, in choked whispers and broken phrases, telling her story as though she was telling it into the darkness, anonymously and without shame. He listened, holding her tightly until she had told all that she could for now.

'Rafael can't find you now,' he said. 'I'll see to that. De Sepúlveda will help.'

She shook her head and looked across the darkness to where the fire was burning. 'He'll find me,' she whispered. 'He won't give up. Believe me, nothing can stop him. Not you, not de Sepúlveda. Rafael can see in the dark. He'll find me no matter where I go.'

He calmed her slowly, wiping her tears away with his hand, then kissing her gently on the lips. When she was properly calm, she came in to him again, and kissed him hard on the lips, and pressed her half-naked body against his.

'Make love to me,' she said. 'Make love to me now.'

And when she came, she cried out loudly, without shame, lending her voice to the many voices of the night.

They found the others asleep when they went back to the camp. Leo fell asleep almost at once. Antonia remained awake for a while, listening to the sounds of the night. She knew that Rokché was watching somewhere close in an attempt to prevent another death.

Sometime around midnight, the drumming and scraping sounds started again, and this time they continued right through till dawn.

That day and the next they walked further than they had walked in forty-eight hours. They were making progress, but the forest was fighting back all the time. On the second morning, they were attacked by a tribe of spider monkeys, who stood in the trees, throwing broken branches down on them. Soon after that, they came across a marney tree and gorged themselves on its sweet, coral-coloured fruit. Their provisions were not lasting as well as they should have done. Because of the other equipment they had to carry, the amount of food allocated to each of them had been seriously below what they should have carried. Their only hope was to make up for this lack by finding food in the forest itself, something which would inevitably slow them down.

That afternoon they came into a swampy area that went on for half a mile or so, bringing them to a shallow mud hole. The mud was cool and inviting, and they stripped and threw themselves into it, plastering their bodies and rubbing it through their hair. When they emerged, they were unrecognizable.

After that, no one dressed completely again, not even the women. Antonia put flowers and other plants in her hair, and one by one the others followed suit, with the exception of Rokché. At their request, he fashioned bows for the men and showed them how to make arrows for themselves. They left behind those parts of their equipment that they no longer deemed necessary to survival.

That night, Rokché taught the men the words of the prayer he had chanted over Barney's grave, and the words of other prayers, and for hours after the sun went down they sat round the fire singing and chanting while the women watched from the side.

They broke off to eat around ten o'clock. Rokché had found a small herd of peccaries soon after they left the mud hole, and had killed one. It had spent most of the evening roasting, and was now ready. Rokché filled their plates with slices of fresh meat, darker and denser than the pork to which they were accustomed. But it tasted wonderful.

'How many more of these can you find, Rokché?' asked Bob.

'Not so many. It could be weeks before we get another sniff of peccary. Today was just a matter of luck. We may go hungry tomorrow.'

As he spoke, something came hurtling out of the darkness and landed heavily, half-bouncing, half-rolling until it came to a halt two or three feet from the fire. Everyone leapt from their seats, spilling roast pig in all directions, scrabbling for weapons. Leo stepped forward to investigate whatever had been thrown into the campsite. It took only moments for recognition to form, and with it the deepest revulsion.

'Leave it,' he said as Steve came towards it from the opposite direction. 'Don't touch it.'

'Why, what is it?'

'It's Barney's head. They've dug him up, the bastards.'

In the end, they did what they had to, digging a deeper hole this time, and placing the head firmly inside. But they all knew that if their tormentors chose to, they could dig him up again. Their prayers sounded hollow, spoken against the darkness. As they spoke them, the scraping began all over, and behind it a man's voice chanting. Leo asked Rokché if he knew what the unseen voice was singing, but he either did not know or would not say. No one slept that night.

They set off again at dawn, ragged and exhausted. The mud on their bodies had caked and was falling off in flakes. Above, the weather did not improve. Everyone knew that their goal was no longer Don Joaquín's lost city, but survival. The moment they could find a way out of the forest, they were leaving.

'What's that ahead?' asked Dorothea.

They could make out something through the trees. Rokché went ahead. He'd gone about ten yards when they saw him come to a complete standstill. Not a muscle moved as he stood, looking straight ahead of him.

'It's a stone building,' said Steve. 'Do you think this could be it?'

'It could be. We've come about the right distance,' Leo answered. He went on forward to where Rokché was standing.

That was when hope left him. They would die in the forest now, he thought, and never be found again. Rokché did not speak. There was no need for words. Directly in front of them was a small clearing, and in the clearing stood the little church that Fray Domingo had built all those centuries ago. They had been walking in a circle.

47

He'd pulled the GPS unit out of its casing in the cockpit, only to find that, bereft of any charge from the engine, it was as dead as his six companions. No amount of twisting and kicking would get the engine to restart, even briefly. Meanwhile, the bodies of the crew had already started to decompose. He knew he had to get moving soon if he was ever to escape from this hell. Digging into the baggage compartment, he found a small compass in Diego's overnight bag.

He was soon able to establish which way north, south, east, and west lay, but he had only the vaguest idea of his position within the forest. His attention had been focused so much on locating some sign of the lost city that he'd allowed himself to grow careless about map references: after all, the GPS was supposed to provide exact readings as and when they were needed. He unfolded the map, a pilotage chart that showed the region in detail and indicated the forest, not surprisingly, as forest. With some effort, he made a mark to show where he thought he must be, and resolved to work from there.

He was not afraid of the forest. The many years he had spent in rainforest very like this, learning to be a shaman, had taught him to regard it as his home. He knew how to hunt, to trap, to cure even the most venomous bites or stings. Accidents apart, he knew he could survive here for months or even years. But survival was not enough. Without him at its helm, the community he had named Sacbe would soon falter and die. That, or one of his lieutenants – quite possibly Juan Amantea, who'd been showing signs of ambition for some time now – would declare him dead and take his place as Nohoch Tata. Rafael had to get out quickly. But he knew there was no point in going back to Europe without at least evidence of what he had promised. A lost city. And a secret that had been lost for centuries.

Time took on new meaning in the rainforest. He had almost forgotten the flexibility of days and years down here where everything seemed timeless, both ancient and newly-formed at the same moment. If he stood still, or sat naked and silent in a glade of cedars, he could sense the forest whirring around him. The processes of birth and death were accelerated here, so that whole cycles of conception and decay might pass in a single day.

His ancestors, the Mayan lords who had ruled at Tikal and Bonampak and Palenque, the shaman kings who had passed from forest to temple and back again, the *nacoms* whose blades of obsidian had opened the breasts of prisoners, ready for them to tear out their hearts, and above all the *chilans* who interpreted the sacred books and foretold the future – they had sought to control time, to make it as much their possession as gold or feathers or human lives.

They had created cycles based on the rise and fall of the sun. A *tun* was 360 days, almost a year. Twenty *tuns* made a *katun*. Twenty *katuns* made a *baktun*. And so it went, each cycle building upon the ones before, until they reached dizzying heights. And still they went on, moving their calendars back and forwards across vast stretches of time, past, and present and future, until no one but the gods could follow them. A stela in the holy city of Tikal, 'the place where spirit voices are heard', recorded a date over five million years in the past. But that was only a beginning. At Quiriguá, one inscription records a specific day ninety million years ago, and another a day four hundred million years ago.

He pondered on all this while the forest moved around him. His ancestors had not even been content to record dates so far in the past. Their imaginations allowed them to do unthinkable things. They created the *alautun*, made up of 160,000 *baktuns*, a cycle of sixty-three million years. And then piled cycle upon cycle on top of that. At Cobá they created fifteen cycles greater than the *alautun*. But a mere two cycles above it had already brought them to a time beyond the age of the universe.

He opened his eyes and saw the forest spinning above him like a galaxy without stars. Then he lowered his gaze.

They were watching him from the edge of the glade, their weapons tight in their hands, their eyes wide. His heart did not even miss a beat as he caught sight of them. How long had they been watching? He had lost track of time. But he knew it had been long enough for them to have killed him several times over.

Slowly, he got to his feet. They carried spears and bows, and their hair fell past their shoulders. Something about them told him at once that they had never been in touch with what the outside world called civilization. They would speak a Mayan language, he was sure of that. One of them carried a spherical object covered in flies. He did not need to ask what it was, but he wondered where they found their victims.

He looked in their eyes, one at a time, impressing

432

on them who he was. When he spoke, he used a single word.

'Kneel,' he said.

One by one, they knelt in front of him.

From his belt, he took a sharp knife, a Chris Reeves product, sharper than the sharpest obsidian. Without once taking his eyes off them, he raised the knife to his chest and cut across in a straight line, just below his nipples. As the blood began to flow, he beckoned to them, one at a time, to come forward. It was a ceremony with which they were familiar. First one, then another came and knelt down in front of him, bending forward to drink from his open wound.

When the last one had returned to his place at the edge of the glade, he asked for a species of moss that grows only on the ceiba tree. One of the Indians was carrying a supply in his pouch. He handed it over, and Rafael placed it on his chest, holding it in place with a bandage he had in his rucksack.

He would spend the night with them, gaining their confidence. Tomorrow they would guide him to his city.

48

Now that he held a single bright thread between his fingers, Declan saw the case begin to unravel before his eyes. The harder he pulled on the thread, the faster the whole thing unravelled. Habermayer had been careless, which was possibly the reason for his execution. Art theft had only been a sideline for him in recent years. His increasing involvement with the Freiheitliche Deutsche Arbeiter Partei had led to his appointment as the group's arms procurement officer. In the main, he relied on his old contacts to get him what he wanted. These were men – and one woman – who would buy or sell anything to make a slender profit: paintings, drugs, pornography, women, arms.

Not all their buying and selling was wholly illegitimate, of course. Most of them had at one time or another served the clandestine interests of governments eager to acquire or sell weapons larger than handguns and pepper sprays. This had brought them into contact with a wide range of government ministers, civil servants, and junior lackeys throughout Europe, Africa, the Middle and Far East, and South America. Men like Arnaud Nougayrède. Women like Sophie Dutheillet.

The threads unravelled and unravelled, forming a pattern at last. Habermayer had been astute in his association with this motley crew of politicians and their suitors, and had it not been for his PDA affiliation, he might have become one of the suitors himself, wealthy beyond his own limited dreams, a name on the scene of international mayhem.

But though these remained his primary contacts, he had tentacles that stretched in other directions. One thread led to France, another to Italy, another to Ireland. He forged close links with the French National Front and, more worryingly, Faisceaux Nationalistes Européens, a right-wing action group that claimed to have infiltrated the police force, created ties with the Belgian Westland New Post organization, the Italian Ordine Nuovo, and the Spanish Fuerza Nueva, and found himself in bed with the Provisional IRA and, above all, Liam O'Neill, their Quartermaster-General.

So far, Habermayer had been developing into little more than a key figure in an extreme-right terrorist network in Europe. Nothing new there, unless it lay in Habermayer's efficiency. But his Spanish connections brought a new dimension to his work. Spanish right-wing thinking embraced a doctrine called *Hispanidad*, which emphasized the need for close ties with Latin-American regimes. Franco had made it the basis of his foreign policy, and his successors made a fetish of it too.

Habermayer already had a different sort of Spanish link in his priestly art collector, de Sepúlveda, and de Sepúlveda had firm ties to Central America. The German began to travel to the New World, where he started to weave new webs of conspiracy, filling his address-book with the names and numbers of ex-SS men, secret policemen, and leading politicians. There was no shortage of fascists or murderers, and no hindrance to the free movement of drugs, arms, and money.

Some time in the early 1990s, Habermayer came into

contact with a shadowy figure whom later documents identified as Rafael. The Indian worked under other names, stuffing his safe with false passports, doctored photographs, and decorations from heads of state.

'I think the rest of this case is going to be fairly straightforward, sir,' Rob Barlow declared, delighted with the sequence of links he'd been able to establish. 'We keep on digging through our files on right-wingers and sooner or later we're going to come up with a bunch of lovely suspects.'

'You think so, do you?' Declan felt less elated. For one thing, he didn't think for a moment this had been a right-wing crime. In his experience, neo-fascists had as much imagination as dough-balls.

'You're ignoring the Mayan links,' he said. 'The tattoos, the removal of the hearts, this man Rafael. Work on him for a while.'

Unconvinced, Rob went to work again. And slowly another picture began to emerge. Declan had been right. It was impossible to fit all the victims into a simple right-wing conspiracy. The Belgian priest de Harduwijn, for example, had been an arch-liberal, an exponent of liberation theology, and a sharp thorn in the side of conservative bishops and reactionary politicians alike. Habermayer's little book of names would have contained plenty who would have gladly seen the back of de Harduwijn, but not as a result of some internal squabble. Why did they share a morgue in Paris?

'Focus on Rafael,' Declan had said. Rob concentrated on him. And for the first time in the investigation, things began to go badly wrong. It was as if control of information had passed out of Rob's hands, out of the hands of his division, out of the hands of Interpol itself. Rafael was more slippery than a tub-full of eels. The closer Rob got to him, the further away he seemed to be. There were hints of him everywhere, nods, winks, allusions; but nothing firm, nothing that could justify a search warrant, let alone sanction an arrest.

And yet . . . As Declan looked over the data Rob had brought to light, it started to become clear just what Rafael was up to.

'We'll need a lot more than this to prove it, and even then I wouldn't be sure he wouldn't just walk away.'

'We can prove he has links.'

'So has a fence. Can you see any of this standing up in court?'

'Maybe not, but it could justify a bigger investigation.'

'I wouldn't bet on that. The moment this man Rafael feels himself threatened, he'll start pulling on strings. As you can see, he has more strings at his disposal than a spider in its web.'

'What exactly is he, then? Some sort of middle-man?'

Declan shook his head. 'No. As I said, he pulls the strings: he doesn't just help somebody else tug them. He's what this is all about. He's doing three or four things at once, all apparently unrelated. First of all, he's stockpiling weapons. Particularly the weapons listed in your Ajax file.'

Rob looked at Declan in disbelief.

'You don't think he's behind . . . ?'

Declan nodded. 'The longer this goes on, the more certain I am of it. It fits in with everything else. You'll see.'

The Ajax file was one that Rob had started compiling after he began to trawl through databases created by a variety of international anti-terrorist agencies and the United States Bureau of Alcohol, Tobacco, and Firearms – the ATF. Habermayer and his associates hadn't just been handling the usual stuff – handguns, rifles, machine-guns, Semtex explosive, and the rest. Their purchases – well concealed until Rob's investigation had started to uncover links no one else had been able to make – had involved much bigger fish than that.

Scattered across Europe, in warehouses, secret dumps, and, for all anyone knew, suburban garages and garden sheds, lay a vast arsenal of some of the most lethal weapons known to man. Habermayer and others had built up stores of M79 and M16 grenade-launchers, Mark 19 automatic grenade-launchers, ex-Soviet ZPU-4 four-barrelled heavy machine-guns, ex-Soviet RPG-7 anti-tank weapons, multiple-launch rocket systems, and small rockets capable of taking out city blocks. There were even indications that they had succeeded in purchasing nerve gas together with the delivery systems necessary to send it into action.

None of this would have come to light had it not been for the Interpol investigation. In every case, documents had been produced to make it seem that the weapons in question, bought from a wide variety of sources, had been sent to regimes in Central and South America. European and American weapons control agencies had lost interest once they thought the guns and bombs and rockets were safely in the hands of governments that could be relied on to use them on their civilian populations.

'Secondly, he has in one way or another gained the trust, or perhaps I should say, the devotion of leading politicians in several countries. These are men who have achieved most things we ask from life: power, money, influence, reputation, even, perhaps, some small measure of immortality. The one thing they cannot have is to live for ever. That is what he offers them.

'Beyond that, he has a core of followers – a few

hundred, perhaps, maybe even a couple of thousand – who will obey any order he gives them.'

'I still don't see how he plans to –'

'It's very simple. When the right moment comes, he will see to it that the various groups controlling these weapons will start using them. There'll be a bombing in a Paris Metro station, perhaps, then a machine-gun attack on pedestrians in a German shopping centre. From there it will gather momentum, until every European country is in a state of near-anarchy.

'At that point, his politicians will declare states of emergency, backed up by well-armed groups of his followers. He could have control of Europe inside a month. After that, it will be time to turn his attention elsewhere.'

Rob was silent for a while. He read the files, he knew just how much weaponry Rafael had assembled.

'Can't we just pick him up now? Surely we have enough evidence against him?'

Declan shrugged. 'That's the problem,' he said. 'We've lost the bugger. He's gone to earth somewhere, and we've no way of knowing when he's going to come out again.'

The invitation was on a plain card, printed on a laser printer.

Hôtel Nompar de Caumont
12 rue de Grenelle
Paris VII
Ce soir à 7.00 heures

Declan returned it to his pocket and pursed his lips. It didn't say, 'You are invited', but it was obvious enough that that was the intent. No opportunity had been offered to decline: it was simply assumed that he would be there at the time indicated. He decided to say nothing to anyone else about it. The area suggested that someone like Sophie Dutheillet had a hand in it, and he didn't want to disturb her or her husband by bringing half of Interpol with him. He glanced at his watch. Just time to change his clothes and catch a fast train to the capital.

The hôtel turned out to be, as Declan had expected, a private house, a fine mansion built in 1727 to a design by François Debias-Aubry, who was also responsible for the nearby Ministry of War. A large but discreet street door led past a gatehouse beyond which lay a wide expanse of freshly-raked gravel that it seemed almost impious to disturb. The house was wreathed in dark green ivy, and Declan was reminded of the words of one writer, 'Even the ivy in the 7th *arrondissement* has more class than in other parts of Paris.' Through an archway on the right, he caught sight of a second, cobbled courtyard and a fountain.

Behind the fanlight of the front door, a yellow light burned. The door itself stood partly open, and after only a momentary hesitation, Declan pushed through it into the entrance hall. His eye took in at once the Savonnerie carpet, and the play of green shadows on the fading gold of the *boiserie*. He could hear voices somewhere behind closed doors. A great staircase lifted itself on his left, offering a half-shadowed glimpse of a landing adorned with paintings.

A baise door opened on his right, and a tall man came out, dressed in butler's uniform.

'*Suivez-moi, monsieur, s'il vous plaît . . .*' he said, heading for the stairs.

An enormous chandelier illuminated the stairwell, suspended by a chain that disappeared into shadow. Declan started climbing behind the butler, wondering more than ever what this was all about.

'Faites attention, monsieur. La tringle est brisée ici.'

The broken stair-rod seemed out of keeping with the whole. Very probably, thought Declan, the house was only used for a short part of the year, or was hired out on a weekly or even a daily basis.

The first-floor landing gave on to three lavishly gilded doors. Each was flanked by delicately-fluted Doric columns holding a pediment within which was carved an intricate, three-dimensional coat of arms.

'C'est le blason du Marquis du Gouffier de Thoix. On a construit la maison pour lui.'

The marquis must have been well pleased with the result, thought Declan. With a half-flourish, the butler opened the middle door and ushered him inside.

It was a large room with ornate panelling that could not, Declan thought, have been designed and worked by anyone other than Nicolas Pineau. This elegant backdrop did not quite harmonize with the rest of the room, which was devoid of the sort of furniture it had been built to house. Instead, some twenty modern chairs of the most utilitarian type had been set out in short rows, as though in expectation of a theatrical performance. They were the type of chairs that are used by the sort of hotel that depends on sales conferences and weddings for the bulk of its income.

The chairs were almost all occupied already. Heads turned to take in Declan as he made his way to the back row, where a single seat awaited him. In the brief glimpse he was afforded, he recognized a couple of his fellow-guests – for he assumed the others had been invited like himself. There was a well-known actress, famous for her roles in some recent films of Rohmer.

And he recognized a senator, a well-known political figure who had survived a scandal a few years ago and still made regular appearances on TV chat shows.

There was no one who was not well-dressed. Well-dressed, Declan thought, in the Parisian, not the American sense – though one or two of the men might have qualified for the Frasier show. The women wore muted colours, velvet scarves, and short hair, the men all wore what looked like the same suit in several shades of black, grey, and beige.

At the top end of the room, a table had been set down to serve as a podium. It was covered with a white cloth, and vases of the most exquisite flowers marched down its length. A single chair had been placed behind it. On the wall behind the chair, a white sheet bore a simple emblem, which Declan recognized as a Mayan hieroglyph.

A few minutes passed, then a door at the top of the room opened and a man of about fifty entered. He was dressed like everyone else in a sober suit, with a tie so understated that it had to be by Armani. His features were Gallic, and Declan reckoned that there wasn't a woman present who wasn't already fantasizing about a night in bed with him. When he spoke, his voice fluttered with melody like a perfectly-strung lute or mandolin. His French accent was unaffected, but touched with an air of aristocratic moodiness.

He spoke for two hours, and during that time nobody took their eyes off him, or whispered to their neighbour, or showed the slightest sign of fidgeting. From the moment he started, his entire audience was in the palm of his hand. Declan had no way of guessing whether any of them had heard him speak before, but he guessed they were mostly, like him, the merest acolytes.

442

The speaker spoke of miracles and angels, gods and demons and doorways to other worlds with such authority that it seemed he must have direct knowledge of them all. He was not selling Jesus, he said, or Buddha, or Muhammad. All that was passé now, all that was flames under a thousand pyres. Happiness, he said, was nearer to them than the breath in their own bodies: he could show them how to unleash it.

There was very little content in all he said, and not much that could not have fallen from the lips of a thousand other New Age gurus. Declan was not, in truth, much impressed. He would have walked away had it not been for the undeniable force of the speaker, whose name remained a secret. Some sort of hypnotic charm lay across the room.

It was not until his summing-up that the speaker referred to Rafael.

'Don't be deceived,' he said. 'I'm just the one who brings this message to you. But there is another one, far above me, who is a guide and a teacher. Living today is much like walking through a deep forest without a compass. We need a guide to see us through to the other side. And if we choose our guide very well, then perhaps he will take us further, out of the forest and into other worlds.

'We are all ignorant, in spite of our worldly knowledge, that we stand in desperate need of a teacher, someone who can educate our hearts and our souls. Today, thousands claim to be such a teacher, to bring all knowledge and all wisdom with them. Do not be deceived. There is only one, and his name is Rafael. He has other names too: his first name was Karinhoti, a Mayan name; but sometimes he calls himself Huitzilopochtli and Tlaloc Tlamacazqui, which are the names of gods.

'You will not see a photograph of him this evening. No photograph can do justice to the divinity that shines out of him. To understand what and who he is, you must meet him in person. A little time will pass, and then you will be ready. But first each of you has a journey to make.'

He spoke of the world and its coming end, of the need to prepare for that event with prayer and sacrifice and whatever other means might be available. And he spoke at the very end in careful phrases about eternal life and how those now present might hope to partake of it, how they might live for ever without dying. And Declan saw them sit up a little straighter, and their heads crane forward to be sure they did not miss a single word.

There were no questions. The speaker bowed and left, exiting the way he had come in. A man dressed all in white invited them to pass into the next room, where champagne and canapés were waiting, and a stall where they could select the various writings of Rafael. On the condition, he said, that they retain them for their own use only and show them to no one else. Everything in this world was by invitation alone. The audience was comfortable with that, they were all people who moved in circles that could not be entered by the uninvited, the poor, the merely rich, or the powerful for a day. They were prominent enough, some of them, and wealthy enough between them, Declan reckoned, to buy entire countries out of debt. But their preference was for the shadows. Whatever Rafael offered them, it would flatter their belief in their own intrinsic worth, their own specialness, their own fitness to be humanity's elite.

Declan felt tired. He got up and started for the rear door, intending to get out that way and beat a hasty retreat to the street. He could be back to his apartment in the Marais by half-past ten or so.

But just as he reached the back of the room, a man came towards him out of nowhere, as it were.

'Monsieur Carberry?'

Declan nodded.

'Would you be so kind as to come this way, please?'

'Well, I was actually planning on an early night. Why don't you leave me your number, and I'll get back to you. Very nice speech, by the way.'

'This will only take a few minutes. If you please.'

The insistence in the man's voice was marked. Declan turned and noticed that a second man had appeared just inside the rear door. No escape that way, then. He cast a glance at the other side of the room and saw a third man sidle into place.

The first man opened a small door near the fireplace and gestured Declan inside. For a moment it seemed like a mistake. The room was cold and empty of furniture. There was no paper on the walls, and the only light fixture was a bare bulb in the centre of the ceiling, well out of reach. The only window was high up, and Declan saw right away that it had been painted black, and that sturdy bars blocked off any hope of a way out. He was about to turn round and tell the man he had made a mistake. Then he heard the key turn in the lock, and he realized there had been no mistake after all.

49

From the journal of Leo Mallory

There was silence last night. We slept in the shadow of the church, and kept fires lit all around the encampment. I sat up most of the night, thinking, or trying to think. Antonia lay beside me, sleeping and waking constantly. She would cry out in her sleep, and each time I whispered to her that her father was dead, and that Rafael would never find her here.

In the morning, I ordered everyone to dress again.

'Look,' I said, 'we're not savages. We can't just let the forest turn us into what it pleases. There's a way out of here, and we can find it.'

I felt as though I'd been asleep and had only just started to wake up. Given time, I realized, the jungle would draw us to itself and kill us, even Rokché, even Antonia. I wasn't going to lose her again, not after all we'd been through.

'We need to find a balance,' I told them, 'some sort of middle point between going right back to a primitive state and acting like civilized morons. Rokché has had experience doing this, the rest of us haven't. He can teach us how to survive for a time, but he can't take us out. That's right, isn't it, Rokché?'

He nodded.

'Too much of the civilizado,' he said, 'and you will die. The civilizado doesn't know how to survive in here. Without help, he can't do anything: he can't gather food or hunt, he

446

can't prepare food, he can't store it, he can't make shelter for himself, or protect himself against animals or insects or plants. He will die very quickly, believe me. But it makes no sense to return to a totally primitive state either. The primitive knows only the jungle. He eats and breathes and sleeps and pisses it. His entire consciousness is taken up with it to the point where, if it cries, he cries, if it is in pain, he is in pain, if it stumbles, he stumbles. He can never escape from it, not even for a moment. He can never even begin to think of getting out. He will pass by a city of stone a thousand times without seeing it, because it is not part of his jungle.

'We have to combine our knowledge. You have to become more Indian, I have to be more civilizado. Otherwise we shall all die in here.'

I told him I'd had an idea about how we could find our bearings and keep them.

'Tracking in the forest depends on knowing where you are to begin with,' I said. 'I've never been here before, and I don't know how to get us out. We need a compass. Since we don't have one, we have to make one.' I turned to Antonia. 'I noticed you were wearing a silk bra. Do you think I could borrow it?'

She burst out laughing, then everyone else fell in. They obviously thought my request was funny. I just waited for them to recover their senses. When they eventually calmed down, Antonia shrugged, unfastened her shirt, and handed over her bra. For some reason, it made me feel uncomfortable, seeing her half-naked like that.

'Thanks,' I managed to say. 'I'll let you have it back.'

'Don't worry, I can manage.' She smiled and buttoned up her shirt again. 'I'm just curious as to how you think you can turn a work of art by Lejaby into a compass.'

'Who's got a sewing needle?' I asked. 'And some thread.'

Dorothy and Dorothea had brought a small pack of sewing equipment. They handed it to me with a smile that seemed to begin on one and end on the other. They were shaking with suppressed laughter.

'OK,' I said. 'What I'm going to do is this. I take a needle – voilà – and stroke it in one direction along the silk. It won't be much, but I guarantee the silk will magnetize it.' I stroked the needle as many times as seemed necessary, then tied it by its middle to a length of thread. The needle began to swing, slowly stabilizing itself to point north.

'Look,' said Steve. 'It's in line with the church. Nothing like the Boy Scouts, eh?' He grinned, but I could see he was impressed.

'Actually, I was in the Boys' Brigade. More church parades on Sunday than trekking through the wilderness. This is just something I picked up somewhere. And it seems to work. Now, we need to steer a course north-west of here. I'll recharge the needle every mile or so, and we can re-orient ourselves in time to stop circling. Let's head on.'

'Wouldn't we be better going south-west or north-east?' asked Bob. 'That way we'd be out of the jungle in no time.'

'We could do that,' I said. 'And perhaps I should put it to a vote. But I came here to search for a Mayan city, and I don't mean to leave until I've given up reasonable hope of finding it.'

'Even if we all die in the attempt?'

I hesitated. It was the last thing I wanted, to cause any more deaths. But I wanted the city. I wanted it badly, more than I'd wanted anything before, except for Antonia.

Bob looked round the others, as though to gather support. But Antonia spoke up in favour of continuing the search for Kaminalhuyú, and the others kept silent. We decided to go on, but I knew I had seen the first seeds of mutiny, and that if things got any worse, there would be more.

13 Cib

I've decided to use the Mayan date, based on a 20-day month called a uinal. *It helps me feel in tune with our search. The thirteen means today is ruled by the lords of the number thirteen. Tomorrow will be one again, because, although there are twenty days in the month, the numbers run on a cycle of thirteen. It will take a total of 260 days (a* tzolkin) *before a combination of names and numbers repeats itself.* Cib *means 'vulture'. I hope that isn't ominous.*

We've found a means of keeping to a straight line, as far as we can tell, but the forest hasn't finished with us yet. Last night we were plagued by vampire bats. Some of them ripped holes in our mosquito nets, and a few of us were bitten. Rokché went out this morning to find some herbs to treat the bites – bats can carry rabies, and we aren't carrying any anti-rabies serum. He hasn't come back yet, but I trust him not to get lost.

Hunting is part of our everyday routine now. It takes up more time than we ever bargained for. Rokché has showed us how to make a variety of traps. We've spent this morning cutting stakes and digging pits. The spears are sharpened and lashed together to form different types of spear trap, relying on great tension and the careful deployment of tripwires. Another trap uses a noose set in a pit, with four sharpened stakes to catch the animal's head. None of these is to be used during the day if we are moving around. But during the night they will bring in peccaries and maybe even a jaguar. We've constructed a smoke tepee on which to dry any excess meat we succeed in killing.

1 Caban. 1 Earthquake

The days have nobler names than we give them. Strictly speaking, each name should be preceded by the word Kub'aal *or Lord, for the days are gods, as are all parts of time to the Maya.*

Screams last night, as our traps took effect. This morning the trap line was filled with corpses. We bagged a kinkajou, a margay, a tapir, and a small deer, as well as various smaller game. This morning, we are all covered in blood as we skin and prepare the meat. We are half naked again as the veneer falls away once more. It will be a struggle to preserve the *civilizado* much longer.

But we will eat well tonight, and there will be smoked meat for everyone's pouch. We have to live by the day, sometimes by the hour.

More vampire bats last night. About midnight, the drumming and scraping sounds again, not as close as before, but none the less ominous.

We all suffer from minor infections or infestations of one kind or another. Bob touched an urticating caterpillar yesterday, when he stretched out a hand to steady himself against a tree trunk. The hand is swollen and red, and itches like hell. I still seem to be attractive to ticks, which means careful work every time we stop, dislodging them so their mouthparts don't remain in my skin, then disinfecting the spot. I've discovered that Antonia's nail polish remover gets them off better than anything; God knows why she brought it on the expedition, though.

Antonia is missing. We don't know when it happened, but probably while we were taking a rest and having a brief siesta. We've looked everywhere, but she's nowhere to be seen, just like when Barney vanished. Rokché says he has found a trail leading away from the camp. Only one person, he says. God knows why she would want to set out on her own. Her packs are still in camp. I've gone through them, and nothing is missing. Except Antonia.

Midnight. Still nothing. They are drumming out there, and I pray she is not with them. The bats whirr and whirr through the branches above us, then they swoop down, intent on sucking our blood. We fight them off as best we can, but our nets are useless, and they get through anyway. I sit here fighting them off helplessly, while they swoop and swoop like maddened birds, afraid of nothing.

2 Etz'nab. 2 Knife. 2 Sacrifice

Today brought another tragedy, one more horrible in its fashion than Barney's disappearance and death. We are all of us still stunned, and are beginning to wonder what sort of fate lies in store for us in this terrible place. While I write, Rokché is praying to his gods for intervention. For my own part, I can only despair of our ever coming through this alive. I wish to God I had never set foot in the forest, nor heard of Kaminalhuyú, nor taken up Mayan archaeology. My chosen career has brought me nothing but pain and grief, and at this moment I would sooner spend the rest of my life waiting tables in the worst greasy spoon London has to offer than to be an archaeologist.

I take that back. Being an archaeologist has brought me one thing I would never want to exchange. Antonia. Beside her, the rest pales into insignificance: the attack at Komchen, the prison, the knifing, this disastrous expedition. I'd go through all of it again if it meant finding her at the end. She's here beside me now, her head on my shoulder, watching me write. She's been devastated by today's events, and in some way holds herself responsible for what happened.

Antonia re-appeared in camp not long after first light, while we were still debating what to do about her. She walked slowly towards us, as though ascending a steep hill, and every step a torment. My heart caught, and I thought I would die. Weary, she seemed very weary. She was naked, and from head to foot she was soaked in blood, and all about her flies swarmed in black battalions, so thick around her we could hear them buzz all the way to our encampment. Her hair was red with blood, as though she had swum in it. I went for her, as though going to fetch in the dead. And as I went I saw that she carried a

451

knife in her hand, and that it was bloody like her, and her hand trembled holding it.

She fell into my arms and put her lips on mine, bloody as they were, and she kissed me with a passion I'd thought gone from her for ever.

'You're hurt,' I said, as I pulled apart from her, trying to see where she was wounded, and how. But she laughed and shook her head.

'It's just blood,' she said. 'It'll wash off.'

We'd found a small stream nearby, and I took her down there while the others waited, and helped her wash the blood off. She'd been right, it came off with a little hard rubbing and scraping. But she'd been wrong in what she'd said just before that. It wasn't just blood. Washing it off wouldn't be enough.

'I'm sorry,' she said. 'I've let you down.'

'It's all right. At least you've come to no harm. We all thought . . .'

She took me in her arms and soothed me. There was something calm about her that had not been there before.

'What happened?' I asked.

She didn't answer straight away, but knelt down over the stream and began washing the blood out of her hair. When she finished, she flipped it back over her shoulders and sat on a fallen log.

'You need a towel,' I said. 'And some clothes.'

She ignored this, and began to tell me what had taken place.

'I got lost,' she said. 'That's how it began. I went out of the camp just to be alone for a while. I wanted to think things through, to think about what happened at the ranch. The bulls. Rafael. All of that. And suddenly I found myself on a track. It wasn't very clear, but I was certain it was used from time to time. Branches were cut, and always at a height that would let a small human being through. It didn't seem

452

like it had been used in ages, so I went on down it. I don't know why.

'I came on a clearing, quite a wide one, full of wild flowers. They attracted me. I wanted to bring some back to camp. There were butterflies above them, blue morphos, flying like wounded birds. Your voices had been swallowed up by the forest. I felt entirely alone, as I'd wanted to be.

'I went up very close, almost to the edge of the clearing. But the closer I got, the more my original impression gave way to something darker. The flowers I'd seen weren't flowers at all, but birds' feathers that had been strewn over the forest floor. Red and blue feathers from macaws and parrots, green feathers from quetzals, masses of them, Leo, all scattered across a carpet of leaves.

'But that wasn't all. I became aware that there were figures sitting in the clearing. My first thought was that they were the Indians who'd attacked us. Then I realized they were too still for that. I couldn't see very clearly. The light was getting worse by the minute. They didn't move, but I kept my distance all the same. I think they're statues of some sort, stone statues, probably Mayan. We may be on the outskirts, Leo. It's round here, I'm sure it is.'

I kissed her forehead and stroked her wet hair and took her to me. Dorothy arrived a few minutes later, bringing some clothes she'd taken from Antonia's pack. I still hadn't found out why she was covered in blood, but I decided it would do no good if I pressed her. Dorothy helped her dress, for Antonia was still a little confused. She didn't seem to know who Dorothy was. Watching them, I noticed something odd about the way Dorothy treated Antonia. My first instinct was to see in it something like a lesbian advance. But a moment later I changed my mind. It was more like veneration, as though Dorothy held Antonia in awe. Whatever it was, I didn't like it.

We went back up to the camp. The others were waiting

impatiently, and a glance was enough to tell me just how worried they had been.

I explained as well as I could what Antonia had found. They listened impassively, but I could detect a degree of disbelief on some faces. Rokché asked her to sit down beside him. Far above our heads, a little tribe of macaws had gathered like a troop of miniature soldiers, screeching and fluttering their coloured wings. I sat down beside Antonia. Rokché took her hand in his. Concern lined his face, and his eyes were troubled as he questioned her.

'It got dark suddenly,' she said. 'I should have known, but the clearing had taken up so much of my attention. I knew right away that I'd be mad to try finding my way back to the camp. I'd be bound to get lost in the dark. So I just stayed where I was, a little way up the trail, as far away from the clearing as I could safely go.

'I tried to sleep, but every time I woke up out of a nightmare. It was always the same nightmare, I was in a field of my father's bulls, slaughtering them with a knife, and at the same moment I was in the great room listening to the cante jondo, and then I was a bull myself, running and running from men with axes.

'Every time I woke up, I found myself covered with spiders and God knows what. So I decided I'd rather stay awake. That was when it occurred to me that the trail I'd found might also be used by animals. I don't know what came over me then. Something in me wanted to act out my dream. I undressed, because I knew there'd be a lot of blood if it went well. Then I dug a pit. The ground was soft, mainly leaf-mulch for a long way down. It still took me ages, but I managed to get about three feet under. Then I covered it with twigs and leaves.

'I had a little food on me, some dried coati meat. I put it on top of the pit, then sat out of the way. Some time went by before I got anything, and I'm afraid I lost all sense of time anyway; but something came along in the end and crashed through the twigs. I was on it before it had a chance to get out. I've no idea what it was, but I managed to hold it down long enough to find its throat and kill it.

'I used some of its meat to bait the trap a second time. And it went on like that all night. I don't know what's out there. I just killed whatever came along.'

She shuddered and bent down with her head between her hands, exhausted, but not sobbing. Rokché looked at her for a while, and I could detect what emotions he was feeling. Eventually, he leaned forward and stroked her head.

'Tell me about the bulls,' he said.

We left about an hour later, travelling in a group down towards the clearing, Antonia going ahead to show the way. I could see Rokché scanning the trail as we pressed along it, his trained eyes catching clues completely invisible to ours.

'Why would there be feathers in a clearing like that?' I asked him; but he said nothing in reply, and just went on with his examination, checking out broken twigs, stopping to sniff a crushed leaf, or run his hand along a branch.

Suddenly, we came on Antonia's pit. All around it were the carcasses of the beasts she'd dispatched during the night. Smallish animals, mostly, except for a grey-coated jaguarundi about four feet in length. Thank God, I thought, she hadn't tackled a full-size jaguar.

'We'll deal with these later,' Rokché said. 'First, I want to take a look at this clearing.'

Antonia led us further along the trail. Suddenly, we turned a corner and I could see, as she had said there would be, the bright colours of bird feathers just beyond a break in the trees.

'Go slowly,' said Rokché. He bent to the ground to examine something, and when he stood up again I could see he was puzzled. Antonia went forward. One or two of the party, eager to see this fabled clearing, fanned out on either side of the trail.

455

We were mere feet away when Rokché held up a hand. He crouched, and gestured to us to do the same. I took the binoculars from my pack and started to scrutinize the figures I could see set all round a nearly circular space. I went from one to the next, trying to make out what they could be. One thing I saw right away: they did not resemble any Mayan statues I had ever seen, whether in the flesh or in photographs.

'Come on, Leo, what's your verdict?' shouted Steve, who was several yards to my right and a little nearer the clearing. 'Why don't we just go straight in?'

'They aren't statues,' I said.

'What are they, then? They're certainly not alive.'

'I'm not entirely sure. It looks like rust more than anything. Yes, that's right, they . . .'

At that moment, I knew what I was looking at. Armour. Suits of Spanish armour, dulled and rusted over centuries. The helmets, the cuirasses, everything suddenly became clear. And when I looked again, I saw something else: a skull grinning out at me from beneath the broad bonnet of a steel helmet.

'I think this is most of Don Joaquín's bodyguard,' I whispered.

'And I think this is where they were brought after they were killed,' said Rokché. 'To be set up as gods and worshipped.'

'Gods?' I looked at the stunted figures in front of me, at their rusting helms and blunted swords. And then I saw the feathers, and I realized that they were not just lying on the ground, as though fallen there by chance, but that they had been stuck into the earth by their points, like little flags.

Were these the only offerings? I wondered. I took up my binoculars once more and started to scan the clearing. And now I saw what had escaped me until then. Among the feathers, and mostly concealed by them, were bones, long, white bones. I might have passed them off as the leg-bones of jaguars or the ribs of peccaries, had it not been for one thing

456

more: scattered among them were dozens of human skulls, their shape perfectly recognizable, their empty eye-sockets screaming at a deaf world.

'This is staggering,' said Bob. He was a couple of yards to my right, and I could see him taking one of his cameras out of the aluminium case he always carried. 'I'm going in to get some shots.'

I looked round, and my eye was caught by Rokché. His head was moving quickly, like a bird's, his eyes darting to right and left, as though he had seen a predator about to swoop on him.

Suddenly he turned to Bob, and I could see his hand lifting and his body begin to twist as he made to run forward, and I heard his voice raised above the forest clamour, screaming high in English.

'Stop!' he cried. 'Don't go any further!'

I don't know whether Bob heard him or not, but in any case it was too late. His foot must have caught on the snare-rope hidden under leaves. There was a snap of something unlatching, then an enormous wooden frame came rushing up out of nowhere. The frame was studded with pitilessly sharp stakes, dozens of them, and five or six of them thudded into Bob with the force of a locomotive. One entered his brain through his right eye, another slammed through his chest cavity.

He was held pinioned there like a moth on a collector's board, his limbs quivering while blood blossomed across his head and torso like red flowers in a florist's window. He was still alive when we got to him. I could hear him murmuring something over and over again, and I wanted him to stop, so that I wouldn't have to listen to him calling on his God or his mother or his wife, so that I wouldn't have to look into that white stained face. But I was paralysed, unable to move a muscle. It was Rokché who cut his throat and gave him the death he was so desperate for.

457

50

Footstep piled on footstep, heartbeat upon heartbeat, as they hacked their way through a dark swathe of forest more tangled and more confusing than ever. In their eagerness to get away from the scene of Bob's murder, they had cut and slashed a narrow path from the camp down into heavy jungle, in the direction they had originally been following.

Long before evening, they grew aware that the terrain across which they were walking was changing, that what had started as a narrow cut in the forest floor was slowly widening into a steep gully, and that the gully was extending itself into a valley with gently sloping sides. As elsewhere, the forest floor was itself almost free of obstructions, but as they descended the slope, humidity, already very high, climbed rapidly, and a proliferation of plants of all sizes struggled for possession of this dark valley world.

Zapotillos, chicarros, and *mescals* tangled their branches with *palo escobos, palo coronas,* and *limoncillos.* Lianas draped themselves round everything. The tree branches groaned with the weight of plants growing on and over them, each one a small garden of orchids, bromeliads, ferns, and moss, complemented by dozens of other plants, some colourful, some drab, some on the verge of some great revelation. Tree ferns a dozen feet tall tickled the lower branches of tall trees, heliconias lifted their vast leaves over the heads of philodendrons and monsteras, and orchids so small they needed a magnifying glass to be seen properly peppered leaves and branches. A strangler fig, having crushed to death the *mescal* round which it had originally grown, now raised its head to find a foot or two of open space in the foliage above.

An undercurrent of abundance and vibrating life ran through everything here. High up, where the branches began to grow heavy, the tadpoles of jungle frogs squirmed in their frenzy to be born, mosquito larvae kicked and wriggled, longing to be free, and tiny birds rustled inside their nests, gobbling down the food their parents brought them, desperate to take wing and fly. Every fallen log concealed a host of spiders, scorpions, and beetles, hollow trees were hosts to whole families of wildlife, the tree canopy quivered with the comings and goings of a million birds.

Leo started as a hummingbird no bigger than his thumb hovered in front of his face. It remained there no longer than a few seconds, hardly enough to permit a proper investigation, then it shot away like a piece of quicksilver given a sudden jolt. Leo smiled, wondering what type of hummingbird it had been. He'd made something of a hobby of them during the time he'd been at Komchen, familiarizing himself with their habits and the ways in which the various species differed one from the other, the hairy hermit from the violet sabre-wing, the green-crowned brilliant from the purple-throated mountain-gem, the constant star-throat from Buffon's plumeteer, Barrot's fairy, or Lucy's emerald. He'd taken photographs of the lovely hummingbird, the charming hummingbird, the admirable hummingbird, and the adorable coquette.

A stream ran along the valley floor, its water warm

to the touch, its banks crowded with low plants that sought to feed on it. Calathea, ferns, and clusters of raffia snarled for their place a little higher up. Tiny silvery fish raced through it, jumping into the air from time to time as they encountered obstructions. On the branch of a white-flowered frangipani tree, a royal heron sat waiting to dart down on its next victim.

'What's going on down here?' Leo asked Rokché. 'It's as if everything's gone into overdrive.'

'I've never seen anything like it. I didn't think the forest had enough room in it for more.'

But it wasn't just more, they could both sense that. In spite of the gloom, the colours of the flowers and the birds seemed brighter and more intense. Individual plants were bigger, or taller, or put out more flowers, or carried more fruit. They passed a papaya covered with unripe green fruit so heavy that the trunk was bent down and seemed ready to break.

Slowly, the ground grew less steep, and they sensed that the valley floor had flattened out on either side of the stream. It was only a sensation, but everyone agreed that something around them was changing.

As they passed on, their first impression of the valley altered. There were fewer flowers, and the branches of trees held less fruit than before, some none at all. Gradually, the sound of birdcalls faded, and when they looked up, the upper branches seemed to be empty of life. No monkeys swung from tree to tree on creepers. No toucans flashed their yellow beaks out of the shadows.

But there seemed to be more insects, more scorpions, more spiders. Almost every tree was covered in snails that were fastened tightly to the bark. Snakes lay coiled openly on the lower branches or curled about ivy-covered trunks. The temperature seemed to drop again. Slowly, a profound silence covered everything. They could hear themselves breathe for the first time in weeks, and if they listened they could make out individual raindrops cutting through the leaves. That was all. It was as if all the birds and beasts that had filled the forest so short a time ago had crept out or flown away, leaving the trees empty of life, but for snakes.

Suddenly, Leo, who had been walking ahead with Rokché, stopped dead in his tracks. He put his hand up to bring the others to a halt, then called out gently to Rokché, summoning him back.

'Can't you feel it?' he asked breathlessly. A strange excitement had taken hold of him. The others looked at him blankly.

'Feel what?' asked Antonia.

'We're there,' he said. He tried to keep his voice steady, but it betrayed him totally. 'We've reached the city,' he continued. 'Kaminalhuyú. At this very moment we're standing in the middle of the ball park.'

They looked at him as if he'd gone mad.

'I can't see anything,' said Steve. 'You're out of your tiny head, Leo. If you'd taken your Horlicks every night as I suggested –'

'Oh, shut up, Steve. I'm perfectly well, in fact I haven't felt this good in ages. We've actually done it. We've found our lost city.'

'What on earth are you twittering on about, man? There's nothing here but forest. These are trees, Leo, just more fucking trees.'

'I was aware of that. Do me a favour, everybody, will you? I want you to spread out, mainly over here' – he pointed to his left – 'and over that way. This spot here can serve as our camp for tonight. It'll be dark in an hour or so anyway. Let's get it cleared and light a fire.'

'You haven't told us how you know this is a ball park,' said Dorothy. 'I mean, Steve's right, this is just another bunch of trees.'

'What did you expect? A main street with the trees lined up neatly on either side? Come on, you remember what it was like at Komchen before we started work.'

'Yeah, but at least we had a pyramid to start with. We don't even have a loose altar or one of those cute little stelae those Mayas kept sticking up all over the place.'

In answer, Leo rummaged inside his pack and brought out a short trenching tool. He bent down and started to dig through the leafmould and humus that had been formed by constant leaf-fall down the centuries. He didn't know how far down he'd have to go, and the deeper he was forced to dig, the more he began to doubt his original instinct. He kept on digging, acutely aware that if he lost face over this, he would also lose what slender control he had of the group.

There was a sudden scraping sound. Leo stiffened, then bent to his task with greater urgency, no longer digging down, but widening the hole and scraping the soil away from a small circle at the bottom.

'There,' he said, straightening and throwing the trenching tool to one side.

Steve bent down and looked into the hole, then pushed his hand down, running his fingers over a dirty white surface.

'Stucco,' he said. 'Fuck me for a nincompoop, it's a bloody stucco floor.'

'Do you believe me now?' asked Leo, feeling hot blasts of relief sweep through him. His hand shook as he brushed the hair back, away from his forehead.

'Let's spread out,' Steve suggested.

'We'll light a fire first,' said Leo. 'No sense in anybody getting lost at this stage.'

When a small clearing had been created and the fire set alight, they broke into two groups and started to cut their way through the trees on both sides. Leo stayed behind to keep an eye on the camp.

The light had just started to fade when there was a cry from the left-hand group, the Minnesota Twins and Rokché.

'Leo, there's something here. We can't get any further forward. It's covered in moss and undergrowth, with some trees higher up. Looks like a wall or something.'

'Scrape some of the moss away.'

Moments later, Rokché's voice boomed out through the trees.

'It *is* a wall. Stone, anyway. It could be some sort of building.'

Minutes later, Steve's voice echoed across the silent forest.

'There's another one here. From where I'm standing, it looks like it's maybe fifteen, twenty feet high. It has a slope to it, from about four feet up. Twenty, maybe thirty degrees. About right for . . .' He paused. 'Hang on, Leo, I've just noticed something. Just as I thought. There's a hoop up above my head, a stone hoop.'

They all knew what that meant. They had stumbled on the city's ball court, where warriors had played the fast and deadly game of *pok-ta-pok*, a game whose losers were dragged off to become sacrificial victims, their heads cut off. As good a place to start as any.

With what light there was left, they identified the court's three aisle-markers, elaborately sculpted discs, one in the centre, one at each end. Steve measured the distance between the two sloping walls, and found they were just over eighty yards apart. That made this court about five yards wider than the biggest at Chichén Itzá, which meant it must be the largest in Central America.

'If they've got a ball court this big, what about the rest of the place?' he asked.

'You guys know nothing about American football,' said one of the twins – in the fading light it wasn't clear which one. 'This place was obviously home to the champs. Headquarters to the Central American Football Association. The Kaminalhuyú Redskins. If we look hard enough, we'll find the Superbowl.'

'Suit yourself, but just hope you don't bump into the team,' said Rokché. 'We Redskins don't give much quarter. One game would be enough to lose all your heads.'

They had barely got back to base when the light dropped from the sky and the forest filled with inky blackness.

Leo shivered as he built up the fire. He could sense it all around him, the vast, slumbering city without eyes or ears, watching and listening by means of its stone. Some people thought stone had memory, that ghosts were nothing more than recordings made in walls and floors. But at that moment, it was more than that to Leo.

The ghosts were dark substances, more than memory or grief, each one complete with its lifetime of hope and suffering. He had come to the City of Sorcerers, where the ghosts of ten thousand sacrifices roamed the tree-choked streets. He could hear bats circling above his head, and an owl crying as it prowled the darkness for its first prey of the night.

51

Paris

He knew there were techniques for coping with this sort
of situation, ways of shutting out the prison walls and
finding liberty of a sort in one's own faintly-beating
heart. He'd had plenty of the techniques in question
used against him by hard-bitten IRA men who refused
to cooperate in their interrogations, and even by the
tougher element in Ireland's criminal elite, resisting his
efforts to make them inform on friends. Now, if they came
to question him, he'd know exactly what to do, he'd give
the bastards a hard run for their money.

But something told him it was not information they
sought from him. He'd lost track of the time he'd been
in the room, the light hadn't been switched off once, and
what sleep he'd been able to snatch had been troubled
and brief, leaving him disoriented when he woke. His
dreams were of Alice and pyramids and bloody hearts.
In them, he cut his way to a pyramid in the jungle, in
the centre of a dark city of stone, but once inside he
found himself in a morgue whose drawers disappeared
into a high ceiling that swarmed with bats. He would
open drawer after drawer and pull back the sheet that
covered the corpse inside, but each one was Alice, no
matter how far he looked. And each time she would

open her soft-lidded eyes and invite him to embrace her. Spiders crawled out from the wound in her chest and there were sweet-tasting maggots on her lips.

Food of a sort was delivered from time to time, and water with it, both shoved in through a little hatch set low in the door. A bell was rung each time to alert him, whether he was asleep or not, but he could never calculate the time between one food call and the next.

He blamed himself for not having taken the most elementary precaution in venturing here, namely to leave details of the appointment with the duty sergeant. They'd have found him by now, and rounded up those responsible for detaining him, assuming they were still on the premises.

When the door opened at last, it wafted a scent of expensive perfume into his tiny, ill-smelling chamber. A woman dressed in a plain black trouser-suit entered the room. She was aged about thirty, short, with dark hair and eyes that showed him no mercy.

'We'll go for a walk, if you don't mind, Monsieur Carberry. It's not too far, and we don't want to keep our friends waiting.'

'If I refuse?'

'Then you'll be taken forcibly. You don't want that.'

She followed him along a corridor, up some stairs, down a second corridor, and at last to a short flight of steps that led to a huge door of mahogany and teak, polished and gilded to perfection.

'Open the door,' she said. He opened it.

A group of men and women were waiting for him, but without particular attention. They were identically dressed in red robes, each tied at the waist with a thin gold cord. Their feet were bare. A few of them seemed self-conscious, and Declan guessed that this might be their first time to appear like this in public.

At the far end of the room, cut off from the rest, sat a man of about thirty. He was naked, and his hands had been tied behind his back. An empty stool awaited Declan, who was made to join the other victim and ordered to undress. He did so with whatever shreds of dignity he could muster, and took his place on the stool, facing out into the room.

This was not a room in the Louis XV style, like the one he had been in when he attended the lecture. The walls were covered in brightly-coloured frescoes similar in style and content to those miraculously-preserved paintings found on the inside of the temple at Bonampak. Declan, who had spent hours poring over reproductions of the Bonampak frescoes, let his gaze wander over these, and found they told much the same story. There were dancers preparing to perform in vast headdresses of *quetzal* feathers, with jaguar skins about their waists and jaguar sandals on their feet. Musicians played on trumpets, turtle shells, and rattles. A dancer dressed as a crab raised fearsome pincers to the sky. A crocodile god sat watching from a raised throne. A shawm player danced with a necklace of human heads dangling from his neck.

But the paintings here, as in the original, gave pride of place to scenes of battle and human sacrifice, to prisoners lined up before a conquering king, ready for execution, to victims laid on low altars with their hearts torn out.

In the middle of the floor stood a low column, on top of which lay a circular stone, its face carved intricately with the masks and glyphs of a Mayan sculpture. He recognized it as a sacrificial altar, identical to the ones depicted in the frescoes.

It was not the only thing he recognized. As his eyes grazed the circle of seventeen red-clad acolytes, he picked

467

out more than one whose face and name were known to him: Commander Patrick Debias-Aubry, a high official in the DGSE, the French General Directorate for External Security; Félix Alphand, the chief of the DCPJ, the Judicial Police Directorate; Gilles-Marie Péguy, a judge noted for his reactionary views on law and order; Charles Sorel, the Deputy Director of Canal 1, France's influential first television channel; the Japanese head of a famous couturier house, and Dick Kraus, an American general who occupied a leading position in NATO's high command. He needed even less introduction to Madame Dutheillet. She looked in his direction, and he thought he saw a little smile of triumph flutter on her dark lips.

The woman in the black suit approached Declan. He recognized the perfume: it was Joy, an old favourite of Concepta's whenever she felt like splashing out. An old joke, that one, but he'd never tired of it. The woman tied his hands tightly behind his back, examined her handiwork briefly, and stepped away, exiting through a door cut through the stone.

Moments later, the door opened again and a man entered the room. It was the man who had delivered the lecture however many nights ago. Today he wore a robe like the others, but white instead of red.

'Welcome,' he said. 'You are all welcome. As you know, it has not been possible for our beloved Rafael to attend this evening's ceremony. It will, therefore, fall to myself and to our newly-created *nacom*, Madame Sophie Dutheillet, to carry out the two openings destined to be performed this evening.'

He paused, then spread his arms.

The congregation held hands and bent their heads, then their leader began to chant a Mayan prayer, his voice rising and falling without accompaniment, filling the room with a sense of mounting dread. Next to Declan, the other naked man started to shiver, his whole body convulsing with spasms of terror.

When the prayer ended, the priest composed himself. Silence filled the chamber. The only sound was a mild whimpering that came from the first victim-to-be.

'Stand up, Jacques Chéramy.'

The naked man stood. His legs seemed hardly capable of holding him upright. He seemed extraordinarily pale, and Declan could see wounds on several parts of his body. He remembered that the ancient Maya had tortured their prisoners for several days before the sacrifice, almost draining them of blood in the process.

'Jacques Chéramy, you have been accused of treason, of having betrayed the Nohoch Tata, our Master Rafael. We have examined your case and found you guilty. Do you have anything to say?'

'I admit it. But I did it for everyone's good, to put an end to the killings.'

'There is a purpose to the killings. Perhaps your own death will help you understand that.'

The chief *nacom* clapped his hands. Behind him, the door swung open, and two women entered, both naked except for a thin cord round their waists. They were exquisitely beautiful. Declan recognized one as the woman in black who had come for him. They took Jacques Chéramy and lifted him over the altar, one holding down his arms from above, the other pulling his legs downwards. These were the *chacs*, junior priestesses whose task was to hold the victim in place.

In a moment, the priest was in position by the victim's side, Sophie Dutheillet facing him. She handed him a long knife of obsidian, its handle wrapped in a white cloth. He incanted several lines of another prayer, then raised the

469

knife and plunged it into Chéramy's chest. The man cried out in anguish, and continued to do so as the priest cut his chest open. Sharper than a scalpel, the dark blade went through fat and flesh like butter. The *nacom* handed the knife back to his assistant, then plunged his hand inside the victim's chest and tore his heart from it still beating. He lifted it above his head, while the body on its cold slab twitched like a frog in a brutal experiment.

The heart was passed from hand to hand round the congregation. No one's hands remained clean. They were all parties to the crime that had been committed, and Declan realized that this must, above all else, represent the hold Rafael had over his followers. They might seek eternal life at his hands, but he knew – and could doubtless prove – that they had participated in murder.

The *chacs* carried the body away, then returned.

'Declan Carberry, please stand.'

Wearily, Declan got to his feet. He wondered which one had cut his Alice open, which one had removed her beating heart. Was it this man? Or had Rafael done it in person? It scarcely mattered now. There was nothing he could do about it.

'Mr Carberry, you have been poking your nose into the affairs of the Sacbe. Misunderstanding our purposes, knowing nothing of the one who guides us, Rafael, and remaining ignorant of our destiny in the world, you have sought to destroy us. For that injustice, you will meet the same fate as Monsieur Chéramy.'

Declan was dragged to the altar. The two women attending him were spattered with blood that had pulsed out during the first execution. Part of Declan was glad it had come to this. They were doing the job for him. If such things happened, he might soon be with Alice. And, if not, he had oblivion to look forward to.

But another part of him rebelled against it all, crying out against the injustice of what was being done, not so much to himself, but to Alice, who might now go unavenged for ever.

This was to be Sophie Dutheillet's first excision. She took the knife, and recited the prayer in French. Declan could see her hand shake. His death would very likely be botched and painful. He struggled against the hands holding him down, but they were too strong for him. The prayer came to an end.

There was a sound of shooting, very near. First, single shots, then a roll as a sub-machine-gun spat into life. Sophie Dutheillet looked round in panic, dropping the knife.

'We've got to get out,' she said. 'Something's wrong.'

The *nacom* lifted the knife and handed it back to her, without its white cloth.

'Continue with the execution,' he said. 'Our guards will take care of any intruders.'

But the congregation was restless. They started to head for the door, when the priest shouted at them, ordering them to return, to watch the next killing. Madame Dutheillet struggled to get a grip on herself. She took the knife tightly in one hand. There was more shooting. It sounded as though it came from the next room.

Madame Dutheillet looked down at Declan.

'I am eternal,' she said. 'You can't take that away from me. Not now.'

She lifted the knife. At that instant, the rear and front doors of the room burst open. The room started to fill with armed men. One detached himself from the rest, knelt, and put a series of bullets through Madame Dutheillet's chest. The force of the shots sent her reeling back against the wall.

Seconds after that, a Kevlar-clad Rob Barlow appeared at Declan's side. While all around them armed policemen made rapid work of arresting everyone in sight, Rob helped Declan to his feet.

'Are you all right, sir? I'm sorry we had to leave it until now, but I only found your diary entry and your invitation to this place three hours ago. We had to get the team set up, then do a proper recce. Didn't expect this, though.'

'Do you realize you've just shot dead the wife of the French President?'

'Is that who she is? Thought she looked familiar. Oh, well, I'm sure he can get another one where that came from. Let's get you home, sir. You really don't look very well.'

52

Kaminalhuyú
Selva Lacandóna

He slept and woke and slept again. In the middle of the
little clearing they had created, the fire burned, and from
time to time he would slip down from his hammock and
replenish it. Each time he did so, he would check that
Antonia was all right, that she was still in her hammock.
He would find her sleeping each time, and would bend
to kiss her cheek or her forehead. He sensed that she was
dreaming, and did not know how to reach wherever it
was her dreams had taken her. His own dreams were
indistinct at first, but as the night deepened they grew
in pace and clarity.

He was in the pyramid at Komchen again, somewhere
on the stairs going downwards. Behind him came men
and women wearing jade masks on their faces, and in
front of him men with plumage like birds danced in the
narrow space. A drum was beating somewhere below,
its steady pounding bruising his heart. He woke and
returned to sleep, and found himself in the same place.
A little further down, and then he woke again. But this
time, when he returned to sleep, he did not wake for a
long time.

They led him downwards, his feet slipping on the

smooth stone. There was no form of handrail, not even a rope with which to steady himself. Above the beating of the drum came a steady chanting, not in the voices of adults, but the small, nervous accents of little children.

And they brought him finally through high doors into a temple painted with bright colours, where the figures of men and gods flickered on the walls, harried into motion by rows of spiralling torches. A roaring fire blazed on the main altar, fed from time to time with bunches of incense. A priest with a crocodile mask kept the flames going. The entire room was thick with perfumed smoke.

Beyond the temple lay another doorway, on the other side of which stood a smaller room, this one packed with priests and children. In its centre stood a stone tomb with a finely-carved lid. The priests were dressed in gaudy feathers, and wore masks to portray themselves as crabs and monkeys, jaguars and toucans. Rich jaguar pelts hung from their shoulders, and their ankles were bound with anklets of shell and coral. In a corner, a drummer sat beating a slow rhythm, and a piper piped a lament that sounded vaguely Irish to Leo's ears.

No sooner had he entered than a pair of priests rushed forward and grabbed one of the children, a little boy. The screaming child was dragged to the sarcophagus and laid down on it, while a third priest wearing a jaguar mask took a claw-shaped knife and plunged it into the child's breast, from which he tore the heart.

Blackness. The night ran through the forest like water, embracing everything. Leo rolled out of his hammock, still half-asleep. A night monkey chattered in the tree above him. There was a cry of alarm further off. Somewhere in the distance, almost too far to be heard, a drum was beating. He crossed to Antonia. She was still asleep.

The fire had almost gone out. He found more wood and

piled it high, thinking all the time of the fire that had burned in the temple of his dream. Satisfied there was enough light to deter predators, he returned to his hammock and tried to settle down.

Darkness, then lights, and he was in the burial room again. But this time he was surrounded by priests dressed as crabs, with giant arms that ended in pincers. They moved about him in a slow dance, and when he looked up he saw he was lying on top of the sarcophagus, and that his breast was naked. They shuffled and turned in the dance, urged by a single drumbeat. And when he looked again, they had changed into monstrous spiders, each the size of a man.

He woke, choking for breath among billows of white smoke from the campfire. The first light of a shadowless dawn was forcing its way down through the foliage above him. Shaking, he lay in his hammock until the dream and its images wore off. Someone fixed the fire. Around him, the camp was slowly coming to life. As he straightened, he saw the pale barks of ghostly *chimones* lifting their crowns high above a battery of corozo palms.

He got down from the hammock just in time to see Rokché emerge from the *champa* he had built for himself the night before. Woven from overlapping corozo fronds, it was watertight and almost impervious to insects. The Indian looked up and caught Leo's eye. He seemed troubled.

Someone had beaten a path down to the stream, which was narrow at this point. Leo followed Rokché down. They stood together in midstream, stripped to the waist, splashing the cold water over their faces and chests. Little silver fish skipped through the translucent water.

'Is everything all right?' Leo asked.

'I don't like this place. There are too many ghosts.'

'Like the Altar of Sacrifices?'

Rokché nodded. 'Like that, but much worse. A different sort of ghost.'

'Rokché, old man, this is the City of Eternal Life.'

'That was Don Joaquín's name for it. Its Mayan name is Kaminalhuyú. The Hill of the Dead.'

'Do you want to leave?'

'I can't go back on my own. None of us can do that. I'll stay until you finish whatever it is you came to do here.'

Leo ducked his head into the stream, then brought it out, spluttering.

'Let's get back,' he said, 'and get a new camp set up north of the ball court. That's our first priority.'

Everyone was keen to get started on exploring the city, but Leo insisted that they first make the camp into something more permanent than the overnight stops they'd been building until then. While Rokché set about instructing Steve and the Filberts on how to build *champas* for the group, Leo started cutting down trees. They'd brought a chainsaw, a Shindaiwa 360, weighing only 8.8 pounds, and enough petrol to get several days' heavy use out of it.

By noon they had a proper centre for their operations. Stage two was to run lines of orange twine for half a mile in four directions out of the camp. They'd be joined later by others, and by signposts as they began to sketch the layout of the city. The first tracks were made by machete. There was no need to make larger pathways with the Shindaiwa until they knew where they were going. Leo prepared a large sheet of squared paper, marking the campsite at the centre, then measuring and entering the two buildings that formed the boundaries of the ball court.

'What sort of thing are we looking for?' asked Rokché.

Leo shrugged. 'To be honest, I don't know. Probably a pyramid or two, some temples. Or maybe not, maybe this place is totally different to anything else. Mayan cities don't conform to a fixed pattern, you know. Have you visited many?'

'Sure, a few. Copán, of course. Quirigua – I went there after college with a girlfriend. Tikal, Palenque, Chichén Itzá. I've been around.'

'Then you'll know this is going to be seat-of-the-pants stuff. There's no routine for working out where typical buildings should be, the way you can with a Roman city. I can't tell you to expect a temple a mile to the east, or a burial site to the west.'

'Something puzzles me. All those places I visited, I never saw anything that made it look like anybody had ever lived there. Just these huge pyramids and temples, plazas, causeways. I mean, some of them had palaces for the kings and their families, but nothing for the masses.'

'That's easily enough explained. The hoi polloi lived in huts all round the city perimeter. Probably large versions of your *champa*. The same was probably true of the markets, which would be set up temporarily. These weren't really cities, Rokché, even if some of them had enormous populations.'

'What were they, then?'

'Religious centres ruled over by kings and administered by priests. Holy places. I imagine there were regular pilgrimages to shrines and temples. Everything was created to further the human link with the gods. The pyramids are just stone hills built to perch a temple on. The acropolises are just collections of temples and altars. Look at the way they're laid out, all those empty spaces, all those stepped walls where people could sit. It was all done for display, so the religious ceremonies could be seen by the largest number of people possible. The sacrifices in particular. They'd kill some poor sod at the top of the pyramid steps, then roll the body down the sides. It must have been an extraordinary spectacle. Feathers and gold.'

'And blood.'

Leo smiled. 'And blood. Let's get to work.'

The two Filberts, Steve, and Antonia had already divided up the four quadrants between themselves. Leo and Rokché busied themselves clearing the campsite, using the chainsaw to remove the larger trees, which fell softly through the upper foliage, scattering birds and monkeys in their wake. The constant cries of disturbed wildlife lent the forest an almost lively air, dispelling some of the gloom that had hung over it previously. There was now a permanent circling of birds above the upper canopy; now that their habitat had been swept away, motmots, jays and manakins, all jostled for space with toucans, macaws and tanagers.

There was a cry somewhere off to the right, down the path Dorothy had taken. With the help of the orange twine, Leo and Rokché got there in minutes. It hadn't been a cry for assistance, just a means of alerting the others that she'd stumbled on something. Antonia and Steve, having worked their way back through the central point of the camp, arrived one after the other several minutes later. Dorothea had either not heard her sister's cry, or had chosen to ignore it.

They set about measuring and clearing a one-storey stucco-covered building with a sloping roof and a stepped arch. The chainsaw whisked away the heavier vegetation, while knives and trowels performed lesser but equally important tasks, uncovering inscriptions and freeing the area around the doorway. The door proper consisted of a heavily inscribed slab bearing the figures of Ah Puch, the skeletal god of death, and Ixtab, the patron goddess of suicides. Beneath each of these deities crouched two smaller figures, each bearing the same glyph, *ahmen*, or 'he who knows', one of the titles given to medicine men and sorcerers.

'Let's get this door off,' Leo suggested. 'It's only held to the wall by concrete that's been crumbling quite badly. Dorothy, could you run back to the camp and bring a maul hammer and one of the bolster chisels? Steve, could you take some photographs before we start work? And, Antonia, why don't you start work on the inscriptions? See if you can find some dates or something.'

Steve had barely finished taking an initial set of photographs – a task he'd taken over from Bob – when Dorothy returned with the hammer and chisel. The masonry was in poor condition, and it took only half an hour to prise the door free from the wall. Thin as it was, it took their combined strength to move the door away from the little building to a safe position against a tree opposite.

Dorothy had thought to bring a torch as well. Leo took it and stepped into the building, swinging the light in front of him. It took some time for his eyes to focus.

'Can you see anything?'

'Not yet, not really. It's as if . . .'

He swung the light from floor to ceiling and back again, then took a second step, playing the torch left and right.

'It's like being outside. Everything's green. There are cobwebs, centuries of them, but that's not . . .' He brought the torch to a halt, letting the light rest on one tiny part of what he had seen. And in moments he understood what he was looking at.

'Skulls,' he said. 'Green skulls.'

Antonia came in behind him. There was a long, narrow passageway that seemed to run the length of the building. On either side of it, sloping back to the walls, and as high as the ceiling, stone racks held thousands of skulls. Green skulls, just as Leo had described them. Jade skulls, each one life-size. The place was packed with them. Their queer hollowed-out sockets stared at them with a malicious triumph, daring the intruders to disturb their centuries-old rest.

Leo watched as a scorpion, its sleep broken, struggled briefly into the light and then crept out of sight among a group of skulls on the right.

'Let's get out of here,' he said.

Steve went in to take some photographs of the skulls *in situ*. He came back out, shaking his head and brushing cobwebs from his hair and clothes.

'What the hell's it all about?' he asked.

Rokché pointed to the door they'd left to one side.

'It's about them,' he said. 'Ah Puch. Ixtab.'

'But why jade skulls?'

'Perhaps . . .'

At that moment, Dorothea appeared, out of breath. Pausing to get her breath back, she pointed north.

'Are you all right?'

Antonia went close to her, trying to read in her face whether there was cause for alarm or not, but Dorothea pushed her away, still struggling to catch her breath. After a couple of minutes, she recovered.

'You've got to come,' she said. 'I've found . . .'

Her face was a shifting canvas of joy and fear and consternation.

'Take it easy. Just slow down and tell us what it is you've found.'

She looked at Antonia, then at the others one by one.

'I've found a pyramid,' she said. 'The biggest fucking pyramid anyone's ever seen.'

53

Declan spent a day in Paris after his release. Part of it was passed clearing up details at the Préfecture de Police, at their Boulevard du Palais headquarters. A RAID unit – the French equivalent of a SWAT team – had effected the spectacular assault that had brought Declan his last-minute deliverance. The unit had been under the overall control of the DGPN, the General Directorate for the National Police, but commanded at ground level by the Préfecture. One of the team had been killed, and now there would have to be a semi-public enquiry.

Declan was questioned by two senior officers, one from the Préfecture, one from the Service de Coopération Technique Internationale de Police, the sub-division of the DGPN which had direct responsibility for the RAID units. He gave them what details of his investigation he deemed it prudent for outsiders to know, and fudged over the rest. They were trained investigators, and Declan's fudge was fairly transparent, but they did not push him: he was, after all, police like themselves, and they knew he would have his operational considerations just as they did.

The main questions were put to him by Jean-Marie Albicoco, an old friend who had spent time in Dublin studying Garda and Ranger anti-terrorist techniques. He knew Declan had been through an ordeal, and he wasn't about to distress him further by pressing hard for answers. If anybody asked for more detailed information in future, the whole thing could be done through Declan's department, without upsetting anyone.

When Declan finally left the office and returned to the street, a late February sun had worked its way down through a haze of snow-clouds and was painting the buildings and thoroughfares with melted honey. Or so it seemed to Declan after his ordeal.

He bought a copy of *Le Monde* at a news stand on the corner of rue de Lutèce. The violent death of Sophie Dutheillet dominated the discreetly-printed front page, as it did in much larger letters every other paper. According to the text, she had been shot by terrorists while addressing a private meeting of a philosophical group that met regularly in the St Germain quarter. First reports suggested that the killers belonged to a Muslim extremist group called al-Jihad al-Islami li-Tahrir Ahl al-Maghrib (Jitam), the Islamic Struggle for the Liberation of the People of North Africa. Several Algerians and a Moroccan had been detained and were currently undergoing questioning at the Paris Préfecture. Nothing had been said to Declan about such arrests, but he had no doubt they had been made, and he would not have been surprised if the individuals concerned were put on trial, if they were not deported before that. Or found dead in their cells.

He lunched alone, in a small café on the Left Bank. Though it had not entirely caught him by surprise, he was still impressed by the speed with which the raid had been covered up. As he ate, he could not suppress a gnawing sensation in his stomach that was linked to his fear of just how far the cover-up would eventually go.

Most of that afternoon was spent with Dr Papadiantis. Declan had refused to go to hospital after his release, insisting that he had not been too badly treated, and was in no need of medical attention. However, before they would let him go, the police had extracted from him a written promise that he would attend his personal doctor for a check-up at the earliest opportunity.

Papadiantis put him through his paces, testing reflexes, measuring blood pressure, checking respiratory function, taking blood and urine samples.

'Just a precaution,' he said, slipping another vial of Declan's blood into a pouch. 'You don't seem to have suffered much physical damage. A little bruising, but that's about it. However, something else has happened since I last saw you, something dramatic.'

'How can you tell?'

'I'm trained to tell. But don't let the homoeopathy mislead you – I'm not psychic.'

Declan stared round the consulting room, unchanged, it seemed, since an earlier generation of doctors. Thick books in French, English, German, and Greek lined one wall. Against another stood a cabinet in which Papadiantis kept his remedies, white pills in little glass vials. Above the cabinet hung portraits of well-known physicians of the past, among which those of Paracelsus, Samuel Hahnemann, and his French wife Melanie took pride of place, side by side with Bernard and Laënnec.

'Someone I . . . loved . . . died.'

'Died?'

'Was killed. Was . . .' He straightened. 'I can't talk about this.'

'That's all right. How are the headaches?'

'A little better.'

'Good. Do you have panic attacks?'

'I . . . Yes.'

'Any time of day in particular?'

'Morning. After I wake.'

'And are they relieved by anything?'

'Just work. Sometimes not even by that.'

'I understand. Does the weather make them more or less frequent? Bad weather, for example?'

'Wet weather, yes.'

'And do you experience anything unusual during these attacks, or afterwards?'

'Only . . .' He hesitated. It was so hard to put into words. 'Sometimes I feel as if I'm made of glass. As if I'll shatter at the slightest touch.'

'And when you were locked up . . .'

So it continued for over an hour, gentle questioning against the wall of steel Declan had built round his heart.

'How do you make any sense of all this?' asked Declan as they drew to a close.

'It's not too difficult. For example . . .' He got up and went to the bookshelves, coming back with a fat volume bound in black leather, entitled *Kent's Final General Repertory*.

'Actually, I do this nowadays with a computer. But this should give you the idea. Here, this is the section on Mind, and you'll see a long sub-division on Delusions.'

He opened the book to the place in question.

'What would happen is that volunteers would be given a drug over a period of time. In due course they'd experience symptoms, which would be recorded and later published in books like this. It's an astonishing collection of what the human mind and body can get up to. Here's an odd one. The subject thought there were animals in his stomach. He'd been given Thuja. This one saw black animals on the walls and furniture.

Here's one who saw cucumbers on the bed. This one's fingernails seemed as large as plates. And here you are – "Has delusions that she is made of glass".'

Declan took the book and looked at the line indicated by Papadiantis.

'And this,' said the doctor, taking the book back and leafing through it, 'is my favourite: "Fancies he is commanded to fall on his knees and confess his sins and rip up his bowels by a mushroom." That one had taken Agaricus.'

'Agaricus?'

'Agaricus Muscarius. It's a poisonous mushroom; in French it is called *champignon fou*.'

'Fly agaric.'

'That's right.'

'And your guinea pig thought . . .'

'A great curiosity. Needless to say, this is not its main characteristic. That thought may only have occurred to a single individual. But who could have resisted recording it?'

Declan nodded, then looked more closely at the book.

'Doctor, is it possible . . . ? If I gave you the names of some Central American herbs, would this book show what they could do?'

'Not this book, no. This gives symptoms and shows which substances cause them. But a *Materia Medica* lists things the other way round. Unfortunately, there are so many of these herbs. But if you give me their names, I'll gladly check them for you.'

'Do you know of anything that would make someone think they could live for ever?'

'Live for ever? That's unusual. I don't think so. Cannabis Indica can make you think that time seems unending. Even a few seconds can seem like an age. And it can

486

make subjects feel superhuman. Does that meet your requirements?'

'It might do. But I'll send you the list.'

He noticed the doctor glance at the clock.

'You have other patients waiting.'

'I'm afraid so.'

They stood and went to the door. As Papadiantis prepared to open it, Declan turned to him.

'She wasn't a delusion, Doctor . . .'

'No, I didn't mean . . .'

'She was very real to me, the realest thing . . . I loved her very much. And now it's as if my life is over.'

'If I had a dozen francs for every time I've heard those words . . . Believe me, you have a lot to live for. Now, take this prescription to the same pharmacy as before. Nothing will bring her back. But this will help.'

He arrived back in Lyon mid-evening, and went straight home, exhausted and in desperate need of sleep.

When he arrived at work the next morning, he found a note on his desk instructing him to report directly to the Secretary-General's office. Dyson was waiting for him as though he had no other demands on his time.

'Carberry. Come in. Take a seat. I want a word with you.'

'Yes, sir. What would you like to know?'

'Don't play the innocent, Carberry. You know perfectly well why I asked you to come here.'

'As a matter of fact, I don't.'

'Then I'll spell it out to you. You may remember that back in November, I gave you very strict instructions to drop a line of enquiry that involved the French President and his foreign minister. You disobeyed me, and now look what has happened. Madame Dutheillet is dead.

Shot down in the course of a botched assault that you brought about.'

'In the course of a rescue mission, sir. When the SWAT team broke in, Madame Dutheillet was –'

'Shut the hell up. You'll speak when I say you can speak. Your actions have caused the most almighty fuss since the Second World War. The president is so angry, you can't begin to imagine. If you value your life, don't for God's sake fall into his hands. But he isn't the only one. Péguy is threatening to prosecute everyone from Interpol to the entire French police force, Debias-Aubry has made it clear that everyone involved in the raid will lose his job and pension, and that some may face long prison terms. The worst is Kraus. Furious isn't the word for it. He wants blood. It doesn't matter a damn to him whether it's French blood or Irish blood, or something in between. I believe he's already spoken with his ambassador. Need I go any further?'

'Sir, you seem to be missing one or two little points.'

'Such as?'

'Well, for one thing, I understood this raid was carried out by a Muslim terrorist group. Did *Le Monde* get it wrong?'

'Of course they did, you idiot. Are you completely simple? That was the first story that came to hand, and for the moment we're sticking to it. But you and I know rather different.'

'Well, I do, sir, but I'm not sure you do.'

'Meaning?'

'Meaning that all the people you just named, including Sophie Dutheillet, are criminals. I can testify that they have all been accessories to murder, and with a proper investigation I may be able to show that some of them have actually committed murder.'

488

Dyson went red. Declan thought his face might explode, so thoroughly puce did his skin become.

'What the fuck are you talking about, man? Are you in your right mind? The people I just named are some of the most respectable residents this country has. General Kraus has Congressional Medals of Honor and God knows what else. He was a Vietnam hero. He almost ran the US counter-insurgency programme down in Central America.'

'The last I saw of the fucker, he was applauding while some poor bastard got his heart ripped out. Grow up, Dyson. If even half of what you say is true, you're just about to commit the biggest cover-up in history. Now, you may be happy with that, but I'm not. I'm warning you now, I'll blow this thing open. I have the evidence, and I can bring every man in that SWAT team on the stand to testify to what was going on in that house.'

'What was going on in that house was a quiet meeting of the Cercle des Philosophes Contemporains, a gathering which you and your whooping savages turned into carnage. The SWAT team of which you speak has now been disbanded, and I doubt if you'll ever be able to make contact with a single one of its members. As for yourself, if you persist in making these allegations, I think you'll find yourself in bigger trouble than you can imagine. Let me put it in simple language: there are people out there who want the skin off your back and the head from your shoulders. They mean business, Carberry, and I wouldn't cross them if I were you.'

'And if I do?'

'You want me to be honest? Do you? I think you'll wind up in some back alley with your throat cut. That's what I think. You aren't dealing with little thugs from the IRA here. These are people who can have you put away just by waving their little finger.'

'And you'd stand by and let that happen?'

'If I had to choose between you and Alain Dutheillet or Dick Kraus, believe me I won't have trouble making up my mind. You should think hard about this, Carberry. In my opinion, you'd do well to consider early retirement and a quiet life fishing for salmon out there in the Irish outback.'

Declan got to his feet. The room was spinning round him. His heart was knocking so hard his ribs hurt. He had never been more angry in his life.

'Dyson, you are, when all is said and done, no more than the little shit I took you for originally.'

'Now, listen here –'

'No, it's time you did some listening. You're a little shit, but you've got fancy ideas through consorting with all those big shits who tell you how to dance, and to what tunes. I couldn't care less for all that. They killed my Alice, which means I don't care what the fuck they do to me. This thing is going public, and if heads roll as a result, I hope yours is the first. You deserve nothing but contempt, but to tell you the truth I don't even have the energy for that. You'll have my resignation on your desk this afternoon.'

He'd just finished typing the resignation letter, which was no more than a few terse lines, when the door opened and Rob Barlow came in, closing the door behind him.

'I thought you'd been spirited away,' said Declan.

'Is that right? Well, I have been offered a post in Toronto. But what's Canada between friends? How are you, sir?'

'I've been better. The doc seems to think I'll live, though. What are we going to do about this mess, then?'

'Well, we could start here.'

'What's that?'

Rob produced a Jaz disk from his pocket and laid it on Declan's desk.

'You'll want to take a look at this, sir. I had a little look round the night of the raid, and I came across this in an office. Among other things.'

Rob slipped the disk into the drive and sat down next to Declan.

'Now, sir, take a look at this.'

He moved the cursor around the screen, clicking from time to time until he opened a file labelled 'Adhérents Français'. Predictably, the file contained the names and details of French members of the Sacbe. Other files contained similar information for other countries.

'I've been through them,' Rob said, 'and you'd be surprised at how many names I recognized. It's not just names, addresses, and telephone numbers either. There are medical records, mainly the results of various blood tests members had to have taken. There are files grouping people according to sex, religion, age, whether they speak Spanish, and so on. And, yes, there's one really weird file that lists twins. It's named in Spanish – here.'

Declan watched as Rob highlighted a file. It was titled in Spanish: 'Gemelos/Gemelas', and inside it had siblings grouped together, with details of their parents, upbringing, and so on, and whether they had been brought up together or apart. Declan scrolled through it casually, wondering what the significance of twins could be, when suddenly his eye caught one of the entries.

'Oh, God.'

'What's wrong, sir?'

'It's nothing,' Declan said. 'I just thought I recognized . . .'

At that moment his office door opened and two unsmiling security guards entered.

'Mr Carberry?' asked one.

Declan nodded.

'We've been asked to escort you off the premises, sir. If you wouldn't mind following us out.'

54

Kaminalhuyú

The pyramid seemed to suck in light from all sides, darkening the forest round it. Very little of it could be seen at first. Its upper courses were lost in a thick covering of bushes and trees, and its sides were hemmed in by ferns and creepers.

'OK, let's spread out,' ordered Leo. 'I want this thing measured and on the map by sunset.'

'Are you crazy, Leo?' Steve waved his arms about in a bemused frenzy. He'd been losing his English cool since entering the forest, and every day it unravelled a bit more. Out of the corner of his eye, he caught sight of a large scorpion creeping into a crack in the pyramid wall. With astonishing nimbleness it squeezed its way through and was gone in seconds.

'I don't think so. Why?'

'It'll take us days. This bastard's covered in trees and stuff. Even with the chainsaw, it's bound to be a long job. We'll never get it done by sunset.'

'We can clear a path down one side, and somebody can get to the top. Look, none of the vegetation on the pyramid itself is very heavy. It was the same back in Komchen, remember? There's not enough soil on the stone to allow anything but shrubs and small trees to grow. You could pull some of them out by hand.'

'OK, I'll try to get up. I'll cut some sort of path.'

'No, you'd better stay down here to operate the theodolite. You'll have to cut back here a bit in order to get some angle. Rokché can take the rod up.'

'What do you want me to do?' Rokché asked.

Steve explained. 'Use your machete to cut a way up,' he said. 'We'll finish the job later with the chainsaw.'

Rokché started climbing, while Steve got down to the business of working his way back from the structure. He'd bring the photo-theodolite down from camp once he'd reached a position from which to work. Meanwhile, Leo and Antonia cut their way along the side of the pyramid in one direction, while the twins went the other way, chipping and chopping at everything in their path, like little dark-haired locusts munching their way through a bean plantation.

It was very nearly dark by the time they all gathered again at the foot of the pyramid. The structure was still barely visible beneath its cloak of heavy leaves and bushes.

'These figures are just provisional,' said Leo, 'until we can do a full survey. But whatever way we look at them, the thing's a monster. The side we measured is just under four hundred feet long. We're all agreed on that. Any adjustments we make later will be tiny. And we reckon the other sides will turn out more or less the same. Now, what about you, Steve? What have you got?'

'Well, I took several readings, and they all seem to tie in with yours. Two hundred and fifty feet high, give or take a foot. I'll take one of the aneroid barometers up tomorrow, and double-check the reading.'

'Are you really sure it's that high?' asked Antonia.

494

'Reasonably.'

'But, Steve, that's higher than Temple IV at Tikal. Higher than the Danta pyramid at El Mirador.'

'Which matches this huge ground plan. You've been along one side, you've seen how long it is: so, work it out. This thing must have been the highest building in the Americas till the Masonic Temple was put up in Chicago.'

'When was that?'

'I'm not sure. Eighteen-nineties, I think.'

'It's getting dark,' interrupted Leo. 'I think we should be getting back to the camp.'

His fears of getting lost were diminishing now that they had the beginnings of a real map. But other fears, less easily defined, had started to spring up in him.

All the next day, and several days thereafter, were spent in clearing as much as possible of the great pyramid. It was hard work, but rewarding. One entire face was cleared from top to bottom, and a pathway swept round the perimeter of the building.

On top, much as they had expected, they found a tall temple that was topped by a crest twice its height. The crest and the temple roof remained inaccessible, and were covered in dense vegetation. A little imagination showed how, from the air, the whole thing would have seemed no more than a thickly-forested hill.

Inside the temple, an opening in the floor gave access to a steep stairway that seemed to head all the way down inside the pyramid, just like the one they had excavated at Komchen. Several of the team were eager to go down in order to explore whatever chambers might lie below, but Leo insisted on a wider survey of the site first. He wanted a broader impression of Kaminalhuyú, and the chance to collect enough inscriptions to build up some idea of the city's age and activities.

And so Kaminalhuyú began to shape itself all round them, as though the forest was turned bit by bit to common stone. The further afield they walked, the deeper they penetrated into a labyrinth that seemed to have neither entrance nor exit. Pyramids, some a mere ninety feet high, others almost the height of the main pyramid that they had designated Temple 1, crowded upon one another in every direction. From time to time they would uncover another building or set of structures, palaces, grain stores, sacrificial platforms, mansions, and what seemed to be an observatory. Many of the buildings and the stelae distributed at random among them retained traces of the red paint with which they had originally been covered. East of the great pyramid lay a cluster of buildings on a high platform, which Leo identified as an acropolis. Inside, it was a warren of windowless rooms, with narrow passageways that led to crumbling staircases.

It was soon clear that to excavate only a tiny proportion of the city would take years if it were done properly. Leo was tempted to call it a day and head westwards out of the jungle. But Kaminalhuyú had begun to exercise an irresistible influence over him, and over the others, each in his or her way. Antonia had started to work on the inscriptions she had found, first copying them on to large sheets of paper she had brought especially for the purpose. Steve had taken over Bob's role as photographer, and spent all day taking a visual record of the city's return to life. The Minnesota Twins had found a cenote, a deep pool of stagnant water, and were busy dredging it for traces of offerings and sacrificial victims.

Leo's whole time was spent planning and measuring.

He surveyed each building in turn, then made tentative site plans, knowing that each one would be complete only until a new discovery was made.

Antonia felt lucky. The inscriptions were in near-perfect condition beneath their coverings of moss, and the glyphs used were relatively standard.

'I've dated seven stelae,' she said. She liked sitting beside Leo while he worked, liked the air of concentration that possessed him, liked to stroke his back and arms in the hope of distracting him.

'Ummm.'

'The earliest – listen to this, Leo – is 14 January 490. And the latest is 9 June 1745. I've gone over them several times, there's no mistake.'

'No,' he said, looking up. 'I didn't think there would be. You know the Mayan calendar better than anyone. What about rulers?'

She did not answer at first.

'Yes?' He put down his pen and gave her his undivided attention.

'On each of the stelae and on the *chacmool*, there are two royal names. One is Oxib Queh and the other Beleheb T'zi. Leo, the same names appear on each stela, and the stelae are separated by centuries in every case. The dates don't lie.'

'But that doesn't make sense.'

'It looks as though they gave their kings the same name in every generation. And not just the kings. Each set of royal names is preceded by two other names.'

'God names.'

'No, that's just the thing. They aren't described as gods, but as Ahkin, priests. Just two names on each inscription. T'o'ohil and Nohoch Tata.'

'More titles than names.'

'Yes, you're right. And beside each priest name the word for twin occurs. *Cuaya*. I think it's some sort of reference to the Hero Twins in the *Popol Vuh*.'

'Perhaps they really were twins. You should tell the Dorothys about this: they'll be chuffed.' Leo chuckled and picked up his pen, planning to get back to work.

'Yes, they'd like that: they have a kind of priestly feel about them.' Antonia made as if to rise, but instead sat down again. She seemed troubled.

'What's wrong, love?' asked Leo.

'Oh, nothing really . . . Just . . . Well, there's something else in the inscriptions. Not just the stelae, but on buildings, monuments . . . wherever I look. It's *aam*, the glyph for "spider", that's all. Haven't you seen it? It's everywhere. The form doesn't alter very much from one inscription to the next. But that's not all: every time the spider appears, it's side by side with two glyphs for eternal life. They're only separated by three dots, the figure three.'

'Yes,' Leo mused. 'I'd noticed the spider glyphs, but I hadn't realized there were so many of them.'

'Have you noticed something else?'

He shook his head, unsure what she meant.

'I haven't seen a spider since we arrived in this city. They were all over the valley on the way in. But I've seen none since then.'

Every day the sky drifted over them, precise and malign, depositing a thin layer of black ash in the open places they had created. They watched it drift down, slow and sullen, and felt it catch in their throats like sand.

Each day, Leo returned to the great pyramid. It haunted him at night, and by day it followed him everywhere. He would look up and see it, towering over him, or he would

498

take a path at random and find himself led to it as though by some form of natural magnetism. And yet he hated it. To tell the truth, the city frightened him, and what was worse, he could not identify what it was about it that unsettled him so much. Antonia felt the same way, but he hadn't spoken with the others. For all he knew, they thought the place was better than Disneyland.

Two days later, he decided to enter the pyramid. It could take years to map the city in its entirety, years and a team of trained surveyors. By then, of course, de Sepúlveda would have lost interest or died. He wanted his secret of eternal life, whether real or surrogate, and if he didn't get it, or a near promise of it, he'd withdraw the funding.

Of course, Leo hardly doubted that funding would be forthcoming from just about every other source the minute word leaked out of the existence of a site on this scale, and of this quality. They could just leave the forest now and fly back to Cambridge or Chicago, or wherever they pleased, and by the end of the year they'd all be back again with an expedition big enough to lay siege to Troy.

But Leo was just as certain that, whoever provided the funding, he would not be put in charge of the enterprise. He was too junior, and too inexperienced in the politics of his profession. There were wheelers and dealers out there who would give their right arms to head the official Kaminalhuyú expedition, and they would see to it that Leo Mallory's name figured as far down the pecking order as was possible.

If, on the other hand, he did more than merely map the site, but brought back artefacts and details of the interiors of two or three major buildings, he might be able to hold on to some of the glory for himself and his team when they returned.

He spoke to the others after dinner that night.

'There's one way in,' he said. 'From the top down. We'll need wooden torches to supplement our electric ones. It's going to be dark down there.'

55

Sandymount Strand
Dublin

From Howth Head to Dalkey, the tide was out, and the early afternoon sun hung above the glistening sand like a sliced lemon, yellow and sickly. On the horizon, a full moon crept skywards, pale and awkward as a thin ghost. There was no warmth in anything. Seabirds huddled together in the shelter of a rotten groyne, their wing-feathers ruffled by a sharp wind.

Declan had used to come here years ago, when he was a student at Trinity College – defying the Archbishop's ban on Catholics studying in that Protestant citadel – and living in digs in Pembroke Road. It was no more than a ten-minute walk from Ballsbridge to Sandymount. Coming on to the beach, it was like dropping off the edge of the city, and the sea spread out in front of you.

He'd felt a desperate need to come here today. The strand stripped so much of the past away, and what it could of the present. He didn't feel young as a result, but he felt a little cleansed, as though the cold wind that swept the sand cut through his body and his soul together. There was frost on the water's edge, and ice had started to form in pools where seaweed lay tangled among dog cockles and tellins and lion's paws, and the long blades of razor shells seemed like some human artefact come ashore from a long-dead wreck.

'Here, good boy, off you go!'

He slipped the dog's leash and watched him run, ears back, across the firm sand at the water's edge. Finn was a Doberman pinscher, a police dog who'd worked with Special Branch and had just been retired. Declan had arrived home on the day of Finn's retirement, and his handler, an old friend called Eamonn Walsh, had more or less foisted the dog on him. Dogs had never been Declan's thing, but he'd said yes, and now he found that Finn was growing on him. For all his size and potential for mayhem, he turned out to be the friendliest dog imaginable, and Declan had taken to going down to the strand with him every afternoon.

Slow clouds, like smoke, crept towards the bay from the west, and the weather, already cold, grew colder. Declan had sold the old house in Killiney, much too large for his present or future needs, and bought a small apartment in Ballsbridge, off Herbert Park. He'd grow old there, he thought, and bitter, and apart, and his only company would be an old dog, limping along behind him.

He looked away to where Finn was cavorting in the distance. Since his return, scarcely five minutes had passed without his thinking of Alice, of what might have been. He had not lost grasp on his original intention, that those responsible would pay. But he knew he would have to lay his plans and set his traps carefully, or else he would get nowhere.

The clouds came scudding faster now, until sun and moon together were obscured, and suddenly hail began to fall, blown hard across the beach by an icy wind. Declan pulled up his collar and buttoned it, but still the hail battered him. He tried whistling, to bring Finn back, but the wind snatched the sound away.

The shoreline was deserted. *It's only an old fool like myself who would come down here on a day like today*, Declan thought. He'd considered taking early retirement, and still might. But Con Dillon had talked him out of that the night of his arrival, over an extremely liquid meal in Doheny & Nesbitt's. Talked him out of it for the time being anyway. Declan hadn't been able to give his old boss a full account of what had happened in France, and why he was back home so soon.

'I'll tell you everything later, Con, when I've had time to collect my thoughts.'

'Are you in trouble, Declan? You look to me like a man in trouble.'

'Well, I suppose I am, so. Which is one of the reasons I don't want anyone else getting drawn into this thing.'

'I'm capable of taking care of myself, Declan. My father fought with Michael Collins, and my uncle Martin was one of the first –'

'Save your breath and drink up, Con. You'd be out of your depth in this business, you and the Pope's sister together.'

'Leave her out of it. Is it serious trouble?'

'Well, let's say I've rubbed some people up the wrong way.'

'What sort of people? Powerful people?'

'The very same.'

'They're the worst, Declan. You can't do worse than get mixed up with that crowd. Tell me about it when you can. In the meantime, I'll fix up some sort of backup for you. I take it that would be acceptable?'

They'd agreed that Declan should select a small group of bodyguards from among officers he'd worked with before, and whom he knew he could trust. Now, looking up and down the long, deserted beach, with the hail bouncing off the hard sand, he wished he'd got round to making his selection. He felt exposed out here. Time he started for home.

Suddenly, about two hundred yards in front of him, in the direction of the martello tower, a man appeared. He was little more than a speck, but he was walking in Declan's direction. Declan called to Finn, as loudly as he could, then looked round towards the beach wall at Strand Road. A second man, closer than the first, was coming his way. He was carrying something black and metallic in his hands.

He looked behind him to see a third man no more than one hundred yards away. And his suspicions were confirmed when a black dinghy swung in from the sea and scraped up on to the beach. A man in black neoprene leapt out and dragged the dinghy further up. Declan saw that the new arrival was carrying a gun, which he now swung round in front of him. It looked like a sub-machine-gun, and so did the stocky black instrument carried by the man coming from the wall.

He'd been an idiot, he thought; and now he'd pay the heaviest of prices for his carelessness. No backup, not even a mobile phone to call for help.

He looked round quickly, trying to see if there was any route of escape, but they had him covered on all sides. Then, glancing off to his left, he saw the hulk of an abandoned boat down near the water's edge. It was no more than a wooden shell, but instinctively he ran for it.

As soon as he started to move, his attackers hurried to close in. The sand that had seemed so firm when walking slowly, sucked his feet down, dragging him back at every step. He glanced round to see the men approaching more rapidly now. They all wore black, with balaclavas on their heads.

The man on his left opened up fire, pouring out a hail of bullets that ripped up the sand right in front of him. Declan pumped his legs harder, turning his head away from the wind, gulping down air. He wasn't fit enough for this, his lungs couldn't take it, and his joints were already protesting. He'd acquired a bad knee years earlier, in the course of a raid on a bomb factory in Dundalk, and now the wound threatened to give and to throw him prostrate and helpless on the wet sand.

The attacker who'd come in from the road was the nearest now. He opened fire with an even, scything motion, and a fistful of hot steel caught Declan in the back, pitching him over the side of the hulk, where he landed heavily in a pool of freezing water.

The killer advanced, his gun held level. The others hung back, letting him finish what he'd begun. He reached the side of the boat and leaned over, bringing his weapon up almost as an afterthought.

Declan's single shot caught him in the mouth and exited in an explosion of brain and blood through the back of his head. Inside the hulk, Declan let himself relax, struggling to contain the rush of adrenalin that pushed through his veins. He'd not been a complete fool. The Kevlar vest and the Beretta had saved his life.

There was a loud growling sound followed by an even louder scream. Declan scrambled to his knees and looked over the boat's edge to see Finn standing over one of the gunmen. The sound of gunfire had triggered the dog's reflexes, and the sight of a man in a black balaclava had brought back memories of endless training sessions out in Bray. The man on the ground screamed, seemingly unable to do anything to get out from under the dog. Yards away, a third man was trying to take aim at the animal without risking his friend's life.

'Kill!' shouted Declan. It was a command no dog handler ever wanted to make use of. But under the circumstances, there was no choice. Finn had been trained on dummies, but now he followed orders on a human being, ripping his victim's throat out in a single action.

The third man, panicking, fired towards Finn, missing him by several feet. Declan stood, took aim, and sent a bullet through his forehead. The body remained standing for several seconds, then toppled backwards with a crash and lay perfectly still on the hail-drenched shore.

By the time Declan scrambled back out of the hulk, the fourth man was legging it back to the dinghy. Moments later, he had it in the water and was dragging on the outboard motor. It came alive at the fifth or sixth pull, then settled into a steady putt-putt that sent the little craft out into the bay.

Declan's back hurt like the proverbial bejaysus. He could imagine the bruises building up, and dreaded taking off the vest. Well, that could wait. He'd a phone-call to make. Watching Finn rip out his would-be killer's throat had made his mind up on one matter. He'd been passive long enough. His enemies might be powerful, but Declan had declared war on them now, and he had determined to take the battle to them, wherever they might be. If they wanted to shut him up, they'd have to come for him again. But next time they'd find him ready and waiting.

11.15 p.m.

He could not sleep. His whole body was tense and nervous, as though he was in the mood for a fight. A police doctor had given him sleeping pills, but he wanted to defer them for a little while. There was a guard outside his door, and others at the back of his house. Tomorrow he'd be moved to a safe house elsewhere in the city. He'd been lucky this time, but the next time he might not be, which was why he had to make sure it was on his own terms.

The telephone rang. He groaned and tried to ignore it, but it just rang on, and in the end he picked up the receiver.

'Carberry.'

'So, I find you at last.' It was Papadiantis, speaking English for a change. Declan automatically reverted to French.

'Doctor. What makes you ring at this time?'

'I tried earlier, but you did not answer. I've had a lot of trouble tracking you down.'

'I was busy. Walking my dog.'

'An Irish wolfhound, yes?'

'Near enough. He's called Finn. What can I do for you?'

'Monsieur Carberry, when we met a few days ago, you asked me what would make someone think he might live for ever. Do you remember?'

'Yes, of course. Have you found something in that *Materia Medica* of yours?'

'Not exactly. I should say that your question rang a bell somewhere in my memory. You need to understand that not all of the information we have about the effects of medicines comes from the last century. Groups of volunteers are still given new substances to try out, and the results are recorded and published in a number of journals. The best material also finds its way on to computer software. This makes it easier to find information you are looking for.

'I think I should also mention that homoeopaths make use of a large number of what are called "spider remedies". They are prepared by macerating an entire spider, a tarantula, for example, and then preparing a tincture which is diluted and diluted to extraordinary lengths.'

Declan broke in. 'You found a spider remedy that makes people feel immortal.'

'Yes. It was proved about ten years ago. The spider in question comes from Guatemala. It's related to the Black Widow, which gives it its Latin name of Latrodectus Reclusa. It's called Recluse because it remains very well hidden under normal circumstances. In fact, it's extremely rare. It's not very large, but it gives a very painful bite which injects a potent venom into the victim's bloodstream.

'According to the information I found on my own software, victims experience hallucinations as a result of which they come to believe they have acquired eternal life.'

'And that's it?'

'Well, no, not exactly. I found a paper that was published in the Guatemalan *Journal of Toxicology*. It's the only one I've been able to find dealing with this particular spider. It's a short paper, in which the authors describe the effects of envenomation on three known victims. For the first few days, they had hallucinations and thought they were immortal. On the third day, they died painful deaths.'

'I see. Thank you, Doctor.'

'I'll send you copies of everything I've found. You'll have to give me your new address.'

'Better send them to my office.' Declan recited the address.

They chatted a little longer, and Papadiantis extracted

a promise from Declan to look up a homoeopath in Dublin. He did not ask why his patient had left Paris so abruptly.

'Doctor, there's one more thing you might be able to help with. What do you know about twins?'

'Twins? Do you mean identical twins?'

'I don't know. Perhaps.'

'Is this connected to feelings of immortality?'

'I think so, yes.'

'I can think of nothing in homoeopathy that relates to this. But in ordinary science, perhaps. Identical siblings constitute a clone. One method of cloning in animals involves producing identical twins. You take a developing embryo from the uterus, and you divide it. Each half is placed into the uterus of an unrelated female, who is to be the surrogate mother. Scientists have already produced identical pairs of sheep, pigs, even horses using this method. To the extent that cloning provides a sort of immortality –'

'Maybe it's not scientific. Are you aware of any other significance given to twins?'

'I'm not sure. Castor and Pollux were immortalized in the night sky.'

'What about further west? The Americas?'

'You'd be better off consulting a real expert. I do know that the Peruvians had twin gods. Apocatequil and Biquerao, or something along those lines. And the great Aztec god Quetzalcoatl was the patron deity of twins.'

'What about the Mayans?'

'No, I don't think so. Unless . . . Oh, yes, they had a legend of Heroic Twins who overcame the gods of the underworld. And became immortal.'

'Thank you, Doctor. Thank you very much indeed. I'd better go now. I have some sleep to catch up on.'

56

Kaminalhuyú

Leo disliked heights, and climbing the southern flank of the pyramid had been an unpleasant ordeal. The steps were both narrow and extremely steep, and if there was a God, He was exactly 1.7 degrees off the perpendicular, for nothing else could explain to Leo how it was possible to climb that staircase and not topple backwards to a certain and pointless death.

If getting to the top brought him close to his Creator, being there brought on an attack of vertigo that only Antonia's presence could calm. Holding her hand tightly in his, he walked round the temple perimeter. Slowly, the vertigo wore off, to be replaced by something akin to awe. Even with the binoculars at their maximum magnification, all he could see, in whatever direction he looked, was an ocean of trees. A troubled breeze shook the forest top from time to time, sending ripples through bright green leaves as if through water. And sometimes a flight of birds emerged, spinning upwards hopefully into a leaden sky.

Ash fell, blacker than ever. Somewhere to the west, another volcano had erupted with full force. A succession of earthquakes had followed in the Sierra Madre, leaving ten thousand dead and many more homeless. Here in the forest, they only knew that ash was falling, and that the sky never changed. None of these things mattered now that they'd be working inside the pyramid.

To make life easier for themselves, they relocated the camp to the main room of the temple. They would sleep and eat and rest in there, without having to climb down to the jungle floor each time.

The stone slab that covered the stairway had been mortared in place and incised with a life-sized figure of the god of death, Ah Puch, and the names of the nine Bolontiku, the dark lords of the nine subterranean worlds. It took a morning to chisel away the mortar and free the stone. And it took another two hours to ease the stone out of the lips on which it was resting and start moving it on to the wooden rollers set to one side. There was an enormous risk that the stone might slip and crash into the stairwell, blocking it indefinitely. They couldn't risk explosives in such a confined space, so the slab was eased from its place by copious amounts of sweat, endless grunts, and straining muscles.

The staircase lay at their feet, as black as hell. The opening was choked with spiders' webs, but of the spiders there was still no trace. Leo ordered torches lit and placed around the opening to prevent anyone falling in.

'Who goes first?' he asked, knowing the answer.

'You do,' answered Steve. 'You're team leader.'

'Rokché's our guide.'

'Rokché's a special asset without whom we'll never find our way back out of this pagan wilderness, Don Leo. You, on the other hand, are a Cambridge don, and therefore expendable. We can find dozens like you anywhere. Every provincial city has its Cambridge Society. I shouldn't be surprised to find a branch here. Dinners twice a year with a guest speaker from Chiapas and breast of *quetzal* on the menu. Consider yourself voted most likely to break your neck, and least likely to notice it. So go on in there, and send us a postcard.'

Antonia kissed him, and he started the descent, taking care to test each step before leaning his weight on it.

'What's it like down there?' shouted Dorothy.

'Dark.'

He felt shut in all at once. Turning the beam of his Mag-lite from narrow to flood, he was able to make out, albeit faintly, the walls and ceiling all around him. To his astonishment, every surface was covered in frescoes, their colours unfaded even after the lapse of a thousand years or more. He did not pause to look at them, but all the way down he was aware of faces staring at him, gods and demons, feathered serpents and grinning crocodiles – and almost everywhere, something he had never seen in a fresco before: spiders. Some were large and striated, clear ancestors of the bird-eating spiders they had encountered on their journey. Others were a little smaller and black, hairy-coated versions of the common tarantula. But more often than not, he saw paintings of a much smaller spider, something very like the Black Widow, but with larger fangs.

The air was stale, ancient, full of dust. He tied a handkerchief across his mouth and nose, but nothing would keep out the smell. It was a dry, bitter odour, not like anything he had smelled before inside an ancient building. He could attach no significance to it as yet, but his eyes darted in all directions, expecting anything. He grew aware of an unpleasant thumping in his chest and realized that, for no particular reason, he was afraid. His movements made him hear things.

A final turn, and the last six steps ended at a wooden door. Leo reached out gingerly and touched it: *chicozapote* wood, an astonishing variety that was virtually impervious to rotting or insects. The Mayans had used it widely, hard though it was to work.

On the wall above the door, the fresco painter had added a bouquet of coloured feathers to a pair of glyphs carved in the stone. Leo had no difficulty in recognizing either: the first was *aam*, the spider glyph, and beside it a single glyph representing Ah Puch, the death god.

He drew a little two-way communicator from a pouch at his waist and switched it on.

'Hi,' he said. 'Anybody up there?'

There was a brief crackling, then Steve's voice rolled through.

'Just us ghosts. You met anybody interesting down there?'

'Not yet. But there's a great portrait gallery. I want some of you down here right away. We're ready to go in. Bring some light tools, that's all. Leave Rokché on top with Dorothy.'

'Actually, Rokché is rather keen to take a look at his ancestors. He's using legal phrases that add up to "We were here first", and he's taking action against Antonia, whose ancestor Hernán Cortés –'

'We know all about that. Tell Rokché he can come down, but he's to keep his distance. I don't know what we've got in here. You can take his place.'

'Thanks very much. Right, that's enough of this. We've got to save our batteries.'

The connection went dead, and Leo was suddenly very alone again. It was tempting to try to open the door, but he knew he ought to wait until the others arrived. He sat down on the second step from the bottom. Examining the door, which was right in front of his nose, he noticed that it had been sealed along all four edges. He picked absent-mindedly at the plaster or mortar, and he saw that there were tiny silver stars embedded in it, and that they still shone when the light of his torch passed over them. They twinkled there in their lonely sky, and Leo wondered who had made them and who had set them in such a place.

The others weren't long in arriving. One at a time, their steps echoed down the staircase. Antonia was the first to arrive. Like the others, she carried a flame torch made of a branch on top of which a mixture of animal fat and petrol was packed inside a metal mesh.

'I've still got that kiss,' he said. 'If you'd like to have it back.'

'Oh, there's more where that one came from. What's the story down here?'

'Not much. I thought you'd all like to see what's on the other side of the door.'

'I hope that's not an indication,' she whispered, nodding towards the glyphs above the lintel.

'Did you bring chisels? There's room for two to work on either side of the door. Be careful with those little stars.'

They set to work, chipping carefully away at the mortar. It took fifteen minutes to cut through on all sides. The door opened in the centre, folding inwards on pins set into the lintel and floor. Leo pushed one side, Antonia the other, while Rokché and Dorothea held torches behind them, shining them into the room beyond.

For a long time no one spoke. Leo took Antonia's hand and held it tightly in his own. In his other hand, he held one of the tiny silver stars that had fallen from the mortar. He pressed his palm on to it until it drew blood, in an effort to remind himself that the door had been sealed tight, that they were the first to stand here in a thousand years or more.

In the centre of the opposite wall, dwarfing a host of smaller figures, was the painted image of a Mayan queen. She was shown full face, her hair obscured by a low headdress, her upper body draped in a *huipil* of many colours. One upraised hand held a skull, and on the flattened palm of the other she held a spider that seemed to be in the act of sinking its fangs into her flesh.

None of this was what attracted their attention. Slowly, they filed into the room and stood in line in front of the portrait.

'What does it mean?' Antonia asked, shading her eyes, as if the painting dazzled her.

'I don't know,' said Leo. 'I've never seen anything like this before.'

'But it is my likeness, isn't it?'

He wanted to deny it, to say it was nothing like her. But the truth was quite the opposite. The truth was that a man, dead long centuries, had dipped his brush in pigment and painted Antonia's face on a temple wall. The question that ran like a hare through Leo's mind was simple: had that long-dead artist painted his queen from the imagination or from life?

'Yes,' he said. 'She could be your mother or your sister.'

'She could be me,' Antonia said.

Dorothea came to her side, and looking at the portrait and then at Antonia's bewildered face, smiled contentedly to herself.

Antonia looked round the empty room. The confidence she had gained since leaving the ranch and coming on the expedition had suddenly left her. Instead, she imagined herself once again in her father's study, and Rafael's insane letter open in front of her: *When God spoke to me last night, He told me that I must fulfil my destiny. He spoke*

515

your daughter's name, and confirmed what I have known for this long time now, that she and none other is eternally proclaimed my heavenly consort, the goddess who will inhabit all the spaces my mind leaves vacant, upon whose body I shall beget the last of those that will die and the first of them that will not die . . .

In the jungle, Rafael and his companions sat and watched. They did not beat drums or play other instruments. They had been watching almost since the arrival of Leo's party at the city. The Indians had long known of the existence of Kaminalhuyú, and some believed they were the direct descendants of the Maya who had lived there. No doubt they were. But until Rafael's arrival, the city had been outside limits for them. Naked fear had kept them away from it. Very long memory had preserved for them its reputation as the City of Sorcerers. They believed that if they entered it they would die.

But Rafael had held out another promise. A promise of life, eternal life. All they had to do was believe in him, and follow him, and do whatever he told them to do. It would soon be time to go in, he thought. He would celebrate his union with Antonia Ramírez here in the heart of the forest, in the heart of the city. And they would live for ever and ever.

57

Set low in a corner of the room was an arched doorway whose centre had been filled up with stones. It did not take long to dismantle. The falling stones dropped into darkness on the other side. When the top half had been opened up, Leo went up close and shone his torch through the opening.

'Can you see anything?'

'Just' – he swung the beam up and down – 'just a passage, really more a tunnel than anything. I can't see the other end.'

They knocked down the rest of the opening, and Leo stepped through, stooping. The tunnel seemed to have been cut through solid stone, which suggested it was an afterthought put in place after the pyramid was constructed. Their voices gave off strange echoes, dying away ahead of them, then returning mysteriously, as though someone down there was whispering, enticing them to join them in a cavern of unknown delights.

The tunnel stretched for five hundred yards or more, then stopped abruptly at a wall. The wall was green, and made up from individual blocks of jade, similar in their depth of colour to the jade skulls they had found outside.

The wall was blank, but on either side of it the stone had been plastered and painted over. Some of the plaster had fallen away, but what was left was quite distinct, a combination of paintings and glyphs. While the others tried to find a way to get through the wall without destroying it, Antonia set about deciphering the rows of inscriptions.

Down here, it felt like being imprisoned in a little tomb. It was not a place for anyone remotely claustrophobic. They all found it hard to breathe, as though wet felt had been placed over their mouths, and the dim and moving light strained their eyes and palled their vision.

The jade wall was built from precisely-cut bricks, each fitted to its neighbour so finely that it was impossible to open up a space between one and another, even by so much as a fine blade or a sheet of paper.

'They must be dovetailed together in some way, probably by means of a hole in the top of one and a protrusion in the bottom of the one over it.' Leo ran his hand over the smooth surface, admiring the skill with which the wall had been made. There was no way in which they could justify simply breaking it down.

'It's extraordinary,' said Dorothea, waving her hand at the wall, then at the walls on either side, 'that they did all this without metal tools.'

'Just their bare hands and a lot of spit,' said Rokché.

'Give us a demonstration.'

'I've lost the touch. That's why I became a lawyer.'

Leo finished his inspection of the wall.

'All right,' he said, 'I think I know what to do. The wall goes into grooves on all sides. These paving stones are the clue. If we can get them up, we can get access to the bottom layer, take it out, and so on to the top.'

The flagstones were easy to dislodge, and after that the bricks came free with the lightest of twists. Slowly, a wide aperture opened above them. So intent were they on working the bricks loose and stacking them along the tunnel wall, that no one bothered to cast a glance into the darkness that stood like a second and less penetrable wall beyond the first.

'The wall's nearly down,' Leo said to Antonia. 'Have you finished there yet?'

There was no answer.

'Antonia?'

She was staring hard at the inscription at which she had been working. Hearing Leo's voice, she turned her head and looked at him with a look of distress.

'What is it, Antonia?' he asked.

'I don't like the look of this,' she said.

'What's wrong.'

'Listen.'

Referring back to her notes, she started to read the main inscription, while the others listened in silence.

'*Eight baktuns, fourteen katuns, three tuns, one uinal, twelve kins, one eb. The fifth Lord of the night.*' She paused. 'That gives us a date of 17 September 320. This place is older than we thought.'

No one said anything. They could feel it where they stood, the age of the stones, the weight of the past over their heads, and the air, full of the breath of long-dead Maya. Antonia resumed her reading.

'*Mak'ina Aam Ahau Chan, the mighty lord, the great sun, the sun-faced king, ruler of Kaminalhuyú, he of the thousand captives, whose face is the mirror of all faces, and whose life is the giver of life to all lives. The great Lord has instructed that it be spoken and written down, that he has built this pyramid and this temple as u y-atoch k'uh, a house of the gods, and as u kanche'k'uh, a seat of the gods.*

'*And he has decreed that the land beneath it be hollowed out, and pillars placed, and stone laid, and a second city built*

*beneath the first city, and all of this to be named Xibalba,
which is the land of the dead, where they have eternal life.
And Mak'ina Aam Ahau Chan shall rule over them eternally,
together with his ancestors, and the Nine Lords that dwell in
darkness.*

*'And he has decreed that there be houses in Xibalba, where
the dead shall be punished eternally. There shall be Quequema-
ha, the House of Gloom; and Xuxulim-ha, the House of Cold;
and Balami-ha, the House of Jaguars; and Zotzi-ha, the House
of Bats; and Chayim-ha, the House of Knives; and Aami-ha,
the House of Spiders. And the dead shall pass between them to
be punished for their misdeeds. And Mak'ina Aam Ahau Chan
shall be their ruler and their God.'*

Antonia lowered her torch. Her words seemed to go on
echoing back and forwards through the narrow tunnel.
Rokché was the first to speak.

'What's that mean?' he asked. 'The king's name.'

Antonia hesitated. Dorothea answered instead.

'It means "Great Sun, Spider Lord Sky".'

'Spider Lord? This place gives me the creeps. We
haven't seen a single spider, yet we can't get away
from them.'

'Let's see what's inside,' said Leo.

For a long stretch there was nothing but darkness. They
had to touch the walls frequently, just to be sure they
were still in the tunnel, that the walls had not opened out
to leave them guideless in some vast open space beneath
the city. As best they could, they kept up a conversation,
seeking reassurance in their own voices.

Without warning, they sensed a shift in the way in
which their voices came back to them hollow and echoing.

'Hang on, everybody. Let's stop here.' Leo halted and

swung his torch in a circle. The tunnel had gone, but it was not clear what had replaced it. He bent down and opened the canvas bag he'd been carrying. From it he took out a battery-operated floodlight. He'd kept it back until now, knowing it burned up batteries faster than a fire melted grease.

Powerful as it was, the new light was swallowed up in darkness as readily as the others. Leo went back several yards in order to nail a ring to the wall at the entrance to the tunnel. To the ring he tied a reel of orange twine. This he handed to Dorothea.

'Just let it run out gently. Don't tug on it. As long as you stay with us, we can always find our way back.'

They went forward, and this time, when Leo swung the floodlight through a long arc, it lit up three separate pillars. Closer inspection revealed that they were in a vast low-ceilinged chamber buttressed by thick stone pillars. Above them stood the city and the forest.

In what appeared to be the centre of the chamber there stood a huge circular altar. It seemed badly stained and filthy, in marked contrast to the altars they had discovered in the city.

'I don't understand this,' said Leo, inspecting the inscription that ran round the outer edge of the circle.

'What's wrong with it?' asked Rokché.

'The size. Look, these holes are obviously intended as anchors for maguey twine or whatever was used to tie victims to the stone. But if the victim was tied like that – the head here, hands over here, feet down there – even if he was quite tall, which would have been unlikely, but even if he was taller than the average, the *nacom* could never have reached him comfortably. Do you see? He couldn't have carried out the job of taking out the heart in the usual way.'

'Perhaps there was a different form of execution. Maybe they cut the victim's head off.'

'Yes, that's possible. But even there, reaching the neck would have presented problems. The longest cutting weapon the Maya had was the obsidian knife. This would require a sword.'

'You're both missing something more obvious,' said Antonia. 'If the jade wall was in place, how on earth did they bring the victims through here? And why? Why not perform the usual ceremonies in the public places built for them up above?'

'I think we can safely say that this place is going to shake up all our preconceptions of pre-Columbian archaeology. There must be at least one other way into this place.'

'What about this staining?' asked Antonia. 'Is it blood?'

'Hard to tell,' said Leo, 'but I'd guess some of it is at least. There's been no rain to wash it off down here.'

'No cleaning ladies either,' joked Dorothea.

Antonia recorded the inscription for later translation. But her mood after writing it down was strained.

Leo fixed a second ring to the altar, and strung the twine through it.

'Let's see if we can get a bit further before we call it a day,' he said, switching the floodlight back on and leading the way out into the unnavigated darkness like Columbus guiding his ships across an uncharted sea.

The pillared chamber came to an abrupt end at a wall of stone.

'OK,' said Leo, 'let's work our way round. Either this marks the back wall, with nothing beyond, or there'll be some sort of doorway.'

No one seemed keen to split off from the others.

522

Leo took Dorothea's hand and headed off to the left. Rokché and Antonia followed, their knuckles grazing the wall, their torches flickering, picking shadows from the unpolished stone.

'What was in the inscription on the stone?' asked Rokché. 'You looked a little anxious.'

'Did I?' She'd been brought up to distrust Indians, to regard them as a different, fallible species. But in the time she'd been with Rokché, any residual prejudice that might have remained in her had been burned away by the sheer force of his personality. She had learned to trust him completely, in ways she would not even have trusted Leo or herself.

'You don't have to talk about it. I was just curious.'

'It's nothing, really. I need more time to work on the inscription. All that staining and filth will have to be cleaned off before I can get a proper look at some of the glyphs.'

'There was something, though, wasn't there?'

'Something, yes . . .'

She took a deep breath, fighting to filter out the fetid, decayed smell that hung everywhere. There should have been no smell, she thought, not in the midst of so much stone.

'There's a small reference,' she said, 'to someone called the Spider Lady or possibly Queen Spider.'

'Spider Lord's wife.'

'Possibly. I think so. But . . .'

'Yes?'

'The glyph for spider is different. Not *aam*, but another form for the same thing, *to'ih*.'

'Any reason for that?'

'Probably, but I can't say exactly what. I think the two terms mean different species of spider.'

'But that's not what's worrying you. Not exactly.'

'No. To be honest, I don't know what is. I think this city used to be the centre for a spider cult. It may even explain how they killed their captives. They may have used that altar stone, tying the victim down, then placing one or more venomous spiders on him. They'd bite him, and then he'd die a slow, painful death. But it's only an idea. The spider may just have been a totem animal, like the jaguar or the *quetzal*.'

'But you don't think so.'

She hesitated. Their feet shuffled along in centuries of dust.

'No,' she said, 'not really.'

Leo called out softly.

'There's an opening here,' he said. He switched the flood on again to reveal an arched tunnel of medium size that opened into the wall and ran off into another expanse of darkness. Leo fitted a third ring and strung the twine on it.

'Are you sure we should go any further?' Rokché asked.

'I want us to get as far as possible on this trip,' Leo said. 'Each time we have to go through the process of climbing down and coming through here wastes batteries and fuel. Let's give it another hour, then call it a day.'

He stepped into the opening. Before the others had a chance to join him, they heard him cry out.

'Jesus Christ! What the hell is this? Get in here quickly. Hurry up!'

Antonia went first, closely followed by Rokché and Dorothea. The interior of the tunnel was brightly illuminated by the floodlight. On either side, crisp and stark in the first light that had touched them in seventeen centuries, stood the mummified bodies of a generation of the kings and aristocrats of Kaminalhuyú.

Naked and half-naked, obsidian-eyed and slack-jawed, they stood in lines that seemed to travel down for ever into the shadows and the solitude of the stone maze to whose embrace they had been translated. Some had stones of jade in their open mouths, some carried little statues in their withered, folded arms, all wore golden bracelets, and necklaces of jade and amethyst, coral and amber, and some had masks of jade and weapons of obsidian, *maquahuitls* and the lance heads known as *chinantla*.

Tunnel branched off from tunnel, and each time Leo played the floodlight along a new corridor, he saw a vista of the dead that stretched well beyond the limits of the torch's beam, into darkness and dust.

'Kaminalhuyú,' he whispered. 'The Hill of the Dead.'

Sometimes the mummies were standing, like the shrivelled poor taken directly from their graves and set up in glass cases in the Museo de las Momias in Guanajuato; sometimes they were stacked horizontally in rows, sleeping, or seeming to sleep like passengers on a rushing train or an ocean liner destined for the bottom of the sea. But without movement, their endless journey was a blissful dream that soothed them while their mouths filled with dust.

Leo and his companions walked, silent and hypnotized, down the long corridors. The passageways were thick with cobwebs, but they saw no sign of spiders anywhere, and though they listened, they heard nothing creep or rustle in the shadows. They found the bodies of men and women, and the thin, astonished mummified remains of tiny children, their mouths open in an eternal scream.

Some of the dead were dressed as royalty or lesser members of the ruling class; some had been warriors; some had been priests.

How many centuries' worth of dried skin was stored up here? Leo looked for signs of changing fashions, clues that would link a jade breastplate from Kaminalhuyú to one from Palenque, say, or Yaxchilán, enabling the trained eye to mark out periods and establish patterns. But down here, very little seemed to have changed from one generation to the next. They looked at hundreds of mummies, but nothing appeared to alter. That suggested that Kaminalhuyú had remained isolated down through the centuries, immune to any outside influence, locked in its old ways from beginning to end.

Antonia took Leo's arm.

'Let's stop here, love. We've seen enough for the moment. There are too many tunnels. And we don't want to get stuck down here in the dark.'

He was inclined to argue, but realized she was right. His enthusiasm was making him take unnecessary risks.

'We'll go back, then. Mapping this place will take more resources than we've got with us. But I'd like Steve to come down later to take some photographs.'

He cut the twine and fastened the end, not to a ring (hammering one in might have shaken and even destroyed nearby mummies) but to a mummy's hand.

'They look so sad,' said Antonia. 'All curled up like exhibits in some gruesome freak-show, dragged out and dumped here. Have you seen the mummies in Guanajuato?'

He shook his head.

'They dig old bodies up from the local cemetery and put them in glass cases. You can go in for a couple of dollars and gawp at them. They look as though they're

526

screaming, the skin around the mouth has dried and shrunk so much. Some of them have hair, many of them still have the clothes they were buried in, the children have little boots. They really don't look human.'

'These guys weren't put here like that, Antonia.'

'No, I know that. I was just making some sort of comparison. They do look very similar. Except . . .'

'Yes?'

'Well, the ones in Guanajuato look desiccated the way you'd expect, with them out in the grave for so long, drying up in the hot sun. But these seem a little different, I don't know. As if . . . as if they'd been sucked dry while alive.'

'Sucked dry?' Leo laughed. It was perhaps the first time anyone had laughed down here in all history. 'By what? Vampire bats?'

'Maybe.'

They went on walking, heading back to the great chamber. They were tired now, and hungry, but stopping to rest was no option.

They made their way back through the empty chamber, Leo's torch picking out the great pillars that upheld the roof. At last, they reached the spot where the twine led back out to the central altar. Leo took out the floodlight and splashed its broad beam across the wall in the direction they had still to explore.

As he was about to switch it off, he noticed a large opening just a few yards away. Slipping across, he tried to see inside, but there was only darkness. The smell they had noticed earlier seemed stronger here.

He stepped back.

That was when Dorothea noticed the first spider.

58

The spider was a black tarantula, rather larger than the average, but no more than that. It had eight hairy legs, a fat body, and prominent fangs, and it scuttled, terrified by the sudden light. Leo caught it as it scurried past him, and ground it with a loud squelch beneath the heel of his boot. Kicking the still jerking remains away from him, he turned his full attention to the corridor in which he stood.

The walls were stained and filthy, just like the altar they had examined earlier. Here and there, Leo could make out what looked like glyphs cut into the stone, but the covering of dirt was too thick to allow a proper examination.

Without a word to anyone, Leo took several paces further down the corridor.

'Hey, Leo, where the hell are you going?' Dorothea shouted. 'We've got to get a move on. These batteries won't last for ever.'

'This could be important. We can afford five minutes to take a look. There's plenty of life left in my floodlight.'

Another spider narrowly missed dropping on his head. He watched it hurry away, its long legs scraping against the stone. It seemed to be a cousin of the Brown Recluse, though almost twice as large. A few more paces, and suddenly the ground in front of him was thick with spiders of all sorts, from Black Widows to bird-eaters, all scurrying away as fast as they could from the oncoming light.

Rokché came up behind Leo.

'I think we should turn back. I've got a bad feeling about this place.'

'Because of the spiders?'

'Perhaps.'

Ahead of them, the tunnel filled again and again with spiders of all sizes. Suddenly, a monster jumped among them, almost three feet across. As it scuttled off, Leo shuddered. Maybe Rokché was right, maybe they should turn back now.

'I think this is the Spider House,' he said. 'I just want confirmation of that, then we can get out of here.'

He had hardly spoken than the short corridor reached its end. He sensed that they had entered another chamber almost as large as the one they had left. Taking a deep breath, he switched on the floodlight.

Spiders everywhere. The floor and walls and ceiling were carpeted with them. *Aami-ha* was no longer a mythological pretence, but a reality in space and time. The carpets rippled and pulsated as spiders walked across them, hundreds at a time. The sudden light, after centuries of darkness, completely disorientated them. Some froze, others tried to outrun the light.

Slowly, Leo lowered the light, and as he did so, he caught sight of something towards the centre of the room. He trained the flood on it. Another altar, he thought, perhaps one dedicated to the worship of spiders.

But it was not an altar. Altars do not move. With a sickening sensation that turned in moments to genuine retching, he identified the source of the vile smell they had detected earlier. It was stronger by far in this place.

And it came directly from the dark, pulsating thing in the centre of the room.

'What is it?' asked Antonia, creeping close to him for comfort.

'It's a spider,' said Leo, 'and it's looking this way.'

His hand shaking violently, he let the beam of his torch play slowly over the legs and body of the giant arachnid. It was hard to guess how big it was, but Leo reckoned it could be perhaps three or four feet high, and maybe eight feet across, longer if its legs were extended. Dark, matted fur covered it, and twin fangs quivered in front of its half-blind face, if it could be said to have a face. Smaller spiders ran up and down its body like servants in close attendance. They must feed it, Leo thought, or perhaps they constitute its prey.

As they watched, it took an uncertain step in their direction. Antonia remembered her remark about the mummies looking as though they'd been sucked dry.

'I think we should get out of here,' said Leo.

No one needed encouraging. While Leo went on playing the light behind them, in order to confuse the spiders, they moved briskly back down the tunnel. In seconds they were back in the altar chamber. Antonia led them to the right, where they could expect to pick up the twine once more.

She reached the spot where the central ring had been hammered into the wall. One length of twine was still tied to it, leading round the wall and into the tunnel that fed into the catacombs.

The twine that led back via the altar to the way out had been cut. Hurriedly, they played their torches all over the floor. There was no sign of the missing twine anywhere.

'Just a moment,' said Leo. 'Where's Dorothea?'

He turned the floodlight on again and swung it in a circle. Dorothea was nowhere to be seen.

At that moment, there was a rattling sound back in the direction they had just come from. And a second sound, louder than the rattle. A loud scraping sound that echoed hollowly off the ancient stone.

59

'Hi, you guys. How are things up here?'

Dorothea emerged from the stairway, grimy, her hair frosted with cobwebs, her eyes reddened with dust.

'You look a fright,' said Dorothy.

'Do I?'

'No, seriously. Doesn't she, Steve?'

Dorothy squeezed Steve's arm, and he smiled. Dorothea could see that her sister had wasted no time while everyone else was underground. That she had seduced Steve was blindingly obvious, you only had to look at her, satisfaction was written all over her face. Their private myth was that, if one Filbert twin had an orgasm, the other would wake up tingling. And, as always, what was Dorothy's was Dorothea's, and vice versa. Some men got turned on just at the thought of making love to two identical twins at once.

'Where are the others?' Steve asked.

'What? Oh, the others . . .' Dorothea smiled. 'They'll be up shortly.'

'Did you find anything down there?'

'Just some tunnels. A couple of burials. Nothing spectacular. No gold or jewellery or anything like that, not so far at least.'

'How long before they come back? Did they say?'

Dorothea shook her dusty head. She looked out across

the treetops, at the emergent layer pushing its way high above the canopy to glimpse the sun. It was getting on for evening. She was hungry and cold after her ordeal below. The question was, how could they keep Steve sweet while letting him remain in ignorance about what had happened to the main party?

'I think we should have a rest and get some food,' she said. 'They may be a little while yet before they come up. It's easy to lose track of time down there in the dark.'

'What are they doing? They can't just be going up and down tunnels.'

'We found an altar. It looks early classic, but Antonia's working on the inscription just to make sure. Now, let's make something to eat. I'm starving.'

The lights went out one by one. First, the wooden torches, then the Mag-lites. Finally, Leo's floodlight, over-used and immensely draining on batteries, began to fade. And still they had not located the way out.

Spiders were flooding into the great chamber now, brown, black, and some a ghastly white – huge albino wolf spiders that crept like ghosts across the floor. And somewhere they could hear the steady oncoming rattle of the monstrous creation from the Spider House.

It had not sucked a human dry in centuries. But it had endured on scraps brought to it through the cracks and interstices of Kaminalhuyú by its army of slaves. Sometimes it had survived by feasting on them as well.

The light flickered twice and went out. They were in total blackness. They dropped their torches, useless now, and held hands.

'Whatever happens, we mustn't let go,' said Leo. 'If we stay calm, we can make it back to the entrance tunnel.'

Rokché reached for Antonia's free hand, drawing all three of them into a tight circle.

'Whatever you do, don't move fast. We're in their element now. They can sense the slightest move we make. Walk on tiptoe, and don't speak.'

A large spider pounced on Leo's boot and started to climb his leg. He threw it off, but no sooner had he done so than a second crawled on to his back, forcing him to shake and beat it down. And already he could feel others swarming round his feet, waiting for their chance to pounce on him.

It was as though they were acting with a single mind. He knew what they were trying to do – the larger ones, who could bite, but who lacked toxins that could do him real harm, would try to cover him and bring him to his knees, leaving room for smaller species to move in and paralyse him with their venom. Once he could no longer move, the Queen Spider would move in and sink her fangs into whichever part of him was easiest to reach, and begin to drain him of his bodily fluids.

They crept on, each of them fighting down an almost overpowering urge to scream and run, fending off the masses of hairy, jointed legs and bloated bodies that filled every spare inch of the floor. One large individual somehow managed to creep into Antonia's hair, quickly tangling itself as it struggled to get free again. Battling against her natural loathing, she grabbed it bodily and forced it from her.

However quickly they knocked the spiders aside, some managed to get close enough to bite. Small ones, less readily noticed, would climb up a leg and somehow insinuate themselves into clothing, where they would begin to sting. The only way to stop these front-line troops was to grab them and crush them between two thicknesses of cloth.

Every step was accompanied by a snapping of spider legs and a squelching of bodies. But still they came, like a constant tide, and the harder Leo and his two companions struggled to fight them off, the weaker they became. Rokché had found the wall, and they were making their way round it slowly, but the entrance seemed as far away as ever. For all they knew, in their disorientation they had started at the wrong spot, so that they might never be entirely sure which opening led to the way out, and which led in to the Spider House again, or to the catacombs, or to something even worse – the Bat House, perhaps, or the House of Knives.

It was then that Leo noticed something ahead of them, a pinpoint glimmering, as though a dark sky without moon or stars or comets was being pierced by light. The pinpoint grew in seconds into something larger. It could only mean that someone was coming through the tunnel.

They threw caution aside and made speed as best they could, hampered only by the swarming spiders. Suddenly, the full beam of a floodlight speared through the dark, and everywhere the spiders scattered, climbing over one another in their desperation to escape the intrusion. The floor ahead of them seemed to clear in moments.

Moments more, and they were at the tunnel mouth. Whoever held the floodlight turned the beam to one side, to avoid blinding them. The next in line was carrying a flaming torch, and after that they could make out several more torches.

'Steve?' Leo had never been happier to see anyone in his life. 'Thank God you came down. We're under siege down here. You can't imagine.'

His gaze was caught by the person carrying the wooden torch.

'Dorothea! We thought you'd got lost. It's a bloody good thing you went back for reinforcements.'

It was then he noticed that, in her other hand, Dorothea was carrying a pistol, and that it was pointed right at Steve's back.

After her came Dorothy, and she too carried a pistol. She was followed by a group of five Indians, all armed with knives and bows, and finally, dressed in Indian garb, Rafael, who carried a second floodlight and a Colt automatic.

He looked them up and down and into their frightened, dust-coated faces. On the floor, spiders still spilled out from the shadows and ran back into them again.

'Hello, Antonia,' he said. 'I'm glad to see you safe.' He turned to Leo. 'And you must be the young man I've heard about, Leo. Perhaps you can introduce me to your friend.'

'My name is Rokché. Don't bother to introduce yourself, I know exactly who and what you are. Do your friends know?'

'Dorothy and Dorothea have been followers of mine for several years now. They know all there is to know about me.'

'I don't mean them. I mean the *hach winick*.'

'They know me better than you. I brought them here to see the city for themselves.'

'I'm glad you came,' said Leo. 'You've saved us from a nasty situation.'

'So I see. Dorothea told me you might have got trapped down here. Unfortunately, I did not come down in order to save you. My purpose is to take Antonia back – out of Kaminalhuyú, out of the jungle, out of the Americas. But she comes with me alone. I have absolutely no use for the rest of you. On the contrary, you would only hamper my own efforts to get back to civilization.'

'Antonia stays with me.' Leo put his arm round her. He sensed her fear, and something more than fear.

'Doctor Mallory, please try not to hold too high an opinion of yourself. I regret that my earlier attempts to have you removed from the scene were ineffective. But perhaps the gods intended it to be this way. Let me show you what this place is and what my ancestors accomplished here.'

He nodded at Steve. Dorothy took the floodlight from him, then dragged him along as Rafael led the way to the altar in the centre of the chamber.

'There is a paradox here, isn't there?' asked Rafael. 'The City of Eternal Life, and the Hill of the Dead. Dorothea tells me you've stumbled on the catacombs. My ancestors are buried there, generation upon generation. Most of them died on this altar, offered up to the Queen. I think you've already set eyes on her.'

He nodded, and Dorothy and Dorothea set to work, stripping Steve of his clothes. When he was entirely naked, they forced him on to the cold stone and tied him down, using the holes they'd noticed earlier.

'Why are you doing this to me?' Steve demanded. 'I haven't done anything to harm you.' He hadn't yet seen what sort of death he was to have, he thought Rafael would butcher him or leave him in the darkness to die of thirst and hunger. No imagination could have encompassed the nightmare that was to come.

They pulled the cords as tight as possible. Dorothy took some of his clothes and pushed them under his neck, so his head was tilted forward.

'Let's fall back a little,' said Rafael. They worked their

way back to the opening that led to the way out. Rafael ordered the lights dimmed, leaving them in almost total darkness.

Almost at once the spiders began their forward progress once more. In what little light there was, their strange, rocking bodies swung between long, queerly-jointed legs.

'For Christ's sake, don't just leave me here!' Steve had started to grow frantic. With each cry, the panic in his voice mounted until it was painful to hear.

'Why can't you just let him go?' asked Leo. In reply, Rafael came to Antonia and kissed her full on the lips. She spat at him, but he merely wiped off her saliva and brushed her cheek with his fingers.

'Look!' One of the twins raised her hand and pointed into the shadows. Something dark moved in them, and moved again, an immense slouching beast groping its fetid way across the gulf between its lair and the altar on which Steve lay, trying to free himself of his bonds. He had yet to set eyes on the great spider, but the sounds it made as it swept its huge body across the floor were enough in themselves to unman the bravest.

'For God's sake, man, cut him free,' cried Leo. 'He's done nothing to deserve this. No one deserves to die like this.'

'This is Xibalba,' answered Rafael. 'What happens here happens according to its own laws.'

'If you have any feelings for me at all,' said Antonia, 'you'll let him go. Or are you just some sick sadist? Is that it? You're some twisted little pervert who gets off on this sort of thing.'

Rafael did not reply. Instead, he lifted the floodlight and played it across the stone, then further back, so Steve could see what was coming.

What he saw at first was a writhing carpet of spiders, thousands upon thousands of them, millions of rustling legs, all converging on him. And then he saw, right in the middle of them and only yards away now, something his worst nightmares had not prepared him for. It was squalid, old, and tattered, its underneath was thick with food it had long ago devoured, on top open wounds gaped like mouths.

Steve began to scream. In seconds, it had passed the limits of any human scream, but still his voice went on, rising in pitch rapidly. Rafael took the floodlight away. The scream died down a little, then suddenly burst out again, no longer a scream, but a hysterical roaring that went on for several minutes.

Antonia put her hands over her ears to block out the screams, but nothing really helped: they were in her head for ever, deep, deep in her brain, never to be uprooted.

It was that screaming that broke the Indians' nerve. They had followed Rafael instinctively, recognizing in him a being with power over the mortal and supernatural realms. He had overcome the most primitive of their fears when he lured them into the city. But bringing them in here and confronting them with a terror beyond their greatest night-time fears had been one move too many. Perhaps he could have persuaded them to stay had this been the outdoors, could he have spoken to them face to face. That was where his power lay. Not in this darkness.

They dropped their weapons and ran quickly back down the tunnel, one carrying a burning torch.

Before his captors could take stock of the situation and keep control, Rokché acted. As Dorothy turned her head to shout at the backs of the Indians, Rokché brought his arm and fist back in a terrific blow that broke her jaw and lifted her bodily from her feet. She fell crashing to the floor, breaking a hip and knocking the breath from her lungs. Rokché dropped to his knees and scrabbled for the gun she'd let fall. As he straightened with the gun in his hand, he saw Dorothea standing over him, her own gun pointed at his head.

Leo still held the reel of unused twine in his hand. With a sudden twist, he threw it with all his strength at Dorothea. It struck her a glancing blow on the temple, not hard enough to wound, but enough to distract her. Rokché used the moment to fire, three shots directly into her heart. The shots rang out among the stone like an alarm, cracking and echoing like whiplashes.

'Where's Rafael?' shouted Antonia.

They looked everywhere, but the shaman had vanished into the shadows. He could be anywhere by now.

At that moment, there was a cracking sound, followed by a long creak and a heavy crash. A stone had been dislodged and had crashed to the ground.

'I think we'd better get out of here,' said Leo. 'Those gunshots have shaken something. I don't think we should hang around.'

They started for the entrance, then Antonia stopped.

'What about Dorothy?'

'Where the hell is she?'

She'd managed to crawl several feet away from where she'd fallen, in an attempt to reach the way out.

Leo bent down. 'Can you walk?'

'I've broken something. It hurts like hell if I try to stand. What about Dorothea? She has to come too.'

'Dorothea's dead,' Antonia told her. 'We can talk about that later, but for the moment –'

There was another crashing sound behind them in the darkness.

'We have to leave her here,' said Rokché. 'There's no way we'll ever get her up those stairs.'

Antonia got to her feet. 'If she stays, then I stay.'

Another rock dislodged itself and crashed to the floor, followed by a long rattle of smaller stones, followed by a silence over everything.

60

If ever there was hell on earth, it must have been what
Dorothy endured in the course of that long climb up the
steep and irregular stairs that wound their way from the
bottom to the top of the great pyramid of Kaminalhuyú.
At first, she cried out terribly, then after a while she
lapsed into semi-consciousness. There was nothing anyone could do to ease the pain. They had no painkillers,
pharmaceutical or herbal, and no means of securing the
break at the top of her leg. At each step, she would breathe
in deeply, and for a moment experience a lessening of
the pain. Then she would have to be half-lifted and
half-pushed on to the step above. To save light, they
went most of the way in darkness. And all the way, they
were accompanied by Steve's screams, ghosts imprinted
on their minds for as long as they might live.

A few times they heard crashes down below, and Leo
and Rokché grew ever more certain that the foundations
of the pyramid were slowly giving way.

Reaching the open air was bliss. They lay flat out on
the paving stones of the temple, taking care only that the
entrance to the stairway was sealed. It was dark outside,
nearly midnight, no moon, no stars. They slept where
they were, like fish on a slab, too exhausted to eat or
dream.

They were woken mid-morning by pitiful cries from

Dorothy. She'd messed herself in the night, and her jaw and hip were hurting unbearably. Antonia helped clean and dress her, while Rokché and Leo set about making breakfast.

When Dorothy was comfortable again – or as comfortable as it was possible to make her, given her injuries – Antonia washed her face and combed her hair.

'Why'd you do it, Dorothy? You and Dorothea, why did you turn on us?'

'You wouldn't understand.'

'Try me.'

'There's not much point. I'm finished anyway. You said my sister's dead.'

'I'm afraid so. She didn't give us any chance.'

'What about . . . ?'

'Rafael?'

'Yes. Is he still down there?'

Antonia shrugged. 'I don't know. He just vanished, which means he could still be down there or that he made it back up here and is out in the jungle somewhere.'

'Dear God, keep him safe.'

There was an intensity and sincerity in this brief entreaty that made Antonia look on Dorothy with new eyes.

'He said you knew him before. That you and Dorothea were followers of his.'

'Was that so hard to guess?' Her words came mangled through her lips, muffled and twisted by the dislocation of her jaw. 'We heard about Sacbe through friends of ours at university. Rafael has a special interest in twins, he regards them as symbols of eternal life. Even if one is dead, he or she will live on in the other.'

'But I don't understand why any of that had to lead to violence. I've seen Rafael at work, he doesn't seem to care about human life, he seems willing to destroy people the way the rest of us destroy flies.'

'Or spiders?'

'Well, yes.'

'That's just it. From Rafael's perspective, the rest of us are nothing more than that. If he needs to kill people in order to achieve his ends, he's perfectly justified.'

'And what do you get out of all this? His followers, I mean.'

'What do you think? The Sacbe isn't just some vague, otherworldly religion. Everything in it is based on firmly-established laws of nature. Rafael has promised us eternal life, and in the end he'll give it to us.'

They went on talking until Dorothy's pains grew unbearable again. Antonia left her to try to sleep. Rokché volunteered to go down to ground level, where he might be able to find some herbs that would give a measure of pain relief.

'We can't stay here long,' said Leo. All morning, there had been occasional rumblings from below, faint sounds of falling masonry. It might not be happening all at once, and it might not happen at all, but it seemed very likely that the foundations of the pyramid and some of the area around it would be undermined, and it would be extremely foolish to be caught on the upper platform when that happened.

'Dorothy, we aren't going to be able to take you with us.' Leo felt no guilt about what had happened, but he didn't want to abandon Dorothy. 'We'll try to get you to the bottom of the pyramid, and as far away from it as we can manage, but that's as much as we can risk. If we don't get out of the jungle in as short a time as possible, we'll all die. But if we can make it out, then someone will come back in to rescue you. I promise that.'

They tried at first to take her down on a stretcher, but the stairway was far too steep to make that either practical or safe. With more ropes, they might have managed something, but what they had would have taken her a quarter of the way down and left her stranded.

In the end, Rokché placed her on his back in a fireman's lift and descended, face inwards, step by agonizing step. She screamed all the way. By the time they got to the bottom, her hip was badly out of joint.

They spent another night in the jungle with her. Rokché's herbs tranquillized her a little. He improvised a splint and tied the broken joint into place as near as was possible. Her jaw was more difficult. Antonia made a bandage, but it kept slipping while she slept. By morning, she was soiled and uncomfortable again.

Rokché built a shelter, and they made her comfortable in it. They left her what supplies they could spare, and a knife. There was a fire, and a huge supply of wood near to hand. Rokché made a water butt for her from a hollow tree stump.

'You won't die of thirst,' he said, pouring in the last container of water.

The last they saw of her, she was sitting upright with her back against the shelter wall, looking out at them as they turned and headed into the undergrowth.

It was on the third day that Rokché first mentioned his misgivings to Leo.

'I think we're being followed,' he said, indicating somewhere vaguely in their rear.

'The Indians?'

'I don't think so. They won't follow us now. What they saw in that place means they'll have nothing to do with anyone associated with it. In their eyes, we're contaminated. Believe me, they're in their encampment somewhere, tearing their hair out for fear the monster from Kaminalhuyú will follow them, or some other bogeyman come in at night to suck their blood. These guys don't dine out, but if they did they've got enough tales to tell to live off caviar for several generations.'

'They probably wouldn't like caviar.'

'Nobody dislikes caviar. Pressed beluga with blinis and soured cream, followed by a rare Chateaubriand steak and a glass of Chassagne-Montrachet ... Irresistible. They'd tell their story every night of their lives for that.'

'Too rich,' retorted Leo. 'Their stomachs aren't made for it. In any case, nothing beats mashed potatoes with black pudding.'

'Black pudding?'

'It's an English blood pudding.'

'Sounds cheap and nasty to me. What about a *feuilleté de langoustines*, or *homard aux truffes*?'

They went on like this for over a mile, swapping dishes and wines. Rokché the lawyer outclassed Leo the academic in his knowledge of good food and fine restaurants. Antonia, who outclassed them both, remained silent. But even her patience snapped in the end.

'Can't you two talk about anything but food?' she asked.

'Can't think about anything else,' said Rokché.

'Well, it's time you did. Who did you say was following us?'

'I didn't. But I know someone is.'

'You think it's Rafael?'

'He's the most likely suspect.'

At that point they hit a clearing. In the centre, speared on a stake, was a human head. Dorothy's head. Or possibly Dorothea's. They went forward. Flies filled the eyes and nose and mouth, making certain identification impossible. All thought of caviar and lobster vanished in an instant.

Rokché examined the site.

'One person,' he decided, after circling the flattened earth around the stake. 'Rafael. I am sure of it.'

There was no point in burying the head, unless they wanted to see it again. So they ploughed on, wondering when he would strike next. He would do nothing rash, since he wanted Antonia alive. At the same time, he most certainly wanted Leo and Rokché dead or worse.

That night, they slept lightly. A little after midnight, there was an almighty crashing sound, and, although they were sleeping in hammocks, they were sure the earth shook. The crashing and roaring went on for several minutes, as fresh sections weakened and fell.

'The pyramid,' whispered Leo. The noise had died down, but the entire forest was in an uproar about them. Every bird, every animal, every insect was in a tumult, running, jumping, cowering, and all calling out in a multitude of alarm cries, shrill and raucous as the demon of the place intended them to be.

In the morning, the turmoil had scarcely calmed down. With so many animals dead or injured or displaced, it would take weeks and months before normality returned to this section of the forest.

Rokché climbed the tallest tree he could find, right into the emergent layer, and used his binoculars to look back towards Kaminalhuyú. Over an area half a mile long and almost as far in width, a shallow crater had opened up, within which a clutter of trees, stones, bushes, and general debris had fallen. The forest would repair its wounds in the end, and Kaminalhuyú would be buried more deeply than ever. *Just as well,* thought Leo, when Rokché came down and told him what he'd seen.

They moved on in the direction they had chosen. Food was already becoming a problem, and they stopped in early afternoon to allow Rokché to set some traps. By evening he had caught nothing.

'They'll be suspicious,' Rokché explained. 'The crash last night frightened even the biggest animals, and they're bound to be cautious for a while.'

He had spent part of the day before and that afternoon making himself another bow, a short bow with as much tension as might be expected from unseasoned wood. There had only been time to make a couple of arrows, but Rokché had no intention of missing.

'There's about an hour to dusk,' he said. 'That'll give my eyes time to adjust to the poor light. I won't go far. Don't worry, I'll be back as soon as it's dark. Get a good fire going.'

The hunt went well. The catastrophe of the night before had left many animals in a state of confusion. He took down a tapir, a *tepezcuintle,* and a male howler monkey. They could eat well for a day or two, and if all went according to plan, he reckoned they could be on their way out of the forest by then.

He stepped into the little clearing where they had made camp. The fire burned less brightly than he had expected. He shrugged: perhaps his friends had taken the opportunity afforded by his absence to engage in a little post-catastrophe sex. Antonia was sitting on her haunches, facing the fire. Leo was standing a little back, just in front of a fig tree.

'What's wrong?' asked Rokché.

'Nothing that can't be put right,' said a familiar voice. Rafael stepped out from the shadows by the fig tree. He had a gun aimed at Leo's head, and when Rokché looked again, he saw that Antonia's hands had been tied behind her back.

'Drop your catch, then throw your bow and arrows out of reach.'

'And if I don't?' Rokché felt defiant. Who was this Rafael to tell them what to do?

'Then I will kill him. He matters less to me than that *tepezcuintle* did to you. Less, really, since the meat of the *tepezcuintle* is tasty, whereas this scraggy object . . .'

He pushed Leo forward and told him to tie Rokché's hands firmly behind him, and when that was done he did the same to Leo himself.

'Now, I think we should sit round the fire.'

Offered no choice, everyone sat as directed.

'Tonight,' said Rafael in a voice as calm as untasted milk, 'Antonia and I shall be made man and wife. There's no need for a priest, for I alone am God's representative on earth. You, Leo, and you, Rokché, will be our witnesses. That is all I ask.'

'She doesn't love you, Rafael, she never has done. She loves me. Even if you take her by force, even if you find a way to legalize your so-called marriage, she will never submit to you, and she will never love you.'

'Well, that's too bad,' said Rafael. 'She's destined to be my partner for all eternity, which will give her plenty of time to reflect on her decision and on her feelings. Perhaps I've not explained that part to you.'

'I'm not really interested,' said Leo. 'You just want to embellish a rape with metaphysics. If she belongs to anyone, she belongs to me: and I belong to her in turn. There's an equality in that you could never understand.'

'On the contrary, there's a cosmic inequality in it.

549

Antonia is not yours by right. From the beginning of creation, from the first *tzolkin*, she was destined to rule hand in hand with me. She is destined to live for ever, just as I am destined. You, on the other hand, can never be more than mortal.'

'Oh, this is a load of crap. You saw what the City of Eternal Life had for us. We're lucky to have got out of it by the skin of our teeth.'

'So, you came away with nothing?'

'Less than nothing. Steve was killed. Your two dumb followers have been killed, one by you. We may not even make it alive out of the jungle, and probably won't now that you've come along. Where's the benefit in any of that?'

'Obviously, you didn't do your homework properly. I thought you were a trained researcher, I thought you might have seen when someone was playing fast and loose with you.'

'Meaning?'

'Meaning de Sepúlveda. You remember him, don't you?'

Leo nodded. He could feel hairs shiver up and down his body.

'He gave you certain documents, which you read, and on the basis of which you conducted this expedition. Did it never occur to you to ask whether what he gave you was everything?'

'No, of course not. What point would there have been in his holding things back from me? He needed me to find Kaminalhuyú, and he could scarcely afford for me to be badly briefed.'

'He gave you what you needed to find the city. But he left you in the dark about its secret.'

'If you mean the spider, I'm more than glad he kept

550

quiet. He would have known that I wouldn't go if I learned about that.'

Rafael laughed. 'That's not quite true, though, is it? You'd never have imagined that anything like that was still alive down there, would you? No, what de Sepúlveda kept from you was the secret of eternal life. It can be attained, you see. You had no idea what you were looking for, and I don't imagine you actually believed for a moment that it really existed. I, on the other hand, knew exactly what to look for. And I found it.'

'Why should I believe any of this?'

'Because I have the paper de Sepúlveda should have given you. And I have what it talks about.'

Reaching into a little pouch at his waist, he took out a folded piece of paper, which he unfolded and held in front of Leo's eyes.

61

Extract from a second letter by Don Joaquín

... not believe all that was in my previous letter, and above all, what was said therein concerning eternal life and the secret thereof. Of our original band, not as many as I wrote were ambushed and killed by the Indians of the forest. More died in the city of Kaminalhuyú, and likewise some of those thought to have perished on the journey home died in the city. For they were made victims of the cult of which I have spoken, and were taken down into the darkness of that terrible habitation.

I have, however, spoken enough of that matter, and will only speak now of the last thing we were privileged to witness during our stay. There was some sort of struggle between the warriors of Kaminalhuyú and the Indians of the forest. Several of the latter were brought back to the city, and that same day they were taken to the temple on the great pyramid and there sacrificed to the heathen gods of that place by having their hearts torn out and their bodies thrown down the steps and fed to the dogs.

This was presided over by the king himself, who was present in the most splendid robes and feathers I have yet seen. When the public ceremony had ended, the king retired to an inner chamber, whither I was ushered some minutes later. By the time I arrived, Kan-Xul had removed his heavy ceremonials and was clad in nothing more than a loincloth. He was surrounded by several priests of the class of Ahmen, and by his sons. Behind them stood the Queen Mother, and the king's wives.

It was declared – and whispered to me at the time – that Mak'ina Kan-Xul Ahau Chan had proved himself worthy of eternal life, and would now set down the burden of kingship in order that the *Ba Ch'ok* or heir to the throne might take it up to rule as he might.

There followed much chanting of hymns, such that I thought they would never end. But like our own Masses, this came to a finish. One of the priests stepped forward and displayed to those present a golden box on whose lid was engraved the figure of a spider. And on the back of the spider was cut what appeared to be the figure of a serpent's head.

The attendant priest drew up the lid, and I saw straightaway that a real spider of some size stood in the box, restrained only by some fine thread which had been tied about its middle. And on its back was a marking that seemed to be a serpent swallowing its tail, which is an ancient symbol of eternity.

When all had seen and admired this spider – which my interpreter told me was marvellously rare and much sought after for its power to bestow immortality through its bite – it was taken to the king, who lay down on a stone bench. And the spider was laid on his naked stomach and allowed to wander freely, though still held by its thread.

Not long passed before the spider struck, sinking

its fangs into the king's breast. It seemed to hurt him, for he rose up a little, but he did not cry out nor address any of our company. The spider bit him a second and a third time, and each time he seemed greatly pained. Whereupon the priest lifted the spider and returned it to its box.

Some time passed after this, during which the king lay prostrate upon his bench, and I truly feared for his life, thinking the spider had envenomed him and filled his veins with its poison. But when about an hour had passed, he came out of his swoon and began to sweat profusely, so that his wives were obliged to wipe his body with cloths. This too wore off in time, and the king sat up, wondrously recovered, and declared himself divine and endowed with immortality. He smiled and laughed, and was very gay, and when he caught sight of me he beckoned me forward and, speaking through our translator, told me that, when proper relations between our people were once established, he would send an embassy to Spain, who would present to our King this same means to eternal life, and a priest to administer it.

I did not see Kan-Xul after that, for we left the next day and were bade farewell by the *Ba Ch'ok*, who still awaited the day of his coronation. And we set our eyes towards the forest, and counted ourselves fortunate to be alive. And yet I thought most keenly, during all that journey back, of the secret that had been divulged to me, of the spider whose bite meant immortality.

'And you believe all this?' Leo asked.

'Why shouldn't I? The city had the reputation. And

without looking too hard, I found a spider of that precise description, with the serpent on its back, just as a violin-back has the outline of a violin.'

He removed a second pouch from his waist and opened it. A large spider fell out and would have scuttled away had he not pulled it back on the cord he'd fastened round its middle.

Antonia had set out plates and cups ready for the meal they had planned. Rafael took a cup and placed the spider inside, covering the opening with a piece of leaf. Holding it tightly, he began to chant a string of shamanistic prayers. To Leo's surprise, there was nothing ersatz, nothing tricky or artful about his performance. In his origins, Rafael had been the real thing, and he could still carry conviction in his singing alone. His voice rose and fell through trees and darkness, touching everything with a little fire. Rafael himself did not know where the words came from, only that he found them in the mind of the forest, where the first words had originated, to which the last would return.

When he had done, he secured the spider inside the cup with a stone, and busied himself tying Leo and Rokché until they could not possibly free themselves. And he did the same to Antonia, for he did not trust her not to try to do him harm, in spite of the gift he was about to present to her.

He lifted the stone and placed the spider on his chest. It bit him almost at once, then again and again, as though angry after its confinement. He did not cry out, but he could not keep his body still either. When he had been bitten several times, he picked up the spider carefully. With his left hand he tore the front of Antonia's shirt, baring her throat and her chest as far as her bra. Then he dropped the spider on her. It did not bite at once, but when it did she cried out quite against herself. Having bitten her once, it seemed to totter, and a moment later fell off and scuttled away into the darkness. Rafael had let go of the cord that held it, but he didn't seem to care. He'd been bitten, he was immortal, that was all there was to it.

So began the longest night Leo had ever spent. Rafael passed in and out of a coma, during which he raved, shouting names and dreams and blood. Antonia, by contrast, fell into a deep sleep out of which no amount of calling and cajoling could waken her. Later, Rafael woke, sweating so hard he was in real danger of dehydration. Antonia sweated too.

After the sweat, Rafael became quite animated. It was light by then, and he talked rapidly and easily with his two male companions. He was now convinced that the spider bites had indeed worked their miracle on him.

'I'm totally changed inside,' he said. 'I feel connected with the universe, and I know I'll go on for ever.'

'You've just come out of a coma,' said Leo. 'You don't know what those bites will do yet.'

'It should be pretty obvious that, if they did harm, the rulers of Kaminalhuyú would hardly have lain back and taken a dose.'

'We didn't find any immortal citizens in there. All we saw were shrivelled remains. I don't think your kings lived for ever, Rafael. I think they died and were left for that thing to devour.'

'You're just jealous. I have your woman, and I have eternal life. You can't help but be jealous.'

He went on all day in this vein. When Antonia finally woke, she too was gripped by the belief that she was immortal. She insisted that Rafael find the vanished spider and administer its bite to Leo. But not to Rokché:

he was not advanced enough. No one argued with her. Leo noticed the red in her eyes and her flushed cheeks, and wondered how long she had to live.

That night, Rafael went into convulsions that lasted for over an hour. And Antonia had a short fit from which she recovered, vomiting heavily. All night long, Rafael raved deliriously, then went very quiet on the edge of dawn. When the light became strong enough to see him by, he had changed out of recognition. His skin had turned black and he was paralysed from head to foot. All that showed he was still alive were his eyes, which opened and closed from time to time, and his mouth, which moved as though in speech, but silently.

Antonia felt much better, though, like Leo and Rokché, she suffered badly from lack of food and drink. Her tongue was swollen, and she experienced severe pins and needles over her body.

'I think my left arm's paralysed,' she said. 'But that could just be because it's tied.'

They reckoned that Rafael died around lunchtime. There were already flies on his corpse by mid-afternoon, and by then the smell had started to become unpleasant.

Their bonds were unbreakable. Rafael had tied them with such skill that no amount of twisting or pulling could undo them. He had tied them hand and foot, so there was no way of reaching one another and getting help that way. They did not see how they could survive another day.

They lay immobile, serenaded by the fly chorus that sang around Rafael's swollen head. Leo and Antonia tried to speak to one another, knowing this would be their last chance, but so swollen were their tongues that neither could form a single word. But as best they could they looked at one another and gained comfort from that.

Rokché remained leaning back, looking up towards the treetops. It was a lot better than looking at Rafael and his army of corruption.

Leo had more or less given up when suddenly he thought the impossible, that he heard voices. He listened attentively, trying to make out what he thought he'd heard from the background murmur of birds, still agitated after the collapse of the city. There, he heard it again, human voices coming nearer.

His heart sank, thinking it was Rafael's Indians come back to find their master. Seeing him black-faced and dead, they would be sure to wreak some sort of revenge on his supposed killers.

The voices seemed to drift away, then returned more clearly than ever. Whoever it was, they were speaking Spanish.

Moments later, two men stumbled into the clearing. They were dressed in flying outfits and carried stout walking sticks in their hands. When they saw the tableau around the campfire, they cried out aloud, and Leo thought they might have turned tail and run had he not at that moment looked at them and smiled.

They were given water to drink as the first helicopter took off. Two choppers had been sent in by the Guatemalan civil defence, CONE, in response to a request from the EAVEG Project run by the National Institute of Seismology, Volcanology, Hydrology and Meteorology. The W. Lee system at INSIVUMEH had picked up two low-level tremors from an area thought devoid of seismic activity, and they were anxious to know just what the hell was going on.

The helicopter team had found a half-collapsed Mayan city, and might have taken off again into the wild blue yonder had it not been for one team member with quick eyes who noticed a trail disappearing into the surrounding forest. Against their colleagues' advice, two team members had pushed on until they stumbled across the camp where Rafael lay dead. His remains had been zipped up in one of the body-bags CONE helicopters regularly carried. Later, it would become the object of much scientific scrutiny and interest.

Leo was next to a window. He looked down as the helicopter dipped, prior to making a turn and heading on the first stage home. They'd been given permission to fly into Mexico, where the emergency room at the main hospital at San Cristóbal de las Casas was getting ready to receive them.

The face of the forest was exposed to him, a seaweed scud of greens across which birds flew like darting fish. And as they tilted again, he saw the great scars sliced into the forest's face. He would never go back, he thought. Kaminalhuyú had been one discovery too many.

The helicopter rose until it touched the clouds, then up again, and so out into sunshine. It was the last sunshine of the day, with the sun almost touching the horizon, turning the dust of a dozen volcanoes to fire. Leo wanted to reach out and touch it. But even as his hand moved, he felt it gripped. He turned and saw Antonia smiling at him, and the helicopter pushed out of the clouds like a fly rising out of a web.

62

Glendalough
15 July

Declan's bodyguard walked several paces behind them. He was irritated by the need for round-the-clock protection, but after the couple of attempts already made on his life, he wasn't prepared to let his enemies have their way.

His visitors had raised his spirits immensely. They had provided him with eye-witness confirmation that Rafael was dead. It might be more difficult persuading the shaman's dedicated followers that their beloved master had met a well-deserved end, but the medical institute in Guatemala City where his body had been examined had been very forthcoming in providing details of dental records and other identifying features.

'I think we'll keep the existence of your city a dark secret, shall we?' Declan suggested. They were out at Glendalough, walking by the still lower lake on a hot summer's day. The grey tower lifted itself above their heads like a great pencil, the surest emblem of Ireland's past.

'It may not be easy,' said Leo. 'It's been put on the map, and in due course someone's bound to want to explore it. I expect there's still a great deal to uncover.'

'All the same, we hardly want that crowd' – by which he meant the unregenerated members of the Sacbe – 'making some sort of shrine of it.'

'Well, nobody but ourselves and our friend Rokché knows about the spider cult or any of that.'

'That's grand. Let's keep it that way.'

They walked on a little way in silence. Antonia had gone ahead of them, enchanted by the green stillness.

'Will your wife recover?' Declan asked, watching her bend to pick a flower with her right hand.

'The doctors think not. She was remarkably lucky to escape with her life at all. There was still a heavy dose of venom in her body when they got her to the hospital.'

'I didn't necessarily mean her arm.'

'No, I suppose not. I really can't say about the rest. What we went through was terrible, and she had some bad experiences before that. There was something with the bulls Rafael killed on her father's ranch, and her father's death, but she'll say very little to me on the subject.'

'If you love her, she'll pick up in time. Don't ask for it all at once. Does she love you as much as I think she does?'

'You'd have to ask her yourself.'

'I will, so.'

'What about you?' asked Leo.

'Oh, I'm all right. I've had it easy over here.'

'That's not what I heard.'

'Well, there's nothing I can't handle.'

'But you don't have anyone to support you. I mean, your wife is dead, isn't she?'

'Concepta? Good heavens, yes. She's been dead a little while. And she was never much of a support to me.'

'And there's no one else, is there?'

Declan did not answer for several paces. He looked out across the heron-enchanted lake, across the weeds and the silver waters, at the remains of the several churches that had once graced the lake's shores, and the faint traces that remained of the monastic city that had once helped make Ireland the light of Europe.

He shook his head.

'No,' he said. 'I'm all right. There's no one else.'